RESURGENCE: THE ARROS SIREN CONFLICTS: BOOK ONE

M.J. Rosay

Cover designed by MiblArt.

ISBN: 978-1-955475-00-6

For John, without his patience and support—none of this would have ever been written down. And to my wonderful friends who kept cheering me on. So grateful for all the support and love.

1

Robert

The melodic hiss—the opening and closing of valves and doors, along with various other things he couldn't make out from his position, set the hairs of his neck on end. *Melodic.* At least that was how his mother once described the sounds. Robert's sensitive hearing earned him a deluge of abuse as a child. His mother promised it would get better later in life—it hadn't.

Frozen at the threshold between his wife and son, he couldn't command his appendages any further. *This is stupid, such a stupid idea.* It had been his idea. He tallied the number of times Julie reminded him since they left the station on the planet below.

"You can do this." Julie's extended hand broke his fixation on the vessels dotting the chamber's walls.

"No..." Robert turned to his son, his arms crossed, unwilling to move aside. He wanted to see her, too. His body trembled in those moments, soon resonating near what Kayla had labeled a seizure. They all knew better than to believe that there was anything *physically* wrong with him. "I can't do this."

"Yes, you can." His wife twined her fingers through his. One swift tug, and his feet thrummed against the interior floor.

"It's okay, Dad." Michael prodded him from behind. "The next six months will go by in a blink. No biggie!"

No biggie! Nerves hardened, his neck rooted in an odd angle—one he knew he would regret later. "Our definitions... Do. Not. Compare—on the matter."

Michael's laugh echoed, only he could hear it with the whir of machinery around them.

"You'll have to forgive him." Julie's frequent apology bled from her perfect composure. She flashed him a smile, shaking her head. "A little too smart for his own good." The technician ignored her attempt to break the ice, so to speak. The Arros rarely cared about the daily lives of their passengers.

The skin around his fingers contracted, pulling them into fists with each pulse of blood denied them. Breaths shuddered between clenched teeth, each step throbbing in his ears. "Breathe Robbie, breathe. Think of Kayla. Think of how excited she will be to see us on the other side." Her whispers threaded through every cavity, the gentle pace of her strides, her eyes constantly grappling for his. "I love you, Robbie. But you're cutting off circulation to my hand."

Twitching the genuine reaction into its proper place, Robert stretched the angry tendons of his right hand. "Sorry."

"It isn't the first time." Soft laughter interrupted her words. "It won't be the last, either."

"This one mine?" Michael's voice drew his attention away from Julie.

Her hand at his wrist prevented Robert from stepping between the stasis technician and their son. "He's fine, he'll be *just* fine."

"You realize," his hands trembled, even under the soothing touch of her fingers. "We'll be essentially—*dead*," he swallowed painfully. "For six months."

Julie inhaled through her nose, exhaling in slow motions. "Robert Erickson, they've been doing this for centuries—with no problems. We'll. Be. Fine."

He could almost hear the sloshing roll of Michael's eyes. "See you in six months!"

His wife's arm around his waist, barely enough to steady him, prevented him from falling to the floor at the sight before them. Michael's limp form, secured to the retracting bench, disappeared beyond the seal of the vessel. "It's okay Robbie, he's fine."

He dropped to his knees, his eyes never leaving the stasis chamber. Michael would never understand why he feared the contraptions. He could never bring himself to regurgitate the memory. They didn't need the fear he lived with every day of his life.

"Probably best to put him out where he is." Julie cleared her throat behind him. "He won't get any closer on his own."

She has the best of intentions. Their entire day—planned by her to perfection—was intended to set him at ease for this very moment. A solitary tear escaped his closed eyes. The prick of the cocktail steadied every nerve in his body, sending him into Julie's arms.

"See you soon."

2

Kayla

Drip, drip, drip. The trickles of water from her face became rivulets as Kayla stared into the mirror. An attempt to wash the frustration away failed with each tear flowing down the perfect curves of her face. Her soft pinkish-white complexion was spattered with rosy spiderweb-like veins of color. She'd been cursed with a beauty she never felt worthy of, a beauty that didn't reach the innermost part of her existence.

Kayla's father warned her of the dangers someone like her would find themselves surrounded by—if she didn't contain herself appropriately. The dangers she faced in the mirror weren't of dire, life-threatening proportions. Well, not if you took her father out of the equation. Not literately, just figuratively. Unfortunately, the morning's communications prevented removing *him* from the situation.

"Kayla, you alright in there?"

She rubbed her sleeves over the tears, but it was little help with the continued flow saturating the sweater. "I'm fine, Roux. I'll be out in a minute."

"Kayla, please tell me you haven't been in there since I left?"

Swallowing, she rubbed the opposite sleeve under her nose. If she admitted she *had* been in there for the duration of his normal morning workout, he'd never leave her alone again. She couldn't take his morning runs from him. It was his only personal time in their cramped living arrangements.

"I'm coming in." The knob rattled with his insisting tone.

Thinking better of leaning against the door, as it opened outward—a terrible design, in her opinion. She shrank into the corner beside the toilet. Arms around her bent knees, Kayla hid her face as best she could.

"Oh, Kayla!" On his knees, before she could look up from where she squeezed herself away, he lifted her chin. "If the message was that bad, you should have used my com. I would have come right back. What happened back home?"

"Nothing happened." She stared at him for several moments, attempting to match the calming breaths he always possessed. "My parents will be ready for us to pick them up at the station tomorrow."

The veins of his eyes to threatened to rupture, at least she thought they might. Roux pinched the bridge of his nose. "I thought you said your dad *hates* traveling?"

"He does..." choking on the words, she rubbed her throat. She couldn't tell him why. She'd promised never to mention it—to anyone.

"Alright. So... we tidy up, let them use the back room. Is *Mikey* coming too?"

Her throat clenched in the laughter. Roux was never good with nicknames. He'd adopted the endearing term she used for her younger brother. Not so young anymore—she hoped Michael didn't mind Roux calling him Mikey. A simple nod was all she could manage.

"Okay, he can have the couch."

"Why are you so calm about *this*?"

"No matter how overbearing you say your dad is, I can guarantee—my parents are much... *worse*."

"He's gonna kill me." *Understatement of the century Kayla... he's going to lock you away for the rest of your life.* She assumed her self loathing translated into her expression when Roux slid her out of her hole into his lap.

"We don't have to tell him." He rubbed the back of his neck, twisting the inch long fibers at the base of his skull. The top was longer, but he kept it styled—out of his face. "Well... We broach that topic, *eventually*. But," he set her down, hopping to his feet. "If we intend to pick them up in time to get back before the storm tomorrow night, we should get started." Kayla couldn't help but laugh as he gathered random garments from various surfaces in their small bathroom.

3

Robert

"Hi Daddy."

The words he'd hoped for. *She knows me too well.* Robert blinked the haze away as he shifted toward the sound of her voice. His daughter put her hands on her hips, sizing him up with a look that said: *No, you weren't misdirected. And YES, you're in one piece.* "Hey, Kayla."

"You could have given me a little more notice about your trip." Eyes rolled back for a moment, she huffed the hair from her face.

"I didn't give myself the opportunity to back out."

"Mom's idea?"

"It usually is."

Laughter burst through the room. She held her hand out to steady him. "She's up next." After helping him to his feet, she guided him to the chair across the room. "What are you dong here, Dad?"

"Your Mom, says it's a much needed vacation." Vision in and out, he struggled to focus on her. A bottle of what he assumed was water materialized in his hand. Followed by a thump against his elbow. "I'll drink it when I can see it clearly."

"Wait here." Kayla stood, warning him not to move with a finger in his direction. A quirk in her lips, she moved back to the center of the room.

The whir sent spikes down his extremities. *Calm down, Robert, we made it.* He focused on his breaths, blinking the last of the black spots from his eyes. It was the only thing preventing him from falling flat on his face as Julie's capsule settled in front of his daughter.

"Breathe through your nose."

"Sometimes I forget what you do for a living." She laughed at his attempt to pretend. Every day since she left for her apprenticeship, he hoped he hadn't made a mistake to sign off on it. Julie insisted on letting her spread her wings. Thankfully, Michael was never interested in spreading his wings. At least he wasn't—yet. He wished Kayla was more like her brother. It was safer to stick close to home.

"I doubt that." He could feel her glare, despite her facing away from him. "Hey Mom!"

"Sweetheart, is your father awake yet?"

Heart pounding at the sound of Julie's voice, Robert swallowed the remnants of the bottle. "Right here, Hun." Kayla averted her eyes from him, assisting his wife to seat herself next to him.

"Something wrong sweetie?" Julie didn't let go of Kayla's hand once she was next to him. "You look a little *off*. I hope we're not too much of a bother."

"Of course not, *Mom*!" Her eyes darted from Julie to her brother, his vessel making its way to the center of the receiving room. "I... I... I just don't like these any more than dad does."

Liar. She'd never been good at lying to him. The smallest vibrations in the vessels of her eyes, the sound of her fingers shifting erratically, and the shortness of breath—that one was relatively infrequent.

"We don't really travel like this very often."

"We?" Staring far longer, and more closely, than any ordinary parent might, he noticed her shortened strides.

"You don't seriously think she does all this work alone, do you Robbie?" Julie was glaring at him. She jabbed his ribs while whispering. "Don't patronize her. We just got here. She'll want us gone before the week is out—if you keep this up."

Kayla cleared her throat next to him. When she had exchanged places with his wife, Robert couldn't recall. His focus locked on the stasis pod Michael sat upright in, engaged in a groggy argument with his mother. He heard every word. Thankfully, they were used to his abnormalities. "I can't believe you let him in one of those *things*. And *Mom*." The smile didn't quite reach her eyes, the engorged veins and blotched complexion finally visible.

He found her hand on the chair between them and gave it a squeeze. "She had them sedate me."

The shake of her shoulders, as the laugh rolled off her tongue, sent vibrations through his veins. "What did she promise you for going through with it?"

"Never pushing it again."

"I'm sorry. I should have visited before now."

"Well, I'm here." Laughing, he stood. "Probably will be, for a while."

Her brows lifted, almost merging. Before he could question her reaction, Michael vaulted between them. "Kayla!"

"Mikey!"

"Can you believe Mom convinced him it wouldn't kill him to travel?"

His daughter shook her head. "The look on his face says that no *real* convincing was done."

Robert bit his tongue, waiting for the imminent sigh from Julie. She remained silent at his side, watching the kids stare at him. Their heartbeats suggested one or both of them would start laughing any second. He couldn't blame them for it. It had been one of his coping mechanisms, too.

"Alright, that is enough out of the two of you!" Julie shook her head, linking her arm through his. "Sweetie, we should probably get out of here." His wife lilted her head toward him. "Have they said if our things were ready to retrieve yet?"

Kayla's heart rate spiked. She swallowed saliva and forced a cough to cover it up. She knew full well he could tell she was anxious about something. The distraction was for the rest of the family. They couldn't read her the way he could.

"Already packed up! All we have to do is get you checked out at the front desk."

The four of them shuffled out of the receiving room, its cacophony of noises remaining behind. He promised himself to ask Kayla if the sensitivity still bothered her, the way it did him. One look at the twitching motions of her hand removed the need. She'd always hid the tick well, only doing it when noises overwhelmed her. The hope that her personal residence was buffered from the everyday assault was unnecessary. His daughter was just as bad as him about muffling every sound imaginable, at least the unwanted ones—or the ones that wouldn't kill someone.

Burying the laugh, he considered the memory of her beating her brother with a pillow for snoring when he crashed on her bedroom floor—after an entire night's worth of vid binging. Kayla looked at him, her eyes rolling quickly enough for the others to miss. They were both thankful Michael inherited his mother's normal hearing and reflexes.

"Okay, let's get out the door before these lights make me scream." She shook her head, nodding at him. "If it's bothering me, it's bothering you."

Robert grimaced with the effort to view the offending bulbs dangling from the ceiling. His ears were still ringing from the bombardment of the receiving room. "Please tell me you have a nice, quiet transport?"

Michael snorted. "Dad, there is no such thing."

"Sure there is!" Kayla laughed, leading them through the retracting doorway. "Roux has one!"

Each time the name fell from her lips, he heard it. Saying it in person, she couldn't quite hide the inflection, the twitch of her smile, and her heart rate.

"I imagine with Dr. Tahali's work, he needs to be relaxed," Julie prodded Michael forward.

"Is he like you and dad?" Michael guzzled the remnants of his water bottle.

"Actually... he's a full blood—like Gran." Her pace quickened, strides taking her across the small patch of flattened earth.

Robert's fingers threatened to retract into permanent fists. A full blood Arros, like his mother, that wasn't exactly comforting. There were so many things wrong with his daughter working with one of *them.* Not wanting to insult her boss, he trudged along the path to where a Dr. Tahali secured the last of their luggage on the bed of the strangest vehicle he'd ever seen. That was saying something, when he considered how many world's he traveled to as a boy. His adult life he'd spent on one of the most mundane human populated planets possible.

He recognized Tahali from the profile on the medical company's records. He signed far too many papers, giving his daughter permission to take the apprenticeship, to skip the biographies of those she would work with. Dr Tahali was a senior medical assistant when Kayla started the program, quickly moving ahead of the others in the apprenticeship.

Julie had called him paranoid for keeping tabs on the others his daughter worked with. Kayla always had a nose for staying out of trouble, and the offered apprenticeship had been a *big* deal. She was only fifteen, far too young for his little girl to be traveling to the known galaxies—but Julie convinced him to relent.

She loved it. Every vid they received from her—was proof of that.

The man standing next to the transport smiled, his hand extended to Julie.

She refused, wrapping both arms around the startled doctor. "Kayla speaks very highly of you. Thank you so much for taking such good care of our little girl."

Unable to parrot the response, Robert stared at the doctor. He was standing a little too close to his daughter. He couldn't decide if the idiot was observant enough to know what he was dealing with, taking on Kayla as his prodigy. It was possible he did. He was a doctor, after all. And with them sharing at least three quarters—similar genetics—he could have been assuming he was mentoring one of his *own*. She was far from normal, even among their own kind.

Throat constricting at the inflection in Tahali's tone. Robert found Julie's free hand. *Don't jump to conclusions Robert, he's fond of his apprentice, nothing more. Stop overreacting.*

"Mr. Erickson." The doctor didn't extend his hand to him. Knowing Kayla, she probably warned Roux about his aversion to touching people he didn't know. That, and it wasn't usually common for Arros to extend the greeting, anyway. *Does he think I prefer my mother's customs?* Shaking off the thought, he almost grumbled. He raised Kayla among humans. The doctor would never consider it without his daughter's input. Tahali flashed a hesitant smile for him, before directing them to the side doors of the transport. "It's a good thing your ship came in yesterday. We're racing a storm home."

With a sigh of relief, Robert found the restraints for the back seat. It explained the hesitation in his tone. They wanted to greet them properly—but didn't have the time to spare.

"Where we are going is about an hour *North* of here."

"*If* you floor it now." Kayla laughed. "Buckle up *quickly*. Roux likes to drive —fast!" She climbed into the seat beside the doctor, fastening her restraint and gripping the bar at her right.

"I'll try not to make any of you sick, but we are trying to get back before the trail is washed out." He laughed, patting Kayla's hand in a manner that set Robert's stomach off.

True to her word, the only sounds heard were the faint scratches of the tires against the terrain. *Yep, he's one of us alright. Poor kid.* Unfortunately, he wasn't a kid. Which made Robert's nerves harden at sight of the attention to his daughter. Not wanting to anger his daughter's boss, he shook the thought off. He looked out the window instead. They left the small outcropping within seconds, alien foliage rising from every angle. How the doctor could stay on the road at the speed he traversed the jungle was beside him. But it was quiet.

That he was thankful for.

The lack of background noises allowed for all four heartbeats to register at a distasteful level, causing him to squint. Tahali was enjoying himself, as was Michael. His wife and daughter—not as much. The effort to differentiate between the two had been easy, even when she was a child. But *this* was different. The erratic nature couldn't be simply explained away by the speed of her mentor's driving. She'd been exposed to it off and on for at least seven years, the last three she'd undoubtedly been exposed to *more* than enough.

With extra effort to tune out the irregularities, he cleared his throat. "So, how's the work coming out here? Staying busy?"

Kayla grimaced, the banking turn shifting all of them in their seats.

"Usually," Tahali adjusted the mirror to allow him to look back at them. "The rain season is just starting, so things will slow down. We won't have as much foot traffic. It's actually the *perfect* time for you to arrive."

Robert could hear the doctor's hands tighten around the steering wheel, accentuating his inflection on the word—perfect. Exhaling, he turned to face Julie. Her raised brow and half frown warned him to be nice.

"And fortunate that you arrived *now*." His voice fluctuated as he swerved around a rock on the trail. How it got there, in the middle of the jungle, Robert didn't want to consider.

"Why's that?" His son chimed, his enjoyment radiating.

"Our assignment here is up in three months, just about when the *rain* season—ends."

"Don't worry Dad, we don't really use the same *travel* methods."

"That would be a waste of valuable time. Gotta research the next assignment en route." Tahali laughed, his hands tightening more on the wheel. The accelerator made little noise as he pressed the pedal to the floor.

The relief pouring from his wife was palpable. Before he could speak, Kayla rattled off curses, words only he and their driver could understand—at least he hoped his parents hadn't taught Michael the words his sister spewed with her eyes fixed on the display in front of her.

"Yeah, I can see it. We'll be cutting it a little close." He reached up and pressed a button above his head. A whir sounded from behind them as a cover shifted over the luggage rack.

Trying to ignore Kayla's choice of curses, Robert stared out the window—again. It shouldn't have bothered him that she was using it, it had been her first language—and his. They never used it at home. His mother often scolded his children, and his younger siblings, with the common phrasing of her native Arros tongue. But anything aside from that—was discouraged by his father. They lived in a heavily human populated settlement. His reasoning had been to prevent the family from being discriminated against, or unnecessary attention drawn to them. No one ever mentioned why to Julie or Michael—they didn't need the added stress.

"What kind of medical emergencies do you get out here?" Michael shifted in his seat, leaning over the console between his sister and Tahali. "It looks pretty desolate."

Dr. Tahali laughed. "You'd be surprised... It took quite a while for most of the locals to be open to coming by. They're not overly fond of outsiders. It's why they don't normally rotate shifts out here as frequently as they do in other locations. But there are miners from various worlds who come and go—we see them more often than you would think, but they have their own medical facilities too."

He recalled his daughter's words on the matter. Their team landed there over three years before. "Is there a reason for the transfer, then? I would think they'd want to keep familiar faces here for longer than you've been here."

Shuddered breaths escaped him, albeit brief, they rivaled by the sharp intake at his side. "Normal rotations *are* much longer. But Roux's specialty isn't normally as useful here."

"We're here because you need the experience." The man laughed, strumming the fingers of his left hand on the steering wheel.

"As if I *need* a reminder." Her tone trembled, despite the laugh she expelled.

Robert stared at his daughter, waiting to see if she would look at him. In the moments that passed, Kayla had kept her gaze on the road or on the readouts of the dash. She occasionally looked at the Doctor.

Julie squeezed his shoulder, reaching behind their son to do so, distracting him from the ragged breaths in the front seat. "You're sure we're not a burden on your travel plans?"

"Of course not, Mrs. Erickson. We called in first thing this morning, amending our arrangements. It was no trouble at all. We're happy to have you here."

Julie kept her eyes on Robert. She stroked his shoulder, smiling.

"How long *exactly* have you been dating my daughter, Dr. Tahali?"

"Robbie!" Julie screeched from her side of the back seat. "What a thing to say!"

Kayla spun in her seat, looking at him for the first time since they'd left the depot. The rapid heartbeats betrayed the innocent look of her eyes. Dr. Tahali's only spiked for an instant. "Dad! Seriously?!"

"Oh, my gosh! You two are soooo dating!" Michael laughed maniacally, leaning back against the seat, ending Julie's ability to glare at Robert without hindrance.

The Doctor's hands tightened around the wheel, the groan of the rubber grip reverberating in small space. He didn't look away from the road, or the darkening skies visible through the foliage. Unlike the others, his heartbeats were steady and deliberate. Robert stared at the back of his head, wondering what exactly this idiot thought he was doing, courting someone like his daughter. He had to know what Kayla was, and yet—he was still interested.

His stomach lurched, his head snapping toward his daughter. He hoped the look he gave her broadcast his thoughts loud and clear. Nostrils flaring, she bared her teeth at him. Shaking her head, Kayla gripped the back of her seat.

"May I suggest we finish this conversation when I'm not driving at unreasonable speeds to avoid a storm? One that we don't want to be stuck out here in, I might add." Roux squeezed Kayla's hand in a moment before he placed both hands on the wheel once more. The gentle stroke of his thumb over the back of Kayla's hand as he pulled away hadn't gone unnoticed. Robert ground his teeth together. They were closer than his daughter or the doctor were willing to let on.

They spent the rest of the drive in relative silence. Robert traded glares with his daughter and the back of her *boyfriend's* head. Kayla wouldn't look directly at him. Julie tapped her fingers on her knees, glancing at Kayla, concern radiating from her. Michael pulled out his tablet, playing a game to ignore the rest of the passengers. Rain began pattering against the roof. Its faint sound would have passed notice for Michael and Julie if it weren't for the drops against the windshield and side windows. The transport shuddered violently with a dragging turn—Kayla once said it was called drifting, brought them near a cluster of buildings. He wouldn't have noticed the structures if not for the glare of their road lights bouncing back to them.

The screech of metal alerted him to the opening of a doorway. The opening retracted toward ground level, wide enough to fit the transport. Tahali maneuvered the vehicle toward the opening just as the sheathe disappeared, stopping mere feet from the end of the space. Looking around the enclosure proved there was enough space for at least three of the vehicles to park side by side. They organized the rest of the space with steel racks secured to the walls and floors. The racks were cluttered with boxes labeled in four different languages—each secured with biometric locks.

Dr. Tahali jumped from his seat, running around the car to open the door for the ladies. "Kayla can take you inside. I'll get your bags."

"Why does the door open that way? Isn't it inconvenient?" Michael watched it rise to a close, clacking loudly once it met the top.

"Prevents wear and tear on the pressure seal if it's under the awning." Kayla laughed. "We'd have to replace it more often than you think with the weather here."

"That, and it prevents the weather from flooding our supply room when that seal fails. This rain would do that pretty fast. Imagine if you opened the door at the wrong time." The doctor grunted, releasing the latch on the cover over their belongings.

"What about the mechanism? Doesn't that take a beating?" Michael remained behind with the doctor.

"There's a guard. It flips up after the door is closed. Sturdier than the interior pressure seal."

Shaking his head, Robert hurried after his wife and daughter. The decision to resist the urge to question her while he was still angry floated as he inspected the store room. The ceiling was at least ten feet high, with shelving spaced far enough apart for a medical gurney to easily traverse the small maze.

Kayla didn't look at him as she waved her hand over the mechanism halfway up the wall. "The place isn't as high-tech inside. We have normal doors, a lot like what you have at home. The outside is primarily to keep the weather out and deter any of the locals from trying to steal the medical supplies."

He stepped in after they entered a decent sized room—appearing to be a communal living space—had modest furnishings spread about. The kitchen was the largest part of the space. It had a decent bar counter and a small table with two chairs off to one side. He eyed his daughter where she skirted the table to reach the fridge.

"Give me a few minutes and I'll get some food going." She didn't look up from her tasks, shuffling through doors in the stark metal cabinetry. He knew it because he stood there, three feet away—waiting for her to acknowledge his presence.

"Robert," Julie whispered from the couch behind him. She pat the seat next to her, her smile forced.

Commanding the nerves of his legs to obey, he trudged across the room to his wife. He could wait until the man in question was present. *Maybe.* He and Michael entered and retreated several times, laden with bags they dropped just inside the doorway.

Eyes on the darkened opening, he watched the man enter with the last of their things. Instead of dropping them to the floor, he continued beyond the couch, his expression blank as the steadiness of his heart. *How is he masking that right now?* Robert had trouble hiding his emotions from his own mother. And this young doctor couldn't be thirty-five by the looks of him. It wasn't a common practice to push that level of composure. *Unless he received his initial medical training in the military...* His spine went rigid at the thought. He knew he'd heard the name Tahali before, a name that screamed of a superior military upbringing.

The doctor disappeared into one of the doors along the back wall, emerging a few moments later—his eyes angled in Robert's direction. *He knows exactly what I'm thinking.* Not that his mother's species could read minds, but most Arros were very good at reading body language, in addition to their heightened senses. Especially for those who'd lived and breathed military command training.

"I hope you don't mind the pull out bed on the couch, Mikey. We only have two rooms." He handed a pile of bedding to Michael. "It should be enough to keep you comfortable—if not, our room is just there. We'll get you anything else you need." Pointing toward the door on the far side of the kitchen, Dr. Tahali made his way to the cupboards.

Robert's throat tightened—fingers twitching, quickly remedied by Julie's hand on his knee. "*Your* room?"

"Yes, Dad. *Our* room." Kayla's voice was muffled as she dipped below the counter.

"Let me get that." The doctor helped her retrieve something from the back of the space. He set it down, helping Robert's daughter stand.

Her heart rate wasn't as concerning as the grimace on her face. It wasn't her usual: 'Back off Dad' expression. No, it was a pained expression he knew too well. Struggling to prevent his legs from carrying him across the room to his daughter's side, Robert cleared his throat.

"To answer your earlier question..." Roux set a metal bowl down on the stove-top. "Five years." He didn't look away from Kayla or their preparations as he spoke.

Robert closed his eyes, swallowing the saliva pooling in his throat. *Five years, she's only been with their organization for eight.* "Well, at least you waited until she was a *legal adult* by human standards."

Julie cursed beside him. "Robert!"

"I don't have the right to know? I'm her father!"

"Do I have to be here for this conversation?" Michael shifted his gaze between the four of them.

Kayla looked up, apology ebbing from her—not for her father. "There's an examination room through there," she pointed to the opposite side of the house from the kitchen. "You can access my collection of vids from the interface by the screen—you can't miss it."

Michael practically ran from their presence, the door closing before his sister finished speaking. Robert's attention turned to Kayla, where she stood with her elbows locked—hands wrapped around the counter's edge.

"Yes, I was a legal adult, and before you ask—I only moved in with him three years ago." Taking the cue from the grimace he failed to suppress, she continued. "I've never used that room. And *no,* I don't want your opinion on the matter." She stormed out of the room.

Julie inhaled a sharp breath at the sound of the door to *their* bedroom slamming closed.

Kayla's boyfriend didn't look up, his eyes and hands busied with their meal. "She wanted to tell you before now. No, moving in with me—wasn't her suggestion." Looking up at him, Roux forced a smile. "And before you ask —I *do* know what she is."

Julie tightened her fingers around Robert's knee. "I'm not sure I like how you're referring to her human heritage."

"That's not what he meant." Patting his wife's hand, he gave her a reassuring smile. "It's a long story, having to do with Kayla's mother, *her* heritage."

Kayla never wanted to be like her mother. His insistence on reminding her of the *troubles* he'd had as a result could have been less forceful. It had felt like the best way to protect her—at the time. Reminding himself that she was a grown woman, capable of making her own decisions, didn't help to ease the sludge of fear creeping through his veins.

Julie stared forward, the hurt resonating from fingers knotting themselves together. He'd never opened up much to her about his first relationship—Kayla's mother. She knew he had his reasons. Before that exact moment, it had seemed fair for neither of them to broach the subject. His wife had her own secrets, too. As far as Julie knew, Kayla's mother had died three years before they'd met. Robert wanted it to stay that way.

He wasn't sure how much detail his daughter had given the young man, refusing to look at him. Did he know who Kayla's mother was? Blinking the thought away, he reminded himself that even Kayla didn't know *that* detail. She was too young to remember, and he'd begged her not to ask about her mother—on more than one occasion.

"It is never easy to lose a mate." The young man rubbed his fingers through the mixture in the smallest of the three bowls in front of him.

Robert would never know the pain a full-blood Arros would in that sense. The young man had to know that he was half human. "And what would you know about it? You aren't you insinuating something about my daughter—are you?"

Dr. Tahali exhaled, pressing his lips into a thin line. "My parents are... I think the human term is—Divorced."

Julie stroked his knee again. She'd believed what their friends had said about Kayla's mother. Heart pounding, he squeezed her hand. Breath caught in his chest, his eyes blurring.

"Breathe, Dad." Kayla knelt in front of him, her hands folded in her lap. She looked at Julie. "Mom, what Roux is trying to say..." she forced the smile, tears threatening to fall. "A full blood Arros marriage isn't like a human marriage. It is a lifelong thing. Even if they decide they don't want to be together anymore." Patting Robert's knee, his daughter stood, the same grimace spreading across her face. Her hand fisted at her mouth, too late to hide it from either of them. "Dad is only half, so he doesn't have the same problem Roux's parents do."

His wife pressed her lips between her teeth, her eyes angling toward him. "Your mother *actually* explained that part while we were dating."

Feeling his eyebrows raise, he turned to face his wife. "Really?"

"And a *bit* more."

His stomach dropped through his digestive track, weighting him deeper into the couch. *Thanks for the warning, Mom!* Groaning internally, he stared at his wife. She hadn't mentioned a word of his mother's behavior for over eighteen years.

"Kayla, sweetheart. Were you planning to tell us you were pregnant before you started showing?" Julie shook her head, laughing softly at Kayla's expression. She shook her finger in Robert's face. "This is her choice, who she spends her life with Robert." Turning back to face his daughter, Julie sighed. "I hope I'm right in assuming neither of you made that decision lightly." She gestured toward Roux. "Especially when considering your experience with your parents."

"Yes Ma'am. Seeing your meaning clearly. I promise you, neither of us was forced into the decision. *And* neither of us jumped into the relationship with *unrealistic* expectations." He dumped the concoction into the pan. It sizzled loudly for several seconds before it died down enough for anyone to speak over it.

Fingers tangling, Kayla's tears fell. "We didn't find out that long ago. Shaking her head, she exhaled. I had fully intended to send a message to you about it. We even recorded it. We made one for Gran too." She motioned toward her mate. "I was going to send it yesterday..."

"But you got word of our arrival instead." Robert bit down on his lower lip. Any harder, and it would bleed. Wanting to avoid any insinuation of not approving, he lessened the pressure of his jaws. "Kayla." He stood up, reaching out with both arms.

His daughter collided with him, tears soaking through his shirt. "We only found out two months ago, Dad. I promise I wasn't trying to keep *it* from you. I just didn't know how to tell you about *us*, before now."

"Oh, sweetie!" Julie stood behind her, joining the embrace. "We didn't exactly give you much notice on our trip, *either*."

"*This* is why we're transferring before the usual time frame. Neither of us feels this planet is conducive to raising our child."

Looking over the shoulders of his wife and daughter. Robert watched his son-in-law swish the food around in the skillet. His eyes never left Kayla.

"I want you to know, Mr. Erickson, that I *do* love your daughter. *Genuinely*."

Shoulders stiffening, he rubbed his hands along his daughter's back. She'd never been one to use what she'd inherited from her mother. He hoped things hadn't changed in the last eight years—for Roux's sake.

"You'd better." Julie turned to face Roux. "You're stuck with her for life. And that means us too!"

4

Kayla

"That should have gone worse."

Roux laughed at her, pulling the blanket back. He fluffed her pillow before heading for their bathroom. "Well, there is always plenty of time for it to become worse. They'll probably be with us for a while, now that they know."

Kayla rolled her eyes and sat down on the bed. She stared through the bathroom door, watching him brush his teeth. Truthfully, most people couldn't differentiate Roux from humans—if they didn't know any better. There were very subtle differences on the outside. The inside, however, was an entirely different story. It was part of her concern about starting the medical apprenticeship. Thankfully, Roux had known right out of the gate, ensuring she was under his wing as a senior intern. The others found out eventually, but it had been on her terms.

"They're not likely to leave now that they know we're having a baby. You know that, right?" Her father's business would run seamlessly, regardless of where he was. He'd worked hard to make it that way. *That,* and her grandfather could fully run things in his absence.

He pointed his toothbrush at her, smiling—toothpaste coating his lips. "Yes, but *eventually,* they'll have a place of their own."

Kayla shook her head at him. "You're okay with this now. Just wait until they're expecting us to have more kids. And you haven't even spent more than a few hours with them—yet. Roux, you do not know what you're getting yourself into."

Roux wiped a cloth across his face. He crossed to her side and sat down with an arm over her shoulder. "My love for you is not determined by whether I can stand your family." He gazed at the door for a few moments. They could both hear Julie speaking to her brother, even with the door muffling it. "When do you think we should tell them we technically got married—*before* we made this decision?"

Laughter burst from her as she shook her head. Knowing it would carry beyond their door, she slapped a hand over her mouth. Her step mother and brother would have to be deaf not to hear it, and she knew for a fact that they weren't. "Lets not mention that, yet." Her father was having a hard enough time dealing with what they told him, knowing she'd legally married Roux in front of their friends and colleagues, three years earlier—without telling him, wouldn't comfort him until she had the chance to explain more.

5

Robert

"Robbie, I think you're overreacting."

"Julie, there are things about Kayla's mother that are too painful to explain. I wish I could, I really do. But I can't." Dropping into the bed fully clothed, not bothering to turn the bed down, he threw the pillow on his side over his face. "There are things about Kayla that she inherited from her mother, things..." shaking his head, he rolled to his stomach.

Her fingers found the tension in his shoulders. She'd always been good at it. Exhaling, he turned his head to her from under the pillow, at least what little the gap allowed. "I really should have told you everything before now. I can't count the times I've tried."

"I know Robbie. Your mother said it was going to be difficult for you. She never promised it would be easy for me to watch you deal with the pain it left." The circular motions of her fingers lulled the muscles into a relaxed state. "I will never force it out of you, you know that. My life wasn't easy before I met you, either. I honestly couldn't believe how wonderful you were to Kayla —even with the pain the memories of her mother caused you. It was the first thing that drew me to you."

He knew it. She'd said it enough times for him to have nearly memorized the notion. But he still loved to hear her say it. He reached for her hand, shifting to pull her down to his chest. "Honey, if you knew half the things I keep to myself... You'd never let Michael out of your sight, you would never have let me sign the release forms for Kayla to leave, and we'd be suck on the most mundane planet for the rest of our lives. I don't want that for you."

The way she stroked his jawline eased every fear from his mind. Meeting her had been the best thing for him—despite his frustrations with his best friend for setting him up on the blind date. "I'm here, and I'm always willing to listen. You know that, dear. Whatever you're worried about. You need to address it with her, before it makes you unbearable." She tapped under his chin before rolling away. "The two of you are going to have to work this out—for the sake of everyone else here."

He maneuvered the pillow behind his head, watching her step out into the front room to check on their son. *Probably reminding him about his medication.* He exhaled, covering his face with his hand when squeezing his eyes shut failed to block the memories. The five months prior to their journey had been especially difficult. His son's sixteenth birthday had been the root cause of the insurgent flashbacks to the year everything changed for him. It wasn't the first time, either. Kayla had left home before her sixteenth birthday, knowing full well what it meant to him. Unfortunately, his daughter's selflessness hadn't paid off as much as she hoped for. He didn't have the heart to tell her. Part of him regretted letting her go. Another knew it wouldn't have made it better to have her there.

Gazing into the dark, he wondered how much she'd told Roux—again. His chest weighed against his organs, breath refusing to draw in for several moments of silence. While Kayla hadn't parted with him on bad terms, it had been a train wreck for him to experience. In the few years before she left their home to help the lesser fortunate civilizations, he'd confessed more about her mother than he should have. He knew it was the driving force behind her decision to leave, and he regretted doing it—every day since.

His beautiful little girl had cried herself to sleep after a difficult discussion. She didn't speak to him for the following week. And while she promised him she wasn't angry, he knew the details he'd given her hurt her. It wasn't his intention. She and her brother were two of the most important things in his life. They kept him sane and gave him hope for the future with every year that passed. A hope for them to never experience life the way he had.

6

Kayla

She hadn't been expecting utter silence when she left the bedroom. Some time in the night, Michael must have dragged the mattress for the pull-out bed into the guest room. For a guy, her little brother was pretty good at catering to their father. He might complain about how protective their father was of them, but he worried about him just as much. Kayla did too. The only difference, she knew *some* details about the nightmares their father dealt with. Holding her breath as she crossed to the kitchen, she hoped Michael never learned the truth about their father's anxieties.

"Good Morning, Dad." She didn't have to see him emerge to know. His gait was something she'd memorized as a little girl.

"Hey, um, is he..." her father nodded toward her bedroom.

"He's writing a report for the head office." She pulled out a jug of water from the fridge, setting it and two cups on the counter. "He can't hear us. He wears headphones to help him tune everything out while he's working on reports." She smiled at him. "Kind of like *someone else* I know."

Chuckling, he took the offered cup. "The *curse* of excellent hearing."

"Are Mom and Mikey still asleep?"

"Neither of them could sleep for a while last night and they didn't want to keep the two of you awake. The booster they took for the trip was a bit of a..." he shook his head, massaging the back of one hand with his thumb. "They'll be fine in a few days."

Sipping the water slowly, she sat down in her usual chair at the table. "If you're hungry, there is plenty to choose from in the fridge."

He crossed to stand behind Roux's chair. "No appetite?"

An understatement, but she wasn't about to admit it to her father. "Pretty much."

He sat down, resting his cup in the center of the small table. "I'm not sure if it would help. But you could ask Julie about what helped her."

"I'm not waking Mom up right now to ask her *that.*"

He shrugged in the same motion to lean back in the chair. "So, uh, Roux... he seems like a pretty decent guy."

Snorting water through her nose wasn't exactly comfortable, but it got a laugh out of her father. "Dad, not now, please. I may throw up on you."

"Be that as it may, I think now might be the only private time we get—for a while."

Her father was right; he was almost *always* right. "Roux's known the whole time. He guessed it on day one." Blowing hair from her face, she shook her head at him. "I don't make him do anything, Dad. I never have."

With a sigh, he leaned forward, resting his elbows on the table. "Kayla, I never said you'd do it intentionally."

"I am *not* like my mother. I would *never* force Roux to do anything."

His brows drew together, lips in a thin line. "I would never accuse you of being *her.*" He reached across the table, taking her by the wrist. "I just want to protect you. Being with someone like him puts you in a very visible position. I worry, because I love you so much, sweetheart."

Someone like him... Daddy, you really don't understand... Tears formed as she focused on the rest of his comment. She cursed her hormones for the effect. She'd always known her father cared a great deal for her. He wouldn't have raised her alone for as long as he did—if he'd blamed her for his life. "Roux is resigning his position for that reason."

"What?"

"We would just stay here, but it is a harsh environment for a child. I couldn't tell you how many times I have treated life-threatening injuries—from many sources. Indigenous creatures, fauna, you name it. I don't want my child living here, any more than Roux does." She blinked tears free, her father's expression blurring. The sound of his breaths continued to rattle through her head.

He slid his chair closer, wrapping an arm around her.

"He's giving up everything for me, for our child, and I've never once asked him to."

Her father tightened his grip around her. "Sounds like he's just trying to protect his family. I would do the same."

Kayla laughed at him. He had done it. She was too young to remember what life had been like before they moved in with his parents, dropping off the grid—entirely. She couldn't bring herself to tell him that Roux hadn't told his family about her. In fact, he hadn't spoken to his family the entire time they'd worked together. She knew about the rift his carrier choice had caused but didn't dare tell her father the intimate details of it.

"I'm sorry for how I acted last night... I just..."

"Faced every fear you have to come here, found out I'm not only living with Roux, but mated with him—Oh, and I'm three months pregnant with his child! Dad, you'd be rather cold-hearted to not freak out about it—after everything you've been through."

He laughed, sliding away from her a short distance. "Yeah, when you put it that way."

"I knew you'd be upset that I didn't tell about you our relationship sooner. Honestly, I should have. But I was afraid of what you'd say about Roux being a full blood Arros. And neither of us expected you to be here," she prodded the table with a single finger. "When we told you."

He rubbed his hands over his face. "Sweetheart, I have nothing against our species. My mother is Arros—*remember*?"

"Yes, but you never talk about it to *anyone*. Mom and Mikey are the only ones outside of *your* family who know that Gran is Arros."

"We've been so worried about anyone finding us." Shaking his head, he tipped back his cup. "Twenty-two years, no incidents, and I still can't bring myself to let it go."

"You'd be stupid if you did."

He snorted in reply, his hands shaking in his lap.

"Dad, Roux doesn't know about all of it. He knows my mother wasn't good to you. But that is all I've said."

"I was wondering about that." Her father cringed, accentuating the word wondering.

Thumbing the table, she turned to face him. "His parents were betrothed when they were children. Some political agenda, on both sides of the family—I think. It worked for a while, but when he was young, they separated. He doesn't talk much about it, just that his parents expected too much from him.

Roux abandoned a military career for what he does. They weren't exactly happy with him when he told them."

"I was going to ask if he'd been in the military. He's pretty *intense,* for a Medical Doctor." He grimaced. Kayla knew he was holding back the hostility he had toward the military.

She slid her chair back, laughing through clenched teeth. "Yeah, I figured you would catch on to that. He is pretty good at controlling his heart rate when he needs to. From what I understand—he started off pretty young."

"How old is he, *exactly*?"

"Thirty-eight."

The look on her father's face was one she knew. He was calculating how old her *husband* was when he'd lived on one of the flourishing worlds that freely mingled between humans and Arros. His parents met on the same planet he'd lived on for most of his life. Until *it* happened. Reaching for his hand, she squeezed it gently. "I doubt his family knows your parents, even if they did—it has been a long time."

"That's..." her father swallowed water with a cringe. "A bit of gap."

"Dad, he's a full blood Arros. The age gap is nothing in the long run."

"Kayla, sweetie, Roux is just a little close to being *my* age—for my comfort."

"Neither of you looks your age, *Dad.*"

The two of them sat in silence. She sipped her water. He stared at the wall—alternating between rubbing each of his hands along the back of his neck. Her father's hair wasn't short, but it wasn't long either, most of it falling to his jawline—if you pulled the curls to full extension. The fibers he fiddled with were only a few inches longer than Roux kept his—preferring something a mite longer than the average military cut.

"Good morning, Mr. Erickson." Roux skirted them at the table, resting his hands on her shoulders.

"Please, Mr. Erickson sounds awful. And don't call me Dad, either, that just makes me feel old."

"I can do that, Robert." Roux pulled a folding chair from behind the false wall at the table. "I'd like to apologize for not requesting permission."

Kayla smiled, resisting the urge to glare at him. The two of them needed to smooth things over. The next few months would be complicated if they didn't.

"As long as you take care of my little girl, I promise I won't make a fuss."

Reaching across the table, Roux grinned. "Deal."

She shook her head at the exchange, making her way to the kitchen. It was going to be the longest rain season—ever. But at least she could sleep better knowing her father would actually acknowledge Roux, enough to take his hand. "The usual?"

"As long as you're feeling up to it. I *can* make it myself—if you don't." Roux sent her a questioning glance. He always ate a light breakfast, claiming it gave him less trouble when he ran. His appetite was always normal for the rest of the day.

The ability to ignore them was impossible. Even frying an egg—or at least what came close to a chicken's egg from Roux's home-world. She watched the near silent exchange between them, cringing every time her husband looked at her. Her father was stiff in his chair. He'd never been good about meeting new people. Surprised he hadn't railed on her more than he had, she poured a glass of water.

Plate in hand, she made her way to the table. "You're going to have to fish more out of the storage on your way back. These are the last two in the fridge."

"Really?" Roux shifted to face her. "How many did I use last night for dinner?"

Eight, he'd used eight. All of which ended up on his plate. Roux always had a healthy appetite, but the presence of her family brought something on in him. She hadn't seen him act that way since they first met. *Is he more nervous than he is telling me?* "I have no idea. I thought we had twelve left yesterday morning, but I could be wrong."

Both brows rising, Roux shook his head. "I guess I ate more than I thought."

She handed him a fork before taking her seat at his side. "You can help yourself to anything you want, Dad. Roux is partial to his small breakfasts before a run."

"Running in this?" Her father cringed. "It is a bit of a mess out there by now, isn't it? I don't think I heard it let up."

"It's not so bad." Roux speared his eggs.

"Ever heard of a treadmill?" Her father shrugged when she scowled at him.

Roux swished the last bite of his breakfast away with a long gulp of water. He swallowed the remnants with a smile. "Yes, but I never use it." Shaking his head, he laughed. "It doesn't quite do it for me." Roux reached for the jacket she held out for him, he kissed her cheek on his way to the door. "I'll be back in a few hours. Oh, and Robert, you're welcome to use the treadmill. It is collecting dust in the exam room closet. Kayla can show you where it is."

Kayla glared at him out of view of the others, walking him to the door. "He's not going to use it either."

He shrugged while he input the code to open it. "Can't say I didn't try to offer what we have."

"Be safe and stay away from the canals. They're supposed to flood today."

"I know how to avoid the trouble spots. Have fun with your family. I'll be back soon." Kissing her again, Roux flipped the hood of his jacket up and disappeared through the doorway.

"Was that Roux leaving?" Her mother poked her head through the doorway to the guest room. "Did it stop raining?"

"Yes, it was. And no. A deluge won't stop him from getting his run in." Shaking her head, she locked the door at the pad and walked back to the table.

"Hasn't he heard of a Treadmill?"

Her father laughed, leaning back in his chair to hand her mother a glass of water. "I just asked him that."

She couldn't help laughing at the normalcy of having her parents there as she sat down across from her father—again. "It's not as bad as it was last night. He'll avoid his normal routes to detour around the flooded areas."

"Seems a little dangerous to me, running in a storm."

"Roux can handle himself, Mom."

"With a *body* like that, I would expect that."

Her father choked, water spewing from his mouth.

"Don't worry, Robbie. I never said it was a trait I find appealing."

"Ew! Was Mom just saying your husband is attractive?" Michael shambled from the bedroom, rubbing his eyes.

"NO!" Their parents responded in unison.

7

Roux

Kayla wouldn't watch him leave, not like she normally did. The presence of her family already held most of her attention. He took advantage of the situation and cut through the trees before the curve in the road he normally used as cover. Thumbing the device in his pocket, blocking his presence from every sensor in range, Roux grimaced. He hated lying to her about where he went on his runs, but it was necessary—until he could explain.

The hood kept most of the moisture away from his face. The light wind helped too. Roux started off at a brisk pace, inhaling the fresh scent that would morph over the next several weeks. The clean air would be musty before the rain season let up.

"Are you running away already? What are the potential in-laws going to think about you?"

Roux grumbled, opening the connection he often left *closed.* "Spying on me again, are you, Farz?"

"Just making sure you're in one piece. I can't imagine her father wanted to leave you whole after he realized you two have been living together for three years."

Roux trudged through the damp undergrowth, avoiding the divots he found early on in their time on the planet. They'd be full of water. The last thing he needed was to show up with socks soaked through with mud. Neither destination would allow him through the door if he couldn't at least maintain a certain amount of cleanliness.

"So... what's he like?"

"An overprotective father. How else would he be?"

"I don't know... considering your girl... a lot of things."

"Almost there."

"Yes, I know."

Farz met him at the door, his eyes scanning him up and down. "Well, you're in once piece *physically*. We'll see about mentally, soon enough." Reaching for the jacket, Roux's brother hung it on the empty peg beside his own. "Hope she didn't give you more than you can stomach today."

Remembering the few times in which she insisted on a full breakfast before he went out in the morning, he groaned. "That hasn't happened in three years." She was only trying to be a good wife, but he couldn't tell his brother that. And he couldn't tell Kayla his brother was living less than four miles from their home. *Omissions will be the death of me...*

8

Robert

Rain, rain, and more rain. When they told him it was a severe storm blowing in, he hadn't expected it to last weeks before it let up. Three boredom driven, weeks. The five of them did more than bump elbows in the fourteen hundred square feet of space—give or take. Occasionally, his daughter and her *husband* would disappear into their medical office, spending a few hours on a project of some sort, coming out looking like both of them spent too much time in front of a screen. Roux went out every morning for his run. Dedicated, but *insane*, in Robert's opinion.

Kayla spent most mornings hiding in their room. Julie helped her out as much as possible. She'd successfully kept *actual* food down for the last few days, her mood improving as a result. Just when he thought things were evening out, allowing him to actually spend time with her, the rain let up. Sort of. Kayla and Roux both insisted that the rain wouldn't let up completely for another few months. A constant mist fell, fogging the exterior windows. Roux had opened the shutters in the front room that morning at the sound of fists pounding against the front door.

With clothing soaked clear through, the short wire haired young man—it could have been a girl—was covered in rivulets of hair and water. The kid spoke so fast in a language Robert wasn't familiar with. Even if he could understand, the frightened thing was speaking so fast—he would have lost every other word.

Roux listened attentively, his head bobbing with each gesture the boy made toward the trees. When their visitor had finished, the doctor called back into the house. Just hearing the man use the language of his birth set Robert's nerves on fire. Roux's words were intended for Kayla. Robert's ability to understand was definitely an afterthought for the doctor—judging by the reddened cheeks of his son-in-law.

"I'll be back before nightfall. Monitor that sensor in the southern quadrant. I think it's on the verge of failing. Let me know if it does. I can swing by and replace it on my way back." He hefted a bag from their medical office to the storage room, doubling as their garage. "If anyone else comes by while I'm gone..."

"As long as it isn't an emergency, I can handle it just fine by myself." Kayla shook her head. "Besides, I have them here to help me out."

Robert's wife stood in the doorway to the guest room they'd commandeered. She bit down on the nail of her left thumb. "Does he leave you alone often?"

"No, if he does, he is never more than a few hours—and that you know about." His daughter closed the door to their storage room. "You three are the only reason he is heading off like *this* without me."

Well, that was good to know. He didn't take her safety on a foreign planet lightly. One day he'd have to explain to his son-in-law just how much trouble they could be in, if Kayla's mother's side of the family ever found them.

"I feel like we're disrupting your routine." Julie apologized for the hundredth time.

"Mom. It isn't a problem. Roux can do his job *without* me hovering."

He smiled at his family from where he continued to pretend he was actually reading the book in his hands. Robert watched them re-arrange the front room to allow space to play the game they started a few days before. They hadn't expected to be couped up in the house the whole time they were there, so the few games they brought along—had been well used.

Though Julie wasn't her mother, Kayla never treated her otherwise. Even from the time they were dating, she'd taken to her. Her brother was her best friend, despite the age difference. The worries about her sanity leaving him behind had been needless. Kayla sent them regular vids, and they sent an exorbitant amount of replies.

"Dad." Kayla prodded him from his thoughts. "I am going to go check the sensor Roux was talking about. He might not be back before dark and I'd rather not have him dealing with it at night."

He shook the daze of memories away, realizing he completely ignored them as they finished their game. He somehow missed the entire conversation between Roux and his daughter. He rarely zoned out that badly. Kayla's expression extended to her brother and stepmother.

"Maybe you should go with her, and not Michael. You look like you need the fresh air more than we do." Julie pressed her lips between her teeth.

"I was just going to suggest it. You okay with that, Mikey?"

"No biggie, I'll just stick here with Mom." Michael nodded toward the door. "Is it safe to wander around the exterior at least?"

Kayla nodded, throwing a slender rod at him. Where it came from, he hadn't seen. "Keep that on you. Press the button in the middle there. It'll make a flashing light that scares off most of the critters, and a high-pitched noise that drives off the bigger ones."

Kayla pulled Robert to his feet, handing him a similar rod before disappearing into the storage room. When she came back with a rifle slung over her shoulder, his spine froze in position. "You expecting trouble?"

"No, but there are some pretty big and nasty things that occasionally think we'd be tasty." She winked at him. "Don't worry, Dad. Roux taught me to use it."

He shook his head at her, failing to hide the grimace. She'd known how to use firearms since she was eight. *That* had been his father's doing. "Are we walking?"

She laughed at him. "We're only going a half mile south. Roux said he'd try to finish up before we do—pick us up on the way back." With a turn to her brother, she winked. "Don't go too far. The weather is going to be bad again tonight, and I don't want to go looking for you in a downpour." She stuck her tongue out, briefly, laughing when Julie shook her head at them.

"Be safe." Julie waved to them from the door, monitoring where their son stretched his legs outdoors. Robert refrained from teasing her for the action. She often gave him a hard time for worrying, but she was just as bad about it.

"Shouldn't be too long, Mom. No worries."

They trudged through thick foliage, starting at least ten yards from the house—if you could call the metal structure a house. Oddly enough, the ground wasn't as soft as he'd expected it to be with so much rain. Kayla had explained the rainy season provided the reservoirs with the water the natives and transplants used for the rest of the year. The ground only softened nearer the roads. The mostly stony ground dried out quickly once the torrents let up.

"So, you do this much?" It didn't seem like the job for two doctors to keep sensors working, but he wasn't sure what exactly they did out there, anyway.

"Sometimes." Kayla continued to lead. The majority of her concentration was fixed on the surrounding sounds. There were quite a few, though most were trees creaking in the distance. "Part of the security net we have out here. An early warning system for just about anything that could go wrong." She snickered softly. "Like the kid who showed up today. *We* knew he was coming before he got close. Roux actually got an alert while he was on his way back from his run—that someone was headed our way."

Not sure if that should have been comforting, he increased his pace to walk at her side—dodging the occasional sapling that came between them. They walked far enough for the house to completely fade from view before she looked at him. "I didn't want to say it in front of them."

Cursing inwardly, Robert stopped. Kayla stopped two strides further.

"Dad, Roux is actually immune to *it*."

His eyes engorging, he stuffed half his fist into his mouth. "That *isn't* possible."

"So most think, but he *is*." She kept walking, adjusting the rifle on her back when it shifted out of position with an unsteady step. "He says it isn't unheard of, but it isn't common. Apparently, there are many people like him. It's just not something that is brought up in normal conversation."

"How?" Heart pounding with the possibilities it could provide, even him, Robert hurried to match her strides.

"He doesn't know how. No one knows why the specific gene presents itself."

"How is it *you* know he's immune, then?"

His daughter laughed through her nose as she avoided a large, slimy rock in their path. "Every time I accidentally use it, he gets what humans consider allergies. His reaction has never been terrible, and the migraines are a fairly recent thing. He thinks it's my hormones messing with him."

"Huh," not the reasoning he expected, but it was better than thinking his daughter had forced the guy to date her at some point—even if accidentally.

"So far, the allergy medications he's taking work better than either of us expected. We've been trying to pinpoint what it is about him that causes his immunity for a while." She plucked a fallen branch from between two stumps and pointed it at him. "Not that I don't enjoy knowing he actually cares about me. And not the *other* way."

He laughed with her, tugging the six-foot stick from her hands—using it and the rod she'd given him as walking sticks. "I'm relieved by that, truly."

"I know." She hopped up onto the short ledge in front of them and offered him her hand. "I just didn't think it was a good idea to mention it in front of Mom and Mikey. I mean..." She shook her head. "They still don't know, right?"

He accepted her help up and over. "No need to apologize for waiting for a private moment, I get it." Pushing the fear he'd suffocated for three weeks fully from his mind, he trudged after her. He imagined he might really enjoy their time together, knowing he didn't have to worry about their relationship. "Well, your Mom likes him and your brother is on the verge of idolizing what the two of you do." They'd heard enough for his son to have his interest peaked, but he hadn't imagined how quickly Michael would start reading the medical resources they had available.

"Almost there." His daughter smiled, pointing off into the distance. "What do *you* think of him, Dad?"

Taken aback by the question, he stopped, his ears pricking at the slightest sound. "I don't know, yet." He hadn't allowed Roux much of a chance, aside from the fact that he had no choice but to accept him as Kayla's mate.

She shook her head, bending to pull something from the ground that he hadn't seen before. "If you haven't noticed, it isn't exactly easy for him—either. He knows what you have been assuming about us, and has kept the matter to himself. Try giving him a little slack, now that you know he isn't some mindless victim."

Sitting on the nearby stump would come back to bite him later, the cold damp threatening to soak through his clothes within moments. He rubbed his hand across his face, nausea setting in.

His daughter slapped her free hand to her face. "I'm sorry, Dad. I didn't mean it like that."

He knew she didn't. She'd snapped at all of them more than once—later blaming it on being hormonally *challenged*. She joined him on the large stump, fiddling with the sensor casing. "No, you're right. I need to stop treating him like he hasn't had a choice in this."

She leaned her head on his shoulder. "I shouldn't have said it like that, all the same. What my mother did... It was terrible, and it was *wrong*."

Robert found his arm around his daughter's wrist, reflexively pulling her from the stump. Her eyes darted in the direction the sound had come from. "That wasn't an animal—was it?"

The silent shake of her head spurred him to pull the release on the rifle's tether over her shoulder. His hands slid into position—despite years of avoiding the contraptions. His father's occupation had exposed him to various renditions of firearms from a young age. Kayla and Michael were both taught basic weapons use by his father for the same reason. It was something Julie never dared to argue against.

"Please tell me that is Roux out there."

Shaking her head again, Kayla wrapped her arms around his left. "Dad?"

He held a finger to his lips, handing his daughter the rod while moving to stand in front of her. Whatever they'd heard was coming closer, but the volume of it faded with each moment. Her fingers twined around his belt, bringing her closer to him with each breath. Sloshed crunches, from all directions, set her wrapping both arms around him—again. The two of them spun in a slow circle, watching the trees.

"Hello, Steven."

His heart thundered at the sound of the voice coming from behind him. Kayla's hands tightened with each audible beat. Peeling her hands away with one hand, he puled her to his chest, holding the trigger of the rifle with the other. His consideration of the thought of shoving her away before he fired a warning shot, even for a moment, was stupid. The man before him wouldn't be alone. All he could hope for was to take enough of them down before they pried the gun from his hands and took his daughter from him.

"Dad?" Her whisper was barely audible against his chest.

The sneer visible from under the hood set Robert's veins boiling. "Come any closer, and I'll put a bullet through your head."

Tisking, the man stepped closer. "Do you think that will stop us, Steven? She'd be very cross with us for giving up—that easily."

Kayla stiffened in his arms, her head pulling back to allow her to stare into his expression. He could only swallow the response she was looking for. His fingers twitched against the trigger, but not enough to engage the mechanism.

"I couldn't believe how fortunate we were to see you at the station. We've waited for some time to make sure we weren't imagining it." He laughed, a familiar disabling laugh Robert had fought to forget.

The sounds rolling toward him sent involuntary vibrations through his knees. *No, no, no. Please, no. Not Marn, not with Kayla here.* The moment he took to look down into her eyes was enough. He pushed her clear of him and fired toward the man approaching him. His daughter dove away, rolling through the damp undergrowth.

9

Kayla

Pain seared through her head before she had the chance to cover her ears. No amount of description could compare to the real thing. She didn't even have the chance to see the device before it sent a shock-wave over her head, her father with it. "Dad!" Her own scream, dull on her ears, felt strange. She rubbed the lobes, her fingers wet with blood running down the side of her face.

It wasn't much more than her burst eardrums. Enough to set her nerves churning. Unable to gage the volume of her screams, she pulled herself to her hands and knees, scrambling to her father's side. Looking over her shoulder, she could see several men converge on them. She struggled to slip her bracelet off—her body blocking the action—shoved it into the sensor and closed the halves before finishing her crawl toward her father.

It didn't matter where she left it. If they weren't there when Roux came to find them, he'd find the sensor. He would know something was *terribly* wrong. Kayla bumped her knees on the rocks, cursing herself for not telling him it would be dangerous if her mother found them. She rolled her father to his back, biting through the pain. Blood ran down his face from the injury of hitting his head on the way down. His pulse was weak, but steady. "Daddy!"

Arms wrapped around her middle, pulling her away from him. She lashed out at the nearest appendage. A muffled cry escaped the man—his wrist breaking in her hands. The last thing she saw was his fist descending on her...

10

Roux

Roux pulled up to the house and rolled his window down. Kayla's brother trudged across the short distance to him. "They went out to repair the sensor."

"Yeah, I told her it would be okay to do it." He shouldn't have relented, but he knew Kayla wanted the time with her father, *alone*. He continued through the door with his brother-in-law following him in.

He winced at the sudden screech bombarding his sensitive ears. Roux jumped through the open window of his transport. He knew that sound. Distance did very little to the effect it had on his kind, unless you were too close. He dove for the weapons by the door, struggling to keep his feet under him with the rain increasing. "Go inside, lock the door! DO NOT OPEN IT FOR ANYONE!"

Michael started the *garage* door, leaving Roux to hop over it as he ran for the tree line. He forced steady breaths, sliding through the foliage faster than he should have with the recent weather. That, and the rain had picked up again. It would be torrential within the hour. Roux cursed himself for not stopping further up the road as he hopped over the ledge in his way. He was hoping to give her a little more time alone with her father to explain their situation. The vehicle was out of the question. It wouldn't have saved him any time to turn around. The roadway didn't cross that sector in a straight line. Putting his adrenaline to good use, his feet thundered toward the sonic blast—the direction Kayla and her father had gone.

"Farz!" The connection hissed with his words as he roared for his brother's help. Unfortunately, his brother couldn't reach the location as quickly as he would. And that was *if* he was ready to run out the door the moment Roux started shouting.

Screams tore through the jungle, a word Kayla often used to describe the foliage. His body shook every time he heard her voice. *I'm coming, hold on!*

"Roux? What's going on?" His brother's voice was lethargic and yet sharp.

"The sensor! Sonic blast!" His heart stopped, time suspended in a moment as he reached the sensor's location. "Kayla!" Breaths fell in ragged motions, retching from him, as he scanned the surrounding area. The sensor lay discarded near the ancient stump covered in moss. His rifle and the rod they used to keep the creatures at bay were half buried in foliage. "Kayla!"

Cursing in five languages, Farz continued to vie for his attention. "Roux! Are you alright?"

Wet leaves sloshed against the soles of shoes behind him. He dropped to the ground, avoiding the slash of a blade. On his back, he thrust both legs into the man as he approached for a better advantage. He pinned his assailant to the ground with his knee in the man's back and roared in his ear. "Where are they?"

The idiot had the nerve to laugh. "You'll never find them. *She* won't let them go so easily this time."

Years of training flowed through him without consent. His only means of finding them suffocated in his grasp. While he grappled with what the man said, Farz continued to curse through the communications link. He stood, echoing his brother's choice of expletives. Back-stepping, he surveyed the clearing, picking up the broken sensor—knowing Farz would replace it. If what he said was true... Roux spun on his heels, forcing his tired limbs to retreat to the house. The means of finding Kayla was there, as were the most vulnerable members of her family. "Farz, I've got to get back to the house!" He hoped whoever took them didn't go there first, urging every ounce of adrenaline left in his system to his legs. Her biological mother was a Siren, and they weren't known to be forgiving. Robert's human wife and their son were in danger, one climbing with each moment they sat waiting for him to return.

11

Michael

His mother sat on the couch, staring at the door, wringing her hands together. She hadn't moved from the spot since he barreled into the room to engage the lock behind him. His sister's husband ran into the tree-line, the same direction his father and sister had gone—not long before. What exactly startled him, Roux hadn't said. But the look on his face was enough to suggest something was terribly wrong.

With an end to his pacing Michael sat down next to his mother, put an arm over her shoulder, and rubbed his hand down hers. He wanted to tell her it was going to be alright, but he knew better. Roux had better hearing than he and his mother could boast. Like his father and Kayla.

Covering his face with his free hand, Michael suppressed the retch that begged to be released. They were only a half mile away. Roux could have heard her screams for help. Imagining it to be the reason his brother-in-law ran like nothing else mattered, he grumbled. For a man in Roux's position—a soon to be father, it could very well have been the case. He propped his elbows on his knees, burring his face in his hands. It wouldn't have done much good to follow him. Roux knew the area surrounding their home. With his luck, Michael knew he'd have fallen and broken his neck before he got far from the house.

The front door opened with an audible hiss from the pressure seals releasing. Roux stormed through, closing it once he was inside. Water dripped from his attire as His fingers flew across the keypad, the sound of metal grinding into place followed.

"Where's Dad and Kayla?"

Roux shook his head. "I don't know, but I have to get you two somewhere safe. Preferably *before* whoever took them comes after you."

"What?" His mother's gasp sent shivers down his spine.

"I'm not sure how much you know about Kayla's mother," he paused for a moment, tearing through the door to the supply room. When he returned, he set three boxes of varying sizes on the table. "Somehow, she knew you were here..." he flipped open one case, pulling out weapons no doctor had *any* reason to own. The array rivaled Michael's grandfather's collection—and then some.

"What are you talking about? Kayla's mother is dead!"

The look in Roux's eyes froze every vein in Michael's body. "If she was dead, why would anyone come for them? Here, of all places?" He motioned for them to stand before kicking out at the couch—sending it back several feet.

Michael watched him, his breath hitching with each step Kayla's husband made. Again at the keypad, Roux entered a series of numbers he couldn't keep up with. A door slid open where the couch had once been.

"Who are you?" His mother's voice wavered. Michael knew she was on the verge of tears.

"The same person I always have been, Julie. I promise you. I will get them back. But I have to keep the two of you safe. Kayla would never forgive me if anything happens to either of you."

His mother nodded, wrapping her hand around Michael's wrist. "What can we do?"

Roux pointed to the darkened passage. "A safe room, at least I think that is what you would recognize it as." He inhaled sharply before urging them to descend the stairs.

Not wanting to argue, Michael dragged his mother down the stairs with him. Roux followed close behind them, his breaths rigid. "Why would they want my dad and my sister?"

Roux merely shook his head as they reached the bottom of the stairs. He closed the doorway behind them. Lights blinked to life, the brightness growing slow enough to allow them to adjust. Michael found a chair for his mother, kneeling in front of her. "Mom, it's going to be okay."

"I need to know if you have contact with Robert's parents."

What kind of question is that? Of course, we know my only living grandparents.

Recalling the arsenal his brother-in-law had on his person, he swallowed saliva in slow gulps. Michael's mother nodded to Roux, her hands shaking harder with every breath.

"Good, I'm hoping they can give me more information on who we're dealing with. There aren't many *living* Siren's in the potential age range for Kayla's mother. The few I can think of..." he sucked air through his teeth. "I don't want to think about some of the possibilities."

"She didn't tell you who her mom was?"

"Your father thought it was best to never tell her who she was." Roux knelt beside Michael, handing his mother something to drink.

That seemed strange to him. Truthfully, Michael always thought his sister's mother had died when she was a baby. He knew for a fact that Kayla used to ask about her mom. His throat collapsed, recalling her sudden disinterest towards the topic in her early teens. He'd been too young to make the connection before.

"Siren..." her voice cut out, sobs replacing the ragged breaths. "Kayla's mother is... a Siren?"

Roux nodded where stood and crossed to the large screen along one wall of the safe room. "You'd better be out there right now, Farz. You owe me."

"Who is Farz?"

"The only one, near enough, that I trust right now."

"And why is that?" Michael demanded. He had every right to know, in his opinion. It was his family at stake.

"He's my brother."

12

Roux

Rubbing the tension from his forehead, Roux relaxed back into the cot. His thumb brushed over the sensor he brought back with him. There were scratches along the sides beneath his fingers. *Did she try to open this?* Once the two halves came apart, something fell onto his chest. He clutched the small band she wore around her wrist in his hand, bolting upright—he ran for the system interface. "Kayla, you're brilliant!"

Startled by his sudden outburst, her mother and brother sat up from the beds he gave them. The shelter was never meant for more than he and Kayla to use, leaving Michael on the floor beside his mother with the mattress he'd used in the guest room. Roux made them stay in the safe room while he retrieved it. "My sister scored higher than every kid in our division—every year of her life, and you're just now realizing this?" Michael rubbed his eyes with fists.

Roux pointed toward the two halves of the sensor, smiling at the reference Kayla often downplayed. "She hid this inside the sensor." He waved the band in the air before pulling it apart and plugging it into the machine. Provided she had the time to activate it, they'd know exactly who took them. *Maybe.*

"Please tell me that is Roux out there."

Julie stiffened at the sound of Robert's voice emitting from the audio. The holographic image projected on the table had her on the verge of tears. Robert held the rifle out, the two of them spooked by whatever they'd heard. The band's range for distance could have been better, though it had more of a range than his connection with his brother—where outside voices were concerned.

"Dad?" The panic in her voice... Roux found himself on equal footing with Julie. He curled his fingers around the table.

Faint sounds were picked up on the feed, Kayla clung to her father—a hooded figure closing in on them.

"Hello, Steven."

Robert's body shuddered enough for the Hologram to fuzz.

Breath caught in his throat. That name, he *knew* that name. *Oh no, no, no. This is very bad!* There was only one Siren, he knew of, whose mate went by the name Steven. Every nerve in his body flared, shakes spreading to his extremities. His brother was going to skewer him for mating with *her* daughter, if he was right about who Kayla's father really was.

The control of his emotions should have been his top priority, especially with Kayla's brother and stepmother in the room. While he kept it to a minimum for most of the recording, he lost all control near the end. His own voice calling out to her, a mere whisper on the recording. She couldn't have heard him, not after being that close when the sonic device went off. Hands trembling, he pulled the band out of the reader before they could see the altercation between him and the grunt left behind to deal with him. Michael and Julie didn't need *all* the details. Steady breaths exhaled, he retraced his earlier steps—dropping into the cot as her brother questioned him.

"Why did he keep calling my father by another name? That has to be a mistake!"

"Michael, sit down. Give him time to think." Julie crossed the room to sit beside Roux, placing a hand on his shoulder. "It wasn't a mistake." Her words were low enough for Michael to miss across from them. "His expression..." the breaths shuddering free, she continued. "He *knew* them."

Pulling her to him, Roux tightened his arms around the woman who raised his wife. The woman who meant everything to her. Unlike his own mother, he would give his life to protect her. He turned his head to watch her son, Kayla's treasured baby brother, hoping it wouldn't come to his life or theirs. Kayla needed *all* of them. "I *will* get them back."

"How? They could be off the planet by now." Julie wiped tears from her face.

"My mother's family is highly connected." Cringing, Roux relinquished his hold—it was an odd feeling. His mother was never affectionate enough to require consoling. "*Technically*, my father's family is too." He left out the detail that most of his family didn't know he was even in a relationship with Kayla, much less married to her, and laid out the plan to wait for his brother—again. She'd been in shock when he dragged them down to the safe room.

While Julie attempted to rest, Michael paced the room. Grappling with the situation hadn't been easy for either of them. Everything they thought they knew about Michael's father—wasn't as it seemed. Roux couldn't really blame Kayla's father for keeping the hard truths away as long as he could. He'd have done the same if their roles were reversed. There was an unfortunate amount of half truths he'd have to amend with Kayla himself—as it was.

"Mikey…"

The boy stopped, extending to his full height—still a good six inches shorter than Roux. "I don't care what your plan is. It will not help us if they take my father and my sister off this planet. Haven't you ever watched the news? When people disappear, they *disappear*!" He stressed each syllable of the word disappear, sending spikes through every nerve in Roux's body. "There isn't some magical way to find them. This isn't some vid. This is real, Roux! They took my father *and* my sister! They tried to kill you for following them! Mom and I are still alive because you dragged us down here." He paused, hands shaking. "Thank you for that."

Sufficing for a nod, Roux stretched his legs. "I don't think they've left yet."

"And why is that?"

"They're bound to realize something they've *missed*."

"And what is that?" Michael growled the words.

"Me."

"I'm *sorry*, but I cannot understand why *you* are so important."

Roux exhaled, stifling the retort he would have given his own brother. The kid didn't know what kind of mess they'd landed in. "Her mother came after them, because your father is her mate—she considers him a *possession*."

The wheels turning in his head, Michael paced away from him and back before he spoke. "When she realizes Kayla is pregnant, she'll come looking for you—because you're her mate. She wouldn't want her daughter to live without something that belongs to her." His eyes were shadowed, what little light reached them showed the horror of his realization. "Your species is seriously messed up."

"Not all of us. But yes, most Sirens—are pretty messed up. There is a reason they don't stick close to our home world." He wasn't about to tell the kid what the reality was. Sirens were hunted.

"Kayla isn't like that."

"No, she isn't. You have your parents to thank for that."

13

Robert

If it had only been the throbbing of his head, he might have kept the contents of his stomach where they belonged. Every few seconds, they hit a bump again, causing every nerve in his body to rage. He'd known Marn didn't like him before, but his intent to drag his transport through every divot, filled with water that sloshed up into the cage he and his daughter were thrown into—soaking them further, was proof his hatred hadn't waned in over twenty years. It was impossible to see completely through the walls wrapped around the bars, the slats barely large enough to stick a finger through. Unfortunately, the top was completely open to the air.

Bile surged upward, his body screaming in pain with the latest bump throwing him against the bars. Thankful for the rain washing away the evidence of his weakness, Robert settled back against the opposite end of their cramped travel space. He'd wondered why they tied his daughter to one rail but left him with hands bound behind his back until Marn laughed manically the first time he was flung across the cart. He'd done it loud enough for Robert to hear him with the damage the sonic device had caused his ears.

Worry soaked through his bones each time his daughter failed to wake with the raucous of the conditions. He shivered with attempted to hold the bar behind him in both hands. The first experience with Marn had been a nightmare. The present situation promised to rival the humiliation of its memory.

He closed his eyes to the bombardment of torrential rainfall and attempted to move closer to his daughter. Keeping her warm was more important than catering to his pain. He'd never forgive himself if she lost her child over his mistake. The urge to curse himself inwardly for coming to see her rumbled as he found her hands—lashed tight against the corner bar. He adjusted his position to face her, forcing his legs as straight as he could. The pain in his knees flared with the motion to press his feet against the opposite corner.

She shifted, her head leaning against him.

"Kayla?" His voice failed to register to his own ears, disconcerting for him on many levels. If his hearing hadn't righted itself, hers wouldn't be any better. She shifted again with the kiss he placed into her sopping hair.

She squinted, the rain pouring down from the grate above them. Tears joined the torrent, barely making her visible. He'd never been especially good at reading lips, but their proximity made it easier. He pressed his forehead to hers, the attempt to encourage her to stay positive. Not that it worked—for either of them.

A sudden lack of deluge forced his attention from his daughter and left his body weighed down to the uneven bed of steel. The outside world was driven away by the looming doors' gradual approach of the other. His body shook, pain returning to every extremity. Kayla prodded his shoulder with her chin. He turned back to her, taking his eyes off the thinning gloom of freedom.

"Breathe, please, just breathe, Daddy." No sound from her lips reached him, though Marn and his lackeys laughed boisterously at her attempt to calm him.

Pulled by his inflamed ankles, his chin hit the bottom of the cage—causing him to bite through his tongue. He could hear her screams, unable to see beyond the blur of his vision, dull against his consciousness.

"Stop it! Leave him alone! Please!"

Falling to the floor, he forced his eyes closed. There was nothing he could do to stop it, much less protect Kayla from them. He knew her connection as his daughter offended them as much as his being a product of his own family did. The damage his father caused to their organization wasn't something Marn would forgive or forget. Ribs cracked under the pressure of someone's foot colliding with him. The assault repeated until someone roared over the commotion. His eyes failed to open when hands, more than one pair, lifted him from the blood he'd expelled.

14

Kayla

The physician wrapped her in a large blanket, its texture like wool. He stooped to ensure she saw his lips as he spoke. "I'm told you speak *human English*. Lay down here, I need to make sure they haven't hurt you, aside from this." He waved toward what she assumed was a large bruise.

Nostrils flaring, she lilted her head toward her father. "My father is bleeding out, and you're worried about me?!" The attempt to scream at him left her throat raw, adding to the pounding of her head.

Not taking her refusal, he lifted her to the table—securing her there. He leaned over her, speaking slowly. "She will not be pleased with their actions." The man ducked away from the scanner before it began its sweep over her body.

Unable to hear anything around her, a sensation that left her shaking, she struggled against the restraints at her wrists. Her legs refused to respond, numb from the chill of being in the rain for an uncertain time frame. Thankfully, the jacket she wore—kept her dry from her thighs up. Her neck groaned as she angled her view to allow the sight of her father.

Every touch of the doctor at his side set his fingers twitching. Tears welling in her eyes, she couldn't turn away from him. He'd been alone the first time they'd found him. She would make certain he knew he would not be alone anymore. Even if it meant she would witness every horror he relived.

His body relaxed into the medical cot, fingers still shaking for several seconds. She cursed herself for leaving home eight years before, biting down on her tongue. All the freedom of being able to travel the known galaxies had only brought her father out of hiding—and full circle into her mother's clutches. *Why couldn't you be happy with what you had, Kayla? Roux doesn't even speak to his family. You could have taken him home with you—a long time ago. This would never have happened if you'd just told them about him years ago!*

A prick behind her exposed ear, she jolted from the sudden bombardment of sound returning. Eyes watering, she turned to glare at the face of a medical technician. The moment of wondering how her mother kept such individuals around fled, the opposite ear receiving the same treatment. Instinct drove her to cover her ears. Unable to do so, she rolled her neck pathetically from side to side. It gave each a minuscule break from the onslaught.

"It will subside in a moment. Be patient."

Patient? He wanted her to be patient, when her ears made every nerve in her body want to flee for safety. Clenching the sides of her confinement, she bit down on her lower lip. An eternity of a moment later, the sounds muted to a dull hum. With the attempt to remind herself that most of their captors were just as sensitive to the sounds as she was, she rolled her eyes at the man looming above her.

"Marn has gone too far this time. He is going to regret his actions." The man shook his head, draping a wet cloth over her brow. "You're carrying a child within you. Thankfully, your vitals aren't dangerous for the child—yet."

Oh, Joy. I get to have my child in captivity. Not daring to vocalize her frustrations, she focused on the ceiling.

"Your father will live. But it may take him some time to heal. In his condition, the serum can only speed his natural healing so much." He shook his head, grumbling about Marn being an idiot.

Unable to keep the growl from rising through her throat, she scowled at him. "If this is how she treats him, there is no wonder why he hid away for twenty years!"

"Marn will suffer consequences for his behavior. Of that, you can be certain." He walked away. She followed him with her eyes to her father's bed.

Dad... this is all my fault. She'd feared it was her fault he lived with the nightmares, and it drove her away from him. All she'd wanted was to give him time to heal, time without seeing her mother in her eyes. What she'd done was worse than staying, worse than reminding him daily of the horrors of her mother, worse than... Tears flowed down her face. He'd never be free. His father wouldn't be capable of finding them. With the travel time, her grandparents wouldn't receive her father's message letting them know they arrived for another five months. By the time they realized something was wrong, they'd have no way of finding them.

Swallowing motions helped to steady her nerves, to some extent. Watching the others tend to her father's extensive injuries sent spikes to her extremities. It should have been her at his side. He'd prefer her aid to theirs. Tears pooled around her, where she pressed her face against the table.

"I'm going to remove the bindings. Please don't make me dull your senses." The man shook his head. "I'd rather have you conscious when your mother arrives. It might lessen her anger."

"If I'm not conscious, will she kill him for it?"

"Marn?" The doctor stiffened, his response causing a choking sound. "Young lady, I wouldn't consider his punishments. It will only stress you. And you need to relax."

"Relax! Relax! That monster dragged us away from my home! He could have killed my father!" The level of her voice rattled components around her. From the corner of perception, she saw her father shake at the recognition of it. The heightened emotions came to an abrupt halt—the prick of a needle in her left arm.

"A relaxant, awake but muddled—you will have to forgive me, but your health is paramount." He helped her to an upright position before starting across the room.

Muddled was an understatement. She couldn't even focus on her own balance, much less—walk across the room where her father lay. The urge to laugh hysterically crossed her mind, nearly falling to her knees when she tried to stand up. Taking the side of the table, she inched her way to her father's side, fully extending her arms as she bridged the gap between them.

They didn't complain about her movement. Thankful for that, she found a chair close to her father to sit in. Her legs felt like jelly as she dropped into it. With her hands in front of her, she buried her face—balancing elbows on shaky knees.

"Where are they?!"

Every nerve in her body stiffened. It was the first female voice she'd heard. With no doubt about who it belonged to, she attempted to slide her chair behind the medical table her father lay on. Using her heels wasn't as futile as she expected it to be. She hadn't noticed the rollers on the bottom of the chair-legs. Unfortunately, the height of the table wasn't enough for her to duck behind without it being obvious. Gripping her father's left hand, she hoped it didn't cause him more pain.

Her mother's eyes widened, jaw lolling open. "Who did this?" She thrust her finger toward Kayla and her father as she roared into the physician's face.

"Marn, and Pittis." His voice felt strange on her ears. The fear he'd had of the *consequences* of her mother finding her unconscious, replaced with a dull whisper. Like she'd forced it from him.

The realization hitting her—it was exactly what she'd done—Kayla hid her shaking hands from view. Focus on the rise and fall of her father's chest allowed her to avoid eye contact with the woman who claimed to be her mother. That title didn't belong to her. Julie Erickson was and always would be her mother.

"Steven."

Startled by the proximity, Kayla's hands found her father's again. With her mother's eyes on her, she stroked the back of his hand. He'd never told her the name his parents had given him at birth. She'd always been afraid to ask him about it. Her own name... Kayla knew he couldn't have kept it as it was. She never wanted to know what her mother had called her.

"I've had enough of this feud of theirs. Bring them here, NOW!"

Not caring if her biological mother was offended by her startled posture, Kayla tugged at her father's arm.

"You do not need to fear me."

I beg to differ.

"Her hearing was damaged when they brought her here, his as well. I believe her posturing is more a reaction to the volume." Again, the doctor's voice held a dullness in it.

Thankful she bit her nails, a habit Roux often teased her about, it wouldn't be as painful—later for her father as she dug her fingers into his arm. The dread of hearing that tone from him made her stomach roil.

"She is with child, likely to be excitable."

A hint of sadness crossed the woman's expression, her eyes turning cold once it passed. "Send for me when he wakes." She disappeared through the door, huffing curses in her native tongue.

"I should give him more now..." the voice, again dull as it was in her mother's presence, shuddered as the doctor made his way to them. Once he'd finished another injection, he left them alone in their corner.

Her face in both hands, Kayla smothered the sobs she could no longer contain. Her body shook with each outburst. For the first time since her father arrived, she allowed the hormones to rage against her. Free to respond in any way they wished. Giving herself the moment to fall apart, she leaned against the hand she held. "I'm so sorry, Daddy. This is all my fault."

"No, it isn't." His voice scratched her ears.

"Dad!" The startled whisper was bound to carry to the men on the other side of the room. She waited for several seconds, watching them go about their business—without so much as looking in her direction. "How long have you been awake?" She tried to keep her voice low as her mouth was level with his ears.

"Long enough to hear you crying, and blaming yourself for *my* mistake."

He turned his head to look at her. The redness of his eyes waned with the bruises on his face. She'd heard of the serum their species used to speed up healing, but she'd never seen it firsthand. The color still made him look like he'd been run over.

Deciding it was best to avoid reminding him of the beating Marn and his friends gave him, she leaned forward to place a kiss on the one spot without a bruise in the middle of his forehead. "Being here isn't your doing—it's theirs. Never take the blame for that again."

The smile he gave her left him cringing. "I want you to know," he coughed for a moment before continuing. "No matter what happens here, I have never blamed you for any of this. You are not your mother, and I will never stop *trying* to protect you from her." He closed his eyes, tightening his hand around hers as he brought it to his lips.

Helping him sit up was an argument she knew she would never win against. In the end—she relented, sitting beside him on the medical bed. "I was worried they'd kill you."

"Marn blames me for a lot of things."

"Let me guess, my mother choosing you is at the top of the list?"

He laughed, bracing his ribs with one hand. "Among other things..." His eyes glazed, fingers twitching. "She's coming."

"How can you..."

He held a finger to her lips, a cringe curdling Kayla's stomach. "She likes to flood her surroundings with her ability."

Folding her lower lip between her teeth wasn't enough to hide the whimper.

Pulled into his arms, her father rubbed a hand down her back. "It's going to take a while for me to be like them." Lilting his head toward the blank faced medical staff, her father exhaled rapid breaths.

"I won't let her do this to you."

"Kayla, there is nothing you can do." He pushed stray hairs from her face and held her tighter to him. "All we can do is hope Roux made it back before *they* went after Michael and Julie."

They both flinched at the sound of the doors hiss, Kayla wrapped her arms around her father. There *was* something she could do, but she wasn't sure if it would work. That, and in her father's condition, it wouldn't help him much.

She couldn't bring herself to look at the woman entering the medical suite. The two men behind her set her father's body into another bout of twitches and flutters. "Whatever happens," he left the rest of his previous words out with the approach of their guests.

"You did this to him?" Her words, spoken in her native tongue, aimed toward the men standing just inside the doorway.

"He had it coming." Marn, he was the one who laughed at her father every time he hurt him. Kayla couldn't help but wish her mother would punish him for what he did.

"Your foolish feud! Steven is not his father. He has harmed none of our people. And as to my choice! It was MINE to make!" She sauntered toward the men. Whatever she was doing to flood her ability about her, it was making her father wince at her side.

"And as for you..." she wrapped an arm around Pittis, hanging a little too close to him for a woman who was so obsessed with her mate. She whispered playfully into his ear, dragging a finger across his chest before the same finger landed on Marn's solid form. Unable to understand the words dropping from her lips, Kayla jolted at the sight of the two going rigid.

Startled by her father's hands over her ears, she gasped louder than she'd intended to. "Look at me, Kayla, don't watch this! Don't look away from me, please!"

Panic raged through her blood, every nerve in her body begging her to run and hide. Obedient to his plea, she buried her face in his chest. The sound of grunts and cries of pain assaulted her senses, her father tightening his grasp around her with every curse on his lips. She made the mistake of pulling away from him at the sound of her mother's laughter, allowing the sight of a bloodied, battered, and lifeless body.

Drawn back into his embrace, he leaned his head against hers. Her mother laughed again at the sound of weapons fire and the slosh of a blade being removed from flesh. All control fled from her extremities. Gasped sobs wracked across her, translating into mirrored tremors in her father's composure.

"Take them to my chambers. And send someone to deal with this mess."

Refusal to look until she they pulled her from her father's side, bile rose through her like the torrential rain outside.

"Kayla!" Her father shoved the doctor aside, helping her to her feet. "Take her from me like that again, and I'll make sure Arzi hears of it!"

Both doctors stepped back, hands held out. "Apologies. We are only following her wishes. Please, this way. You will be more comfortable with her arrangements for you."

Additional voices merged with those of the doctors, all held the same dull tone. It made her stomach turn, worsened by the look in her father's eyes when he noticed her reaction. The guards hurried them out of the room and down too many corridors for her to keep track of. By the time they left them alone in the opulent space, her legs nearly gave way. How her father stayed upright, his extensive injuries still healing, she dared not ask.

He laughed, pain turning it to a wince as he helped her to a bench on the farthest wall. "At least I don't have to worry about Marn and Pittis lingering around the corners anymore."

Unable to do anything but stare at him, Kayla gripped the lip of the bench.

"And they won't be around to hurt you, either." He wiped a tear from her face. "I know it sounds harsh, but they were always like that—and I was anxious that they'd treat you the same way."

15

Robert

Being able to hear her voice might have been comforting if his daughter wasn't crying. It wasn't her fault. Their experience was anything but pleasant up to that point. He didn't think she'd ever seen anything as brutally sadistic as Arzi made them watch in the Medical Suite. Saying her name had left a bitter taste on his tongue. But it got his point across to the mindless medics under her control. Nothing would stop him from protecting Kayla from her mother, not even the effect her mother had on him.

That was the tricky part. But he knew her ability could only control so much. The will to resist anything she required of him would completely fade in time, but he would still care about their daughter. He doubted Arzi would ever expect him to change on that matter. Her insistence for him to protect her before he and Kayla were taken home had bothered his parents. They feared his affections were residual, from long-term exposure to Arzi. But it wasn't. Thankfully, it didn't take them long to realize it.

With Marn and Pittis dead, he could at least rest easy. They couldn't hurt Kayla—or her baby. But... Arzi *could* have punished them elsewhere. No, it was a reminder to him—and everyone else. The Siren was the one in control. She wouldn't hurt them. He was her mate, and it wasn't as if she could have another. Robert held his breath, pleading in silence. If she didn't know already, Arzi would find out about his wife and son—soon enough. She'd stop at nothing to remove them both from his life, giving him nothing to run to—nothing left to fight against her for.

His hands trembled, sweat building between his fingers. She'd get everything she needed from him, and he'd have no way to stop her.

Upon notice of his internal struggle, Kayla took both of his hands in hers. "Dad, I have an idea." Her eyes toward him, she bit her lip and turned away. "But I don't think you're going to like it."

He retracted his left hand and bit down on his knuckles. His head rattling, he took her hands again. "No, Kayla, I won't ask you to do *that*." His breaths bordered hyperventilation, hands sweating profusely. That path could pose a much larger problem for his daughter. There was a reason most Sirens were hunted and killed. The power and control their abilities gave them was addicting. At least, it was what his mother had warned him about. None of them wanted their sweet Kayla to evolve into the monsters her mother and grandmother were.

"Dad, if I don't, she can force you to say anything, *anything*! And that includes how to manipulate Julie into exposing herself. I won't let her hurt Mom, and I don't even want to consider what she might do to my brother."

"Kayla, you don't understand. I can't let you."

"You'll forgive me—one day. I promise."

She moved too quickly for him to react. His sluggish pace was because of the injuries that only further doses of the serum would remedy. Unfortunately, they'd given him too much, too close together—as it was. "Kayla, don't..."

Flooded with the raw emotions running off her, she enveloped him with her essence in a way he'd never experienced from her. *Has she been practicing?* His mind raced in the moments he had control of, promising himself that if Roux had encouraged it—he would kill him. Mate or not, his daughter wasn't a tool for others to use on a whim. Having never experienced this from her in such quantity, he wasn't able to resist the urge to move closer to her—inhaling the scent she pushed with it. When their ordeal was over, if it was ever over, he intended to have a long discussion about her never doing it again—ever!

It felt so wrong to be drawn in by the thinnest of threads to the little girl he raised. But it wasn't an attraction, not in a romantic sense in the slightest. More akin to his will being won over by her control. He tried to speak again, his words rolling in his throat, with no sound escaping. *Kayla, please don't do this!*

"If you are asked about your life, you will never mention Julie. You will never mention Michael. If asked of them directly, you will not respond. You will act as if they do not matter to you." Her words were soft in his ear, though they thundered through him with each breath of her aura. "If anyone asks about Roux, my mate, my husband or any reference of the like, you will not speak of it. You will act like you do not know yet about my child or their father. You will not mention any conversation we had in private regarding Roux. No one can ever know he is *Immune*."

As swiftly as the influx began, Kayla withdrew her ability. His head spun, sending him to his knees. "Kayla, what did you just do?"

His daughter dropped unsteadily to aid him, tears streaming down her face. "I'm so sorry, Daddy. I had to. It was the only thing either of us could do. You know what will happen if she uses them against us."

The forefront of his mind went blank, the suddenness of it forced air from his lungs. *How could you do that to me?* Unable to even utter their names, Robert clenched his teeth in frustration. The flow of tears raging down her face grew with each moment, knowing exactly what she'd done to him. She'd told him he couldn't mention the other members of their family to anyone. That, unfortunately, meant he couldn't even mention them to Kayla. The ability to show how he felt about them was ripped away alongside their names.

Still capable of drawing the entirety to his conscious thought, he couldn't even thank her for leaving that. Anger for what she'd done was off the table, too. He could feel it all he wanted. His body and its reactions would never show it. A brilliant plan, one he never intended to confess the appreciation of —even if he could.

16

Roux

"You look terrible, little brother."

"I don't recall letting you in." Groaning, Roux sat up in his cot. His brother leaned against the stairwell, watching Kayla's brother where he glared up at their unannounced guest.

"You forget I built this hide-y-hole of yours, little brother. I can get in with, or without, your authorization." He sauntered to Roux's bedside, a hint of laughter in the whisper only Roux could hear.

With a glance down the edge of his nose as he stood, Roux huffed into his brother's face. They were only two hours apart in age, but Farz had always insisted on calling him his *little brother.* "That isn't comforting, Farz. I have a life. One that shouldn't include you dropping in on me at the wrong times."

Farz laughed, his chest bouncing with each breath. "What? Worried that I'd walk in on you and that girl of yours that you insist I keep out of every conversation back home?"

"Wait… your family doesn't know?" Kayla's stepmother crossed the room, her arms folded in a stance to match the growing scowl on her face.

If he smacked Farz upside the head, it would only traumatize them further —considering it would start an all-out brawl between them. A glare spreading, Roux turned to face his mother-in-law. "No, they don't. It was with the best intentions. Unfortunately, it will not stay that way."

Farz laughed again, doubling over. "Honestly, little brother. I think they're going to find it amusing—*eventually*."

"Why would they find your relationship with my sister amusing?" Michael joined his mother in the growling stance.

Farz slapped him on the back. "Go on, little brother. Tell them why you don't want anyone back home to know about her."

His eyes closed, Roux imagined the things he could—and would do to Farz for his involvement—later. "I mentioned the situation with Kayla's mother." He exhaled, pinching the bridge of his nose. "Well, um, my family..." he couldn't say the words. He hadn't even mentioned the unfortunate detail to Kayla. She wouldn't be *thrilled* when she found out who his family was.

"My brother and I hunt down Corrupt Sirens." Farz was all business in that moment, his arms spread across his chest. "Unfortunately, that kind of comes with the territory of *being* a Siren."

"No, it doesn't!" Roux snapped, growling in his brother's face. They'd had the conversation too many times already. It was a waste of time to rehash it for her family. Time they could use to find Kayla and her father.

"Right," laughing again, Farz poked Roux in the chest. "Your girl is different. I'll give you that."

"She has a name!" Michael spat, standing at Roux's side.

Restraint prevented him from allowing the internal smile to show as Roux pat Michael on the shoulder. Kayla had mentioned how over protective her little brother was of her, frequently. "He knows her name. He's just trying to get me to hit him."

"Why?"

"It's a long story. Farz, we don't have time for this." Arms motioning toward the display, he rolled his eyes at his twin brother. "Did you relay the information I sent you?"

"Yes, Mother seemed especially interested in the family members you sent her after. She thinks she might know them."

His throat tightened. He'd been hoping for the opposite. "That isn't comforting. I was hoping we don't know Robert's family. Because if we do,"

"Your problem will be much bigger than just getting her and her father back." It wasn't uncommon for Farz to agree with him, just not for him to admit to it—with witnesses, no less.

"You don't look like you're much younger than him." Michael glared in Farz' direction.

"I'm not. This meat-head considers two hours, enough to gloat over."

"Oh my goodness, you're Identical twins." Julie moved closer to them, the light allowing her to see how much the two of them really looked alike, aside from Farz' insistence on keeping his hair much shorter. Her posture wasn't as frightened as Roux expected it to be, considering the revelation of what he and his brother were. Shaking it off, he nodded in response to her comment.

Farz ignored them, flipping through the security footage from the house. "I had to avoid two guys earlier. Not sure who they were, but they were hanging around the house."

"I thought you came through the *other* way?"

"I did, but that doesn't mean I wouldn't scout out the house first." Farz groaned. "You're losing your edge, *little brother.*"

"Farz, shut up! I'm not hashing this out in front of them, regardless of your need to blow off steam."

"And what about yours?"

Face concealed with both hands, Roux shook his head. "Not the best idea, either. I'd probably kill you."

"You wish."

His brother watched the feed from Kayla's bracelet on his hand-held device, several times, the audio low enough that only the two of them could hear it. Painful chills ran up up his arms every time Kayla spoke.

"Roux," Farz kept his voice low, looking over his shoulder. "So, uh..." he cleared his throat. "How you holding up?"

There were audible clicks of his eyelids cascading into each other. It was enough for Farz to shake his head. His brother could have asked before. It wasn't like him to hold off as long as he did. "My mate is being held against her will. She could be dead for all we know, and our child with her."

His brother's jaw locked, air hissing between his teeth. "You didn't tell me you two had gone *that* far yet."

"Oh, and I'm supposed to have your *permission* to do that, am I?"

Farz glared at him. "You and I both require permission from *her* to break the contracts issued for us."

"Mother knows I never intended to go through with it. I told her as much when I left." Careful not to add the words Farz already had bouncing around in his head, Roux glared at his brother. They'd discussed the potential of the relationship before he started dating Kayla. Farz hadn't been keen on letting him go forward with it, but he hadn't disagreed either.

His brother shook his head, sucking air through clenched teeth. "It was one thing to have her as your fling, Roux. But *you* mating with a Siren, *before* you had time to smooth things over back home, is bound to be a bit… *troublesome* with our family."

"If our Mother is right, and she's Caya's granddaughter… I am within my right in choosing her."

"Are you forgetting who her mother is, *if* she really is Caya Morris' granddaughter?"

"I think it's time you explain who you think my husband is." Julie sat with her legs crossed, pressing creases from the blanket she sat on. "He and Kayla are in danger, in case you've forgotten. I have a right to know what is happening to my family."

Roux took several breaths before he faced her. "I had my suspicions when I first watched the recording Kayla left behind."

"And what are those?" Motioning with her hands, she directed Michael to sit at her side. He obeyed with a scowl on his face.

"Steven Morris."

"Who is he?"

"Let him finish, Michael!"

"Twenty-six years ago, our people were working together with a group of humans. Their efforts to stop an organization known to be behind various disappearances for monetary reasons—among others—caught the attention of the wrong people."

"Alan Morris was the human representative assigned to work alongside our military. His appointment was because he was married to a high-ranking member of our society." It was something his mother couldn't argue with, if Kayla was, in fact, Caya's granddaughter. Their families weren't on the same footing, but it was close enough to prevent arguments about the match—at least from a political standpoint. *If* they didn't take into consideration that his mate was a Siren. "Their son was sixteen at the time the disappearances escalated. They considered the situation and sent him to live with his sister until things settled—as a precaution."

"Sister? He has another sister, and I don't know about her?"

"Another?" Their voices merged. Michael and his mother stared at them. Roux looked at his brother. It had been so many years since he considered how much they actually sounded alike.

"Aunt Eva is my age." Michael grumbled, rubbing his hands over his elbows.

Farz covered his face. "How many kids do they have now?"

Julie's eyes found the floor. "I've only ever known about Eva and Brandt—he's eleven."

His brother began pacing the room, curses rattling over the distance. "*This* just got worse! Do you have any idea what *she* will do if she finds out *he* has a brother?"

"We don't know for sure yet, if it is *her*."

"What happened to Alan and Caya's son? You never finished what you were saying." Michael's expression darkened.

"Vivianne was Alan's daughter from his previous marriage—to a *human*." Michael glowered at Farz' inflection. "They sent Steven to live with her until things settled."

Fingers pressed against both sides of her face, Julie exhaled heavy breaths. "He... he never made it to his sister, did he?"

With a rattle of his head in unison with Farz, Roux ran a hand through his hair. The details of the raid had been part of their training in their teens. It should have been a red-flag with Kayla, but her story didn't quite match up with it. Unfortunately, her father hadn't given her enough information. Either that, or she hadn't given enough to him. His lungs sagged at the thought of both of them living half truths with the other.

"That is why he... why he hates traveling?" She covered her mouth, barely muffling the sobs.

Michael wrapped his arms around her, a fire growing behind his eyes. "They took him because of his father's involvement?"

Trapped by the situation in his head, Roux nodded. "They threatened to kill him." *Among other things...* His eyes closed of their own accord. There was much more to the story he wasn't willing to share. Their mother had related information given to her by her *friend*.

"Alan never gave up finding his boy. It drove him crazy that he couldn't protect Steven from the monsters who plagued our people. It only got worse once they found him. And that didn't happen until three years *after* he was taken." Farz' voice rang in his head. He knew the entire story, but hearing it with a new light—made the world around him spin.

"They brought him back, with Kayla," Julie's eyes fixed on the floor, welling with tears she refused to allow.

"It wasn't the name I've been told since I was a boy." Roux lifted her chin. "I honestly did not know. If I did, I would never have let her leave his side, or yours, eight years ago."

"But you've been dating Kayla for five years! Shouldn't something have seemed off?" Michael's growl set his mother trembling beside him.

His skin seethed. It should have felt that way, but he was trying to help her see there was more to her life than fearing what she was. "I would have taken her home to you, if I'd known before now." And he would have stayed with her to ensure Arzi never found her.

"So they changed their names and disappeared, to hide from Kayla's mom?" Michael shook his head. "Like I said before, your species is messed up."

"I'd like to agree with you there, kid." Farz stepped away, giving them time to absorb his words.

"What was her name?"

Farz made eye contact with him. Roux shook his head in response. His brother grunted, turning toward Kayla's brother. "Best not think about it, kid. It doesn't change who she is to you. I don't think your father would want to hear the name again, especially from you."

They knew the name his wife had before, though Roux refused to utter it. She was and always would be Kayla to him. "Farz, what did you see while you were out there?" It wasn't like Farz to go completely silent. Even when they were on missions together, he always had a running commentary for Roux's benefit or annoyance—depending on his brother's mood.

"Wherever they're holding them, they haven't left the planet—yet. I saw nothing out of the norm—but that doesn't mean much here."

Looking up from his mother, Michael howled his displeasure at being left out. "How do you know that? You couldn't possibly have gotten here soon enough to know!"

"I don't stray too far from my brother," Farz grimaced for Roux's benefit. "So yes, I was here. *And* I know because I've been watching for any change."

"If you don't stray too far from your brother, why weren't you there to stop this from happening?"

It was a good question, though Roux knew the answer already. Waiting for his brother's reply, he mentally fought the guilt of telling Farz to let Kayla do something *he* should have been doing.

"I was a little *preoccupied*."

Silencing the groan, Roux glared at him. *Really? Of all times, you idiot?!* Sighing, Roux crossed to his console. He would berate his brother for his *personal* choices in private. The topographic map of the surrounding areas wasn't much of a distraction. He couldn't count the number of times he'd stared at it in the last while, having set the computer to search for any logical location for the organization to hide. *She's still out there, somewhere.*

His brother moved closer, keeping his eyes on the display. *"If you'd told me!"* Though his voice was lower than Julie or Michael could hear, it was amplified for Roux with the proximity. "I wouldn't have been doing *other things* when she was out there with her father!"

Frowning at the terrain, he considered the volume of his reply. "*If* I told you! Farz, you knew my intentions—a *long* time ago!"

"I'd never have let you two out of my sight if I knew she was pregnant." Shaking his head, Farz pointed to the display. "There was some erratic traffic going on here." His fingers migrated toward a trail they knew well. It ended near a small village that rarely let them enter.

"We both know the locals are fairly busy during the rain season. They're extremely aggressive in that region. It wouldn't be easy for anyone to hide in their territory without the local authorities being involved. Plus, I've been there enough. I think I'd recognize that face if I'd seen it before."

"They saw her father at the depot, so we're not dealing with locals. They get their supply dump just like everyone else who squats here." Ignoring the glare from Roux, he rotated the image on the screen. "The hills have potential."

"If you ignore the beasts who roam freely there."

"Carry around enough firepower, and you can deal with *them*."

His stomach clenched at the thought of Kayla being there. The injuries she and her father suffered would drive the wild animals into whatever camp they made it to. "But there isn't a settlement out there? At least not a foreign one. I would know. We get reports of people who want to be included on the medical rosters when the camps are set up." With the natural resources on the planet, it wasn't the most lucrative job, but miners were willing to come all the same.

17

Kayla

The sound of the door opening set the hairs of her arms on end. Her father sat across from her, struggling to keep his eyes away from the entrance to their prison. With her back to the door, she had a perfect angle to observe her father's reaction to their guest.

His fingers twitched along the edges of the table where they'd been eating. Another drone of a male had delivered their meal twenty minutes before. His presence was a further glimpse of what her father's fate would be—the longer they remained. Reaching for his hand, she squeezed it—hoping he would realize she would not leave him at Arzi's mercy. She forced a shaky smile.

Arzi seated herself at Kayla's right at the square table. "I'm happy to see the two of you get along." The plate offered her forced Kayla to relinquish her father's hand.

The smile twitched into place as her father spoke. "And why wouldn't we?"

Arzi laughed. Though it was pleasant to Kayla's ears, it took everything to stay in her seat and remain silent. Her mother took possession of her father's hand, the hand Kayla held moments before. His disgust at her touch showed for only a moment.

"It is so good to see you again, Steven." She kissed his hand, smiling cruelly as she stroked her fingers across the back of his thumb.

The muscles of his neck flinched in his attempt to turn away from her.

"Oh Steven, don't fight it. I do recall that you used to enjoy my company."

His eyes shifted from Arzi to Kayla. He blinked slowly before turning his head to face her mother. "You know I didn't."

Arzi laughed. "Not at first, but you did, and will."

Forced to watch her mother piece at the decadence before her, Kayla's stomach soured. She couldn't tell if her mother was actively using her ability. Unfortunate in her consideration. It would have been helpful, being around another siren, to know when she needed to be on her guard. The only evidence of her mother's aura was in her father's eyes and actions. Unlike the others in the room, her father actively fought the effects of it. She didn't know if it was normal for any male to fight it, or if he did it because she was in the room with them. Kayla couldn't handle it if it was the latter. She did her best to avoid eye contact with either of them.

"Now, Ahni, I think we need to discuss something."

Kayla swirled her fork in the remnants of her plate, trying to ignore whoever she was talking to. She didn't care to know the names of the drones circling them at all times.

"Ahni! Look at me when I am speaking to you!"

"That isn't her name!" Her father growled from across the table, his hands fisting.

"It is the name we gave her when I birthed her. And the only name I will ever use." Arzi leaned closer to him, fire in her eyes. "You will not interfere in this discussion unless I ask it of you."

His nostrils flared in rapid breaths, his eyes blazing in Arzi's direction.

Unable to watch, Kayla slammed her palm against the table. "Leave him alone!"

She had the gall to laugh in her face. An actual gut laugh that rolled through the room. "Ahni... you should understand this at your age." She turned to Kayla's father, gripping the underside of his chin. "If you love our daughter, you will stay your tongue for the rest of the evening, unless I give you permission to speak." Her sneer at his struggled reaction was enough to set Kayla's nerves on fire.

"Stop it!"

Arzi ignored her complaints. She shifted in her chair, leaning delicately against the table. "Now Ahni, about your condition."

"Condition! My condition! I don't see how my condition is any of your business!"

"I intend to retrieve your chosen mate. All I need is a name, and he'll be here within the night."

Her throat constricting, Kayla wrapped fingers around the arms of her chair. "I don't know what you're talking about."

Arzi laughed. "Oh Steven, you didn't tell her, did you?" She tapped his shoulder playfully before returning her attention to Kayla.

His expression was blank. Knowing it was her own fault, she bit her lip. The tang of blood mixing with saliva was enough to distract her from the haughty expression her mother kept giving her father.

"You wouldn't be pregnant if you hadn't mated with the male who did it to you." Arzi folded her hands in her lap. "Mating is a mutual agreement. He had to know you were doing it and agree to it."

Like you did? When you forced the decision from my father, you mean? She thought better of of saying it as she watched his reaction. He closed his eyes, unable to turn away. Tears welled, but didn't fall from his lashes. He hadn't agreed willingly, and she knew it.

Arzi tapped the table with her nails. "I won't allow them to behave the way Marn and Pittis did. I don't think I need to remind anyone what happens when I'm angry." She turned to face Kayla's father. "Is he the young doctor she works with?"

Life returned to his eyes, not quite the way Kayla was expecting. His brows lifted high, his mouth taut, completing the confused look she knew well. The moment of truth, or something like it. Kayla held her breath, hoping whatever she'd done to him wouldn't cause him too much discomfort under her mother's influence.

"I did not know she was even pregnant."

Arzi's brows lifted. "It would seem both of us are surprised by this, then." She tisked in repeated motions with her fingers. "Not the best way to learn we're to be grandparents, is it? Maybe she will listen to you, ask her to tell you who he is."

Her father stared, bewilderment couldn't even come close to describe it. Though her plan had worked, it didn't settle the sour taste of having done it to him. Kayla worried her bottom lip, averting her gaze from him.

"Kayla..."

"Stop calling her that dreadful name, Steven."

He glared at her mother for a split second. The emotion dissolved into one she didn't want to see from him so quickly, causing her to lose control of her stomach.

"Ahni!" The name fell from his lips as he slid his chair back.

Unable to bear it, she stumbled from her chair, the remaining contents of her stomach cascading to the floor.

Her mother shoved away from the table. She cursed their attendants at the top of her lungs to assist them. Her father was at her side, cradling her head, stroking her hair with his thumbs.

"This conversation is no longer necessary. Stay with her, Steven. I will return shortly."

He handed Kayla a wet cloth while helping her to her feet. She wiped it across her face, shuddering at the taste still in her mouth. He took it and handed her a glass of water. Relenting, she took a mouthful, swished it around, and spit it back into the glass. Her father cringed, handing the glass to the nearest drone, shaking his head at her.

"I guess *that* could have—gone better."

Her father nodded. The usual smirk he loved to taunt her with spreading across his face. Shaking his head, he led her to the bench—again.

"I think I'm going to hate this bench."

He pressed his lips together, rolling his eyes and raising both brows.

Kayla slammed her palm into her face, remembering the words her mother enjoyed toying with. "You can't say anything, because of how she said it, can you?"

Sighing, inhaling and exhaling through his nose, he shook his head.

Her chin dropped to her chest. She'd accidentally done it to him when she was a teenager. He spent a few hours trying to get her to notice what she'd done. Once she realized it, she spent the next week in a slew of profuse apologies and favors to make it up to him. Unable to remember the details of their argument made it worse. It wasn't even something worthwhile in the long run. "I'm sorry, Daddy."

With a snap of his fingers in her face, he directed her attention to his rolling eyes. He pointed a single finger in her direction and shook his head.

"I know. You don't think this is my fault."

He pointed at himself first before he thrust both palms out. He did it three times, then pointed at her before motioning around them.

"I don't get it."

Inhaling and exhaling through his nose, again, he pointed at himself and her. Then fisted both hands, making them connect—repeatedly. He then repeated his earlier motion of thrusting his palms out toward her.

The meaning dawning on her, she almost cried. "You didn't push me away,

I just," she couldn't say it. Truthfully, he had pushed her away. But not in the sense of how he perceived it. She released a choppy laugh. "I needed space. But it wasn't because of you."

Smiling for her, he pulled her into a hug. With her father's arms around her, she almost felt safe. Part of her was happy for his silence. It meant he really loved her. But another part of her wanted to cry until she had nothing left. "I love you too, Daddy."

18

Roux

"I understand why she wants Robert. But why take Kayla? She can't make her do anything, can she?"

Rocking his jaw from side to side, Roux arched his brow. He didn't want to scare Julie with the potential outcome of their situation. Robert hadn't emerged unscathed from the first encounter he had with Kayla's biological mother. Not wanting to think about it hadn't prevented the action for himself. The woman who raised his wife deserved to know what she'd be dealing with when they were reunited. "No, she can't make her do anything, not like she can with Robert. But she'll find out, soon enough, that Kayla would do anything to protect her father. Her mother *will* use that to her advantage."

Rubbing fingers across her brow, Julie exhaled shaky breaths. "Kayla will never accept that. She'll push back."

"I know." He didn't want to think of what direction she was headed. He'd already traveled that train of thought repeatedly. "We'll get them out."

"She kept my husband locked away for *three years,* Roux. I can't sit here waiting that long for help to come."

"Neither can I."

"I know that look, and I don't like it." Farz shoved him against the wall. "You're not even going to consider giving yourself up. I won't let you."

"It may be our only choice."

"No, we're going to wait here until Mother says otherwise. Like we were told."

"Farz, if it was your mate, I wouldn't stop you from protecting her."

"When our mother realizes you mated with Arzi's daughter, she's going to flip. I'm not adding you to the list of reasons she wants to skin me alive."

"It was my choice."

Michael cleared his throat behind them. "Um, I hate to state the obvious. But you said my sister is a Siren, right?"

He and Farz both nodded.

"So... um, how is it you think you had a choice in mating with her? I mean, my dad didn't really have a choice with Kayla's mother. Why would you be any different?"

Farz laughed like a maniac, holding his chest with one hand. "I like him."

"Of course you would." Scowling at his brother, he turned to hers. "I'm immune."

That drew Julie's attention from where she retreated. "How? I didn't think that was possible."

"That is a mystery. Well, sort of..." Farz snorted. "Our people have been trying to combat the effects Sirens have on our males. We," he motioned to Roux and himself. "Were just kids when they realized Roux was immune. No one can figure out why it was just him, and they've been trying to recreate the result—without success."

"Our scientists haven't been able to pinpoint the recessive gene responsible for immunity. They are hoping *I* pass it down to my posterity, but it doesn't always work that way." It was a painful fact he'd hoped to have left behind with the life he once lived. But his mother hadn't relinquished her old on him —or his brother. He doubted she ever would.

"And your kid will die the moment Arzi finds out you're immune." Farz shuddered. "Not to mention any chance of you having more."

Roux thrust his hand out, intending to hit him, Farz dodged. "You don't have to point it out. I'm already aware of what it could mean for Kayla."

"And it's also a *big* reason I'm not letting you anywhere near those crackpots when we find out where they're keeping her."

"You're saying they'd kill my sister if her mother knows about your immunity?"

"I don't know what she would do."

"Here's to hoping it's a female, otherwise we're screwed." Farz held a bottle up, tipping it back in one swig.

19

Robert

By the time Arzi returned to her chambers, Kayla had fallen asleep in his lap. He couldn't help but glare. Her delicate form sauntering toward him made his stomach churn.

"I see she's feeling well enough to rest."

He nodded at her *astute* observation with less enthusiasm than his mate preferred. Robert wished for the ability to add a snide comment along with it.

"Oh, come now. Is that how you wish to treat the mother of your child? A child you seem attached to." She dismissed the two men who'd been watching them, continuing her movements toward him.

"I have missed the sound of your voice, Steven. I really have. Tell me something. Do you see me every time you look at our daughter? Or is your mother's reflection in her, the reason you didn't abandon her?"

"I didn't abandon her, because she's my daughter. She had no part in what you've done." Thankful she'd asked for an honest answer, he glared up at her. As liberating as it was, her response was going to leave him regretting it.

Hand gripping his jaw, she squeezed the still tender muscles. The attempt to pull away only jarred complaints from his other injuries. "It is time we showed our daughter to her room. Carefully now, we don't want to wake her."

Swallowing the pain away, he tried his best to remain seated.

Her eyes were on him an instant later. "Steven, I want you to carry our daughter to her room. Just this way."

It would've been better if he did what she said the first time. Her aura was difficult to handle in large quantities and she was making it hard for him to breathe, as it was. He lifted Kayla in his arms and followed Arzi. His steps were slow and steady, following her command to an extent he knew would annoy her. She had said not to wake her. It didn't help that every part of his body still ached from Marn's abuse.

"I've always found it sweet how hard you fight. I wonder if it is your mother's line that gives you the strength the rest of them don't possess."

One breath from her and every man in range would bend to her will, but he *had* to fight her. It had been his downfall before. "Please don't hurt Ahni's mate. I don't know who he is, but she's partial to him. In a way you aren't with me."

"Oh, Steven. I *am* partial to you." She activated the door, turning to him in the same motion. "Her mate is vital to our plans. As are you, Steven. Convince her of his need to be here by her side. She'll tell us when she realizes his importance to all of us. Everyone on this planet will die before we leave it—that should give her incentive." She smiled at him, her eyes wide with delight.

The two halves of him battled the words. She was trying to get him to say something, test his resolve. Only, the inability wasn't his doing. Part of him wanted to scream, threaten her for endangering the lives of his wife and son. But that part couldn't communicate. He crossed into the room, the silent anger consuming his ability to fight Arzi's commands.

"Set her on the bed."

Doing as directed, he turned to face her. "What is it you want, Arzi?"

"Time." She laughed, standing with her body a whisper's distance from him. She stole the kiss from him before he could move. It left him feeling dirty when she released his mouth. "You're not ready, and our daughter needs a guardian. I don't want any of the others near Ahni. You will stay by her side at all times. Protect her, and I may let *that* woman and her son live."

His body convulsed as the door closed behind her. He wouldn't be much of a guardian for at least a few days. Growling under his breath, he rubbed the image of her lips on his from his mind. Protecting his daughter was something she didn't have to demand. She knew it, but she'd done it, anyway. Some part of him wondered if she really was worried about what the others would do, now that she wasn't the only siren present. He sighed, glanced around the room, flipped the light off, and made his way to the second bed farther from the door. Arzi never said he couldn't rest, though her threats guaranteed he wouldn't.

20

Mina Forran

"You'll have to excuse me, Caya, Alan." A nod of her head, as was customary for their status—and hers, Mina turned to leave them. "I promise, you will be the first to know when we have any information about Steven and his daughter."

The corner of her perception viewed the pained reactions of her once friends. Their arms around the other, Caya buried her face in her husband's chest. She shook off the concern for the friend she'd known far longer than the man she'd chosen as her mate. Mina trudged through the door. Why Caya had chosen a human, and not one of their own, she would never understand. Alan wasn't frail by any means, his intelligence and spark were definitely admirable. But he was a *human*. Their lifespans would be nothing comparable. With the privileges allowed by Caya's status, Alan received treatments to extend his lifespan. Had he been just any foreign dignitary, Mina knew their society would never have allowed it.

Her private quarters aboard the vessel were silent as she entered. She sealed the doorway and pulled the chair out from under her personal communications station. Mina released several shaky breaths, willing the urge to pound her fists against the table to pass. All the years spent training the twins to be the most formidable weapon in their arsenal, and they'd fallen into the worst mess of their entire lives. They were men, not bumbling toddlers—they should have known better.

Tapping her fingers along the display, she input the code to reach the only individual who could help them out of their mess. It wasn't someone she *often* wanted to speak to. But he would drop everything to help Farz and Roux get themselves out of trouble. Groaning, she knew he would find the predicament amusing.

"Mina, do you have any idea what hour it is here?" His voice trailed off, nothing appearing on the screen before her.

"Do you have *any* idea what *they* have gotten themselves into?"

He laughed. Mina was thankful she couldn't see the smug reaction through the audio. He was always smug when she had to come to him for help. "Tell me. What have *they* done to upset you now? And what exactly are you expecting *me* to do about it?"

21

Roux

"Why is it we haven't contacted these *local authorities* you keep talking about?" Michael sat up on the couch, his legs still draped over the arm. They'd moved it to sit along the wall in the last few hours. Farz had confirmed the house hadn't been breached, allowing them to ascend from the basement he created for Roux.

"It would cause more problems than you think, Michael." Julie hadn't left the guest room for hours. She left open to allow her to hear their voices. "She's a Siren, if anyone found out…" She stood up from the bed, walking to the door —leaning against the frame. "They'd take her away."

Farz growled from the kitchen. "Thats if they even cared to help us. After they figure out what she is, they're likely to tell us to get off their planet and take our trouble with us."

Roux leaned against the wall by the table, the back of his head thumping against it in slow, repeated motions. He had hoped to avoid anything of the sort by going so far from Arros.

"My little brother would lose his medical license for hiding her, and I'd be stuck taking him home to deal with the consequences."

"I wouldn't be the only one." Roux's voice was slurred with the motions of his fingers against his tired jaw.

"I don't know why you doctors insist on being so stupid. What did they think they could do? Keep her hidden here with *you*—forever?"

"They were trying to help her, to help us. She isn't like the others. They know her too well to think of her any other way." Roux closed his eyes, focusing on his breathing. His brother would know something else was behind the reason he and Kayla came to the planet if he wasn't careful about his reaction.

"If I didn't know you were immune, I would laugh at you right now. But this isn't funny—and you're an idiot."

"Wait! You're saying it's illegal to be a Siren?" Michael stormed across the room, his feet planted on the hatch to the safe room.

The urge to have Farz open the door, let him fall and close it behind him—crossed his mind for an instant. One look at his brother proved he'd noticed the kid's unfortunate choice of location. They both shook their heads. Kayla would rip them to shreds if they treated her little brother badly. Regardless of how much he deserved it.

"No. But considering her mother is on the top of a very short list of *highly* dangerous Sirens…" Farz shook his head.

"Honestly. The only reason I'd lose my license is for not reporting her as being a Siren. Our government likes to keep tabs on them when they can. And the company *we* work for is strictly hands off in *this* department."

Michael shook his head, eyes rolling. The words he'd repeated often written all over his face. "I'm wondering what my sister sees in you." Storming away, he slammed the door to the guest room.

"Let him be angry."

"It isn't the entire story, Farz."

"No, but with how he was raised, he will never understand." His brother went about opening various cupboards, and the fridge more than once, his voice low enough for Michael and Julie to miss everything. "She's a kid, Roux. Did you really think about any of the consequences *before* you two did this?"

"This…" Roux motioned in a circle downward with the fingers of both hands. "Isn't the situation either of us intended from the beginning, if that is what you were asking?"

"She's a kid, Roux!" Repeating the harsh whisper, his brother turned to face him. "What were *you* thinking? I *thought* you were planning to wait until she was *older*? She doesn't have the training to survive our life. Throw in the fact that she's a Siren…" Not waiting for a response, Farz dropped a plate on the table in front of him. "Eat. You are no use to her if you keep starving yourself."

Glaring at the food in front of him, he slid it away. "You think I can eat right now?"

Grunting at him, Farz shook his head. "I get that you two have always liked each other. You and I both have had relationships before, little brother. You knew it was a bad idea going into it. No relationship survives *her.*"

He rolled his eyes slow enough for Farz to snort in response. He'd cut off most connection with their mother, but she still sent him messages via his brother—even when he stopped responding to them. "Have you heard from Mother?"

"Yes. And yes, they are Caya and Alan. So yes, your decision won't make waves. As far as political connections are concerned. But they're bound to use your relationship with *her* to their advantage—somehow." His brother shook his head, biting into a sandwich his mouth barely fit over. For a glutton, he didn't chew as loudly as he should. Not that any of their species did. Sensitive ears and all, some more than others.

Thinking about it reminded him of why Kayla and her father were so sensitive to it. "Caya! That's it!" He slapped his hand down on the table. "That is why they're so sensitive. She passed that down to them!"

"What am I missing here? Other than my ability to eat in peace."

"She's a Skym?"

"Wait, what? What makes you think she's a Skym?"

Skym was a slang term, referring to a less common form of Siren. They couldn't control the opposite sex, but they had the power of persuasion. It often led to positions where they mediated for the government, because they could smooth out frustrations—without taking the individual's choice away. The problem being, most people didn't know. Which is why the term was used loosely to describe women who were good at calming others, or convincing people to change their minds on minor matters.

"That's a stretch, little brother."

"Not really. Think about it, Farz. Why did they drop off the grid so well? Aside from having a little help from friends in high places."

"Because she persuaded the appropriate people to let them leave." Farz slapped himself in the face. "Why didn't Mother mention that?"

Raising both brows, Roux rolled his eyes. "Even she has her secrets."

"I'll give you that, but how does this help us?"

"It buys us time."

The wheels turned behind his brother's eyes, a smile spread across his face. "She can't completely control him, and he doesn't know it—does he?"

"I doubt it." Finally, all the years of sitting through lectures about their species were paying off. It had bored them to tears on more than one occasion. He and Farz were careful to never mention that fact to their mother.

"She won't kill your kid, even if it's a male." Farz shook his head, sliding the plate with his sandwich away. "And you being immune won't matter if this is going the direction I think it is."

It wouldn't. But it also meant Kayla was far more important to her mother than he'd originally expected. It also put her in and their child in a very dangerous position. His people hunted Arzi's organization. The chances of getting stuck in the cross-hairs were high, especially if they came out of hiding. Leaving the planet wouldn't turn heads. But his mother knew who they were trying to find. As long as she didn't report their having located Arzi to the fleet, they had an advantage. "Did you tell her?"

"She knows who Kayla is."

Glaring, he folded his arms over his chest. "Did you *tell* her?"

"She isn't exactly happy with you right now." Farz lifted his cup to his lips, muttering as the fluids left it. "But she is glad you decided to reproduce before she dies of old age." He smiled from behind the cup.

Great! The entire fleet will know by now. "I hate you."

"Hey, I wasn't the one who had the *bright idea* to mate with a Siren." He laughed, stuffing another bite between his teeth. "Speaking of… *how long* have you been keeping it from me?"

Grumbling, Roux looked away from him. If his brother couldn't guess, then he didn't deserve the answer.

"Roux," Farz set his food down, swallowing his recent bite. His eyes widened more with each moment of silence between them. "Dammit, Roux, that's why *we* came here—isn't it?"

Growling, he gave his brother the look both of them used to warn about their volume. He didn't need her family knowing how long they'd kept the truth from them. He already regretted the decision to take the present assignment—when they could have gone home to her family.

Farz shook his head. "The fact that you're giving me *that* look," he stuffed the sandwich back into his mouth, chewed loudly, and set it back down. "They think this is a recent thing, don't they?"

Sucking his lips back between his teeth, he stared across the table at his brother.

"You could have told me, Roux. I wouldn't have said *anything* to Mother." He shook his head. "To you, I sure as hell would have." Rubbing his palm over his face, he pointed a finger at Roux. "I should have known you were up to more than you said you were."

"It was Father's idea."

Farz blinked at him, the whites of his eyes getting smaller with every moment. "*Father* knows you mated with a Siren?"

"Yes." He didn't dare mention their father had been present for the small ceremony they'd had with their colleagues. Kayla hadn't realized he was family. His father had been kind enough to make up some reason he'd be present for their wedding.

"He pulled the strings to get the two of you here, didn't he?"

Nodding, Roux stood up from the table.

"So much for *me* being your lifeline. How long have you two been in contact?"

"Since I left."

"Does *she* know? Does Mother?" Farz dropped his hands to the table, pushing himself up to join Roux.

"No."

Farz slapped a hand over his forehead. "Roux, you've got to stop lying to your mate."

"I haven't lied to her."

"Omissions aren't any better, little brother."

"I need to speak with Mother." The faster communication transmission technology their species used was restricted. Only the military was allowed to have access to it. Being that he resigned his military position to become a doctor, he couldn't use it—without permission. Which was why Farz was never allowed far from him. Their mother refused to let him off that easily. An umbilical he and his brother hated.

Farz pointed toward the safe room door. "She wants it to be *private,* when you do."

22

Kayla

The raucous from the door pulled her from the strangest dream. Roux was there, and then he wasn't. Alone with the cacophony blaring from the entrance to a room she didn't remember, panic flared through her. An attempt to untangle from the bedding left her falling to her knees. Vision adjusting with each breath, she moved closer to the door.

When she found the control for the light, she slid her hand over it. Her eyes stung as it brightened faster than she had meant to set it. "Who is it?"

"Your father's serum... Arzi asked me to bring it to you."

Why? She scanned the room, her eyes falling on him—curled away from the light with a pillow barricading him from the bombardment. "Dad?" *Did he bring me in here?* She couldn't find the handle for the door. "Um, I can't open it from in here."

"Apologies, My Lady, it slipped my mind." A moment later, a slot opened below the panel by the door. A drawer extended with the syringe.

She lifted the metal casing, trembling with the thought of what she had to do. "Dad, are you awake?" Not waiting for his answer, Kayla hurried to his side, setting the vial on the shelf conveniently at his bedside.

She withdrew the pillow from his grasp, cringing at the sight of him. The discoloring of the bruises had yet to fade, if anything—they looked worse than they did the night before. "Daddy?" Carefully lifting the hem of his shirt, she unbuttoned it from the bottom up. Each inch revealed the extensive damage Marn and Pittis caused.

Kayla covered her mouth to stifle the sobs, laying half of his shirt back over his chest. Instinct brought her right hand to the syringe. She wanted nothing more than to throw it across the room.

"Throw it. I'd rather heal on my own."

She set it on the table and knelt beside him. "Dad! This is terrible. The swelling alone. How are you even breathing?"

He held two fingers out. "They gave it to me twice yesterday, remember?" Opening the small drawer below the surface with one hand, she rolled the syringe in with a flick of her fingers and slammed it closed. "The longer it takes for me to heal, the better off we are."

She hung her head, breaths falling raggedly.

"I'm not sure I can sit up." He coughed. "Can I have the pillow back now?"

She retrieved it from the floor with one hand, wiping her eyes with the other. "She's going to know you are refusing it."

"We have bigger problems."

"Such as?"

"She plans to do something. I don't know what yet. But whatever it is, no one left on this planet will walk away from it."

Cursing under her breath, Kayla turned away from him. She sat on the floor facing the door and leaned against the bed. "She's threatening to kill everyone if I don't tell her?"

"No, she's going to kill everyone, *anyway*. She just wants to make sure your mate isn't one of them." Her father growled the words.

Knowing he couldn't voice the emotion behind what he was really thinking, Kayla turned to face him again. "How are we going to get them off the planet if we can't warn them?"

"Tell her who he is, Ahni. It is the only way to save your child's father."

"You know why I can't! If I tell her, she'll find them! I won't be the one who throws them under a bus." Her head rattled. The groan escaping her rivaled one of her childhood tantrums. She stood up and paced the room.

"Ahni, everyone on this planet is going to die. Unless you tell her, and we give *him* a chance to warn others."

That name on his lips, again, riled every nerve in her body. She stomped her feet with each step, huffing loudly. She couldn't blame him for the use. It was her mother's fault. She'd told him to stop calling her by the name he'd given her. But using the name Ahni bothered him. His eyes begged for her forgiveness. It was hope. Hope she intended to hold on to with everything she had. Her father could still fight Arzi. Shoulders falling, she dropped to her knees. "Daddy, if I tell her, she'll bring him here. I can't do that to him."

"Sweetheart, if you don't," his eyes welled with tears. She knew he was trying to say it, something he couldn't say—because of her.

"Wait… Dad, you're fighting what she's doing to you. Why can't you do that with me?"

"Because you actually thought through the loopholes when you said what you did. Arzi isn't patient enough to think it through first."

There had to be more to it. It couldn't have been that simple. Her mother was doing it for far longer than she was. Or maybe it was that simple, and her mother was only playing with him to see how much he would fight it. *She disgusts me.*

"Look at me, Sweetheart." He lay there, pain creasing his brow, inducing tears to flow down her cheeks. "Your mother doesn't want me to leave your side. I'd say it is safe to assume there is more going on here than either of us is privy to."

"She also locked us in. Even the idiot bringing that…" she thrust her finger toward the drawer. "Couldn't open the door."

Sighing, he leaned back into his pillow. "The only choice you have to keep *anyone* safe is to get him here—and not reveal what you are keeping from her."

"See what I mean?" Kayla lunged toward her father, wrapping her arms around him. The apology in her expression wasn't enough to wipe the wince from him. "You're finding the loopholes in mine."

"Sort of." He smiled through the pain, nudging her off him.

23

Roux

Farz watched him sort through the things in the bedroom, throwing the less important items out of his way. He placed everything of sentimental value in the box he'd emptied from the storage room. The entire time, he looked up once—maybe twice. His brother sat on the end of the bed. His eyes divided between Roux and Kayla's family. Julie and Michael were gathering their things, tossing full bags down the open hatch to the safe room. He couldn't blame them for trying to take at least what they thought they would need.

"You never said how the *talk* went." His brother motioned behind his right ear, turning the action into a half hearted scratch.

Choosing to ignore him, Roux entered the bathroom. There was very little in there he needed and even less Kayla would need if the plan worked—but it still smelled of her. His eyes trailed along the wall to where she squeezed into the corner the day she found out her family had arrived. The wish to relive that day and the days following would only make his task exponentially harder than it already was.

"Roux." Farz stood in the doorway, his right hand outstretched. "You've already got everything you need. What are you doing in here?"

"Leave me alone, Farz."

His brother raised his hands in defeat before hefting the box from the bed. "I'll just take this down for you, then."

Roux leaned against the basin below the mirror, burying his his face in his hands.

"It *is* going to work, little brother."

He refused to acknowledge him, instead slamming the bathroom door closed. The conversation with his mother hadn't gone well. Their father agreed with the plan he and his brother devised, but their mother was insistent that both of them return home with Julie and Michael. The Morris' were anxious to be reunited with at least part of their family. He couldn't blame them for that. Caya and Alan were worried about their son and his daughter. And *that* was the tipping point.

His breathing ricocheted against the mirror, leaving blotches of fog behind. For three years they'd shared the space, taking the time to know the other in ways he'd given up knowing anyone. The life he left behind promised little in the attachments department—going back to it without his wife wasn't at the top of his priorities. He wasn't keen on abandoning her to her mother's organization either. Roaring over the pestering of his brother through the communications link, surgically implanted in the tissue behind his right ear, Roux threw his fist into the mirror.

"You okay in there, *Little Brother*?" He could hear Julie's tense words from Farz's end.

He and Farz were cursed with constant communication since they were boys. It was very little of a burden when they were kids. Though, over the last three years, he'd found it highly distracting. Thankfully, Farz didn't intrude on him often, leaving Roux to initiate the conversation. He could cut the outgoing connection at will, but preventing incoming from Farz wasn't possible. His brother rarely cut his own outgoing connection. For someone who lived by himself on a ship in orbit half the time, he talked a little too much some days.

He walked out of the bathroom, finding three concerned faces. Julie's eyes found his hand, blood coating his knuckles and fingers. "Oh, my goodness! Are you alright?"

Farz rolled his eyes, leaving her to fuss over Roux's stupidity. "If you're so hyped, why don't you load everything into the pod while I give your family the rundown?" His voice was low enough to avoid the others from hearing him.

"I'm fine. Really."

"That doesn't look fine. Roux, I know you're frustrated, we are too. But hurting yourself will not bring them back." Her head rattled from side to side as she pulled a pillowcase from the bed to wrap around right his hand.

"Farz has some of the more advanced medical supplies on his ship. It'll heal before we break orbit."

She bit her lip, arms folded over her chest. "Roux, I know what you're going through. More than you think I do."

He passed by her, dropping his chin to his chest. "Farz wants to give the two of you another rundown of the plan. I'm going to take our things to the pod."

"Roux," her hand latched to his wrist, preventing him from leaving the room. "We'll get them back."

"I'm not giving up. I'll never do that to them."

"That makes two of us."

"Farz isn't patient, Julie. I should go."

"Does he always take charge?" She smiled, laughing at his shrugged response.

Roux took the stairs three at a time. He found the pile of bags loaded on the cart, ready to go down the tunnel. A last look around the room, he secured the tethers tighter. With one hand on the grip, he slapped the panel on the wall—revealing the passage to the escape pod. It was a long drop, one he didn't intend to take ahead of their things. He pushed the cart forward, holding the rod with both hands. Once over the threshold, he jumped and put both feet on the bottom rung. It wasn't a long trip. The magnetic rails also doubled as a ladder, which would be his way back up and their way down.

He waited for the incline to level before he jumped from the cart and trudged off the momentum. Farz had the shuttle ready hours ago, doing his preflight checklists before anyone was awake. He was by the book with everything—*most of the time*. The cart passed him before he made it to the shuttle, rolling to a stop at the bottom of the ramp.

Breaking the tethers from their lines caused his right hand to twinge. He tossed the soiled material away and sucked at the sensitive fissures. It wouldn't be a good idea to continue using the hand for a while. He hefted two bags with his left, reminding himself to check the shuttle for medical supplies once he finished. It was going to be a tight fit for the four of them, being that it wasn't designed to have more than he and his brother aboard. Though Farz had taken the notion that one day he'd need to drag Kayla with them, and added another command chair.

Almost laughing at the thought, he crossed to the chairs. Farz's surprise wasn't unexpected, but he knew what was going to happen—*eventually*. Kayla's pregnancy would only have gone unnoticed for a short time. His brother only argued for the sake of arguing. That, and he often took it upon himself to play the Devil's advocate. It wasn't really much of an addition, bolted to the floor behind Roux's designated position. He ran his hands along the makeshift apparatus, fingers trailing the entire height of it. *Farz had too much time on his hands.* The fourth member of their party would spend their assent strapped to a shock harness in the back with their things. He'd volunteered for it, but Farz refused. In the end, it was Michael who said he didn't mind.

With the bags secured, Roux made himself trudge toward the ladder. His brother's constant rumblings of the plan played out in his head. Sometimes he thought his brother liked the sound of his voice, a little too much. He began climbing the ramp; the world spinning and his head pounding from the shriek of metal above him.

"Farz! What was that?"

With no response, Roux fought for a better grip on the rails above him. Voices rumbled through the tunnel, followed by the light of the safe room blinking from existence. All sound ceased with it, aside from his brother's moan.

"Roux, get out of here..."

"Farz?" He was only halfway up the ramp, his hands failing to grasp the wrung above him. "Farz? Answer me!" The near silence Farz had kept while investigating the details of Kayla and her father's disappearance had been disconcerting, to some extent. But the present complete lack of response had Roux scrambling up the rails. "Farz!"

Static overwhelmed him, well you couldn't really call it static when you heard other voices over the connection. Garbling occasionally happened when the voices were too far to register on the implant. The voices grew to a volume that nearly set Roux falling down the fifty-foot drop.

"Load them up. *She* will be upset if we take our time here."

"Farz!" He knew it was useless to yell. If his brother was conscious, he'd hear him. But he wouldn't answer if there was anyone who might assume there was someone else below their feet. He slammed his good hand against the eight inch thick steel wall between him and the safe room.

He listened to the banter coming through the link. Roux tried to focus on the voices, but none of them were members of his family. He balanced himself with one hand on the wrung, biting back the anger.

Concentrate, Roux, remember your training. Farz can be tracked by the pod!

He used both hands to slide down the rail, wincing with the pain in his right hand. He didn't have time to bemoan punching the mirror, or the lack of speed he had returning. Feet on the ground level, at least eighty feet below the surface of the planet, he used his momentum to run up the ramp—closing it behind him.

"C'mon Farz, wake up." Promising to never close the connection again, except in times it would be uncomfortable for Kayla, he sat in his brother's seat. Shaking off the years of neglecting to keep up on his piloting skills, Roux punched the recall button halfway. A full depression would send him back to his brother's ship, and he didn't want that—yet.

The shuttle hovered above the ground four miles from his home. He blanched at the sight of the smoke rising from the trees. His brother's location flecked to life on the display, Roux's hands streaking across the console. He covered his face. "You were so off Farz, they're not going to the hills."

They were heading directly toward the station, but there was no way they'd possibly be able to hide that way. *Unless they built something beyond it, or below it.* He jumped from the pilot's chair to rip the cabinet doors open. The two suits hanging there were a stark reminder of what he'd once spent his life doing. Roux shuddered as he pulled his gear from the rack. It wouldn't be like the past. He wasn't dropping in, removing his target, and heading back home. And there would be no fist-bump for luck this time.

24

Robert

His daughter rolled away from him at the sound of the door opening. He regretted his inability to pull her back to his side in the attempt to sit up—wincing loud enough for Kayla to stop her trudge toward the door. She stood in front of him, blocking his view of her mother.

Air huffed from her lips. He didn't need to see her face to know what it meant. He girded himself for the verbal abuse, causing another bout of coughs—his winces deafening to him. The hope it was only his condition flew through the window as both his mate and daughter rushed to his side.

"You didn't give him the serum?" Arzi cursed, spittle reaching him on the bed.

"He refused it! I'm not like you. I don't force him to do anything!"

Her mother shoved her aside with little care about how hard she was doing it. "You're going to kill yourself if you don't take it."

Robert bit back the pain, glaring at his mate. "I'd say that's preferable, at present." Kayla's gasp had their attention before either could continue the argument.

"You fool, do you think your life means nothing to me?"

"Yes," the words fell from his lips. His eyes never took in her expression. Kayla's fear kept everything else away from the forefront of his mind.

Arzi wrenched his jaw, forcing him to look at her. "Where did she put it?"

Pain flared through every nerve in his body. He wasn't sure how that was possible with the treatment he remembered, but he hadn't been awake for all of it. Unable to resist the command, his eyes trailed toward the drawer. She wasted no time wrenching it open. Syringe in hand, she thrust it into his shoulder. It added further pain to his present state—for only a moment.

"Marn poisoned you, you idiot! I didn't tell you before, because I wasn't sure." Arzi flung the spent vial away, her body shifting to face their daughter. "If you want your father to live, you'll never let him skip another dose."

His daughter shook with every breath, her legs failing her. Everything he'd thought about Arzi fled his mind when she caught Kayla before she fell to the floor. "Marn didn't dare touch you, Ahni. He knew I'd make him pay for it. Instead, he thought he'd torment your father. He'll live, Ahni. But please, do nothing so stupid—again."

The clarity that fled with the pain returned slowly. Agony lessened with every breath. He closed his eyes, not wanting to see any sign of Arzi's emotions. She'd done it to him before, she'd do it again. Her feelings only went so far. His daughter's tears jarred his recent memory. He hadn't meant to scare her—wishing for death.

"Ahni," his voice trembled with the attempt to speak.

"Daddy." Kayla scooted on her knees to him. Behind her, he saw the brief sadness in her mother's eyes, quickly replaced by the icy stare he knew too well. "How would a poison work despite the serum? I thought it was supposed to be advanced?"

"It is, but the poison won't be completely through his system for a few days. Marn knew we'd give him the serum. I doubt he expected either of you would try to skip a dose." Arzi shook her head, fury burning behind her eyes.

"I'm glad he's gone." His daughter buried her face against his side.

Arzi wasn't. She'd been fond of Marn since long before they met. One of the major reasons Marn hated him. He watched her reaction, waiting for her to curse their daughter for hating a man she loved more than she loved anything else.

"Don't look at me like that, Steven. I wouldn't have killed him myself—if I didn't care about what he was doing to you."

Kayla rubbed softly against his arm, her attempt to ease the trembles the way Julie often did. He didn't dare ask her to stop. Anything that helped her remain calm, in their present situation, was better than the alternative. Even if what she was doing did very little to help him.

"Your mate will be here soon. I wish you'd told me it was the young doctor when I asked it of you." Arzi's tone was flat, her heart-rate fluctuating beyond her normal inflection. "This was my reason for coming to you." After glancing his direction, she turned away from them—leaving them in their cage once more.

His daughter lost control of her tears at the sound of the lock engaging. Sobs wracked from her, a little too close to his ears. He rolled to face her, strangely free of the pain from moments prior. "Breathe, Ahni."

"I hate that name."

"I know. I'm sorry, Sweetheart." Unable to cry with her, though their concerns were the same, he tugged her by the arm. "I don't think she'll hurt him."

"Dad, there is no way whoever she sent didn't find Mom and Michael there." Meeting his blank expression forced torrents from her eyes. "Are you're at least as frightened as I am?"

"Yes." It was the only word he could muster. He tugged at her hand once more. "Look at me," waiting for her eyes to rest on his, he stroked her face. "Can you fix it?"

Rubbing the tears from her face, Kayla nodded.

With no use keeping the inevitable bomb from her mother, she wouldn't deny him the pain wreaking an internal havoc. "Everything I said before is useless now. I relieve you of the obligation of obeying what I told you to do, Mom, Michael, Roux, all of it. She'll find out soon enough that he's immune."

With the sudden release of his memory, and the control of everything involved, he pulled his daughter into his arms. "Sweetheart, try not to panic." Despite his words, everything within him threatened to do the exact opposite. Arzi already knew who they were. All they could do was hope she left them alive—as she promised. "She said nothing about your Mom and Michael."

"That isn't a good sign, Dad."

She was right. Closing his eyes, tears wet the hair closest to him. Wrapping both arms tighter around her, his body shook—fear overtaking both of them in the moments following. Silent for what seemed like an eternity, Kayla sat up. She slid away from him and began pacing. As he watched each step, every tick of her reactions, it reminded him of someone else. "Julie does that when she's mad at me."

Kayla turned to him, her eyes red and puffy. "She's never mad at you."

The laugh didn't cause him pain. Neither did sitting up in his bed. "You weren't always home, sweetheart. And you were avoiding me during one of the worst arguments we've had." He laughed harder, shaking his finger in her direction. "In fact, that one was actually *your* fault." It was funny, as an afterthought. Though he'd been furious when it happened.

His daughter covered her eyes with one hand. The other she shoved halfway into her mouth, for only a moment. "It had to be *that* day, didn't it?"

"You were twelve, and upset about something that was legitimately important to you." He decided against standing. Instead, he folded his legs in front of him. "She did not know what you'd done, *accidentally,* and thought I was avoiding speaking to her on purpose."

"It was stupid, and I am sorry for it."

"Sweetheart, it was *eleven* years ago." He'd never explained the situation to Julie. In hindsight, it would have been the perfect time to explain Kayla's differences from Michael.

"It was still stupid."

"I'll concede to your point about that." Patting the bed next to him, he waited for her to climb up. "It was the start of a tough time for you. I'm sorry for pushing you away—the way I did."

"Given our present situation, Dad. I can't really blame you for pushing me away. And I prevented you from saying or doing anything that could endanger Mom and Mikey for *two* days."

He couldn't bring himself to be upset with her. She was desperate to protect all of them from her mother's wrath. Lifting his arm over her shoulder, he felt a mild twinge of pain compared to earlier. "Sweetheart, I can't fault you for trying. But there has to be some other way. Maybe there is something I can do to keep them safe." Even if he had to promise never to fight her again, he'd keep Julie and Michael safe from Kayla's mother.

25

Roux

Heavy breaths registered, breaths that weren't his own. Tuning out the rain, falling in droplets the size of his fingertips, he wiped the moisture from his visor. "Farz, if you can hear me, cough." He waited a few seconds before the dry heaves assaulted his auditory sensors. "You had me scared for a minute there." Listening to his brother cough again, he held his breath. "I really hope that isn't a bad sign."

"You and me both." Farz groaned, his voice cracking. "I'm alone."

"Figured that."

"Where are you, little brother?"

"Not far behind you."

"Her mother and brother are here, neither are conscious."

"Status?"

Grunts escalated for several seconds, followed by his brother blowing air through his teeth. "Breathing. It looks like our friendly Siren drudges have drugged them. Feels like I was, but they're not like us."

Roux restrained his impatience. Knowing the reason for that already, he bit down on his lip. He could see the convoy responsible for destroying his home, and taking his family, from where he perched beneath the canopy. Even without his camouflage active, they'd have trouble spotting him in the branches.

"How long was I out?"

"Two hours, maybe more."

"Hills?"

"Not even close."

"Where?"

"From what I can tell, you're headed back to the station."

Farz cursed, his words slurring between four different languages. "You sure?"

"Of course not. I can just see it from where I'm standing, and you're headed that way."

"Y'know, when I said I missed *actually* doing this with you—I didn't mean *this*."

Heavy breaths of his own, Roux balanced on the branch—taking hold of another. "Farz, once we get you and my family out of there, I'm never doing *this* again."

His brother laughed. "We'll see about that."

"I meant it ten years ago, Farz." He meant it even more in that moment. If they succeeded, he'd be a father soon enough. Kayla deserved better than what their old life could give her. Not wanting to consider what his mother would put his mate to use doing, Roux lunged for another branch.

"She'd be quite the asset to the team."

"You so much as mention it to our mother, and I'll never speak to you again."

"I've heard that before." Farz groaned. "What exactly do they have us in?"

"Looks like a shipping container."

"That would explain why I can't hear anything from outside. Wait, are we turning?"

Glancing toward the convoy, Roux cursed. "Yes, you're headed south of the station now."

"Roux, there isn't much of anything south of the station, for a *reason*."

He stifled the roar long enough to cut his outgoing connection. Roux struck the tree with his fist. Bark split and fell away into the deluge. So much for Michael's hope the local authorities would help—if they hadn't been dealing with a Siren. The bunker housing most of the planet's policing force was the only thing between the station and the barren lands. Nothing survived the rain season in the badlands.

"Roux, get out while you can."

"Not on your life."

"If they figure out, I'm not you... It could very well be your mate's life on the line."

"And yours, Farz."

"All the more reason for you to get your ass back in the shuttle, and get the hell out of here."

"I'm not leaving."

"I'll do my best to keep her safe, Roux."

"Farz?" He cursed as loudly as possible. Roux dropped to the ground, his knees bending and hands forward to prevent his fall. "Don't you dare cut your connection! Not now!"

His run through the trees and keeping the convoy in sight would have been difficult without the suit. Warnings flashed every time he came a little too close to one of the giant trunks. Rain pelted him with each breath. Protected within the suit, the sounds were a mere echo of what they would have been. His use of the silence to fuel his speed wasn't a wise move. If it weren't for the torrent of rainfall, they'd hear him from the distance he kept.

He ducked through the underbrush, close enough to see the lock on the container. "Farz," he couldn't say it. Of all the things he swore he hated about their lives, his brother never made that list. Any closer in the daylight—especially with the rain—would make it too easy for anyone to find him. *Unless... no Roux, don't be stupid, they'd spot you before you climbed under that thing.*

"On the bright side... it looks like we found out why no one has found their base of operations."

"Please tell me you're not close."

"Close enough to tell you—it's a biometric lock."

Farz cursed. "You can't get caught up in this too, little brother."

"They have Kayla. I'm already so deep that it doesn't matter."

"This is serious, Roux. No one walks away from these guys. Get out while you can."

That wasn't true. Robert walked away twenty-three years before. Granted, he wasn't safe, but he was free—until she found him. "Tell me to leave again, and I'll make you regret it."

His brother laughed. The sound of thumping against his confinement wasn't audible from the outside. "I've never seen one of these things from the inside."

"Farz, what happened back there?"

His brother ground his teeth together. "We didn't have any warning. Every sensor out there should have picked them up before they got that close. But, *considering* we just figured out where they are taking us, that's not exactly surprising. They blew the front door." He hissed. "Hurt like hell, by the way. She and the kid were far enough back, but they're beat up. They'll live through it. Not that I can guarantee any of us will survive Arzi. She's nuts, you know that—right?"

"Yeah."

"Roux,"

"Don't say it again. I'll beat you senseless for it."

Farz rapped against the interior of the shipping container, his laugh rebounding over the connection. "You already sent the pod back, didn't you?"

An effort to concentrate on his footing, he cut across the road. Roux laughed for his brother's benefit before starting up the ledge. With only one access road, the cliff face hiding behind the foliage was the fastest way to cut off the convoy. It would take them an additional forty minutes to navigate the switchbacks.

"You did..." His brother mirrored the laughter. "Mother won't be happy with you."

"When is she *ever* happy with me?" Farz had always been their mother's favored child, despite Roux being immune to Sirens. It was one of the many reasons he'd chosen their father's name when he left.

"How many people do you think they pull through this place in a year?"

"I don't want to think about the amount of locals they've stolen, Farz." There were too many ways to explain away disappearances. He knew of at least seven young kids who had turned up missing in the three years he and Kayla had been there. Some of them could have been legitimate deaths to misadventure. The thought of the others caused his stomach to sour. By using shipping containers, they could easily hide contraband intermixed with mining shipments headed elsewhere.

"What do you want me to tell her?"

"Can this wait? I'm trying to not fall to my death right now." Without his suit, finding grips for his ascent would have been impossible.

"How far up are you?"

"I'd be farther if you stopped distracting me."

"I wonder what your mate would think of you doing this?" Farz's voice echoed.

Kayla would think he was insane, but it wasn't as if he hadn't explained at least some of his tactical training. "Best not explain what I'm having to do to keep up with the truck. She'd probably blame you for it."

"Fair enough."

Smiling at the mental image of his brother relaxing with his hands behind his head—legs crossed in front of him—he dug his hands deeper into the wall above him. If it weren't for the trees reaching far above the cliff face, and those growing at the edge, he wouldn't have considered the climb. The fact that it gave him a little more cover was the least of his concerns as he kept his neck bent forward and head turned away from the rivulets of runoff.

"But seriously, little brother. You scaled Totus when you were ten, and that was at least what—fifty times bigger?"

"In my defense, Father was with me on that trip." He grunted with the effort to duck below a ledge, avoiding the debris breaking free above him. "And Totus doesn't have torrential rainfall—ever." It was a freaking desert. The region hadn't seen decent rain in four thousand years. He gaged the water running between the fingers of his suit before shifting to avoid the worst of the deluge.

"True."

His arms shook, taking the last grip to hoist himself over the edge. Laying in the underbrush for several seconds, he let the stupidity of what he'd just done sink in. He couldn't mention the situation to Kayla—if any of them survived their encounter with her mother's organization. She'd threaten to have his head examined. Laughing as the rain assaulted him, he rolled away from the edge.

"You make it up, little brother?"

"Nope, I'm laughing at the bottom of the ravine—with my back broken."

"I've missed this side of you."

Not willing to mirror the sentiment, he made his way up the nearest tree. The two of them had been inseparable—until he'd had enough. It wasn't his brother's doing. They'd been raised for a task, one his brother still loved. A life he couldn't pursue with a family waiting for him. Glancing down, he could make out the truck along the road. *Plenty of time, Roux.* He could scout for the facility before they reached the top.

26

Farz

The effort to brace himself with the shift in the container was difficult with two unconscious occupants beside him. The boy rolled over him, still in a dead sleep. Farz cringed about what his brother would have to say about it as he waited for their prison to steady.

Roux hadn't checked in with him for the last half hour. Not that he could blame him. The question of what he should say when they dragged him to his brother's mate, believing he was in fact the man she would have no trouble differentiating him from—had shaken his once iron stomached brother. If she was as dedicated to their relationship as Roux said, Farz knew she would call him on it. He just hoped the woman who held their lives in the balance wasn't present when she did.

He moved Michael back to his mother's side. Roux would be less anxious about their situation as long as Farz breathed deep enough for him to hear it. He kept the banter going for Roux's benefit, despite the arguments in both directions. If his brother fell apart over the situation, they were all dead. "You still out there, little brother?"

No response from his brother wasn't unexpected. His nerves wouldn't settle until he stood with his brother again. Even if he succeeded in getting in when the truck dragging the shipping container behind it did, that didn't mean Roux would get to him—before Arzi killed all of them.

The sudden stop jolted him from his thoughts. Farz knelt between Kayla's family and the opening, the height of the container was a few inches shy of allowing him to stand. He hoped to reason with their captors. They wouldn't be expecting any of them to be conscious, even most full bloods couldn't withstand the things he and his brother could.

Bombarded by light and sound, he squinted with his hands over his ears. Armed grunts lined the opening to the container, their eyes on him and not the woman and her son behind him. He swallowed the comment for his brother and held his hands up. *Looks like they did some research before going after you, little brother.* Tahali, their father's family name, wasn't an uncommon surname. Though, their mother's—Forran—was bound to turn heads when these people found out Roux was related to them.

Dragged from the shipping container, they bound his wrists behind him. Grunting in response to the *gentleness* of the reception, he scanned the receiving room of an underground facility. They'd have to have used some serious tech to keep it hidden from the sensor readings he ran as a precaution—regularly.

"There are too many of them, Farz. I can't get much closer." His brother's voice was low, but still registering on the implant's audio. No one around him could hear the incoming message, but Roux had to keep his voice down with this many of their species hovering.

Farz forced a smile. Wherever his brother was, he hoped he could see the twitch of uncertainty in it. A guard thrust the butt of his weapon into the sensitive area of his stomach. He'd taken shrapnel and failed to mention it to his brother. The brunt of the attack ruptured what little healing he'd managed. Blood ran down his side, a line of fresh crimson along what had dried since they found him. He bit down on his tongue to prevent himself from responding to his brother's heavy breathing.

"You didn't mention that!" Roux's whisper distracted him from another thrust against his injury.

The groan was impossible to stifle as two guards pushed through the line in front of him. "Take him to Arzi."

"She won't be happy about the injury."

"Happened in the blast. Nothing we could do about it."

Not looking up from the ground, he couldn't even put pressure on his own wound. The guards dragged him away, closing the door to the container—leaving Michael and Julie inside. Even if he tried to argue with them wouldn't do him any good, and it would only draw attention to how important their other prisoners were—if they didn't know already.

Pushed and pulled down the corridors, his ability to maintain a compass failed with the loss of blood. Despite the concern in his breaths, his brother was unlikely to follow him. Kayla's family would be in more danger than he was—they would need their location first. That, and the tracker built into his implant would remove the immediate need to know where they were taking *him.*

Thrown to his knees, he blinked the haze free. One pair of legs, the only thing visible in front of him. A woman, one who growled down at him.

"Why is he bleeding?"

"Shrapnel. He was in the wrong place at the wrong time when the door gave. The medic removed it already."

The hiss left his ears ringing. "Give him *more.*"

Delicate fingers wrapped around his left arm, pulling him to his feet. A minor distraction from the injection into his abdomen. Glaring into her eyes, Farz considered the outdated image they had on file for Kayla's mother.

She pulled him toward her, gripping his right arm with her free hand. She laughed in his face—a soft and yet threatening laugh—looking him over. "At least she has good taste." She released his left arm, dragging him further into the facility.

No one near him spoke, Arzi flooding her aura around her. It pulsed in his head with every step. His gut twisted at the thought of how long these men were under her influence. If the blank and glazed stares of those bringing up the rear were anything to go by, it was far too long.

The whir of a door brought his attention to his escort again. "Where is she?" His attempt to sound demanding came out in a grumbled hiss.

Arzi sneered, bringing her face too close to him. "Leave us!"

Startled by the volume of her command, he attempted to turn away from her. *Oh, now that is not cool.*

"Not you." She tugged at his arm again and pulled him toward another doorway. "Stay by her side at all times. Give her what comfort you can, and I might just overlook where you came from."

It felt like his lungs were dropping through his body. Farz struggled to remain upright. His brother's complaints in his head were the only things keeping him from madness. "Please, just *try* to keep your hands off her." Tugged through the second doorway, the Siren severed his bindings. The gasped greeting brought his eyes up to the young woman he'd yet to be properly introduced to.

"The injury was sustained *unintentionally.*" Arzi was quick on the draw, taking in the same expression Farz did. The Siren released her grip and pushed him into the arms of his sister-in-law.

Kayla gave him one look, her face shifting from the shock of their entry to a confusion he couldn't blame her for. The elder Siren laughed, folding her arms across her chest. "What I would give to see your mother's face when she realizes one of her precious boys—mated with my daughter."

She stiffened in his arms, for which he gave himself a mental slap. He hadn't even realized he was holding her. "You know Roux's mother?"

Arzi placed her hands on her hips. "Your choice has done more for us than you could ever imagine, daughter of mine. *She* will be less of an obstacle with her son at your side." She left them in the room without another word.

Kayla untangled herself from his arms. She left him leaned against the bed before taking careful steps away from him. Her father looked terrible. He was laying in another bed across the room. He considered his own treatment by the guards for his family affiliations. Robert couldn't have escaped it. Alan Morris was responsible for many setbacks, deaths even, among the organization the Sirens hid behind. But it was nothing when compared to the involvement he and his brother added to the scales. There was something about the way he guarded himself that told Farz they'd been insulted by his abandoning Arzi over twenty years before.

"I don't know who you are to him, but you are *not* Roux." Her father sat up, wincing. He pulled her closer to his bedside. Kayla didn't fight the attention. Instead, taking his hands in hers. He couldn't imagine watching her father recover was pleasant for the kid. Roux insisted she was close with her father, despite the years and distance.

He took a deep breath, ignoring Roux's complaints, and held his palms out. "The name is Farz."

She approached him with a gasp, fear draining from her eyes. "Roux's older brother?"

The smile spread on his lips. He could almost hear his brother slap a hand over his face with the way he grunted at his mate's use of the term. "Oh, he's mentioned me? Here I thought you hated it when I called you, *little brother*."

"Farz, shut it."

He couldn't help but laugh, holding his abdomen when the pain flared. "Oh, I so won't be shutting it, any time soon—little brother."

Kayla stood there, staring at him. He'd seen that expression before, on more than one woman's face. Neither of them had the best of timing when it came to interrupting the other. "I will say one thing for you. She definitely looks better closer up than she does from a distance."

"Farz,"

"You've seen me before." She squinted. "Wait, are you talking to Roux right now?"

He pointed behind his right ear with one finger and braced his stomach through another laugh. "Yeah, the curse of being who we are. I can't get him to shut up right now." The smile plastered on his face was undoubtedly a disconcerting one for his brother's mate.

"Is she alright? Is she hurt? Does she look alright?" Roux's panic wasn't unexpected. He hadn't seen her in almost four days. Any man separated from their pregnant wife, especially when that separation wasn't voluntary, would be the same. At least he hoped they would.

"He wants to know if you're alright."

She nodded shakily, rubbing her hands against her elbows.

"You can't see it, but she's nodding. Honestly, I think I'm more worried about her father right now."

"He's doing better than he was. But you, I'd like to look at that, just to be sure." Kayla pat the bed her father wasn't laying on. "Take your shirt off."

"I'm not sure this is a good idea..."

"Please tell me she's not telling you to lie in a bed she's been using?"

"No can do."

"Need I remind you that you keep referring to my mate as a *child*?"

Farz grumbled to himself. He knew Kayla wasn't a kid. But she *was* young. Especially with her not knowing much about Arros society.

Huffing at his words, not realizing they were intended for Roux, she pointed to the bed. "You may have stopped bleeding, and I'm guessing that has to do with one of their injections, but I'd like to make sure. You and your sister are the only family Roux really talks about, *and* I just met you. If you are really talking to him right now, I think he'd agree with me."

"Not about where she wants to do the examining, Farz, her mother just..."

"I know what Arzi just insisted I do. It was only minutes ago. You don't have to remind me."

She laughed hesitantly before looking at her father. He slid from the bed he was on, an audible wince breaking free. He motioned to the space with a grunt. "I think I agree with your brother."

"Don't make me *insist*."

"Yes, Farz, please don't. The more she uses it intentionally, the less you'll be able to resist her."

He pressed his lips into a straight line, lifting his shirt over his head and crossed the room. It ended up being more difficult, with the recent bruising, so much that Kayla helped him into the bed when he failed to hop up without holding pressure on the wound.

He stared at the ceiling, repeating the mantra of his brother's admonition in his head. Her delicate touch sent trembles down every nerve surrounding the injury. "It's closed again, but I don't like how this looks. I think this is going to scar, even with the advanced healing."

"Wouldn't be the first one." He didn't know if she was aware of what she was doing. Roux had said she'd flood her surroundings, unintentionally, something to do with her being pregnant. But her father didn't seem phased by the increase. Farz groaned for his luck. If you called having the tail end of the genetics when compared to his brother—lucky, he held his tongue between his teeth.

Kayla withdrew her fingers from his stomach, urging him to rotate his neck to face her. Her fingers trailed along the unmarred skin behind his right ear. "I'm guessing it isn't a complete neural connection, otherwise he wouldn't be asking how I looked." She probed the surface a little longer, her hands coiling away when she noticed the look in his eyes. "I can't tell it's there."

"That's kind of the point." He sat up, threw his legs over the side of the bed, and walked as far away from her as his body would allow. *Stupid aura is intoxicating.* He didn't dare point that out to his brother while he struggled to put his bloodied shirt back on. As far as Roux was immune, unfortunately—Farz was the exact opposite, making him far more sensitive than most of their species. He gave it a few hours in her presence, considering her current inability to keep the aura contained, before the need to please her in every way started getting progressively more difficult for him to fight off. Unfortunately, her mother made that even harder to do.

"His is the same?"

Farz rubbed the tingling from his arms with a nod. Grateful his brother couldn't see the shudder in his composure, he scratched the area behind his ear. "We can cut the outgoing connection at will, but the incoming doesn't have that option. You should know that Roux blocks his connection often. But I'm not so shy about what he hears."

She turned red, moving to lean against her bed—where her father had deposited himself. He really looked awful, though he complained little about it. "That explains a lot." She rubbed her nose, tucking her lower lip between her teeth.

Roux's lack of input was a bit unnerving. Either he was listening and steaming over what he thought was happening, or he'd shut the connection down from his end because he was too close to someone who might overhear him. He once admitted it removed the temptation to cuss Farz out—if the connection wasn't active.

"Where is he?"

"Last he had the chance to say, he was waiting to see where they take your brother and his mother. He can track me at any point he wants to, as long as he doesn't draw attention doing it."

Her father practically fell from the bed, his legs failing to respond to the information his head registered. "Are they alright?"

"They were alive when the guards brought me here. Roux hasn't said if they moved them from the shipping container, yet."

Eyes shifting focus between the door and his daughter, the man waged an internal battle. Arzi leaving them where they were wasn't a good sign. Disappearances weren't overly common, but their own history with it—her father's especially—left no room for false assurances.

"Why wasn't Roux with you when they came for you?"

Farz waited a fraction of a second to see if he was getting anything, anything at all from his brother, he cleared his throat. "We'd received orders to take them back with us. He was loading my pod below the safe room when your mother's grunts blew the front door open."

"Safe room?" Both of them stared at him, their eyes widening with each breath.

"Uh, yeah, I, um, sort of built that for him before the two of you moved into your place. It was supposed to be for emergencies."

"He never told me about it..." she paced the room, mumbling something he assumed was another human language he didn't know.

"I hid the entrance under your couch." The look on her face would have made him laugh if his brother weren't listening to every word coming out of her mouth. The range of any external voices wasn't the best, but the room was small. Short, bursting breaths reached him through his brother's end. He didn't want to know what they'd done on that couch if it made his brother uncomfortable to admit the location of the hatch to his mate.

Her father's head snapped toward him, a growl leaving his lips as he pushed between them. "Farz, and Roux..." Robert thrashed his head from side to side. "*Forran*?"

His stomach twisted, the foul glare from her father threatening to bore holes through him. Swallowing, he nodded. "I was wondering *if* you would catch on to that."

"Dad?" Kayla's voice trembled.

"Shit! How does he even remember us?" Roux's voice was a harsh whisper in his head. He took a second to consider what might be happening where his brother was, diverting his attention from the fist thrown in his direction. The distraction wasn't enough to allow it to connect. He twisted the arm behind Robert's back.

"What are you doing? Stop it! You're hurting him!"

He obeyed the command, her father falling to his knees. She joined Robert before he could climb to his feet.

"Farz! What did you do?"

"Stay away from my daughter!" Eyes glaring daggers in his direction, Robert wrapped an arm around her.

"Dad, why did you call him that? Their name is Tahali."

"No, it isn't. *Tahali* is their father's name, isn't it?"

Fighting the inability to lash out, Farz nodded. "Roux took our father's name when he resigned."

"From the military?" She shook her head at them. "Dad, what is it you think is so terrible about them?"

"The Roux and Farz Forran, I know of, were trained to hunt and *kill*—Sirens."

"How? What? Are you serious? But you've met Roux! Dad, he's a doctor—he doesn't kill *anyone*. Why would you say such a thing?"

"Because we were, and yes, we did." Answering for her father, Farz attempted to step closer to them with his hands outstretched.

Roux spewed curses in his ear, low enough to remain silent within the confines of his suit—as long as no one was standing directly next to him.

"Take another step and I'll call for Arzi. I have no issue telling her who you really are." He used her support to stand, taking a gigantic step backwards with Kayla wrapped in his arms. Her eyes reddened with each breath, head rattling from side to side.

"That's why he doesn't speak to them..."

"Partially."

"Farz..." his brother was on the verge of breaking. He had every reason to

—even if it was his own fault.

"Kayla, he resigned ten years ago. He'd had enough of what we do. Honestly, he should have warned you about it, *before* now. Because it was bound to come out at some point."

"I didn't, *because*—I hoped the need would never arise."

Hiccuped breaths escaped her, her gaze trading between the two of them. "I don't understand. Dad, how did you know?"

Farz sneered, gesturing toward him with the hand not bracing for his injury. "Would you like to tell her, or should I?"

"Farz, don't taunt him. You said he was injured. You'll only make this worse."

"NO, little brother! *You* made this worse by not telling your mate the life we both gave up when you resigned!"

"Their mother, Mina Forran... my mother grew up with her." Robert watched him like an avian waiting for its prey to make a fatal mistake. The muscles of his throat twitched as he tightened his grip around his daughter. "It appalled my mother when she found out what Mina's boys were being trained to do."

"In my brother's defense, he wouldn't have recognized your father. We were kids the last time we saw the Morris'. Close to thirty years can make a big difference, even for our kind." Shaking his head, he glared back at her father. "Your disappearance only fueled our mother's need to train us to stop every Siren in existence."

Robert sneered, sliding himself between Farz and his daughter. "The number of years aren't enough to completely strip the memory away."

"You're also a little older than we are," Farz rolled his wrist for emphasis, feeling a little like the dignitaries his mother mingled with. "And with our training, we didn't always pay much attention to Mother's friends—or their families."

"They're moving Julie and Michael." Breaths ragged, his brother grumbled about the need to stop taunting her father.

"And what about Kayla? She doesn't have a choice here?"

"Dad..." They both looked at her, eyes clenched shut, fingers digging into her forehead.

"You should know, Roux is on the move. They've finally turned their attention to your wife and son."

Covering her mouth with both hands, she backed away. With the small door behind her, she lowered one hand to open it—disappearing behind it with a sob.

"Farz, she did this the day we found out they arrived. Don't leave her in there like that—please." Not taking the moment to question what exactly he'd heard and why Farz had read nothing into the strange behavior of a distraught woman, he forced the door open.

His brother's mate sat on the floor, hugging her knees to her chest, burying her face behind them. "This won't solve our problem. Roux won't let anything happen to them. If he can intervene—he will."

"You don't understand!" Her tears magnified the cries. "She forced the men who attacked my father to kill each other. One of them succeeded—and *then* she killed the one who survived. She won't hesitate to kill my mom and my brother, and she'll kill Roux if she catches him."

As unsurprising as it was to hear of such things happening among the drudges Sirens kept around, he hadn't expected Roux's reaction. "Roux, keep it together." He pulled Kayla to her feet. Against his wishes, his arms wrapped around her—again.

"Farz, if this goes south..."

Clearing his throat was enough to get him to shut up. He would not let his brother down, regardless.

Outside the bathroom, her father stared at the exterior door. His nostrils flared, blotches peppering his face. "I won't let her hurt them."

"Don't let her father do anything stupid!"

"I was about to tell you the same thing."

"I've got this, Farz. Just make sure they do nothing to attract Arzi's attention."

27

Roux

Don't think about it, Roux. This is like breathing. Or it was. The effort in reminding himself wasn't doing as much as he hoped it would. Though, he considered it was the sobs he could hear through his connection to Farz causing most of the problem.

"Farz, I need you to shut down your link. Tell her..." the sudden silence nearly brought him to his knees. "I'll be with her when I can."

Of all the times for his brother to actually care enough to shut his connection down when asked, he'd never felt unnerved by it quite like he was in that instant. She was with him. And while that meant she was in excellent hands. It also meant she was in his arms. He wasn't entirely comfortable with that. Especially since Farz had no way of resisting her.

First order of business—steady breaths and pace. The task at hand—protecting Julie and Michael. He almost ran down the corridor after the guards dragging his wife's brother and mother. Neither of them were conscious—not a good sign. Farz hadn't known what their attackers used on them, but whatever it was, it would not end well for either of them if he couldn't keep up.

That being considered, he couldn't just bump into the idiots who did not know he was behind them. Grumbles to himself for being off his game wouldn't help him, either.

Easing through the door behind the guards was a close call. It nearly caught on his foot. Farz would scream at him for it later—if he'd witnessed it.

Roux, stop thinking about Kayla. You're going to get yourself killed.

He cringed, watching the idiots dump their charges into the cells. He bit down on his tongue to stifle the anger. Julie wouldn't be faring as well as her son. She was human, and with it—came the unfortunate frailties of her species. Michael wouldn't do as well as his sister—their genetic ratios flipped as they were. Though he was thankful, the guards left him there with her family. He growled at the thought of Kayla being treated the way they'd just treated her mother and brother.

A quick scan of the interior proved they didn't have visible cameras. One registered on the sensor of his heads up display. It was on the far right wall. As long as he didn't remove the helmet of his suit, no one would know he was there.

"Farz, they're in a cell, but don't tell Kayla and her father that. Not sure what they gave them, but they're still out and I think it would be best if I stick around."

"Agreed."

Roux closed his own connection, his nerves shuddering with the silence of the space. Even with Kayla around, there was some sort of noise. Her heart rate and breaths were often the only things he wanted to hear. They built the entire facility beneath the surface of the planet to absorb sounds. Not surprising, when taking into consideration who built the place. In his time away from almost all of his own species, he'd learned to tune out most of the normal things those around him couldn't hear—to an extent.

Jagged breaths rattled from his mother-in-law. She propped herself up on unsteady limbs, dropping to the floor again when they failed her. Three steps closer to the division, Roux gripped the bars with both hands, leaning his head against them. "Julie," his voice was steady, despite the nerves roiling beneath his skin. "Julie, can you hear me?"

She rolled to her side, rubbing at her eyes. "Roux?"

"Don't look for me, you can't see me and the camera behind you will make it obvious you're looking for someone."

Her hands closed into fists, her body tensing. He could hear the acceleration of her heart rate and breaths as if she were standing directly in front of him, instead of the middle of a cell—four feet away.

Roux backed away from the cell with the sound of the door opening behind him. Julie's eyes locked on the woman sauntering toward the bars. Barely at arm's length from the woman responsible for taking Kayla from him, Roux fought the urge to end her life—the way he'd done for countless others. His suit kept the inevitable migraine at bay, even if his nose tingled from Arzi's proximity. Her guards filled the space, leaving him taking silent steps away from Julie.

Whispering a warning to Farz would only give away his position and risk Julie's life. He held his breath with each step, finding the wall far too close for the present situation. One misstep and they would know he was there.

"So, you're the one who stole his heart?"

Roux forced his eyes closed. The sounds of his mother-in-law scrambling to her knees left his own shaking. *Please don't make her angry. I'll never be able to live with myself if I watch you die.* He couldn't stop Arzi. There were too many guards to deal with. Taking out the Siren would only cause more trouble for his brother—and Kayla.

"Where are they?" Her voice scratched against his ears with every breath shaking from her. "What have you done with them?"

"Brave, or stupid." Arzi's voice brought the threat of another, more excruciating, headache. Kayla's unintentional use of her own aura was nothing compared to the full-blown exposure of her mother's. "I'll give you a chance." She stroked the bars between them, laughing at the struggles before her. "I see an opportunity. One that requires your cooperation, and his."

"I won't make a deal with you, and I won't let him, either."

"Not even if it allowed your son to live?"

Roux's eyelids sprang fully open, his heart rate threatening to spike. *Keep it in control Roux, she can't know you are here.* Julie's breaths ricocheted through his head, her expression burning into his retinas. She slid closer to the division between her and Michael.

"You harm my son, and Robert will fight you—harder than I know he already is."

"You think he can?" Arzi laughed, turning to the guard closest to Roux. Her smile playing with the attention ebbing from him.

"I know he can." Her eyes threatened to tear the Siren apart with each breath.

Arzi stepped back from the bars. "It is only a matter of time before he cannot do so. I *could* just wait for that moment to kill both of you."

"And what of Kayla? Do you think she'll forgive you for taking her brother's life?"

"My daughter's name is Ahni. You will not use the filthy name given to her."

The smile grew across her face, the grinding of teeth visible between parted lips. "You might be able to prevent my husband from using the name *he* gave her, but I will never use the name *you* did."

Roux planted his feet, readying to move between them as the door to her cell opened. The smile on Julie's face prevented any action. She angled her eyes toward the woman grasping her throat. Not even bothering to struggle, Julie smiled wider as every curse spewed from the Siren's lips. Restraint ebbed away from him with every breath, making his way closer to the women.

Arzi released her grip, jolting away from the other woman in the cell. "You... you're... No, it isn't Possible!" Releasing shaky breaths, the Siren left the cell—slamming the door behind her. She stood there, her eyes fixed on her prisoners for what felt like an eternity to Roux.

Frozen two steps from Arzi, he fought to control his breathing, willing his heart to lull below what was audible for the full bloods around him. His suit dampened it to an extent, though he wasn't willing to chance them finding him—before he got everyone out.

"He doesn't know, does he?" Arzi laughed hesitantly. Crossing her arms over her chest, she moved to view Julie's expression. "You've played your hand. You won't enjoy mine."

Four guards followed the Siren from the room, an audible breath leaving Julie once the door was closed. "Roux?"

"Still here." Every instinct fought against his need to ensure her safety. He couldn't chance moving closer or speaking any louder with the little distance given. Keeping his whisper below what she could hear, he opened his connection to his brother. "Farz, I think Arzi is coming. Be careful."

"Noted."

"How's Kayla?"

"Stay focused, Roux."

Shuddering, his mother-in-law leaned against the bars of her cell with her legs out in front of her. "Have you seen them?"

"Farz is with them."

Her eyes widened, searching the darkness for him. "They think he is you?"

"Yes."

She covered her face, breathing into her hands. "I shouldn't have done that..."

"What *did* you do?" Another closer to the cell, Roux tapped the bar directly in front of him with his fingertips—giving Julie something to look at. "As long as your back is to the camera, look here. They won't see the movement of your lips."

"Full bloods don't want to listen to the pain they cause." She shook her head, rubbing the strain from her eyes.

"Something I've never been grateful for until now."

"Kayla and Robert, are they…"

"I haven't seen them yet. I wanted to ensure you two were safe. Farz can hold his own."

"Roux, your brother is the exact opposite of you. He can't resist Kayla or her mother."

"How did you know that?"

"You can see it in how he regards your immunity. But there are things I've kept to myself for a long time, things that would have been much harder to hide *if* I'd inherited my father's hearing."

Cursing in his native tongue, he tightened his grip around the bars. "Who was he?"

A single tear slid down her face. "Liorn Vassen."

"Son of *Golan Vassen*?" His breath caught in his throat with the slight dip of her chin. Eyes blinking in rapid motions, he focused on the controlled breathing coming from the woman who raised his wife. She'd been able to understand his private comments with Kayla the whole time. Thankful she couldn't see the flush of his expression, he shook his head. "You knew Kayla was a Siren…"

"Kind of hard to miss." She shook from the soft laughter, turning away from him to watch her son's chest rise and fall.

"How the hell did you end up on Tinall?" Her family was almost as connected as the Forran's were. He'd known there was some sort of trouble when he was a boy, something to do with Golan's son and his family being killed on the fringes over a dispute. "You're supposed to be dead!"

"I'm the only one who made it out." Julie situated herself against the bars to face him again. She shuddered. "What did they do to Michael?"

"They dosed the three of you. Farz isn't sure what they used." Resisting the urge to punch the bar in front of him, he clicked his tongue. "But if you're really who you say you are, then you will both be fine."

"Robert doesn't know."

"Obviously!" His eyes pulsed with every moment. He'd thought his own omissions were bad. The woman who'd been married to Kayla's father for eighteen years hadn't told him she was half blooded, too. "Does Caya know?"

"I didn't realize it was her. I'd heard stories about the Morris'. But I'd never actually met them." She shook her head, pressing the back of her skull against the bar. "I haven't been involved with Arros society since before my father died. What happened to my husband happened *after* I went into hiding. I didn't know any of it until you told us."

"Julie,"

"Arzi will use this against him. Use *us* against him."

"I won't let her hurt either of you."

"You can't promise that, Roux," Julie pulled her legs to her chest and wrapped her arms around her knees.

"Kayla does that."

"Unfortunately, something she learned from me. I can't always be the positive one. It can be rather exhausting to keep going."

Breath held, refraining from the curses that tossed about in his head, Roux leaned his helmet against the cell bars. "You're a Skym."

She leaned forward; her scowl threatening to slap him across the face if she could see him. "That is a derogatory term, young man."

"Forgive me, it is the only term I've ever been familiar with."

"That's because they've buried the original term, which even I don't know. What with Sirens making a bad name for the rest of us." She cupped her hands over her face, whispering into her palms. "They've also forgotten... It isn't a female exclusive trait. If that were the case, I wouldn't have the *luxury*."

"I knew it passed through the male lines, but not that they..." he shook his head, before remembering she couldn't see him. "Julie, are you saying Robert..."

She lifted her head, a smile spreading. "Yes, but he never noticed when he was doing it for the kids." Her body shook with the soft sobs emanating from her.

"But you *did*." He shouldn't have been surprised, a Skym finding another like her on a heavily human populated world. There was no wonder why she chose Robert, and him her.

"How is it you knew about Caya's ability?"

Exhaling, he smiled behind the safety of his visor. "My reasoning wasn't as sound as I first thought. All of my species has sensitive hearing, Sk..." He stopped himself short. "Those with your *qualities* are normally far more sensitive. But you..."

Julie rubbed her throat, wincing through a smile. "You're right."

"Someone is coming." Biting down on the words he couldn't give her, he retreated to the wall as the door opened.

Julie pulled herself upright, turning to face the last person either of them expected to see.

"Mom!" Kayla sprinted across the walkway, gripping the bars with both hands.

"Kayla!"

Roux battled the need to be at her side, strangling the relief at seeing her. He closed his eyes, folding both lips between his teeth. *Farz, you'd better have a good reason for not warning me.*

"Mom, I'm so sorry! I... I..."

"Kayla, this isn't your fault."

He opened his eyes, trembles threatening to reach his extremities as he watched Julie reach through the bars.

"Make your decision, Ahni."

His wife froze, her heart rate spiking. "She wants me to decide between you or Michael. She won't let me take both of you back with me. Not if... not if I want *Roux* safe."

Not good. Roux braced himself, readying to move in when he could.

"What did she do?"

"She..." Kayla wiped tears from her face. "I, I, thought it was only the serum to help them heal, but they..."

"Heal? Kayla, what did she do to your father?" Julie's expression paled. She tightened her grip on the bars.

"Neither of them will wake until you make your decision, Ahni."

The growl on the tip of his tongue was silent as he opened his mouth to gain the breath, not realizing he'd held it too long. *That* was why Farz hadn't warned him.

Glaring over Kayla's shoulder, Julie's body shook with the anger Roux could hear boiling through her veins. "Take your brother."

"But Mom," sobs raged from his wife. "I can't leave either of you here."

"I'll be fine where I am. Tell your father I'm sorry."

"Sorry for what?" Kayla turned to face the woman, laughing behind her, scowling. Roux had seen that expression many times before. Not being on the receiving end—was only *slightly* comforting. "This is funny to you? And you wonder why he left *willingly*?"

"Have you decided?"

She lowered her gaze and turned toward her brother, tears engulfing her face. "My brother."

At Arzi's command, the guards hefted the still unconscious Michael from his cell. One remained behind at the Siren's side.

"If you hurt my mother, I will never forgive you." Kayla's eyes scanned the surrounding darkness. Assuming she was looking for any sign of his presence, Roux held his breath again. "And neither will my father."

"Given enough time, your father won't want her." Arzi lilted her head toward Kayla. The guard at her side dragged Roux's wife toward the door. Waiting for them to pass her, Arzi sauntered toward the cell. "A pity she didn't choose you. I would have enjoyed breaking him." She laughed, causing Julie to grind her teeth. The sneer on her face set the hairs of his arms on end. Her laughter echoed through the door before silence settled in its wake.

Watching wasn't much help. He had to get Julie out. Not having to worry about Michael made it a *little* easier. It meant he would have to leave the compound and the others behind. With no way to know what Arzi would do when she found Julie gone, he couldn't risk going too far. Cursing himself for not taking Arzi's life both times she was within his reach, Roux crossed to the cell. "Julie..."

"What are we going to do?"

"Hold still." He took the palm sized cannister from the pocket of his belt and put his hand through the bars. Fumbling with the release valve in his gloves, he wasn't as coordinated with his gear—another downfall of not using it outside of training for the last ten years. Roux didn't give her time to step away.

"What?" Coughing through the plume, Julie blinked tears from her eyes. "What... is... that?"

"Turn around. I need to coat you with it."

Still coughing, Julie obeyed.

"It will render you invisible to their cameras and sensors. Not permanently, but long enough to get you out." They'd have to run for it once they got outside. As useful as the chemical was, it wouldn't last five seconds in the deluge.

"Why didn't we do that before they came back?"

"Because I couldn't get both of you out this way." He could have, though it would have been much harder than what he was about to do.

With his free hand, he retrieved the explosive putty from his belt. Tucking the canister back in its place, he molded the stabilized goop around a single bar in two places. Julie wasn't small, but she wasn't large either. The gap would be plenty large enough for her.

Julie eyed the visible concoction with wide eyes. "Don't you think they will hear that?"

"Nope. Back up a little." Activating the substance from the interface of his suit, Roux forced the bar from the cell.

Not waiting for instructions, Kayla's mother slithered through the opening. "I can't leave them, Roux."

"Neither can I. Stick close. We need to move quickly."

28

Kayla

Labels of varying degrees of anger didn't quite meet the mark. She watched the guards dump her brother on the floor next to her father and Farz with enough to force to the further flow of her tears. But she didn't dare argue with her mother present.

"You can give them each this." Arzi handed her three vials. "When you're ready to face them." She smiled at her, causing every nerve in Kayla's body to shudder.

She fell to her knees with the sound of the lock engaging on the door. The curse of trading one mother for another wasn't fair. Arzi would never be the mother Julie was to her. The hope that Roux had a plan didn't soothe her nerves. She'd been so close to him, knowing he was in the room hadn't helped her fears. Unable to even acknowledge his presence was excruciating. Somehow, Julie knew. The brief glance behind Kayla—not at Arzi—was proof of that.

Kayla inched toward Farz, crawling over her brother to reach him. Her limbs thrust the vial into his chest—just above his heart would give the concoction a boost. He was a full blood Arros. The surge of adrenaline wouldn't kill him. She'd have to be more careful about how she used the other two vials on her brother and father.

Roux's brother convulsed with the puncture, gasping loud enough Kayla had to cover her ears. He cursed at a similar volume, tossing from side to side as he assessed his surroundings. "What the hell happened?" Noticing her brother on the floor behind her, his eyes widened.

"She made me decide between my mother and my brother. What was I supposed to say: take my brother and do whatever horrible things you have in mind?"

Farz wrapped both arms around her, panting from the continued surge through his veins. "Roux, what happened?"

The attempt she made to wait for his nerves to settle was silly, seeing as it never happened. His heart rate was likely to be erratic for at least an hour. Though she wasn't expecting it to spike higher. "Is he answering you?"

He held one hand up to quiet her. "Roux, get her out before they realize what you did." He paused, shaking his head at her questioning glance. "Yes, he's here. No, they're both still out. Well... I'd imagine she woke me up first to check on you... why else would she?" Farz looked at her, his expression darkening. "You can tell her yourself. I'm not doing that for you."

She shoved herself away from him, sliding back on her butt, holding both hands over her mouth. It did little to stifle the sobs. But she hoped it was enough to prevent it from carrying over the connection to Roux.

Farz was standing above her a moment later, nudging her with a finger. "I know you're trained on how to use those..." he pointed to the unspent vials. "But I think it's better if I do this." It took little for her to relinquish her hold. She watched him skirt her brother. "There is a trick to this. Half-bloods have a bit of a difference here." He pointed toward her father's collar bone. "Judging by how much it still hurts, I'm guessing you injected me right where it would do the most good."

She nodded. "But you can't do that for them. It could kill them both. Michael isn't even half Arros."

Farz had the nerve to laugh as he knelt beside her brother. If she'd been closer, she would have hit him. "Roux says otherwise." He huffed with an eye roll. "Can you say something to ease him before I shut down my connection? He's going to drive me crazy."

She rose to her knees and shuffled toward him. It felt strange wrapping both arms around Roux's brother's neck, pulling him down the few inches to place her cheek even with his. Farz shuddered with the contact, but didn't argue. "Roux, get her out of here, please. We'll be alright. Just don't get yourself killed. Okay?"

Farz pulled her from his neck and pushed her to arm's length, smiling at whatever response his brother had given. "I'm pretty sure the feeling is mutual, *little brother.*"

She cringed, failing to turn away from him as he shifted between her father and Michael. "What did you mean when you said *Roux says otherwise?*"

Vial in hand, Farz trailed along the exposed skin of her brother's arm. "Apparently, your stepmother is half-blooded." With the short sleeve rolled up, he punctured Michael's shoulder. "So they'll both survive this." He waved the empty vial in the air moments before her brother's body convulsed.

Kayla flung herself to his side to hold Michael still. "Did *she* tell him that?!"

He nodded, thrusting the remaining dose into her father's shoulder. "It's a major artery, but it will not be as instantaneous as what you did to me." He laughed. "Thanks for that, by the way. I'll probably be up all night."

29

Roux

Not bothering to apologize for the death-grip on Julie's arm, he ran through the corridor with her struggling to keep up. "Arzi locked them in Kayla's room with my brother and Robert."

"How are you expecting to get us out of here? I can't even see you. How am I supposed to know what way you're..." she grunted with the force of him tugging her to the side. "Going?"

"I'm not about to let you go, so don't worry about that." He grumbled to himself about the tone he'd used. It was too late to amend the comments. Even if he tried, it wouldn't wipe the glare from her face. She barely knew him. And it was his own fault. "Try to keep your voice down."

"Do you have more of that *stuff*?"

"Yes, but it will not do us any good if someone hears us."

"Sorry."

"Don't apologize."

She bobbed her head, eyelids trembling.

The side entrance he'd found while waiting for the convoy would be guarded, though he didn't imagine the inside would be the problem. The guards inside the six-foot corridor to the exterior door would be easy enough, but it meant he'd have either shove Julie in a corner or use her as bait and take out the guards. Either way was going to give them very little time to make the tree line before Arzi sent reinforcements.

He couldn't control the pod from inside the bunker, but he could at least start the course command if he'd had a free hand. Not willing to release his grip on her arm, sure to leave a bruise, he continued forward—debating if he should tell her what would work best for getting them out along the way.

They ducked into a shadowed corner. Roux put himself between Julie and the walkway. He pressed a finger to her lips for good measure. Her heart rate lulled faster than he'd expected, but he couldn't focus on that. The effort to keep his hands in appropriate places to keep her against him was the only thing he could manage—in the few seconds he had. She had to be close enough to him for the suit to register the wall behind her for the camouflage. They both held their breath while the men walked by them. Still holding her right shoulder, he held her against the wall while he checked to make sure they were gone.

Her eyes darted around them the further they moved. Smiling with the familiar sensation coming off her, Roux tried to push away the memories of Kayla trying to calm him. He would definitely berate himself for not noticing that she'd inherited Caya's ability along with her mother's—later. The need to recognize it was one of his jobs. But he'd overlooked it, sensing the greater problem when he met Kayla. She was just a kid, frightened of what she could do to those around her, nothing like the mother he had to save her from.

The pocket for the compound flipped open with a slight touch of gloved fingers. He released Julie, pressing the fingers of his left hand to her lips—as gently as possible in his haste. Using both hands, he spread the putty around the door. Satisfied it was enough, he took her arm again—pulling her behind him as the door fell into the corridor beyond.

Both guards flailed for their weapons, spinning on their heels. Once again letting go of her arm—cringing at the gasp breaking free of her lips—he dispatched the distracted guards.

"Roux?" Her pulse skyrocketed when he took her arm again. "A little warning might be nice!"

"One more door. Once we're out, we can't stop." He flung the hunk of acidic paste across the door, he blocked Julie's view. The spark was going to be brighter than the other times he'd used it. It wouldn't blind her permanently, but he would not risk the temporary effect. The door, or what was left of it, hadn't touched the ground when he threw his mother-in-law over his shoulder and vaulted through the hole—alarms deafening him.

Not caring what sound he made, he forced a pace he couldn't keep up with Julie on his shoulder. He didn't need to keep it up for long, just enough to get into the trees. He reached over her legs, sending the command for the pod.

Farz assumed he'd sent it back to the ship. He almost laughed as he calculated the three hundred yards to the ravine—give or take. He could do it with his eyes closed, if he weren't carrying someone. The last time he'd made a run for it, Farz laughed at him the entire way. They'd both been running at their max to avoid the impending explosion. Julie wasn't a living weapon like Farz. She couldn't keep up—or protect herself.

He breathed heavily through his nose, keeping his focus on the trees ahead of him. *C'mon Roux, you're almost there.* He'd have to slow his pace, to some extent, once he broke through the foliage. That was the least of his concerns with the sound of voices coming from the compound. He shifted her into his arms as he broke through the bushes. "Try not to panic when I jump off this ledge."

"What?!" She struggled in his arms, pushing against him. "Are you serious?" Her voice barely carried to him, the rain falling heavily around them.

"We're not there—yet. Just thought I would warn you."

Her arms shot up, hands searching for his neck. Once she'd accustomed herself to the shape of the suit, she latched her hands together behind his helmet.

The shuttle pulled into position on the display, taking up half of his visor. He tightened his grip around Julie. Muscle memory took over his breaths with each twist and turn to avoid the trees. He mumbled the distance aloud for her sake.

Falling. The worst sensation he'd ever experienced. It would never be enjoyable for him. Even with the perfect placement of the shuttle's open upper hatch. He landed on his feet, careful to bend his knees—it still hurt like hell with the dampening effect of his boots. Pain filled grunts escaped him as he let Julie down. He shuffled for the first few steps before flinging his helmet into the open cabinet. Deactivation of the camouflage gave her the first look at the extravagance of his father's creations. If his sons were going to risk their lives as specialized ground troops, he at least wanted them to have the best equipment available.

"Are you alright?"

"No, but I can deal with that later." He dropped into the pilot's chair, letting the restraints shoot out around him. The removal of his gloves wasn't necessary, but he did it anyway. "Sit down. This is going to be a ride. They don't know where we are, but they sure as hell know we're out here."

30

Farz

Ow! The back of his head hit the wall—again. Arzi ordered the idiot pinning him to the wall to hit him—again. Kayla's arguments on the matter were ignored—again. Robert stood guard over his children, watching the beating with wide eyes. Farz knew he would have done it, even if the wretched Siren hadn't ordered him to.

"Where is your brother Farz? What was he doing here?"

Twitching with the inhale of her aura, Farz smiled at her. "I don't have a brother named Farz." Unless she asked in another manner, he would continue to answer her that way. He almost laughed at her insistence on using the same words over and over. She did not know who she had her little henchmen beating on. If she hadn't given him a direct order to stop fighting her idiot minion, Farz would have handled him in seconds.

As it was, he was stuck taking a beating that wasn't anywhere near the one he would have dished out in return. *Even Roux hits harder than this idiot. Ow!* Roux could pull his punches, but this guy definitely had power behind it. Farz spewed blood on the floor, his lips and gums bleeding from the continued assault.

"Then how do you explain the loss of my prisoner, Dr. Tahali?"

"Did you lose someone?" Farz was almost hysterical with the combined essences flowing around him. He made a mental note to mention how nauseating and dizzying it was to be around both of them. Her father and brother appeared to be fine—to some extent. Both of them looked glassy eyed, but they were standing without difficulty.

The poor kid wrapped his arms defensively around his older sister. After the last four days, Farz couldn't blame him. Waking up and finding out where he was, not to mention hearing that his mother was missing from Arzi's prison cell, was a little much for a sixteen-year-old who'd never heard of Sirens before. Farz was pretty sure he'd be reacting similarly—if their roles were reversed.

Fist to his ribcage, Farz doubled over. Thankfully, his injury had healed over enough to prevent the barrage from splitting it—again. The grunt dropped him to the ground, kicking him repeatedly. The muffled screams of his sister-in-law pounded in his head with every attack on him.

"Stop it! Please! Stop!"

"Instill in him the need to tell me where his brother is, and maybe I'll consider it."

"He has told you repeatedly! He doesn't have a brother named Farz!"

The assault ended as abruptly as it started, with Farz laying in his own blood. The sound of a vial clinking against the floor registered in a moment, followed by the light of the room being blocked out.

"When I come back, you'd better be willing to answer. My daughter's mate, or not, I will not tolerate resistance."

A gentle caress traced the bruises of his face, the anger bleeding from him. *Holy shit, she really is a Skym too!* Farz stared at her, feeling his eyes widen with each moment. Roux's theory was looking to be a reality, something he didn't plan to admit to his brother. He was always a little too smart for his own good.

"She's gone Farz. I need to give you the serum... but I am worried about how many of these she has given you—so close together."

"I've lived through worse." His words slurred, his heavily bruised jaw, the most likely culprit.

"Please tell me Roux didn't hear any of that."

"He didn't." Though he rarely cut his connection, before they shoved the crazy week in his face, it seemed the right thing to do. His brother would have just been a distraction otherwise. Roux would never have let him suffer alone. In fact, he'd have probably come back and turned himself in to prevent further abuse. He was always the sentimental one, not that Farz couldn't feel or show emotion. It was quite the opposite. He was just a little stupid about it, compared to Roux's reserved nature.

Using her sleeve, Kayla wiped the blood from his face. "I'm sorry, this isn't much of a first experience with you. You probably think I'm terrible."

"Roux would never have chosen you—if you were." Truthfully, he *knew* she wasn't terrible. But he couldn't tell her that.

Tears welled in her eyes. She twirled the vial between fingers, a shy smile parting her lips. "This might hurt."

Bracing himself for the injection, Farz ground his teeth together. He knew the damage had to be severe with the amount of clarity failing him. While the injection pushed most of the pain away, it also left him losing consciousness—a little too quickly.

31

Roux

He wrung his hands around the railing as he stared out through the view-port. They couldn't see the station or the compound from orbit, but he knew exactly where they were. He'd set the computer to monitor movement of any kind on the surface and the space surrounding the planet. Roux abandoned the futile attempt to sort through the refuse of unwanted information.

"Whats the plan?"

He couldn't bring himself to take his eyes off the planet as his wife's mother entered the room. "Farz isn't answering me." Either his brother was purposely preventing his connection, or he was unconscious. Both options were unsettling.

"Maybe they're with others and can't say anything?"

"If that were the case, he'd be letting me hear what was going on. Not ignoring me completely."

"Maybe you're out of range?"

An eyebrow raised, he turned to her. He jabbed his finger behind his right ear, grumbling. "The ship amplifies this… He could hear me if I was eight to ten hours at full speed from here."

"Ah."

"We also happen to be in an orbital loop around this planet, which prevents either of us from being out of range with the amplification."

"He's been watching you all these years, hasn't he?"

He returned his attention to the view-port. "Mother's ultimatum. My leaving could only happen if Farz was nearby—at all times." Farz had always insisted it did not bother him. Roux knew better than to believe him.

"Oh." Julie folded her lips between her teeth.

"Fortunately, he doesn't intrude in my life often. At least not physically."

"Must be difficult for him, not having anyone around."

Roux made his way to the console in the middle of the room. He almost laughed at the absurdity of the assumption. Julie knew nothing about his brother. Neither did his wife. "He only comes up here when he needs time alone—mostly."

"You mean he lives down there too?"

"It's connected to the same escape route I used to get out after Arzi's grunts came after you." He'd never told Kayla about the residence four miles from them. They'd passed it several times during their duties. She wondered aloud, once, about who lived there. He hadn't even considered a response, using their assignment as a distraction.

"Does Kayla know?"

The slow pivot of his neck was all he could convey, his attention on the computer's filtered data.

"Why?"

Roux looked up from the screen, blinking. "My brother and I hunted Sirens for a living, before I met her." Farz had known about Kayla. But that didn't mean Roux wanted his brother anywhere near the woman he'd have no control resisting—the woman Roux loved more than anything.

"But you haven't for ten years. I don't think she would judge either of you for it. Especially knowing that neither of you really had a choice in the matter."

"Do you have any idea what my mother and her *friends* would have done if they knew I was protecting her?"

"I don't want to think about it." Her gaze dropped to the floor, she scuffed her toes.

Roux forced his eyes shut as he dug his fingers into the back of the console. "They will never accept her among our species. *That* is why I brought her here."

"But your mother knows about Kayla."

"Yes, she does now. But they can't do anything to her now."

"Will your mother really defend her, simply because you've mated?"

"*Our* posterity may be the key to preventing Sirens from continuing their conquest. I am the only one capable of protecting Kayla from the others back home. I knew it the first day I met her."

Her eyes flared for an instant, softening at the realization of what he meant. "You've loved her that long?"

His eyes lolled back with an exhale. He grumbled internally. If he told her mother what happened when met her, they wouldn't make him popular with Kayla's father. He saw her as an equal, despite being ignorant of the Arros way of doing things. Someone he could start over with. Someone who would never judge him by his immunity. "I only wanted to protect her. I never expected her to become what she is to me now." It was only half true. He turned away from Julie, walking toward the corridor outside the observation deck. She followed him out.

"It was fairly obvious you two cared about each other when we arrived. I'm sorry for the way Robert reacted. I think he's always feared she would become her mother."

"He pushed her away with that fear. If she'd run into anyone other than me…" he cringed at the thought of what would have happened to her without his help. Roux quickened his pace. Truthfully, Robert's fear drove Kayla's. She wanted to protect her father from the memory, something she could never tell him herself.

"Roux, wait!" Huffing to keep up, Julie took hold of his wrist.

"Kayla will never be like her mother."

"Robert knows that. He might not show it, but he does. Please don't judge him for his fear of Arzi."

"All male Arros fear Arzi. They fear what she, and those like her, are a representation of. I'm not making accusations of any kind. He did what he thought was best. I don't have a daughter. I don't know what he has dealt with. But one day, I may yet have one. I hope to avoid the mistakes he's made. I will never urge my daughters to fear what they are."

Julie released her hold but not her gaze. "I let him bear it alone. I should have told him I knew. He was trying to keep it to himself, to keep all of us safe."

He couldn't condemn the man for his efforts. Even if he wanted to. "There is something I need you to do for me." Not waiting for her to respond, Roux continued down the passage.

"I don't see how much good I can do in this situation."

They stopped outside the shuttle. He held up a hand for her to wait. They'd moved almost Everything from the shuttle arrived. The container remaining in the cargo hold of Farz's shuttle housed the belongings he and Kayla held dear. Unable to bring it aboard, he'd dug through it for necessities while Julie was sleeping. It was still open.

Roux knelt in front of the box, lifting the clothing from the top of the stack. It allowed access to the small case his wife kept her most precious things in. He stroked it with his fingertips, heart rate elevating with each breath. Shaking off the emotion, he wrapped his fingers around the edges and pulled it clear.

With the latch open, it only took a scoop of his fingers to retrieve what he was looking for. Closing his fist, he pocketed the rest of Kayla's keepsakes. No amount of planning would change his mind about what he needed to do. He wasn't bound to be popular with her father for what he was about to admit, much less what he planned to do.

He drew in a bolstered breath before he returned to Julie. "I need you to keep a hold of these." Roux opened his hand above hers, dropping the polished loops into her hand. "Kayla will skewer me if I lose them."

Her breath vacated her body, leaving her shuddering with the weight of his confession. "You married her?" Her gaze lifted from the rings. She stared wide eyed at him. "You told us you'd only mated with her."

Roux pressed his lips together, exhaling through his nose. "I did..." fisting both hands, he began walking toward the command deck of his brother's ship. "Three years ago."

She was pale at his side, staring at her open hand. The fingers of her opposite hand twitched with each step.

"Julie, I meant it when I told Robert that I genuinely love her."

"I don't doubt your word. The last few days have been enough to prove it." She exhaled, pressing fingers into her forehead. "I know why you didn't tell us then. He would have gone ballistic over her getting married without telling him. But you let Robert believe you got his daughter pregnant and didn't marry her first."

"She was planning to explain more once she had time to discuss my immunity with him." Pausing his pace to consider the situation, Roux rubbed his left hand over his mouth and jaw. "She didn't want to scare you with all the details. Neither of us were expecting *this* to happen."

"Why did you get me out? You could have grabbed Kayla and ran when you had the chance."

"Do you think you mean that little to her?"

"I know how Kayla feels, Roux. I raised her."

"Arzi means nothing to her. *You* are her mother, Julie. She'd never forgive me if I left you there."

"You and Farz, you were supposed to be officers, weren't you?"

He nodded before continuing away from her, keeping his eyes on the floor ahead of them.

"That is why you both have the implant. I suspected it at the house, but I didn't dare mention it."

Roux turned down the corridor, laughing softly. "You were pretty good at keeping what you knew to yourself. I couldn't even tell you were hiding anything—and that isn't easy for anyone to get past me."

"Over twenty-five years of pretending to be human makes it a little easier to act dumb about things you *shouldn't* know."

"Caya never told you about mating, did she?"

"*Actually,*" Julie dropped into the seat he normally used when he traveled with Farz. "She *did.* I just made her think I didn't know those details beforehand."

Sitting down across from her, he couldn't help but laugh. "Yeah. I bet that was quite the *talk.*"

Julie turned red. "You have *no* idea."

"In hindsight, I should have taken her home to you—after we married."

"Everything is easier to consider—in *hindsight,* Roux. You were trying to give her a good life. That's what matters."

They sat in silence for several moments. Julie watched him alter the orbit, her eyes questioning his plan—again. He couldn't tell her where he was planning to send her. She wouldn't be happy with the plan he had, either.

"Roux, the Tahali's aren't front line warriors. Is it because you were immune?"

Retracting his hands from the controls, he cringed for her benefit. "Unfortunately." He and Farz were slated for command school. Their training for it had begun when they were very young. That started with the conditioning needed for their communications implants. It wasn't until they were eleven years old that they discovered his immunity through normal testing of all Arros, throwing them into the hell that was their lives before he resigned. "Tahali is my father's side of the family."

"I can't imagine your father's family being thrilled about that." Swiveling her seat from side to side, Julie strummed her fingers along her knees.

"No. But my father *was* supportive of my choice to leave that life behind. I think my decision to carry his name amused him. He has never rescinded his support."

"Either your father has excellent connections, or he's one of the upper echelons himself."

Smiling, Roux tried to ignore the comment. He knew what she was getting at, but he couldn't give her the answer she wanted. There was a reason few knew who his father really was. Political connections aside, the match would have drawn far too much attention. While it was fairly common knowledge that the Tahali line was a very *military* family, few outside the family really understood what that meant. "He called in several favors when I told him I planned to marry Kayla." Exhaling a laugh, he watched Julie's reaction.

"The position here?"

He nodded. "She wished you and Robert could have been there. My father was there, but Kayla doesn't know it was him I introduced her to."

"Roux, there is no way your father doesn't know who she is."

"That thought has crossed my mind." Reciting the number of times wasn't necessary. He couldn't blame his father for keeping it from him, even if it had caused more harm than good—for both of them. The urge to grumble about the omissions passed with each breath.

"Secrets and *Lies*. This is feeling just like home."

Roux couldn't restrain the laughter, because she was right.

Had his dreams been pleasant, he might have complained about the rude awakening. The cacophony assaulting his sensitive auditory nerves set his unsteady limbs into a frenzy. Rolling out of bed was something Kayla did. He'd always had a terrible habit of leaping over her to reach the bathroom first. It wasn't much different from his behavior at that moment, aside from the destination.

Strides Roux rarely used, with his wife around, brought him to the command deck of his brother's ship—faster than necessary. The unprecedented heavy footfalls were bound to wake his mother-in-law—even with the superior design intended to absorb most of the sounds.

Digesting the specifics the computer spit out faster than any human would be comfortable with, Roux shifted in Farz's chair. Knuckles whitened with every breath. His brother's absence seeped through his veins, blood thickened with every detail scrolling across the feed. *Not good. So. Not. Good.* He rubbed his fingers across his temple, bracing himself against the console.

The slew of curses roiling through his head would never find fruition, or wouldn't have—if Kayla had been present. Her absence, and the data glaring back at him, forced the articulation.

"How bad is it?"

Gasping at the sudden surge of blood to his extremities, Roux tightened his grip on the chair. "Farz! What happened to you?"

His brother cleared his throat, groaning with whatever movements he was attempting. "Well, I'm in here alone now. So I do not know."

Refraining from cursing was impossible.

"The last thing I remember…" Farz coughed. "Arzi still believes I am you. She was asking about where you'd have gone and why you were here." He laughed, causing another bought of coughing. "But that serum she gave me should have fixed the damage."

"Damage?" The vessels of his eyes threatened to overtake his vision with each breath. "What did *Arzi* do to you?"

"Don't think too much about it, *little brother.*"

"This isn't a game, Farz!"

"Don't I know it? But you still haven't answered my question."

"*She* has a ship in orbit. If these readings are correct, it's a dreadnought. I don't know how you missed it."

"I was looking for something that *shouldn't* be there, little brother. No one in their right mind, outside of the military, comes here. I was expecting a slight military presence on a piddling mining planet four weeks from the nearest military installation. *That* one comes and goes."

"You didn't think I needed to know about a dreadnought in orbit?"

"It isn't always there."

"And that is supposed to make me feel better?"

"The beast is readying engines, isn't it?"

Swallowing the pool of saliva, he groaned. "Yes." Withholding further grumbles, Roux punched the coordinates into the console. "I'll get as close as I can. But there is no way I can stop that thing."

"You'd better not go near it, Roux. You *lied* about sending the pod back as is,"

"I didn't lie… I failed to confirm your suspicions."

"Omissions are going to be the death of you, little brother. But I see why you did it."

"I answered your question. Now answer mine."

"One of her drones beat the crap out of me, because I wouldn't tell her where my brother *Farz* was." His brother laughed, coughed again, then groaned.

"How does she know about you?"

"Probably should have mentioned that by now… her grunts did their research… knows who our mother is. I'd bet a fortune she knows you're immune. She seems to think I am, because I won't tell her where *Farz* is."

Pinching the loose skin of his forehead, Roux echoed his brother's groan. "You'd better hope she doesn't decide to learn patience and start rephrasing how she says it."

"I never thought all the stories about her were *this* accurate." Farz laughed again. His connection cut with the induced coughs.

"Farz, how bad is it?"

"My jaw isn't as bad as it could be. I think he busted one of my knees, some broken ribs, probably a punctured lung."

"She's not treating you for it?"

"Kayla thought the vial Arzi left was the serum. *Obviously,* it wasn't. I don't know how long I've been out."

"Four hours. Yes, I've been counting them."

"Aw, that is sweet, little brother. Here, I thought you hated me poking my nose into your life."

"Shut up, Farz."

32

Kayla

Her father's expression weighed her down to the chair. Michael cringed at her side, fearing any word spoken against the Siren would increase the discomfort her mother would dump on them. She couldn't blame her brother for fearing Arzi. Though she hadn't given him any command, they all knew it wouldn't stay that way.

Kayla wanted to throw her plate at Arzi. It took every bit of control to keep most of her attention away from the conversation her mother was trying to have with her father. Either she was letting him off easily, or her father was actively fighting her control over him. Either way, watching the exchange was excruciating for his children. She reached for her brother's hand, squeezing it under the shelter of the table.

Their shared glance ended with the struggled words falling from their father's lips, the location of their grandparents on Tinall. Breaths ripped from him, heaving with each blink of his eyes. "Arzi, please… they have nothing to do with…"

"Enough, I won't have them miss the birth of our grandchild."

Tears ebbed from his clenched eyes, his chin resting against his chest. No one outside the family knew they were his parents. Their slower aging had the family introducing their grandfather as their father's brother. They'd worked so hard to keep the illusion alive. Their father's younger brother and sister often still called him uncle Robbert in private.

Michael tugged her hand, still clasped in his. Using a single finger, he tapped their childish code into her palm. *Roux's Mother has them.*

Masking her erratic heart-rate would be easy enough, if she toned it down—a little. Relief flooded every nerve in her body, her fingers grappling to respond. *Thank You.*

"Stop that. You'll make the children think I hate them."

"You *do* hate him." Their father's voice cracked, his hands trembling.

"My *mother* hates him. I never liked my grandmother." She laughed, her hands covering her face. "Your father was not *directly* involved in her death. He may have taken part in the orchestration, but he wasn't there to be *involved.*"

Stomach dropping through the chair, Kayla slid away from the table. Her father had mentioned his father's efforts to stop the abductions and murders carried out by the organization her mother was part of. But he'd failed to tell her just how involved he was.

"Ahni, are you alright?"

"Feeling a little ill."

Her father and brother both stood. Closer to her, Michael pulled her chair away and wrapped an arm around her.

"It will pass with time." Arzi smiled, shaking her head at the fussing of the men in the room. "There is something I need to speak to you about before I leave you."

Nerves seizing, Kayla pushed her arms to full extension. She nudged Michael back. Shaking her head for his benefit, she turned to face her mother. "Haven't you done enough?" Kayla thrust an arm toward the bedroom. "He isn't healing well. All you did was knock him out. And now, you insist on bringing my father's parents here. What does that serve? Can't you see what it's doing to him? Do you *not* care?"

Her father's cringe was visible in her peripherals. She couldn't bite her tongue, not when Arzi was threatening everything they cared about.

"I care a great deal," Arzi pushed back from the table, taking the few steps to reach them. "Your father is my mate. I know what his parents mean to him, and what all of you mean to them." She sneered, checking the nails of one hand.

"If you cared, you wouldn't do this to him."

"Look at me, Ahni," she growled for emphasis. "I care about your father, the same way you care for your child's father."

An internal eye roll was all she could manage. She'd already made her mother angry. Any more would only get her father and the others in more trouble.

"If you want your mate to live, you will do what I tell you."

Nostrils flared with each word thrown in her face. All Kayla could do was clench her fists. Her mother was insane. Arzi still didn't realize that Farz wasn't who she thought he was. She couldn't tell her the truth. It would get Roux's brother killed. For the moment, she had to pretend he was Roux, to keep them both alive.

"You'd let him die?"

"Ahni, you retain part of your father's human genetics. As such, you are not bound by the same physical barriers I am." Arzi smiled over her shoulder.

Kayla's father put himself between Arzi and Michael. "There is no guarantee she isn't."

"A theory I won't test." Glaring back at Kayla, she placed both hands on her hips. "As long as you convince him to tell me where his brother is."

"You think I will make him sacrifice his brother? I don't even know who Farz is! He's never introduced me to his family."

Arzi laughed softly. "Ahni, you're so naïve. That would be your father's doing." She lifted one hand from her hip and stroked Kayla's cheek. "They hunt Sirens, Ahni. Your mate and his brother *kill* our kind. Do you really want the boy running around free? When we could use both of them to keep their mother away from us?"

Air shivered through her lips, her head rattling from left to right. "Roux is a doctor. He would never kill anyone."

The corners of Arzi's mouth lifted, increasing the churning of Kayla's stomach. "Oh, but he did. I don't know what made him change the course of his life," her laugh grated against Kayla's ears. A chanced glance behind her mother proved that both her father and brother didn't enjoy it, either. "And I don't know how you took hold of Mina's *immune* son," Arzi continued to stroke Kayla's jawline. "But the child he's given you is exactly what we need, going forward. Talk to your mate, make him see reason. If he is interested in keeping his brother alive, he'll cooperate. Because if he doesn't tell us where to find him, I will kill them both. Your mate is, of course, the *easier* target."

Dropping to her knees, Kayla covered her mouth with both hands. Tears cascaded over her fingers, running along her wrists to wet the sleeves of her jacket.

"Give this to the boy. I think he's suffered enough for her to realize I'm serious." Her father took the serum, his hands trembling at Arzi's touch. The grit of his teeth was audible with the siren's attention on Kayla's brother. "He looks just like you did when we first met. His use will come, for now, keep your children safe. I have preparations to make."

He didn't move until the door closed behind her; the lock engaging. Her father handed Michael the serum, nodding toward the other door. "It doesn't matter where you inject him. Just make sure you don't do more damage to his injuries."

"Why didn't she lock us in the room?" Michale's voice jostled with each step.

"I don't know. Just be glad the four of us have more space to roam." He shook his head, a half smile lifting his lips. He dropped to his knees in front of Kayla, lifting her chin. "Tell her he isn't Roux."

"Why didn't you?"

Brow rising, he curled his lips in a half groan. "She'd assume you told me to say it. And that wouldn't go over well."

Kayla wrapped both arms around her father. He stood slowly, using his arms to steady her. "How does she know Roux is immune?"

Her father tightened his grip around her. "I don't want to know how she knows. Your mother has connections. Just leave it at that. It was why we went through the efforts we did." He adjusted his hold, pressing his cheek to her hair. "I should never have let you leave for the apprenticeship."

"And I should have come home when I married Roux."

Her father stiffened in her arms. "What?" He took hold of her shoulders, gently pushing her away. His eyes wavered with every breath of silence between them.

"He married me three years ago, before we came here, and I was afraid to tell you. Because... I thought you wouldn't believe he was immune."

His hands at his side, her father's shoulders dropped.

"It wasn't Roux's idea to keep it from you. He argued against it for a *long* time. But it *was* his idea to come here. He thought it would be less suspicious for him to take the position here, and less visible for me."

"Hypocrite."

They both spun toward the bedroom doorway.

Farz leaned against one side, the opposite arm wrapped around his chest. "Him, not you." His head pivoted slowly. "He never told me he married you. Though, I think our father knows. In fact, Roux told me—back at your place, that our father set up everything the three of us needed to come here."

"The three of us?"

"The house Roux always ignores. It's mine."

Blood drained from her face. "The house I've asked him about?" The same house he never even acknowledged she questioned him about. Trembling nerves had her seeking her father's embrace.

Farz nodded. "Before you get upset with him over it. I was here to keep the two of you safe. I just didn't know you were already his wife."

"Can he hear us?"

"No, he's a little busy right now. He doesn't need the distraction."

"That never stopped you before." Her face heating, she turned toward the bench—the dreaded bench she wanted to burn. "Your connection explains some of the *strange* reactions I've had from him."

Farz grimaced. "To be fair, he didn't open his end often. Come to think of it, if you were around, he was more likely to keep it off."

"And you were rude enough to not take the hint?" Her father groaned, taking a seat next to her. "You sound like your mother."

"Hey, I like to think I'm not as bad as her."

"*Slightly*." Her father scowled. "From what I remember, she's a piece of work."

"She can't be that bad, if she's Gran's friend?" Michael handed a glass of water to Farz, remaining within reach if he lost control of his hand.

"Not everyone stays friends when they're adults, Mikey." Kayla grumbled, leaning against her father's shoulder.

His cheek on her head, Kayla couldn't see his expression. His heart rate stuttered briefly. "Mina was always jealous of my mother."

"I don't recall that." Farz guzzled the fluids, his eyes never leaving them.

"My mother told me there was a young man they both liked when they were kids."

"And who might that be?" Farz shook his head, a smile spreading across his face. "Our mother is never very open about her childhood."

Kayla didn't want to think about what he had going on in his head. They might have been twins, but everything she'd seen of him was nothing like his brother.

"I've only ever known his first name... Rivan."

Kayla turned to look at him. The name sounded familiar, but she couldn't place it.

Roux's brother slid from the doorway, catching himself with his hands before he fell on his face. Michael caught the cup before Farz could crush it. "Rivan?" Farz's voice cracked, arms trembling under his weight. Kayla's brother discarded the cup, struggling to help Roux's brother sit upright. Farz choked, responding to her father's nod. "*Rivan* Tahali, is *our* father..."

Her father sat up, fidgeting. "That explains a few things. *Apparently*, your father was my mother's best friend."

Michael turned toward them, his eyes widening. "Please tell me you're not saying what I think you just said? Because if you... and these two are siblings, I may lose whatever it was she just fed us."

"Our father was promised to our mother when they were very young. And they're full blood Arros, which means Roux and I *can't* be your uncles." Farz grunted, shifting his position to sit against the wall. "It's a mate for life thing with us full bloods. Something you don't have to stress over, kid." He shook his head, the laugh inducing coughs from him.

"She never told me Rivan was Mina's mate." Shaking his head, her father folded both lips between his teeth. "That makes a lot more sense, knowing that." He laughed through his nose, looking up at Michael. "Your Gran insists it was never a romantic thing between them, Michael. He always had an attitude she couldn't handle." There was more going on in his head, Kayla knew better than to ask. He smiled, knowing her expression well. "I *can* verify your grandfather *is* my father."

Kayla slapped her palm to her face. "You're an idiot, Mikey. You both look just like grandpa." Right down to the curly brown hair atop their heads. Granted, Michael rarely let his grow out enough to show more than a slight wave.

"Hey," he held his hands out. "I was just wanting it clarified, for my benefit. *Okay*?"

"My father knows who you are. He has to." Farz tried to stand, but abandoned the effort—he dropped to his back. "Roux, was father there when you married her?" He laughed again, holding both hands against his ribcage. "Yes, her father knows—now. Something you should have mentioned to me back at your place, *little brother*." He rolled to his side, eyes scrambling to focus on Kayla. "Roux, he isn't being honest with you. Trust me, he didn't tell you he recognized her... Shut up for a second, and I can explain... *Father* had a *thing* for Caya—apparently... Oh, I know you're busy, but I thought you should know that your girl here, looks like the image we have on file for Caya... Yes... I checked it before Arzi's idiots blew your house to crap!"

"What?" Kayla gasped, her eyes locking onto her brother's shrugging expression.

"Yeah, they blew the front door open, and then some." Michael cringed.

Completely ignoring their side of the conversation, Farz growled at Roux to listen to him. "If what her father is telling me is *true*, then he knows. It makes complete sense, if you consider how he feels about our *Mother's* insistence to push us toward what she did. Roux... I am absolutely certain, if he didn't know before, he knew who she was the minute you introduced him to her."

"Wait? What? I've never met your father."

Farz exhaled through his nose, glaring toward her. His eyes were unfocused. Roux made the same expression frequently. "Roux didn't introduce him as our *father*. But he said his name was Rivan. Do you remember?"

Breath fled her lungs, her head spinning. *That was where I heard the name.* She slapped her hand over her mouth, her fingers giving way to a faint whine. "Yes."

33

Roux

Julie was right about a lot of things. Roux wiped the smile from his face before his mother-in-law could see it and locked his helmet in place. They'd been over the plan several times. She had every reason to be worried about it. *He* was worried about it.

"You'll be safe. I've sent word to someone I know I can trust. They'll pick you up before you reach the base on Vorn."

"I don't like this, Roux. Vorn is a month's journey from here. If she really does have connections with the Arros military, can we really trust anyone?"

"No one can see *this* ship. No one but my contact will even know you are out here."

"How will I know this *friend* of yours?"

Roux held his breath, resisting the urge to grumble, and smiled for her. He couldn't tell her who he was talking about. *He* was strict about who spoke of him in a professional matter, regardless of the setting. Even with their superior technology—there was no guarantee someone wasn't listening—or at least trying to listen. Either way, it wasn't worth the risk. The details would be easier for her when she met his contact, face to face. "They'll know exactly where to find you. And I promise it will be *obvious* why, *when* they find you."

"You expect your friend to be satisfied with me leaving you behind?"

"They will understand."

"This contact is aware you're going after Kayla, aren't they?"

Roux crossed the threshold with a nod. He didn't wait for her response, pressing the command for the airlock. He rapped the back of his glove against the small window before using the com to speak through the on-board system. "After you are out of range of me, don't use the communications system—for any reason. My friend will come aboard. It's *their* design, so there is nothing preventing them from accessing the controls."

"Roux, be careful."

He extended his thumb, steady as possible, turning away from her. With the command entered using his suit, Roux braced himself for the rush. They were already too close to the dreadnought. Use of his thrusters at anything above five percent capacity would draw attention. It meant they had to sidle very close to the beast of modern warfare. The thrust from the air vacating the access hatch would give him enough momentum to bring him within range for the minimum capacity thrust he was willing to use. Close enough to potentially damage the engines—without them knowing.

He'd left the channel open to the ship, and fully intended to keep it that way until she was out of range. The need to lock her out of the autopilot capabilities was a low blow, but he couldn't risk her getting herself killed trying to help him. She needed to be far from Arzi. Especially if his plan didn't work as intended.

"It's a stupid idea. You should have gone with her."

Roux ignored his brother's grumbling, hoping his wife wasn't listening to him. She didn't need the added stress. Her explanation of Arzi's ultimatum was hard enough to digest. He didn't need her panicking over what he intended to do. Not being willing to admit the full plan to his brother would not go over well, either.

"Farz, you'll disappear for good if I don't slow them down—give the others time to track us."

"Mother won't write us off that easily, little brother. She might be a frigid woman, but she isn't *that* callous."

Roux regretted the choice of nutrients immediately, forcing his concentration away from his brother's words. His stomach twisted in the moments he was propelled—end over end—from the ship. He counted the seconds in his head, waiting for the moment to activate his thrusters. Stabilizing his trajectory was like breathing. *That,* at least, wasn't as difficult after years of neglect.

"Don't get yourself killed up there." Farz grumbled before cutting his connection.

"Tell Robert, I'm sorry." Julie's voice shuddered over the link.

Roux cringed, focusing on the distance left. No use hiding the intent of his relative *suicide* mission. He laughed for her benefit. She wasn't the only one guilty of the attempt to protect those she loved from the truth. "Tell Caya and Alan the same for me."

"Roux?"

"At this rate, you see them before I do, even if this doesn't go terribly wrong."

"Roux, this isn't your fault. You didn't purposely go looking for Kayla's mother."

The muscles of his face twitched. It might not have been his fault directly, but he blamed himself for not pushing back with his wife over the decision to stay away from her family. She and their child would be safe on Tinall, with the entire family. Arzi would never have found them, his brother wouldn't be risking his life, and his own parents wouldn't be expending every resource trying to get to them before the Siren disappeared again—taking two of their children with her.

"Robert thinks his father would like you."

He closed his eyes, breaths failing to leave his lungs. "He did."

"You knew him?"

"It was a long time ago. Honestly, I haven't thought about it in *years*. But yes, I knew Robert's parents, briefly." Memories he'd somehow repressed surfaced over the last week. They were the reason for his nightmares. His father had trusted him with bringing Caya and Alan the documents they needed to disappear. The rest of the details were still fuzzy. It was only their first step in the journey. None of the details of Kayla's entire childhood would've been known to him, even if he did remember everything.

The realization that he'd met Kayla before the day he welcomed the younger members of their organization was hard to swallow. His father had a hand in it, secrets and lies... Even the flicker of a memory wouldn't have been enough for him to connect his wife to the family he helped his father smuggle away. It should have been obvious his father knew. Farz was right—he wasn't telling him everything. He'd told his father everything from the very first day. How he felt around her, what she meant to him—all of it.

"Farz, I think Father meant for me to find Kayla."

His brother's muffled groan was followed with a thwack.

"What was that?"

"It's the sound of a pillow removing my air supply." His brother moaned angrily. "You've always defended him, but he's just as bad as our Mother—in his own ways."

Roux couldn't bring himself to disagree. "She doesn't deserve this."

"I'll agree with you there. She's a good kid. Scared as hell right now, but she's stronger than she looks."

"Don't tell her what I said."

"Wasn't planning on it. Not that she doesn't already know she's married into the most dysfunctional family our species has to offer."

"I'm not sure I would classify our parents in that category. There are several, much worse, families to choose from."

"Her mother's family doesn't count."

He laughed harder than he had in a long time, letting himself drift closer to the dreadnought.

"You think it's funny, but *dude*... you *married* into *that* family."

"Not intentionally."

"The same could be said of her and ours."

"Fair enough. Keep an eye on things. I have work to do."

"If you mean keep an eye on your wife, sure, she's not too bad to look at."

"Farz..."

His brother didn't answer him, closing his portion of the communications off. Roux exhaled and did the same. The not-so-subtle hints from Farz were always entertaining, even when they were kids. With the effort to shake off the image of his brother staring at Kayla, he activated the thrusters in his suit to minimum capacity.

Roux kept his eyes on the display and the planet below him. Somewhere on the surface, his wife was most likely pacing the confines of her prison. She didn't know what he was up to, as long as his brother kept his mouth shut. She could make him tell her. But that wasn't Kayla's way, she wasn't like most of the other Sirens out there. If they survived this, Roux hoped to give her daughters. It would take a long time for their species to accept there could be peace between Sirens and everyone else, but it would be a start.

Hand holds weren't difficult to find as he approached the exterior of the vessel. Roux tugged his way towards the underbelly of the ship, shutting down his thrusters. It was a common design, one he wouldn't be able to cripple from the outside—with what he had on him. He made his way toward the shuttle bay, the grumble inaudible for anyone. If they were preparing to break orbit, there were going to be inbound transports.

Why Arzi hadn't moved his brother and the others yet, he wasn't sure. The last he'd heard from Farz, they were still in the underground bunker. If Arzi knew who their mother was, she couldn't be stupid enough to stick around and wait for a fight—especially with a dreadnought in orbit at her disposal. Of course, he could be wrong about who had control of the ship. But he doubted they'd be that lucky.

The wait wasn't an issue. Moments after reaching the hatch—it opened. Taking advantage of the situation, he pulled himself into the bay. He continued holding the exterior walls for stability. The last thing he needed was to get caught because he couldn't avoid a collision with the incoming transport. His path to the landing platform was easy. The cloaking system built into his suit was fully functional with his thrusters lowering him to the deck. Not taking the time to inspect the arrival, he ducked through the open door once the exterior hatch sealed.

Farz was going to rail on him for entering an unknown vessel. It was asking for trouble, in his opinion. But Farz liked trouble more than he was willing to admit. Roux imagined his brother was probably jealous it wasn't him who had the pleasure of *trying* to cripple the beast. Stifling the laugh, he followed the corridor towards the engine room.

He didn't see anyone in the passages the entire way there. *Strange, there should be at least a hundred men aboard a ship like this.* And that was just the minimum. His father drilled them on the necessities of manpower needed to keep various models at peak working condition—and dormant care-taking. He shook it off, moving slowly towards his destination. It wouldn't bode well for him if he made more noise, even if the vessel was working with its minimum crew count.

Roux crossed into the antechamber, his hands attempting to cover his ears. With a mental slap, he adjusted the dampening of his suit. Eyes watering from the bombardment, he back stepped—nearly falling over. Cursing, he turned on his heels, running back the way he'd come. That wasn't the sounds of whirring machinery. The ship shouldn't have a security measure like it, but he knew the sound of a sonic alarm. His ears groaned, blood ebbing from them —despite the dampening preventing his complete loss of balance.

The reflection of his pupils threatened to consume his irises with the sound of bulkhead doors slamming closed ahead of him. The explosive compound wouldn't do him any good. It would only give them a trail to follow. He needed to get somewhere off the main passage, away from the sweep they would do to find him.

Heaving, he cursed himself for not considering Arzi would know someone might try to disable the ship. But she couldn't have known he was out here, the last she knew he'd taken Julie and ran. *Unless...* he bit down on his lower lip. She could have done sweeps of the jungle around the bunker, realizing he wasn't on the ground, and concluded that he, too, had a ship in orbit.

Another bulkhead slammed closed in front of him, narrowly missing taking his hand with it. At full speed toward the bellows of the ship's alarm, Roux flung himself into the engine room. He dug into the pouch on his left hip, finding what he was looking for. Tucking it behind the nearest access hatch, he waited for the acidic paste to do its work before placing the communications port in the small hole it created. No one would see it from that angle, his gloved fingers barely reaching through.

He returned to the corridor, more thuds assaulting him. He laughed. They didn't know which way he would try to go. The doors were closing at random. *At least I can toy with them—sort of.* He chose the passage left from the engine room. He avoided another door, snapping shut behind him. Unsure of what exact part of the ship he'd trapped himself in, Roux scanned the walls for the customary sector markings.

E3T, E4T, and E5T were visible before another door slammed closed in front of him. Engineering billets. It wasn't surprising. Many of the Arros ships in use had their engineering crews housed close to their duties. Every door he passed was locked, also unsurprising. Opening one would most likely alert the idiot closing the doors at random, giving them his exact location.

The sound of crackling grew louder with each door he inspected. He turned to face the open passage, towards the alarm that had died out. It was too late to change his mind about breaking through one of the doors. The electric current arching between the girders was traveling faster than he could break through. It wouldn't do him any good either. Without the insulation of the door's perfect seal—the incoming barrage would rip through the opening. Backing towards the last blast door, Roux redirected the suit's energies to the shielding. Praying wasn't his style, it never had been. But he threw bias out the window as he plastered himself to the bulkhead, hoping for the best.

34

Alan

The cold steel threatened to leave a permanent mark on Alan's forehead. He didn't care, but Caya might. He grumbled as he moved away from the wall to look in the mirror. The reddened patch of skin was proof enough. He rubbed the fingers of one hand across the offending mark and dipped the other into the basin. The warm water wouldn't erase the mild bruising he would have later, but it would at least allow him to have dinner with the family, and Mina, without testifying to his own frustrations on loud-speaker.

Brandt stood outside the lavatory. His nose scrunched and eyes were wide. "You look like you smacked your face against the shower head again."

At some point, he knew he needed another excuse. His height made avoiding the spigot difficult, but he was used to those challenges. All four of his children, even the one he hadn't seen since before Steven was taken, knew he wasn't a novice with space travel facilities. "I wasn't thinking about it." He rubbed his forehead again. *So much for making it go away.*

"None of us are *here* mentally, Dad." His eleven-year-old sighed, trudging toward the door to their lodging aboard Mina's ship. "Mom is going to think you're doing it on purpose."

Echoing his youngest's movements, Alan reached for the mechanism. "Maybe I am."

Brandt grimaced, his fingers weaved together behind his head. "Yeah. She won't like that answer, Dad."

"It's not your fault, Daddy." Eva Hurried from the side room. She kissed his cheek before wrapping both arms around him. "He didn't exactly warn us he was going to see Kayla." She rolled her eyes for his benefit. "Telling us with a delayed vid—was stupid. He knew you would have talked him out of it."

They'd all held their breath over the six months' time-frame it would take them to reach the planet his granddaughter lived on. Pinching the bridge of his nose, Alan pat his daughter on the shoulder. "It isn't your brother's either." The unfortunate situation his eldest son found himself in might have been avoided if he'd stayed home, but none of them blamed him for the need to see Kayla. She hadn't come home in over eight years. It wore on all of them, even with the frequent letters home.

"It was stupid! He's the reason all of us pretend we belong on Tinall!" Eva shook her head, her face reddening with each word.

"Sweetheart, I would have done the same if it were you—avoiding me."

His sixteen-year-old daughter plowed into him. It muffled her sobs against his chest. "I'm sorry, Daddy."

He stroked a hand through her waist length hair, cooing her name. She was almost to maturity, but she still adored the attention he gave her. Grappling with the loss of contact with their half sister, Alan had latched onto the children he had left. Vivian understood, more than her younger siblings, why they went dark. Having just married into an *extensive* family, she couldn't drag her budding family into the mess her brother's situation created. As a result, she wasn't even aware of Eva and Brandt's existence. Sighing, he lifted Eva's chin. "We're all worried about them."

Lilting his head toward the door, Alan raised a brow over Brandt's reaction. He knew better than to judge Eva for her emotions. The three of them made their way down the corridor, attempting the best composure for their hostess. Mina wasn't an emotional woman, at least not in the difficult ones. Anger and annoyance, she did quite well with.

Caya barely looked up from the table, her eyes fixed on the screen of a tablet he didn't recognize. Assuming Mina had news, Alan gestured for their children to take their seats. Sliding back the chair beside his wife, he took her hand in his. "Anything new?"

"That depends on your definition." Mina rolled her eyes in a moment, her composure returning with Caya's attention on her.

He could never understand why the two of them were friends, knowing the story in its entirety didn't help matters. Caya squeezed his hand, gaining his attention. "Two messages. One from Kayla, sent the day before she found out they were coming. The other from Robert, two days later." Her voice wavered on the name they'd used for their son for over twenty years. Eva and Brandt had never been told what their names were. They'd agreed it was safer that way.

"Your granddaughter, mated with *my* son. She's carrying his child."

Blood vessels enlarged, causing haze in his vision. "What?"

"The doctor she has been working with all these years..." Caya swallowed four times. "Roux Tahali, he's Mina's son."

He knew the significance of Roux, to Mina, from their earlier conversations neither of them would discuss in her presence. But his having claimed their granddaughter—a siren, no less—that wasn't bound to make their friendship last. "When did this happen?"

Caya slid the tablet toward him, replaying the message. Kayla's familiar conflicted expression came to life, her eyes angled away from the camera. "Roux, sit down before I change my mind and decide not to send this." The young man relented, his expression one of a man resigned to his fate.

"Gran, I'm sending this to you first, because I know dad is going to go ballistic over it." She straightened the camera angle, centering her and the young man in the picture. "Roux and I are married. I know it's a sudden thing to drop on you, but it really isn't. He and I got married three years ago." The boy raised his brows, his smile spreading.

"I'm telling you now, because Roux and I found out we're going to be parents." Roux reached for her hand, squeezing it with a much larger smile growing. "By the time this reaches you, we'll have moved on to another assignment. One that will give us a better atmosphere in which to raise our child. Please don't be upset with me for waiting to tell you. I didn't want Dad jumping to conclusions, and he would have if I told you and not him—before now."

"Roux is immune. None of our decisions have been single sided. I know dad would assume everything we've done is." She grimaced. "Say hello to everyone for us. I promise, in a few years, once we're a little less chaotic, we'll make the trip to visit you."

"What the he..."

"EVA!" He and his wife warned from across the table. Their daughter had a bad habit of using human jargon and swearing when she was angry.

"She got married and didn't tell us! What do you expect me to say?"

"Kayla is an adult."

"Who has been hiding from her biological mother since she was a baby!"

Eva glared from across the table.

"Play the next message." Caya exhaled through her nose, shaking her head at their daughter's raised shoulders.

Their son slid into view in a rolling chair. "We made it…" bouncing his eyes at the voices in the background, he hollered over his shoulder. "If you want to say something, get your butt over here and say it."

Michael hopped in behind him, laughing. "Can't believe you're not freaking out more right now." Turning his attention to the camera, their grandson smiled. "Hey Gran, Grandpa. This place is super weird." Someone called him from another room. He waved before disappearing outside the camera frame.

"I should have given you more warning." Robert exhaled, his head rattling. "That being said, you're never going to believe what we found out when we got here."

"Robert, be nice about it." Julie scolded from the other side of the room. She threw a suitcase on the bed behind him.

"Kayla's pregnant." The words fell from him like a child's complaints of bitter food. "She's mated with the doctor here. What's worse, he's a full blood Arros."

"Robert…"

Raising his hands, he exhaled. "Okay, he's not so bad. I just wish she'd told me about this *relationship*—sooner. *Apparently*, they've been dating for five years and moved in together when this assignment came up for *Roux*." Their son pressed his lips together, sighing over his wife's scolding. "So, we're not going to be here more than a few months. We'll have forwarding set up for anything that comes through after we leave. It will probably be a few years before we come home. Julie wants to be here for Kayla and the baby."

His wife slapped the back of his head. "It isn't just me!"

He laughed, "Yeah, but I'm sticking around for another reason entirely."

Their daughter-in-law sat down on the bed behind him, leaning forward to make herself visible. "He isn't as upset as he sounds. I *made* them work it out."

Robert laughed again. "You'd probably like this guy, Dad. He's ex-military. Not surprising with the name Tahali. Doesn't mom know a few Tahali's? I know it's a common name in the military, probably stupid to ask."

Heart twisting, Alan covered his face. Roux was from the one Tahali family they knew well. Odds were never in their favor.

"Anyway. We got here. *Transition* wasn't the problem."

Alan felt his stomach churn, the inflection of his son's voice bringing terrible memories back.

"Kayla says hello. She's not feeling very well at the moment. She'll send another message when she's up to it. Tell Eva, Kayla wants opinions on baby names. The next assignment isn't as far out as this *place* is. You might be able to send a few suggestions in time." Julie leaned in over his shoulder, whispering in his ear. "Take care of yourselves. We promise we'll be careful out here."

"Careful to walk right into Arzi's hands."

"EVA!"

Their daughter pushed back from the table. "That crazy woman has my brother! If you expect me to keep my opinions to myself, I'll just stay in my room."

"There's more." Mina interjected, pulling the device from Alan's grasp. Pecking away at the screen, she groaned. "My sons haven't reported in since I ordered them back here. They should have left the planet by now." Mina pressed her lips into a slim line, her face paling. "The connection is closed. Farz never closes the connection to his ship."

Eva sat down, fingers curling around the end of the table.

"We believe Arzi found them."

The children gasped. Alan's heart sank further.

"She'll kill Julie!" Eva covered her face, tears falling.

Brandt slid his chair closer, wrapping an arm over her shoulder.

Resting his elbows on the table, Alan hid his face from Mina. Her anger was present again, but she sounded concerned about more than the disappearance of her children. That wasn't like her, not the Mina Forran he'd hated associating with all those years ago. He'd only put up with her for Caya's benefit.

"I don't think she will, Eva." His wife closed her eyes, tears begging to cross the threshold of her eyelids. "She'll use Julie and Michael to pressure him to do anything to keep them safe."

"Is that supposed to make me feel better?" Their daughter stood, pointing her finger toward their host. "She doesn't even care about the fact that our family is suffering here. All she cares about is her sons." No one spoke while their daughter roared her complaints. "It doesn't take Arros hearing to know she despises the fact that Kayla chose her son! I know you all heard it!"

"Eva..." Alan's voice cracked, his hands trembling. Following her from the room, he caught up with her halfway to their accommodations. "Eva," taking her by the arm, he pulled her from her rampage. "She might not approve, but she has no choice. Roux willingly chose Kayla. Their fates rest as heavily on her as they do for us. Kayla's child is her son's. She might not be the most feeling woman, but she cares what happens to Roux, and that means Kayla by extension."

"She could at least show a bit more remorse. We might never see any of them again. And she's rubbing your decision to hide away in your faces."

"Sweetheart, no one knew Arzi was there. She's been hiding just as much as we have."

"Rotten luck for us," tears cascaded beyond her chin. "Our lives are laden with it."

"Eva," Alan wrapped his arms around her, kissing the top of her head. "If anyone is to blame, that would be me."

She shoved away from him. "No, Dad! Blaming yourself is silly. You were just doing your job, trying to protect innocents. Trying to stop horrible people from doing terrible things. *They* are the ones who took my brother from you all those years ago! *They* are to blame for this, not you, Daddy."

If only it were so easy to dismiss the blame he'd lived with for twenty-six years. "Your mother needs you in there. Not out here, Eva. Please, don't abandon her to this news."

Nodding, his daughter wiped tears away with her sleeves. "As long as that *woman* keeps her mouth shut, I'll concede."

His laughter allowed the flow of his own tears. "I shouldn't have told you how much I hate her."

"What's done, is done. I can't blame you for it." Eva growled, pushing by him. "She is terrible. I hope her son isn't like this, for Kayla's sake. I'll never want to meet him—if he is."

"Do you really think Kayla would marry someone who is as *terrible* as Mina?" They both laughed, shaking their heads. "I'll deal with them, if you will."

"Fine." His daughter rolled her eyes. "But If you insult her, I get to."

"Deal."

35

Arzi

Pain was often more amusing than it was effective. Watching Mina Forran's son writhe was far more entertaining than anyone else she'd had the pleasure with. He was strong, not that it surprised her. Both of Mina's sons were trained for it from a very young age. But she expected more from the son who remained part of the military.

Each breath increased the flow of blood from his mouth and nose. The young man wouldn't even look at her. She wondered if both of Mina's boys were immune to her. It would be just like *her* to flaunt one child's abilities, and not the other.

"It's a pity your armor was destroyed." Tisking, she crossed toward him.

His upper lip twitched, causing blood to flow over it.

"I would have liked to study what technology they used for it."

"I would have destroyed it myself, before I let you use it against Arros." The boy had the gall to spit blood on the floor.

"You think you're saving our people from us, do you?" Arzi took in his physique with a shake of her head. She gripped his jaw, forcing him to look at her. His eyes threatened things he wasn't capable of in his state, chained to the wall. He was definitely very similar to his brother, but her daughter's mate lacked the luster in his expression. Not what she expected of the loner he supposedly was.

A smile tugged at her lips. She released her hold, noting what she had failed to see in the *other* son. "Tell me," Arzi motioned to the guard at the door to join her. "Is it difficult to be away from your mate, forced to look after your brother and his?"

The boy stiffened. It was far from an apt description, but thirty-eight cycles was still young for an Arros male. "I don't know what you're talking about."

"It must have been a good match," Arzi snapped her fingers—waving them around her face. "Few arranged matings leave the young man in your state." Her inability to resist the laughter left his expression fluctuating—even if just slightly—at her revelation.

Her man, she couldn't remember his name, handed her the metal case from his inside pocket. Her mother had gifted some of her drudges to her. Thankfully, they weren't entirely useless—but their names were unimportant. The sheath fell away to reveal the large syringe. She'd intended to use it to confirm his identity, but the resemblance to the young man she'd left with her daughter negated it.

Lips curving upward, Arzi produced the implement for the boy's benefit. "There is one way to know for certain. But I hear it is very painful." The jolt in his stiff posture drew laughter from her again. *Oh, how wonderful he knows it will be.* This discovery promised to be far more enjoyable than she'd first anticipated. *We'll see if I'm right about who you really are...*

The guard held the injured Arros against the wall, blood sputtering from him with each complaint. Recollection of her studies of their anatomy, Arzi thrust the needle into his chest. As long as she wasn't off by the short span of error, she'd strike the sensitive portion of his adrenal glands. The same portion responsible for the cursed permanent mating in all Arros.

His gasps sent blood in droplets over her hands. Each draw from the tissue forced deafening howls from him. Arzi shook the temporary discomfort away, withdrew the syringe—designed to tear the tissue away—and wiped in on her sleeve. "Take this to the physician." She would have her answer before the results came back, of that, she was certain.

The young Arros was limp in his restraints, blinking in rapid motions—heaving, strangled breaths. His eyes locked on hers, burning with another threat of something he'd never be capable of doing—even if she removed his bindings. It would take hours to recover from what she'd just done, and that was *if* she consented to giving him the serum. Given his condition, and her need to prove who he was, he'd die if she left him there. She intended to keep him alive, but she wanted answers first.

Hollering to the guard over her shoulder, Arzi smiled. "See to it, they test my daughter. I want to ensure the other one is indeed her mate."

"No!" The boy shuddered in his restraints. "You can't do that! You..." his body shook, adrenaline coursing through his system to compensate for the extraction. "Know what that will do!"

"If you are who you claim to be, it is no concern of yours."

Fisting his hands, he coughed blood between them. "In her condition, you could kill..." his breath faltered from him, fingers shaking with every attempt to speak. "Both of them..."

"Does a Siren, and her child, really matter to you? To you, who hunts our kind?"

"Please, don't do this..."

Her smile spread wider with the strength ebbing from him. Unable to hold himself upright, they could all hear his wrists crackle angrily. "Disregard the last request. I have my answer." The shadow of her guard nodded. He remained in the doorway, awaiting further orders. "I think you've earned a reprieve." Snickering, she shifted on her heels—allowing her to see both of them. "Take Dr. Tahali to his accommodations." The taste of his defeat would sate the itch for some time. It answered more questions than she realized she had. Her daughter's mate was the one to take the woman who raised her from the compound. His brother wouldn't likely have cared. *It was a trivial attempt to give them hope.*

36

Roux

Nerves lit under the weight of hands clamped around his shoulders. Muscles failed to respond to his commands, leaving his feet trailing on the floor behind him. With the Siren's expression burned into his retinas, Roux clenched his eyes shut. She laughed at his vain attempts to free himself from their grasp.

"Make sure there isn't a mark left on him."

Pain surged through him with each step the massive drudges took. He blacked out more than he could count, the adrenaline in his system failing to compensate. Dropped to the floor, the guards left him alone. His body shaking with each breath, Roux opened his connection to his brother.

"Farz..." his voice failed to reach his own ears, hissing and sputtering with each attempt to speak.

"Roux, what happened?" Panic rattled through his brother's tone.

"She..." coughing blood into his hands, Roux rolled to his side. "Knows..."

"Roux, what's going on?"

"Caught." Breaths stuck to the sides of his throat, leaving Roux heaving between words. "Arzi... knows..." he rested his cheek on the floor, blood pooling around him. Not enough to obscure the guards returning.

"Roux!"

He couldn't answer his brother, not with witnesses in the room. The disconnection of his side brought physical pain with it for the first time since he was a young boy. Initial reactions to the implants hadn't been easy for either of them. He forced the agony from his mind as he watched the men Arzi entrusted with his care skirt him—repeatedly. Their words were muffled, his head spinning.

The Siren's idea of torture bordered on barbaric. The act was often such. But she took an unnatural pleasure in every arc of his muscles, every drop of blood she drew from him, every groan of agony. How she'd known who he was, he couldn't fathom. He had done nothing to suggest he was Kayla's mate. Every word and action could easily have been construed as a brother's concern. It was in every way for Farz. Her threats to draw tissue from Kayla broke his resolve, and she knew how he would react.

Appendages shuddered with each breath capable of breaking through his lips. His chest trembled with each pulse of blood. He'd lost enough to be concerning. Extremities would become difficult to feel soon enough. Focus was fruitless, his body struggling to compensate for what Arzi took from him.

Unable to fight them, they pulled him from the ground. The ability to judge the distance failed with each gushing breath. It was too much damage, the pathetic serum would never keep up. If they did not get him to a surgeon, he would bleed out. He knew what the inside of an infirmary looked like. He wasn't in one.

Roux spent his remaining strength at the sound of something heavy dropping to the floor, turning his head toward his momentum. Curses roiled in his throat, unwilling to form on his tongue. The effort to reestablish his connection to Farz left him incapable of speaking, much less expend the energy to turn it off again.

The vessels of his eyes engorged. His brother was going to listen to him die, and there was nothing he could do about it as they tossed him into the water. Arms heavy, his hands slipped from the edges of the tank. He barely had time to withdraw his fingers before they closed the chamber and darkness enveloped him.

Air rushed from his lungs. Fluid filled the void with each attempt to rise above the surface. The continuous flow pushed the remaining adrenaline through his system, rage fueling his limbs.

His brother called to him, his voice breaking up each time. Farz's tone wasn't the usual joking manner, and the influx of water muffled his own attempts to speak. Struggling with continued convulsions, he barely managed his brother's name. When he did, it unfortunately sounded like he'd been trying to insult him. Kayla's voice, her concern ebbing through the connection on Farz's end, rattled through his consciousness.

He hit the bottom of the tank back first, limbs following close behind, his chest still rising with each draw of fluid into his lungs. The cooling sensation as he opened his eyes left his mind reeling. *No, not drowning.* Roux cursed to himself. He willed the use of her name. Farz had to know he was still breathing. He had to let his brother know he was alive.

Only managing mere gurgles, he bent his arm. Pain seared every muscle in the appendage, forcing him to abandon the attempt to strike the side of the tank. Roux closed his eyes again, letting the Niffen chamber do its work. Whatever Arzi had planned, she wanted him alive.

37

Farz

"Farz..."

Sputtered winces rattled through his head. Farz jolted upright from the bench. Thankfully, his reflexes had recovered enough to prevent a repeat of the embarrassing display for the others. "Roux, what happened?"

"She..." coughs assaulted his auditory nerves. "Knows..."

"Roux, what's going on?"

"Caught." His brother's breathing forced the hairs of Farz's arms to stand on end. "Arzi... knows..."

Feeling his irises enlarge, Farz struggled to keep his feet under him with Roux's withdrawal. "Roux!"

"Whats going on?" Kayla emerged from the bedroom, blanket wrapped around her. Her eyes went wide, taking in his reaction to Roux's warning.

"Your mother has Roux."

"How? He was with Julie!"

Farz turned to steady her. "He was trying to cripple the dreadnought your mother has waiting for us."

Her jaw trembled, her hands wrenching his from her arms. "He did what?!"

Farz covered his eyes in the attempt to explain Roux's plan—emphasizing his own arguments against it. "I don't know how he was caught. He wasn't broadcasting anything until just now."

"What about my mom?" Michael rushed from the room, their father at his side.

"He set the ship to take her to someone we can trust. She should be *very* far from here by now."

"Should be?" Robert growled. The longer he was around the man, the grumpier he seemed—none of it was *ever* directed toward his children. A good thing, in *his* opinion. If Farz gave the man the means of blowing off steam, all the better. *They* needed their father, not a man breaking from the influence of a Siren.

"Look, you have no reason *not* to trust me. For the last eight years, I have been the one keeping them off the radar. I have never, *once,* done anything to endanger your daughter, *or* my brother. I might have even taken out a few pirates over the years." Truthfully, the pirates had been for sport, but Robert didn't know that. While it was Robert's fault for arriving unannounced, giving Farz little time to prepare for any potential issues, he couldn't say that to them. Unless he wanted to make the man angrier than he already was. "Julie is safe."

"Who is he sending her to?"

He pressed his lips into a thin line, shaking his head. One didn't speak of this contact on a professional matter, it wasn't done. Farz knew exactly who his brother would turn to. Roux didn't trust their mother with Kayla, he wasn't likely to send Kayla's step-mother to her either. "As a matter of principle, we can't share that information. But I assure you, she is safer with *them* than she would be here."

Robert fisted his hands, shaking with the breaths falling from him.

"Dad, I trust Roux's judgment on this."

"Do you? He's been lying to you the whole time."

Kayla tugged the sides of the blanket closed. "He never lied to me dad, he might not have mentioned everything—but neither did I."

Farz turned away from them, pacing past the table. *C'mon Roux, what happened to you? Say something.* A splash ricocheted through his head, followed by gargles breaking through the link, forcing air from his lungs. "Roux! What's going on? Roux?"

"Farz?" The blanket fluttered to the ground beside him, Kayla's hands at his shoulders. "What is *she* doing to him?"

Every nerve in his body froze, the sounds coming from his communications link driving him to his knees. He couldn't tell her what he was hearing. She'd panic—Roux wouldn't approve. Her mother had threatened to kill both of them if he didn't tell her where to find his brother. But she hadn't even returned to ask the question. He was prepared to give her the coordinates of where the ship was, knowing Roux would have changed the orbit—it would have at least bought them time.

"Farz!" The sting flared on both sides of his face before he looked at her. "What is going on?"

His jaw moved uselessly, words failing him with the garbled clamor coming from Roux. Only one thing could cause the combination: his brother was *drowning* and Farz had no way to save him. "Roux..." the rapid motion of his eyelids blurred his vision.

His brother called out for him, and Kayla, his steady breaths breaking through the link—combined with the rush of the water Roux thrashed to free himself of. *He's on a ship. Why would they consider drowning him?* He covered his face with both hands, pressing his fingertips against his forehead.

The struggles ceased, but his brother's breathing didn't stop. Drawing one hand away, far enough to pull the palm at full force against himself, Farz groaned. *They have a Niffen vessel...* his brother's initial reaction was similar. But seeing as he was still breathing beneath the fluid they'd forced him into, he calmed—leaving the connection open for Farz's benefit. With an attempt to steady his own shuddered breaths, he shook the image from his mind.

"Farz," his brother's wife knelt in front of him, her hands shaking over her mouth.

"He's alive." Farz gulped for air, stretching his jaw from side to side. "Sounded like he was *drowning* for a minute there."

Her eyes widened. "A Niffen? Aren't they..."

"Illegal..." He nodded, slumping to sit on his ankles. Several steadying breaths, Farz closed his eyes. Niffen chambers were hard to regulate, cutting corners on their composition resulted in deaths. Rather than continue—and fail—to enforce proper procedures for their construction, their government had outlawed the use of them.

Her arms grappled around his neck, pulling him into her. "Are you alright?"

Unable to do anything other than shrug, Farz wrapped his arms around her. He knew Roux wouldn't begrudge him the moment, both of them having feared they were losing him. If he complained about where Farz' hands were in that moment, he would give him what for—*later.*

"I thought we were losing him, you..." Kayla shuddered in his arms. "You were so pale."

Disguising his cough with a laugh, Farz pushed back from her. "It would be pretty vacant in here—without him." Prodding his ear, he stood—extending a hand to her.

Kayla shook her head at him, accepting his help to stand. Tears spilled from her eyes with the sputtered laugh. "He'd probably say the same for you."

Drawing blood from his lower lip, Farz nodded. Neither of them were good at expressing their emotions—at least where the other was concerned. They'd spent most of their lives together, hadn't been apart much in the physical manner, until Roux met Kayla. Even then, Farz never gave his brother the break he deserved.

38

Roux

Two fingers against his brow, Roux massaged the budding migraine. *She* was there. He couldn't bring himself to open his eyes, acknowledging her presence would only encourage the behavior he dreaded. He rolled toward the wall. She, or her drudges, had moved him from the Niffen chamber at some point. The bed he lay in, and the lack of sopping clothes, the first evidence of it. He groaned upon realizing he didn't have any clothes on, feeling around for the edge of the sheet covering the lower half of his body.

Thankful for whoever had thought to provide it, he pulled it over his shoulders. Arzi never made a sound. Either she really thought he was still mostly out of it, from his bout with the Niffen chamber, or she thought she could toy with him—again. He folded his arms over his chest, attempting to secure the sheet in place. In doing so, he brushed against something cold as the surrounding room. Colder, when he pressed his fingers against it.

"You'll have to get used to it."

Roux stiffened as he rolled to face her. "What are you talking about?" He shifted under the sheet, hoping she assumed he was concerned about his attire—he clenched his hands around the edges.

Arzi tapped the closure of her shirt, just below her collarbone, the exact place he'd felt the foreign texture affixed to his skin. "Grafted in place."

Taking the moment to inspect his chest, he grumbled at the sight of the device. He knew she would find some way to keep him in line, but he hadn't expected *that*. "What do you want, Arzi?"

"Oh, good. You know who I am." She smiled. While it was a similarly marked expression he'd seen from her daughter, her eyes lacked the sincerity Kayla's held. "I was worried *they* waited too long to use the chamber." She crossed the room with a laugh, enticing him to hold tighter to the minuscule covering. "I doubt Ahni would appreciate it if your injuries damaged your memory."

"*Kayla*, won't appreciate any of this."

Her mother sneered, spinning on her heels. "*My daughter* doesn't have a choice. This was the life *they* denied her. I will see to it—she accepts it."

"By using me."

Fixing her gaze on him, Arzi laughed. "*If* I have to, yes."

"And my brother?"

"You do as I tell you, and I won't punish him for his charade."

He sat up, careful to keep hold of the sheet. "You threatened to kill your own daughter, to get answers from me. And you think I'm going to believe you would let Farz live, simply for doing as I'm told."

Eyes icing over, her sneer grew. She opened a cabinet on the far side of the room. "Oh, I'll let him live—either way. But if you want what is left of his life to be as painless as possible, you'll do exactly as I tell you." She sauntered back to him, holding a pile of clothing. "You have time to decide if the *quality* of your brother's life is worth the effort." Arzi set the clothes on the end of the bed, turning towards the door. "When I return with Ahni, I *expect* your cooperation."

Dropping the sheet into his lap, he dug his fingers into his forehead. The pain of the migraine wasn't as bad as he expected it to be. But Arzi knew he was immune. She wasn't likely to spend the energy to compel him in ways she knew wouldn't work.

"What exactly did she threaten to do to Kayla?"

Wincing, Roux dropped back against the pillow. "Adrenal extraction."

Farz cursed. The sound of a door closing preceded further grumbles. "Please, tell me she didn't do that to you." His silence induced another bout of curses. "Now I know why they used a Niffen." He grumbled again. "Thanks, by the way, for that disturbing revelation. You scared the hell out of both of us."

"As if you haven't given me some highly distracting images with your *behavior*."

"*That* is different. *We* thought you were dying!"

Not bothering to say he was, he reached for the clothing at his feet.

"She messed you up so bad you couldn't turn it off, could you?"

Struggling with the shirt, Roux grumbled.

"I *told* you she was crazy, *little brother*."

"How much of what she just said did you hear?"

"Don't let her use me against you. She wants both of us alive, and I highly doubt it will be painless—for either of us."

"Farz, I can't let her do the things she has in mind."

"I can handle it."

"No, you can't. Need I remind you *she's* insane?" Finishing his ensemble, Roux sat up again. Surveying his *accommodations* didn't take long. Arzi left him in what amounted to a crewman's billet. He groaned. He couldn't even relieve himself without leaving the room. Arzi made *that* impossible with the restraining device grafted to his collarbone. A second glance left him sighing. There was a door—not a closet. He stood up, his muscles stiff, and crossed to it.

"She can't hear me. She's sleeping and I've locked myself in the bathroom—for now."

Clenching his eyes shut, Roux slammed the door to the closet of a bathroom. He fought the urge to scream. "Please tell me you weren't in bed with my wife."

"As pleasant a thought as that is," Farz gagged. "I was on the floor by her bed, with her brother between us. She's been pretty freaked out since your little *incident*."

"How is she *not* getting to you by now?"

"Oh, she *is*. But you were right when you said she has it pretty well under control—most of the time."

"Give her a heads up. I don't want her to panic when she sees what Arzi has done to keep me in this *room*."

The sound of his brother's hand slapping against his face induced a chortle. "She seriously put a restraining unit on you?"

"Three fingers wide, two high." He didn't want to know how far deep the nodes went. Different types of restraints were used for different purposes. He hadn't seen enough of them to know what exact model they affixed to his chest. Normally he would have considered the ignorance a good thing. But that was before someone gifted him the particular disadvantage.

"Is it somewhere she will see it?"

Sighing, Roux lifted the neckline of his shirt—looking down at the device again. "Left side, below my collarbone."

"Okay, so just leave your shirt on until she wraps her head around the idea."

"*My* shirt is nowhere to be seen, neither is anything else I *was* wearing."

"Didn't need that image."

Roux laughed at him. His brother was known for giving him the worst images possible—at the worst times. Payback was going to be fun... Or would be if their situation wasn't life threatening. "Surprisingly, she left me decent."

Farz cleared his throat. "I'm *leaving* the bathroom now. Try to get some sleep before we are dragged up there."

"Farz,"

"Yeah,"

"Thanks for taking care of her. I..."

"Arzi isn't going to hurt her, Roux. She hasn't even done anything to her father, or her brother, since I got here. All she's done is insist we all keep her safe and we all would do *that* without being compelled to."

"How is Robert doing?"

"Much better, not sure what they did to him when he got here, but they'd have to have done a real number on him for it to take so long for him to heal. Arzi was giving him at least one dose a day." Farz laughed. "I might tell him what you went through to keep Kayla alive. Maybe then he'd stop grumbling about being stuck with you as part of the family."

He didn't have the energy to argue. It could go any number of ways. Almost all of them were worse than the predicament he already had. "Kayla is the one who insisted we not tell them."

His brother closed his portion of the link, the sound of his head thumping against a pillow preceding it. *I'd give my life for her, Farz.* He didn't need to say it aloud. His brother knew how bullheaded and determined he could be. "I'm going to leave mine open, as long as you don't mind." The lack of response sent him against his own pillow. Farz wouldn't sleep, even if he'd intended to.

39

Kayla

Kayla climbed from her bed, stepping over her brother and Farz in her haste to the bathroom. Once inside, she inspected the puffy eyed disaster she knew they'd find when they woke. Locking the door, she turned on the crammed shower. The room filled with steam, hiding her reflection in the mirror.

Farz's side of the conversation was bad enough, she'd spent most of what remained of the night worrying about the things she couldn't hear from Roux. Unable to bring herself to tell Farz she was awake when he went into the bathroom. It had taken hours to silently cry herself to sleep. Whatever her mother had done, it hadn't been easy for her husband.

She reminded herself that he was alive and waiting for her as she stood under the shower. With no choice but to rush through her routine; the heat causing her nausea to flare, she finished as quickly as possible. Dried and dressed—in the clothes provided—Kayla stepped out into the room.

Farz leaned against the doorway, facing the exterior room. "You could have told me you were up last night." He shook his head with a brief snort.

"I was trying to let you sleep."

Rattling his head, he grimaced. "Wasn't going to happen, after what he told me." Striding into the larger space, he motioned for her to follow him. "I was keeping an ear out for him. He needed the sleep more than I did."

Following him, Kayla rubbed a hand over her stomach. "I hate her."

"You can't let your mother hear you say that."

"She isn't my *mother*."

"Maybe not in the right aspects, but she *is* your *mother*. And she's not likely to cut Roux any slack if you keep pushing back in ways *she* will notice immediately."

Planting her butt on the bench, she fanned herself. The vain attempt to stave off tears only brought them faster. Farz sat down beside her, his hands on his knees.

"None of this is going to be easy for you. But Roux is alive, and he is up there waiting for us. We just need to try not to piss *her* off *before* we get up there to make sure he's being honest with us."

"She put a restraining unit on him, Farz. What's stopping her from doing that to all of you once we get up there?"

His pupils dilated. "Nothing."

Tears flowed as she pulled her wet hair back. "Farz,"

"Hm?" Roux's brother held a hand over his mouth, rubbing his thumb and fingers over both sides of his jaw.

After gaining his attention, Kayla bit her lower lip. She had to ask, even if she didn't want the answer. "Be honest with me, please. Is he alright?"

Shrugging, he shook his head. "Mentally or physically?"

Pressing her fingers to her forehead, Kayla shoved him with her free hand. He barely budged with the effort she forced against him. "What did she do to him, that she threatened to do to me?"

"I'm *not* mentioning that. Please don't make me say it."

Swallowing, Kayla shook her head. "I won't do that to you... She doesn't care about us, Farz. She only cares about her way of life being the way *she* wants it."

"I can't say she does or doesn't care. But I know she's done nothing but order the three of us to keep you safe." Running his fingers through the short hair on his neck, Farz exhaled. "It has to count for something."

"Farz, she just wants my baby. She's all but directly said it, more than once."

"We're both going to be here. We won't let her use your kid like that."

"Neither of you will be able to stop it."

Placing one hand under her chin, Farz shook his head. He leaned forward to whisper in her ear. "Roux sent Julie to our father," his words barely audible, he continued. "Normally I wouldn't say it. Our father doesn't like anyone to use his profession in casual conversation. But Roux and I aren't from just any military family. Our father has the means to find us. I swear it to you."

Leaning into him, Kayla cried. Her body shook with each breath. "I can't tell my dad, can I?"

"No." Farz shook his head, exhaling heavy breaths. "But being my brother's mate, *you* needed to know, deserved to know—Roux should have told you long before now."

"How did she find out you weren't him?"

"She threatened to do, to you, what she did to him." Farz wrapped both arms around her before she could collapse. "Breathe, Kayla. Roux doesn't want me to tell you, for this reason."

Her hands shook, no amount of steady breaths she'd attempted could calm her nerves.

"Sweetheart, look at me." Her father's voice drew her attention to the door they'd left open. Three leaping strides brought him to her side, kneeling in front of her. "Breathe, it's going to be okay, I promise."

Farz shuddered beside her, stifling a laugh. "You honestly do not know what you are doing, do you?"

Scowling, her father stood. He pulled Kayla into his arms. "Trying to calm her down, because—yet again—*you've* upset her!"

Farz laughed again. "Um yeah, *that*." He shook his head. "You really don't know it, do you? It's why she wants you, it's why she is completely fine taking your son in, and why she isn't willing to let Kayla's child go."

Kayla stared at him, her arms twinging at the pressure her father increased with his fingers. "What are you talking about?"

"The fact that your father is also like his mother, and both you—*and* your brother inherited it from *him*." He nodded to her father, standing to make his way back to the room.

"No, it's a female exclusive..."

"If that were the case, how do you explain what you just did right there? She was having a panic attack. Is she *now*? And no, it's not just because I'm distracting her with this conversation."

"Why would she want my mother's bloodline?" Her father's expression fell. "She... made me tell her where to find my parents."

Returning the favor, Kayla held both hands on the sides of his face. "Daddy, they're not on Tinall. Michael warned me when you told her. Roux and Farz's mother already have them." Her father's pulse steadied, breaths regulating. He wrapped both arms around her, pulling her into a tight hug.

"*See*, your daughter knows she's doing it. But you clearly haven't taken the hint."

Burying her face in his shoulder, Kayla lowered her hands to wrap them around her father. "I never considered it. I should have realized it before now."

"Pretty sure, Arzi already does."

Her father leaned away from her, glaring at Farz. "How is it *you* knew?"

"You disappeared a little too easily. Roux and I thought that maybe your mother used her ability to urge a few people to let you drop off the grid."

Her father's face shifted in that instant. He growled at the reference of his mother forcing people to let her disappear. Her grandmother did nothing like that. Kayla doubted she would have, even then. "Farz, your father was there when we disappeared... I didn't realize it until *after* you mentioned Rivan being your father."

"Dad, if he was there... Why didn't you know who Roux was the first time you saw him? They look like their father." The image of the man her husband introduced her to sat in the forefront of her mind. She'd explained it away as a distant relation.

"It was a long time ago. I can't picture Rivan's face, but I do remember him *and* his son being there."

"My *brother*?" Farz shook his head. "No, we were in the middle of training. The two of us barely spent minutes apart until we were..." Farz covered his face. "Roux, is any of this sounding familiar to you?"

Kayla dug her fingers into her father's arm, heart rate making it difficult for her to breathe. "Roux, did you know who I was before I came to orientation on Tinall?" Blood rushed to her extremities, surging in every direction but where she needed it to be.

"Get all that? He says you were there, *with Father...* Is that why you said what you did, about the *thing* you didn't want me to mention to Kayla?" Farz cursed. "Roux... Don't you realize what that means? He drugged you! You weren't meant to remember you helped him get his childhood girlfriend off the radar. You don't remember it—because he doesn't want you to!"

"Your father sounds like he's a piece of shit." Michael rubbed his eyes, limping into the room. He rubbed his foot before trudging the rest of the way to them. Kayla assumed it was still numb from how he'd tucked it under himself in his sleep. "Why are you guys yelling at each other?"

"We weren't yelling *that* loud, Mikey." Kayla felt her eyes roll.

Her brother rubbed his fingers along the creases of his forehead. "Tell that to my aching head."

Kayla, her father, and Farz stared at him.

"We were actually *not* yelling until just *now*." Farz pointed at Kayla, then at her father. "Are you sure he doesn't have Arros hearing?"

"Um, what?"

"He's never been sensitive to it before." Their father stared at Michael, his lips barely moving. "Mikey, you look terrible. Maybe you should go back to bed."

Kayla heard the whisper. She knew Farz heard it—his eyes rolling at the effort her father made. But Michael's grimaced reply was something she never expected.

"I'm not going to be able to sleep with you three yelling at Roux, for *whatever* it is he did."

"What's changed?" Their voices merged, forcing her brother to cringe—again.

"I don't understand... I heard you tell me to go back to bed..."

"He whispered at a range you shouldn't have been able to hear." Kayla stared at her brother. The mental rotation of medical explanations dismissing themselves with each thought that didn't explain why her brother would suddenly start having sensitive hearing.

"So, uh, Mike... when was the last time you had your medication?" The three of them stared at Farz. He pointed at his ear. "Roux tells me you had plenty of it while you were at his place, and it was all packed in the shuttle."

"What are you saying?" Her father paled, pulling Michael toward him with his right hand—the left hand still clutching Kayla's. "You couldn't possibly be suggesting that my wife would give him something to alter his hearing."

"No, no, that isn't what he is saying. *Apparently*, certain human medications do weird things to *us*."

"But mom uses the same thing though... We both have the same genetic disorder." Michael traded glances with the three of them.

Kayla's hands flew to her mouth. "Mom's been taking that since before we met her..."

Her father looked at her, then Farz, his eyes widening with every breath. "Julie's been taking it since she was two, which was about the same time Michael started showing signs of the same immune disorder she has."

"Do you think she knows?" Farz paced, rattling his head from side to side. "She seriously thinks she doesn't have the sensitive hearing either?"

"Wait, are you suggesting my wife is Arros?"

"Half, but yes, that *is* what we are suggesting. And it's because she actually told Roux she was." Farz grimaced, holding both hands out in front of him.

"Dad," Kayla tugged at his hand. "Farz mentioned it when Roux was trying to get mom out of here. He says it's why Michael survived the adrenaline shot we used to wake the two of you up."

"And you didn't think to tell me *then*?"

Farz nodded toward them, grumbling to himself. "Do you think her parents chose that *specific* medication on purpose? I mean, you *said* her mom was human."

"*She* actually said she was half Arros?"

Farz nodded. "Roux says he'll relate the story in full when we get up there." He pointed for emphasis. "He says this…" his back-and-forth motions drew a snicker from Kayla. Roux always preferred a hands on approach to everything. "Is too complicated." Holding a hand up, Farz continued. "But, he says there is a certain genetic disorder that has been known to present itself in half Arros kids. It isn't life threatening, but it can be a pain to deal with. He isn't sure what they usually prescribe for it, off the top of his head. The condition isn't as common as you would think, but it isn't rare either."

"You mean I could take something else, and still have hearing like Dad and Kayla?" Michael's eyes glowed with the prospect. He'd often been jealous of Kayla's ability to eavesdrop on their parents.

"Should be. We've gotta have something for it, right?"

"Can't you just ask mom?"

"She's out of range." Farz cringed, his entire body flinching. "And Roux says you're going to have to explain the need to Arzi, because he really *shouldn't* be off his meds."

Some medical assistant I am, Kayla grumbled, leading Michael back to the room. She hadn't even considered the medication with everything else going on. "Mikey, I feel awful. I never even thought about it."

"You aren't the only one."

They could hear their father arguing with Farz in the other room, even after the door closed behind them. "How you feeling?"

"Eh, like I've been sleeping funny and need something less *disgusting* to eat."

"I'm an awful sister."

"No, you're not. I've been taking it most of my life, Kayla. Plus, you've been gone for eight years. It isn't like mom has to force feed it to me anymore." He laughed for her benefit, sitting down on the edge of her bed. "This is super weird. Mom and I both had boosters before we left Tinall, and started taking the normal dose when we got here." Michael turned toward the door. Their father stood there, attempting his best smile for them. "Dad, why wouldn't she tell us?"

"Mikey, Dad and I didn't exactly tell you about *our* past."

"Yeah, but you and Dad had a pretty legitimate reason for that. What kind of reason could she have, to lie about being half Arros?"

"She's a Vassen. They killed her entire family a *very* long time ago. Somehow, your mother got out alive. A good friend of the family made sure she disappeared, to protect her from the individuals who wanted her dead."

"Is that what she told Roux?"

Their father nodded. He crossed to sit opposite of Kayla, beside her brother. "I don't think she knew the medication was inhibiting your hearing, Michael. She wouldn't do that to you—not intentionally." He exhaled, rubbing his chest with one hand. "I want you both to know. I knew she had things she didn't want to talk about, and she knew I had my own. Neither of us has ever pushed it."

"Keeping it from you, that she's exactly the same as you are, that's a bit rough." Michael shook his head, fidgeting with the blanket.

"I never told her I was mated to a Siren and fled for my life—and your sister's."

"Justifiable."

"Mom's story is too." Kayla nudged him with her elbow.

"Yeah, I can't really blame her for not talking about it. But it has gotta suck for her, to not at *least* talk about it with us."

Their father stood up, pushing them apart to sit between them. With one arm over each of their shoulders, he pulled Kayla and her brother close. "Going forward, no more secrets."

"Agreed." They echoed their father's affirmation. Kayla was silently hoping for the chance to see Julie again, fairly certain her father and brother were doing the same thing.

40

Robert

Stretching the kink in his neck from sleeping upright with both Kayla and Michal at his sides, Robert winced as quietly as he could. He pulled the blanket higher with what little span he could use his arms and glanced toward Farz—asleep in the other bed. He promised himself to thank him for the thought later.

He laughed softly, considering how many years it had been since Kayla had last fallen asleep like she was. Curled into a ball at his side, she held his shirt with both hands. Michael was using the opposite shoulder as a pillow, sprawled across the other half of the bed. They'd grown up too fast for his liking, especially Kayla. But that was his fault.

Resting his head against the wall, he begged sleep to overtake him. They hadn't seen daylight since Arzi brought them to the facility. Nights and days blurred. He didn't even know how long it was since he last saw his wife, or how long she'd been free of Arzi. He owed Roux and his brother for their efforts. But he knew nothing would ever erase the way he'd treated both of them.

Faint memories cycled every time he closed his eyes. He knew he'd been right about seeing Roux somewhere before, but he hadn't been able to place where. His mother's social circle, before they went underground, wasn't a small one—he could have seen Roux anywhere. *Why did he have to be one of Mina's boys?* Grumbling to himself, letting the memories replay in his head, Robert drifted off.

"My father's sister has a young daughter." The boy trilled a short tune for Steven's daughter. "They're *excessively* vulnerable at this stage."

Steven rolled his eyes and pushed between the boy and the crib. He'd never met his mother's friend before. He didn't share her trust in the ghost of her past, but he trusted his parents to choose someone who could help. They wouldn't let anything happen to him, or his daughter. He Scrunched his nose, avoiding the itching sensation the young man's presence brought him and moved to watch his daughter.

"That is why I am here." He turned, gazing into the darkened hallway. "Once we reach our destination, your daughter's protection will be your responsibility. Time, unfortunately, doesn't allow for much more than my father is providing."

"I don't see why your father is risking his life, and yours, for my family."

The young man shrugged. "He has his reasons. It isn't my place to question."

"So much trust for such little information."

"My father isn't as difficult as you think," he laughed. "My mother is much worse." His attention on the baby, the dark-haired young man grimaced. "It's time to go."

Fingers shaking, Steven pulled his daughter from the bed. He wrapped her in the dark blanket, tethering her against his chest. She snuggled against him, barely stirring from her sleep.

The boy waved him toward the door. "Stick close."

Flinching awake, Robert blinked in rapid movements. The expression from his dream burned into the back of his eyelids. It was the same expression Roux gave him when he promised Robert his feelings for Kayla were genuine. He wasn't wrong about it. If what Farz said was true, his mother's trust in their father wasn't misplaced—even if he did obscure Roux's memory of it.

Swallowing the air compressed in his throat, he cringed. Roux was Michael's age. He'd never consider doing what Rivan had done to his son. Military training aside, Roux was a kid. It was barbaric, no matter how you reasoned for it. Even if Rivan had assured Roux knew what was expected going into it, Robert couldn't and wouldn't do the same for Michael.

The effort to keep his nerves steady was bound to wake his children. Robert inhaled through his nose, focusing on their breathing—hoping to match their cadence. For being half siblings, they had more in common than either of them were willing to admit. He ran fingers through Kayla's hair, smiling at the memories of trying to style it when she was young—before Julie stepped in to help him. She'd never been one to fuss over her appearance. His daughter was like his mother in that aspect.

"Thinking of your mother?"

His gaze lifting, he closed his eyes for a moment—hoping he hadn't heard *her* voice. Roux had warned them Arzi was coming back, but he'd hoped for a little more time.

"You forget, I've seen that look before."

"I'm surprised you remember." Matching the level of her whispers, Robert attempted to look away from her.

She leaned against the doorway; her smile causing tingles to spread across his arms. "There are some things I have never let go of."

Glaring, he tightened his arms around his son and daughter.

"They denied me seeing this side of you. It is *appealing*, watching you care for your children—even at their age."

His breaths caught in his chest, causing Kayla to stir. Thankfully, she remained asleep. It didn't matter how old his children were, he'd never deny them what they needed from him.

"I didn't want to disturb *this*." She gestured toward him. "However, we only have so much time to prepare for our departure."

"Departure?" Keeping his facial muscles in check became increasingly difficult with her presence. He couldn't afford to let her know Roux had already told them about the ship.

"We're leaving this *pathetic* planet." Rolling her eyes, she turned toward Farz.

"Arzi," a fire ebbed from her eyes in the moments her gaze tarried on Roux's brother. "She believes he isn't Roux,"

Her eyes widened, taking in his words. "Are you sure?"

He nodded. "Ahni meant to tell you when you returned, but you've been gone for so long—we weren't expecting you to be."

"How is it she knows?"

Robert swallowed the snide remark he could have given her, exhaling through his nose. They'd all gone over how to react to her arrival, and what to say. Her efforts to push the words from him made it easier than he anticipated. "She asked him who he was, when he didn't respond the way Roux would have. It was something personal, something only Roux would know. I don't think he could tell you where Roux is. She's already tried."

Her expression softened. "Is this why they..." she gestured toward his children.

Grateful for Kayla's insistence to use her ability, despite his own concerns on the matter, he nodded. "She's worried about Roux. You threatened to kill them both if he wouldn't tell you where to find his brother."

"She does not need to worry about her mate. He is found and is awaiting her arrival."

"Is he alright?"

"He is whole, and will be for as long as Ahni wishes him to be."

The genuine relief flooded from him, Arzi drawing her ability back for a moment. "She will be glad to hear of it." Fear roiled beneath his skin, the words he needed to say caught in his throat. "Arzi,"

"Yes?"

"My son hasn't had his medication since you brought him here." Guilt ebbed from him, an honest emotion. He, too, had failed to consider Michael's medical condition with everything going on. Poor Kayla, she'd spent hours beating herself up over forgetting. Much to Robert's dismay, Michael had forgotten, too. It wasn't uncommon for his son to forget, despite the time he'd been using it. Julie was consonantly reminding their son to take it when he was younger.

She raised her brow, angling her eyes toward Robert's son. "I believe I know what condition you speak of, but I do not have the treatments here."

Flinching, Robert slid his hand away from view—fisting it behind Michael's back. She already knew about Michael's medical needs. *Is she keeping it from him intentionally?* His chest threatened to collapse. Roux was right in saying it wasn't life threatening, but it wasn't a comfortable condition to deal with. He'd seen it enough when Michael missed doses before.

Arzi came closer to him, the light illuminating the concern in her expression. "I will make sure he receives it when we board the vessel awaiting us." Shaking her head, she turned away from him. "Wake them. I will return shortly. Make sure they are ready to depart."

"And Farz?"

"I will deal with him *later*."

He waited for her essence to fade before nudging them awake. "Time to get moving. She's back."

Kayla grumbled, hiding her face under the blanket. "She came and went, already?"

Robert shifted his weight, dumping Michael from his shoulder. "I told her what we agreed on. It worked, but I think we need to keep an eye on *him*." He nodded toward her brother-in-law. Kayla had mentioned the lack of sleep he'd been getting to keep an *ear* out for trouble Roux might run into. He never intended to admit his behavior towards Farz had been cruel. The kid might have been trying to protect them, for his brother's sake, but he and his brother were still trained assassins. *That* would never set well with him.

Hoping for more answers when they reached the ship in orbit, Robert jabbed a finger into Michael. "Get up before she comes in here and makes you regret it."

Michael stood up and almost fell over. "Does Dad's voice always sound like that when he drags us out of bed?"

"Yep." Kayla laughed at him, poking a finger into his ribcage, just below where Robert had. "Better get used to it."

"Farz," only three years older than Farz, it felt strange to rouse him the way he would his children. His connection to Kayla's husband would forever prevent Robert from considering him a peer. He raised his voice, calling the young man's name again.

"I'm getting there..." he rolled from the bed, stood up and barged between them, heading into the bathroom to splash water in his face.

"Roux kept you awake?" Kayla shuddered beside Robert, closing her eyes.

"More or less," rubbing his face, Farz looked up at her. "I don't think he'll sleep well until after he sees you himself and knows you're okay."

Kayla grumbled about never being okay again before shuffling her way into the exterior room.

"Did you tell her?"

Robert stood between Farz and the door.

"You didn't have any other choice." After drying his face, he stood in front of Robert. "What did she say about Michael's medication?"

"Not available down here."

"She could be lying, to see if you are."

"Considered that already, I don't want to think about it."

He cringed. "Can't blame you for that."

Farz ran wet fingers through his hair, causing the short hair to spike.

Where Roux kept his a few inches long, Farz kept his somewhere shy of an inch—not surprising for a military man. Robert's father had been strict about his own style before they went into hiding. Since then, he and his father had less patience for cropping their hair. The longest portion of his own hair was at his jawline. If you stretched the wavy locks to their full extent—Julie liked it the way he kept it.

Shuddering, Robert moved away from the door. His peripherals gave a clear view of the same reaction from Farz. Arzi was coming back. *She wasn't kidding about having little time.*

41

Farz

Hands clenched into fists, Farz attempted to close the door to the bathroom. The dreaded aura clouded his mind with every breath. Thankful Kayla didn't do the same, he abandoned the attempt to hide. Trudging through the opening, he stood as close to Kayla as he could bring himself to. If things went wrong, he wanted to make sure Arzi didn't hurt her.

Three guards entered behind Kayla's mother, their eyes on one person—him. Smiling, Farz thought of several things he could say. None of them were appropriate for mixed company. All of them would have made Kayla growl at him over his words the night before. *Don't piss her off. Get Kayla to Roux.* He repeated the mantra with every step the guards made in his direction.

Arzi shook her head, eying Kayla's proximity to him. "So you believe *he* is Roux's brother?"

An audible gulp, fingers sliding together, and the grind of her teeth, Kayla moved to stand in front of him. Farz cursed, holding his hand out to stop her. "Kayla, don't."

She shook her head at him, continuing to stand directly between him and the guards. "I know he isn't Roux, if that's what you mean. But I won't let you hurt him, simply for you not realizing it when you brought him here."

Arzi sneered, a laugh on the tip of her tongue.

"Everything he did, *you* made him do. You never asked him if he was Roux, did you?"

The Siren stopped, her eyes turned to ice. "How was I to know he would be there?"

"Exactly. He didn't think you'd drag them out of the house, and you didn't know Farz lived nearby, or that Roux was most likely out looking for me."

Farz cringed. If she wasn't careful, she'd give away the connection he had to Roux. That wouldn't bode well. The damage she'd cause ripping out their implants would do more than even the Niffen chamber could repair.

Her gaze cooled, hands folding across her chest. "You would defend a man who kills our kind."

"I defend a man who has done nothing but protect me from the moment you brought him to me."

Arzi smiled, looking beyond Kayla to view him better. "That is true. But I still don't trust him to not hurt you—without extra care to prevent it."

Robert pulled his daughter to his side with one hand, the other he used to keep Michael from interjecting. "Arzi, he was a kid—you know Mina didn't give him, or Roux, a choice."

Blood rushed through the veins in his eyes. Farz blinked at Robert. *Is he seriously defending me?* Forced to abandon the thought, he watched Arzi stride closer to him.

"I don't plan to give him one—either." Arzi's expression hardened, her ability flooding the room. Robert groaned, faintly audible to Farz. She was directing the majority of it on him. Unable to move away, he grimaced—inducing her to laugh. "Once her child is born, you will take her as your mate."

"What!" The Erickson's voiced their complaints as one. Other words spoken against her plan were incomprehensible, the Siren drawing Farz's full attention.

Blood curdled beneath his skin with the sound of his brother's roar. Mentally kicking himself for not shutting off the connection, Farz twitched under Arzi's command. The muscles of his throat curled against him, preventing the retort he would otherwise have given the woman staring at him. "And if she declines?" His voice cracked with each syllable. *Or can't do what you think she can.* Farz hoped it was the latter, for Kayla's sake.

"She won't decline. Your brother will not enjoy the consequences—*if* she does."

"And if she can't?" Robert roared from the defensive position in front of his children.

The moment of distraction, Arzi pulled her aura away—giving Farz the ability to see Robert's posture. He'd know Steven Morris wasn't exactly feeble, not with the line of work his father lived and breathed. But the fire in his eyes guaranteed he might actually fight his mate over the situation. *But is your ability enough to give you control? Could you win?*

"That will be obvious *if* the problem presents itself." Arzi turned away, her steps louder than normal. "Bring them."

"Farz?" Kayla's voice shook, her father wrapping an arm around her.

Feeling the blood drain from his head, he rattled himself from the daze. Her eyes widened with each step they made toward the doorway. Unable to fight the pull, he joined them—bringing up the rear with two of the guards.

Roux cursed wildly. His voice added to the muddled movements Farz made towards the others. "I can't believe she would do that," he grumbled. "No, I can. Farz... this isn't good."

Wishing for the privacy to agree with his brother wouldn't ease the rise of his blood pressure. He didn't like her that way, even with the effects of what her mother had done—or the few times she'd accidentally given off a little too much for him to handle. She was too naïve, too nice for his temperament. If they didn't find a way to get their father where he needed to be, Farz was going to drive the poor girl crazy for the rest of their lives—however long or short that was going to be.

Imagining his brother might *actually* kill him before letting him mate with his wife, he cringed. She'd been his brother's girl from the moment he laid eyes on her. Farz saw it then, never taking the moment to question his brother's judgment on the matter. Wishing he had, Farz followed the group towards *wherever* it was they were going.

Robert glanced over his shoulder, his expression frozen as it was during Arzi's mandate. "You alright?" He kept his voice low, his tone wavering with his steps.

"Ask me later."

Robert turned away from Farz—tightening his hold on Kayla.

42

Kayla

Sitting across from Farz, Kayla studied the blank expression he allowed. She knew Roux made conscious attempts to ease her concerns in the beginning. The two of them hadn't been given much chance to interact with *normal* people. If you could call any Arros, normal.

His features wavered, noticing her attention on him. "Kayla, I don't..." his eyelids slammed against each other. "Roux is going to kill me for this."

"It's not your fault." Her father grumbled from beside her.

Michael remained silent, his gaze locked on Farz. None of them had expected Arzi to demand it from him. Her keeping him around to protect Kayla wasn't off the table, but what her mother suggested—made her sick.

"I guess the bright side," Farz laughed, glancing toward the doorway her mother disappeared through—moments before. "If we don't get out of this... I'll be here to keep you sane, by driving you *insane*—every day."

Her father held a hand to his face. "That isn't reassuring."

"Or funny, okay, so maybe a *little* funny." Michael laughed, leaning forward to look at Kayla. "You okay, Sis?"

Her body shook, every breath denying her the calm she fought for. "No." Kayla secured her harness.

"He isn't either." Farz stared past her, his eyes struggling to focus.

"He heard that?"

Face muscles twitching, Farz nodded.

Kayla's father wrapped his right arm over her, their harnesses preventing the full hug she knew he would have given. Feeling the calm rush through her, she leaned against his shoulder. "Thanks, Dad."

He nodded, closing his eyes. "I wish I could do more."

"Doing *that,* intentionally, is probably the best thing any of you *can* do right now." Farz swallowed, his body shuddering.

Her father shrugged, nudging Michael with his left elbow. "Put it on."

Another grumble about his head, Michael fastened his restraints.

They didn't have to be touching for the calming effect to work, though it turned out better any time she did it that way. Her grandmother once told her that with familial connections, touch often broadened the effect—intensifying it to a level they were incapable of with others. Focusing on Michael, she breathed deeply.

"I'm fine Kayla, don't waste your energy." Their father flicked his ear at the same time Farz kicked out with his right leg, hitting Michael's shin at an angle. "OW! What was that for?"

"Give your sister a break. She's trying to help." Her father groaned from beside her.

Farz nodded his agreement, tapping Kayla's foot with the toe of his boot. "Remember what I told you."

She managed a smile, for his benefit, but it was harder than she would have hoped. His brows converged, the way Roux's often did. Coupled with the hazed look in his eyes, she knew he was listening to whatever his brother had to say on the matter.

"He can't be upset with you for it. You were trying to help."

Her father nudged her and kicked Farz the way he had with Michael. Farz just shook his head, mouthing the words: *Your mother is on her way back.*

"Ahni," Arzi tisked, motioning toward the seat across from her father. Her father opened his mouth to argue. "No, Steven, she needs to get used to this."

Farz closed his eyes, hanging his head.

Kayla unfastened her harness and stood. Her mother smiled, nodding toward the vacant seat by Farz. There were eight seats in the compartment her mother left them in—to do whatever it was she was *preparing.* The insistence for her to sit directly next to Farz was salt on the wound for them both—and unfortunately, Roux by proxy. She dropped into the seat next to him, glaring at her mother.

One of drudges sat down on the opposite side of her, another crossed behind Farz to sit on the only vacant seat in their row. Heavy breaths expelled. He looked at Kayla. She put a hand on his knee. Unsure if the physical contact could calm him the way it did for his brother, she left it there until his nerves began to race.

"I know you weren't meaning to do that. It's okay." Farz's voice sounded strange, so close to her ear. He shuddered when she retracted her hand.

Arzi laughed from her seat. Kayla's father blanched, his knuckles turning white from the grip on his harness. "It will get easier with time, Ahni."

"Being like you, or being forced to love both of them?" The words were sour on her tongue.

Her mother laughed. "So you understand what *it* entails?" She shook her head, crossing one leg over the other. "How long has Dr. Tahali been your mate?"

Jaw clamping shut, Kayla's gaze met her father's. She told him they were married first, but she'd failed to mention the *other* details taking place shortly after.

Farz laughed through his nose. "Your research seems a bit shoddy. You know who my brother and I are, who our mother is, but you *didn't* know they've been living together—since they got here."

Kayla elbowed him. *So much for not making her angry.*

Her mother snarled from beside her father, beckoning the remaining guard with a finger. "I *was* going to wait until your brother could see you to do this."

Kayla jolted with the motion of the guards. The one beside her moved to hold her in place. Farz cursed, grabbing her left hand. With one guard holding him down, the other gagging him, Arzi pulled the collar of his shirt aside. The motions happened so fast, Kayla's head spun. Roux's brother howled, muffled by the object shoved down his throat, his grip threatening to crush the bones in her hand.

The pain in her ears, and her hand, prevented her from looking until after Arzi stepped away—wiping her hand on his shirt. "Farz..." her harness falling away, Kayla stood in front of him. Blood flowed down the front of his buckle, stemming from the restraining unit protruding from the left side of his chest. His own harness was off kilter with the positioning of the device.

She lifted her hands to his face and called his name again. His eyes trembled, head lolling to the side when the guard released him. Kayla removed the gag and threw it at the retreating guard. Her hands shook, assessing the damage around the device. Even with criminals, they sedated them before affixing the device meant to keep them confined. Farz wasn't a saint, but he wasn't evil—her mother held that title.

Standard restraining units came in many varieties. Her mother's choice was anything but standard and urged the contents of her stomach into a constant rumble. The oblong device had prongs that punctured the skin with no for medical equipment. Protected by the same razor sharp prongs were nodes—remotely operated to connect to internal organs and nerves.

Kayla placed her right hand over her mouth and nose in the attempt to stifle the nausea. She removed her light jacket and held it—gently—over the edges of the unit. The flow would stem soon enough on its own, the unit being designed to cauterize everything once it was in place, but she wouldn't let her mother cause more troubles for him. Blood loss, pain aside, would muddle his ability to protect them. Unfortunately, the device *also* did that. Her mother could cause him extreme pain with the press of a button—if she saw fit.

Kayla called his name again. Unsure of Roux's ability to hear them, she stroked behind his right ear. "What is wrong with you? You could have killed him." Pain shot through her right arm, dulling after a moment. Turning toward her mother, Kayla glanced down at the blood ebbing from the cut on her arm.

"It will allow him to go anywhere you do. Without it, he can't go anywhere." Waving the implement through the air, she laughed. "You will heal fast enough, but he needs a *little* more." Arzi nodded to the guard again.

Farz groaned, inducing her to turn to him. Witnessing the withdrawal of the needle in his shoulder, she stooped in front of him. "Farz?" He grimaced, his motions excruciatingly slow.

"Ahni, take your seat."

Forcing steady breaths, wiping the tears from her face, Kayla did as she was asked. He found her hand, stroking it with a single finger. It was something Roux did when he was busy working. His way of saying everything was going to be fine. He'd always said it was better than not paying her any attention, despite the proximity, when others were around. Unless Farz paid a lot more attention to the way Roux behaved around her, much closer than she was comfortable considering, it meant her husband was listening—telling his brother what would help her.

Her mother laughed, crossing her legs—again. "At least he is resigned to his fate." She smiled at Kayla's father. He grimaced in a moment—shuddering.

She couldn't look at her father, much less Michael, for the entire duration of the ascent. Their heart rates synced periodically. Her brother's pulse was steady in its elevation, their father's strum was more erratic. Unable to blame them, she focused on the techniques Roux used—hoping to ease their concern.

Out of the corner of her eye, she noticed a twitch in Farz's expression. He was still pretty lethargic, but he was paying more attention to her than she realized. The hesitant smile faded from his face with her mother's attention on them.

Arzi laughed, removed her harness, and walked away. She stopped by the open hatch, laughing over her shoulder, before she kept walking.

"I hate her." Michael grunted, pressing his fingers against his forehead.

Their father dropped his head into both hands. "Please, don't let her hear you say that. I'm having a hard enough time dealing with her. I don't need her making your life miserable, too."

Kayla watched the way her brother rubbed circles with his fingertips. She nudged Farz with a finger, tilting her head toward Michael. He shrugged.

"How long have you had a headache, Mikey?"

"Couple days." Michael rolled his shoulders. "It gets worse when she's around."

Choking, Kayla lost her grip on the harness she'd been unfastening.

"What?" Eyes going wide, Kayla's father slipped from his harness. He shifted in his seat toward Michael. "How bad is it? Do I need to get her in here? She said she would have access to something for you when we get to the ship."

"Dad..." hands on her elbows, Kayla watched Farz's expression. He shook his head, angling his eyes toward the doorway.

"I'm not going to promise her anything for..." he stopped, his eyes locked on the exchanged between Kayla and Farz. "What?"

"She might not have what we need." Farz grimaced, tugging the buckle of his seat away from him. His eyes lingered on the blood coated straps as he rubbed his hands along his pants. It was dry, as were the stains on his clothes. Kayla watched him pull at the collar of his shirt, covering the device —but not the evidence of the blood-loss. The jacket she'd used to stem the flow lay discarded at his feet.

Fingers twitching, she calculated the number of hours since her mother's guard gave him the serum. She doubted he would be strong enough to stand, much less walk wherever it was to their semi permanent dwellings. With her left arm held in front of him, Kayla shook her head. "You shouldn't move, yet."

He raised a single brow.

She bit back the laugh. "I'm pretty sure you two get this all the time, but..."

she smiled. "He does that too."

Grumbling under his breath caused a chuckle from Michael. "He never told Kayla you were twins, did he?"

"No," they both answered.

"It is a bit..." Kayla cleared her throat. "Unsettling."

"Wasn't my idea." Farz laughed. He stopped short, seeing the glare on her father's face.

"It's okay Dad, I wasn't entirely upfront with him either. He doesn't know about..." Kayla mumbled the names Eva and Brandt.

"He does now..." Michael shook his head, blinking the pain away. "Mom told them when we were stuck in that *hide-y-hole*."

Her brother's chortle caused Farz to roll his eyes. "You were listening when I said that?" He held a hand over his face, rubbing around his eyes.

"Dude, I was right behind you." Michael squinted, shaking his head again. "Though... it had been a day or two since I took my meds when you were griping at Roux for not telling you he mated with my sister."

"She's coming back." Farz and her father both whispered. Their eyes glazed in that instant.

Michael shook his head. "How..."

Kayla held her hand up to silence him, her mind reeling. She watched him squint, dipping his head to the side as he pressed fingers against his sinuses. Processing the events of the past week, she cringed. It wasn't a coincidence. She should have noticed it sooner. Though, she assured herself; it had been eight years since she spent enough time around her brother. It wouldn't have been something she knew about him before.

43

Robert

Whispering to a guard over her shoulder, Arzi beckoned them with a motion toward the door, her smile widening at the sight of Kayla's attention to Farz—who barely restrained a growl when he heard mention of his brother. Why she insisted on whispering so close to them, when they could all hear her, Robert would never understand. Arzi had always liked to toy with people.

Robert stood, extending an arm to help Kayla's brother-in-law stand. He nodded, accepting the help with a grunt. Kayla shook her head before draping his right arm over her shoulders. He took his daughter's actions to mean the boy had lost too much blood,—to make the effort himself—he moved to brace the opposite side. Michael stood behind them, his grim expression visible in Robert's peripherals.

Their steps were slow for a while, crossing the docking bay threshold into the large passageways of the ship. His height left Robert taking most of his weight, though Farz did intentionally lean some towards Kayla. He spent the entire time glaring at the back of Arzi's head.

One of the guards stopped ahead of them, his hands flickering across a screen. The door beside him opened. Arzi slipped through with a laugh while the other guards kept them in the corridor. "Have you made your decision?"

Before they could hear the response, the guards ushered them through the door. Robert nudged Kayla away with his hand, the doorway only wide enough for the two of them. Arzi had already made her way across the room small room, taunting the man with his back to them. Farz stiffened, two steps in, his breaths shaking from him.

Kayla stepped around them, gasping at the sight before her. "Roux!"

Roux spun in place, his gaze immediately landing on Robert's daughter. "Kayla…" there was a definite difference between Farz and Roux—looks aside. The initial proximity to Kayla had startled Farz. But Roux—*he* lost all composure at their entrance. He practically sprinted across the gap between them to wrap his arms around his wife. Finding himself transfixed, he watched Roux grapple with their arrival. Kayla's husband trembled with every breath, something Robert hadn't expected from the military man he once was. The actions that followed differentiated the twins even more.

Farz's brother held Kayla's face in his hands, taking in every inch of her with his eyes. He then dropped to his knees, took her hands, and pressed an ear to her abdomen. With each moment, he steadied, wrapping his arms around Kayla's waist. Whatever happened, whatever Arzi had done—or said—made him fear for his wife and child.

Robert swallowed saliva, his heart shuddering at the thought of what Arzi used to threaten Roux into cooperating. He couldn't bring himself to watch the reaction Kayla's mother had to their reunion. The soft laughter with each step toward them—was hard enough. Every part of him wanted to rush to his daughter's side, be the barrier she needed between her and her mother. But he couldn't bring himself to move away from Farz—or Michael.

After ensuring Kayla was whole, Roux looked up from her—his eyes icing over at the sight of his brother. The blood coating Farz's clothing was gruesome, even in Robert's peripherals. Dr. Tahali tightened his hold on Kayla before he turned to face Arzi. She stood only a few paces from them, her arms folded across her chest. "What did you do to him?"

"I thought waiting would be the best reaction," she laughed, covering her face with one hand. "But this…" Arzi gestured toward them. "This is still *entertaining*."

Robert shifted his stance, compensating for the movements Farz made. His position blocked the view Roux's brother had of Arzi. Making sure Farz was looking at him, he mouthed, *Not now*—drawing a defeated expression from the young man. Michael moved forward to stand next to them, his gaze on the floor. Robert groaned internally as he turned away from them. His desire to get them away from Arzi wasn't enough to break through the hold she had on him.

"Make yourselves comfortable." Arzi sneered, brushing past Kayla and Roux. "You'll be coming with me, Steven."

Robert held a hand out to stop Michael's objection. Kayla's voice slurred through his perception, her motions halted by Roux's grip on her shoulders. Michael anticipated the shift in his stance would throw Farz's balance off, quickly taking the position Kayla had before they entered. With a half smile in his son's direction, Robert turned away from them—his steps matching Arzi's.

He knew it wouldn't bode well to ask Arzi why he she chose that moment to separate him from the others. Even if she answered him, she wouldn't be honest, not in front of his children. With the threshold behind him, he glanced over his shoulder. Kayla's protests prevented Arzi from holding complete control over his actions, but he couldn't let her know that. Robert continued forward, the image of Roux holding his daughter back burning into memory. The last of the motion allowed for him to see his son attempt to hold Farz up. The larger man fell to his knees as the door closed—snuffing out every sound the others made.

"Don't look so put out," Arzi looped her arm through his. "We're not going far."

True to her word, they stopped one door down. A glance around the much smaller room, Robert noted the reinforced door along the right wall. It differed from the other doorway—open straight ahead of them, leading toward the facilities. His scan of the room ended with the bed on the left side. Closing his eyes, exhaling, he turned away from Arzi.

Arzi sidled close to him, breathing softly in his ear. "This is your home now, Steven. You should get some rest while you can."

44

Roux

Fear, pain, or anguish? Roux wasn't sure which emotions to pin to the sobs Kayla expelled, tremors surging with each breath. It could have been all three. Though he hoped that pain had nothing to do with it. She looked whole. There wasn't a mark on her, and their child's heartbeat was steady. Noticing Robert's attention on him, when he made the assessment, hadn't given him any reason to change his mind. They all needed to know if she and the baby were alright. It wasn't the first time he'd done it, though the necessity to hear their child was greater. It *had* been the first time anyone witnessed the action —aside from his wife.

Lifting Kayla in his arms—she leaned against his chest—Roux made his way to the right wall. He kicked the mechanism at its base, stepping back several feet. A single bunk slid out, its linens clean—but disheveled. Keeping his wife against him, he tugged at the blanket. It came free with little effort. An internal grumble, Roux glanced over his shoulder. If anyone in the military had made the bed, it wouldn't have pulled free that easily. He set Kayla down and wrapped the blanket over her shoulders.

Kneeling in front of her, Roux brushed hair from her face—tucking it behind her ears. "I need to make sure Farz is alright."

Kayla nodded, pulling the blanket tight around her.

Each step away from his wife was excruciating, on an emotional and semi-physical level. His father had warned him about it frequently. If he ever found himself thrown back into his *previous* profession, it would keep him away from his mate. Those separations would eventually cause less of a burden on him, but they'd never been apart for more than a few hours since making *that* decision. Until her *mother* showed up.

He rubbed his hand over his face, trying not to think of the incessant need to stay near Kayla. She was only ten feet away, but it felt like she was back on the planet while they confined him to the billet.

"You, aright?" His brother's words came with the sound of his teeth grinding together.

"I'll be fine." Roux motioned to Michael. "Help me get him over there."

The two of them pulled Farz to his feet, inching across the gap towards the wall—again. Once they reached Kayla, Roux moved to press a mechanism in the middle of the wall—right of the bunk he'd already activated. Two bunks slid out, one two feet off the ground—like the other bunk he'd activated—the other was four feet above the lower. Thankfully, the ceilings were at least nine feet high in the barren room Arzi abandoned them in. The previous compartment was *maybe* seven feet high. Michael would have more than enough room—if he was comfortable sleeping on the top bunk.

Michael approached with Farz, who dropped into the bunk with a grumble. "Remind me to kill her once this *thing* is out."

Roux suppressed his comments, pulling the collar of his brother's shirt back.

"Why would she do that without the proper precautions?" Michael's voice trembled.

"Because she's sadistic." The three of them glanced at Kayla. She'd pulled her legs up into the bunk and leaned against the wall. Her head shook in rapid motions. "You all know I'm not exaggerating."

Despite agreeing with her, Roux said nothing. Instead, he returned his attention to his brother. Farz knew him too well to argue when he pulled the shirt off him. The bloodied garment fell to the floor as he inspected the tissue around the restraining unit. Unlike his own, Farz's showed the signs of his struggle. He closed his eyes, curling his fingers against his palms.

He'd heard what happened, but seeing it—Roux struggled to stay calm. Even if their military could find them before Arzi did worse, or Kayla had the baby, their lives would be *difficult*. He calculated the hours since Arzi had given his brother the serum in his head as he stood to pace the confines of their space. As long as he did what she asked of him, she'd return with more. And *hopefully*—Michael's medication.

His brother rested his head against the meager pillow of his bunk, eyes closed. Instinct drove Roux to check his pockets for the earplugs he'd designed to tune out everything. He grumbled loudly, remembering they were on the ship—with Julie.

"Roux... He's immune..." Farz groaned, covering his eyes with one hand.

He stopped his continual trudge and glared across the room. Michael traded glances with the three of them, his face contorted with each breath. "No, *he* isn't... haven't you been paying attention to how easily she makes our father do *anything* she asks of him?"

"I wasn't talking about *him*."

Roux's gaze fell on his wife. She focused on her nose, rubbing fingers along her knees. His head to the side, Roux crossed to kneel in front of her. "How long have you known?"

"An hour, maybe..." she shook her head. "I'm not sure how I didn't know before..."

He lifted her chin while brushing the strands hair away from her eyes. "Kayla. I was eleven when they realized I was." Her younger brother was eight years old when she started the internship. Roux rubbed a hand over his face. She would blame herself for not knowing, even though it wouldn't have been obvious.

Michael cursed from behind him, shoving Roux away. "Wait... You're saying *I'm* immune?!"

Folding both lips between her teeth, Kayla nodded to her brother. She opened her mouth to speak, three times, before any words were intelligible. "The headaches... Roux, gets them too... and... and... I think Arzi knows..."

"Farz, has she told Michael to do *anything*?"

"No. Not a single order, or request, made of him *directly*."

Michael backed away from the bunks, his head rattling almost violently. "How can I be immune when Dad isn't?"

"It's a recessive gene," Farz sat up. "They still don't know why *I'm* not immune..." flinging his arms forward, he ground his teeth together—again. "And we're twins! If *that* can happen when we're *almost* identical, you sure as hell can be, when your father isn't."

"Farz..."

"I'm not sugar coating it for him!"

"Farz..."

"This isn't anyone's fault. But we could have avoided it. We're all mixed up in this because you *had* to have her—the moment you laid eyes on her!"

"What?" Michael joined them, his hands fisted. "You told *us* you started dating *five* years ago."

"Michael, shut up!" Kayla snapped, the vessels of her eyes flaring.

"No! You've been lying to us the whole time we've been here! Don't even try to tell me to shut up!"

The kid didn't know who he was dealing with, coming far too close to striking range with his sister. Knowing they were close and registering the potential altercation were two different things. Michael was on the floor with both hands behind his back before he could take another step toward her. Kayla's shouts halted instantly, Farz's laughter replacing them—with increased volume.

"Roux!" Kayla was at his side, tugging him away from her brother. "He wouldn't have hit me."

The instant his hands left her brother's wrists, Michael rolled to his back, sliding away on his butt until he reached the wall. His pupils widened with each rattled breath. The kid stared at him for several seconds before glaring in Farz's direction. "He just attacked me, and you're laughing?" Michael locked his gaze on Roux again. "You're both *insane*!"

"Let me give you a basic education on Arros Biology, kid." Farz attempted to stop laughing, winces interspersed, before he continued. "You just came pretty darn close to *his* mate, and you looked like you wanted to hit her. Consider the fact that they have separated him from her for over a week, and she's pregnant... that's like trying to poke a bear cub while its mother is sitting right next to you."

Roux covered his face with both hands. He mumbled through his fingers. It was an apt description, but it didn't excuse the behavior. "I'm sorry Michael, I didn't mean to do that."

Kayla exhaled steadily, walking to stand next to her brother. "You have to remember they're full Arros, Mikey. They're *not* human, and that means there are a lot of differences you don't know about."

"Full Arros, who were trained to kill Sirens." He took his sister's extended hand and stood between her and Roux, looking over his shoulder at Kayla. "And that *doesn't* bother you?"

Her chin dropped to her chest, breaths wavering with each moment of silence. "It *does,* Mikey..."

Unable to watch the devastation on her face, Roux turned away. His strides put as much space between them as possible. He pressed his forehead against the wall, ribs aching with each draw of breath. While he knew would have to face her, now that she knew, it hadn't helped his nerves. He never intended to tell her about his past unless it was necessary. If he'd deemed it necessary, he intended to be the one who did the telling.

"You should have told her…"

"You know why I didn't."

"I told you before, hiding it from her wasn't going to end well…"

"I didn't want your advice on the matter the first time. What makes you think I want it now?"

"You two realize we can hear you, right?"

"Careful kid. You've set him off worse than I've seen him in a long time. Don't push him farther… He's trying really hard to keep his hands off you, for your sister's sake—right now." Judging by the sounds, he could tell Farz sat up in his bunk again. "Yes, we were trained to kill Sirens. But your sister isn't the type we hunt. We both knew that when *he* met her. Neither of us wanted to see her become what we hunted."

With the angle of his neck, Roux could see the Farz's expression. He wasn't looking at Michael or Kayla. He bit down on his tongue before moving back to this previous position. His skull pounded with every noise from the others. The ship, like every other built by Arros, was nearly silent. Though, being locked in a twelve foot box, give or take a few feet, with three others wasn't bound to be good for his sanity—or theirs.

"I'm not moving."

"Yes, you are."

"Kayla, he's been lying to you…"

"Mikey… he never lied to me." He knew she moved toward him, her words gaining volume with each step. "I knew he was in the military, and I knew he didn't enjoy what he did."

"I did lie…" a lot more than she should have, a lot more than he'd intended to. She was going to rail on him for it, and he'd deserve every word.

"About your father?" She huffed, planting her feet at his side. "Farz already explained a little about that."

"Kayla…" Roux rotated to face her, pulling her close to him—where she belonged. Her fingers stroked the tissue behind his right ear. He closed his eyes again, pressing his forehead against hers. Disconnecting from the link, he braced himself for the potential pain he had experienced a few days prior. When it didn't come, he leaned further against her touch. "We were six." Her gasp induced him to pull her closer. "I can't honestly remember not having it… not well, at least."

"I don't think I'd like your mother."

"Trust me, you will *hate* her." Farz laughed from the bunk.

Keeping his head against hers, he pivoted. The sneer he threw at his brother for the interruption wasn't as much of a deterrent—Farz only laughed harder.

"A pillow will muffle it to some extent…" Farz shook his head, plopping back down on his—he folded it up over his ears.

Michael's nose twitched, his glare fixed on Roux.

Kayla pulled away, keeping her arms around him. "I'm not angry with you…"

"You should be."

"Roux…" she ground her teeth together, tugging him to look at her. "I never expected you to talk about it." Gulping, Kayla pushed him back. "Yes, I was a little freaked out at first, because I wasn't expecting you to be a *hunter*."

Chin against his chest, Roux backed away. The term was common knowledge, though the actual numbers were not. "I would never hurt *you*, Kayla."

"Really…" Kayla huffed, crossing her arms over her chest. It accentuated the subtle bump. Her build hid the evidence to some extent. If she turned to the side, it was more obvious. Noticing his attention, she rolled her eyes. "You think I would believe you could hurt me, after *eight* years?"

"I… I wanted to protect you—from all of it."

"Even Farz?"

"I didn't tell you, because you would involve him in…" he swallowed saliva. "*Everything*." Roux watched her brother climb up to the third bunk, the kid's gaze threatening to bore a hole through him. "Kayla, I know how much you missed Michael." She'd always regretted leaving her little brother behind. Now that he understood some anxieties tied to the regrets, he wanted to beat himself for not seeing the signs.

She glared at him, her hands dropping to her side. "Roux… he's your brother. And you've been keeping him at a distance for *eight* years!"

"The more time he spends around you, the harder it is going to be to keep him *off* you."

"You got that right!" Farz poked the bottom of Michael's mattress. "Try humming, *quietly*…"

Kayla rolled her eyes at their brothers. The attempt to give them privacy wasn't much use. "And *before* all of this?"

"Um…" he bit down on his lower lip, eying the pillow his brother pressed against his ears. Exhaling, he pulled her back to him. "That was actually *his* decision."

Both brows lifted. Roux loved the expression on her. It wasn't often he could surprise her with details. Unfortunately, he was going to see the expression quite a bit over the next while. She'd want to know everything he'd kept from her. Thankfully, he had been as open as he could, without shedding light on what or who he was before. The omissions weren't anywhere near what Farz accused him of.

"I gave him the opportunity to meet you eight years ago." Roux grumbled. His brother wouldn't see the glare he intended to plaster on his face. "You already know that Farz isn't immune."

"Obviously…" she extended her hand toward the bunks with a flourish, rolling her eyes at the laugh his brother expelled.

"He didn't think it was a good idea to tell you he was around." Which ultimately led to Roux never mentioning it.

She turned, glaring at Farz. He rolled away gingerly, covering his exposed ear with the pillow. "*He* didn't mention that."

Puffing his cheeks for a moment, he released the air in a huff—making the longer fibers on his brow dance. "Farz likes to pin most of everything on me. He's done it since we were kids. Besides, if he didn't meet you, it was easier for him to avoid mentioning your involvement in my life—to our mother."

Her eyes widened.

"Technically, I wasn't fully honest with him about it, *either*." He pulled his wife into his arms again. "I didn't exactly tell him about how far we'd gone, and I was afraid to tell you how much time I was spending with him." He grumbled about the latter half, bracing himself for her rebuke.

"Your morning runs. You were with Farz." Kayla sighed, shaking her head at him. "You could have told me. If you'd explained he wasn't immune—I would have understood. You know I would have."

"I should have been honest—with both of you. But I didn't want him trying to talk me out of *anything*." Rubbing a hand over her stomach, he smiled. "I don't regret any of it."

Kayla ran her fingers over his chest, a grimace forming when she reached the restraining unit. "I'm sorry about all of this, Roux."

He lifted her chin with his hand and pulled her to his chest. "Kayla, your father never told you who she was. I wouldn't have known Arzi was your mother. But truthfully, if I knew a *little* more—I would have taken you back home a *long* time ago."

She buried her face in his chest, tears soaking through it. "Why do you think I *never* mentioned it?"

"Hey, I didn't mean I would have left you there. You don't think I'd give you up after everything we'd gone through together, do you?"

"You wouldn't have married me..."

He strangled the laugh before she could hit him and lifted her into his arms. "Farz is right, you know. I've wanted you as my wife from the moment I met you. No amount of family *difficulties* will ever change that." He shook his head before setting her down on the single bunk. "I know a thing or two about how to avoid Sirens."

"Says the man who moved his family to a planet where one was hiding."

Both Michael and Farz laughed, albeit briefly.

"So *if* I'm immune, *and* Arzi knows. What does that mean for me?" Michael sat up in his bunk. His words were to Roux, but his eyes never left his sister.

Kayla shuddered, blinking tears free. "I don't know, Mikey."

"Just go with it, kid, otherwise she'll use one of these on you." Farz pounded on his chest, wincing. "Trust me, they're not meant for show."

Michael's gulp was audible, his hands shaking. "Where did she take our father? Why choose now to separate us?"

Roux's wife covered her face, barely muffling her sobs. It wouldn't help any of them tune it out, but at least she was trying. Sitting on her left, he lifted his right arm over her. Pulling her to his side, Roux angled his eyes to view Kayla's brother. "I'm not sure any of us want those answers."

45

Farz

Farz stretched his arms, sitting up in his bunk. His eyes roved the entire room before landing on his brother. The pain was ebbing… thanks to the serum the wench jabbed him with several hours before. *Alright, maybe she isn't a wench… but she works for a Siren. Willingly!* The woman hadn't made any motions to befriend his medical minded brother—either.

Her inspection of his scarring was brief. His brother had looked at it multiple times since their arrival—cringing each time. The absence of a delicate touch when she injected the syringe directly into his chest didn't help matters. Michael's medication was practically thrown at him, no effort to assist him with the dosing made. The last strike against her… Farz cringed at the memory of it.

Unfortunately, the woman was trusted enough that Arzi allowed her control of the retraining units he and his brother were *gifted*. Her appraisal of Kayla's health was less than savory, inducing Roux's attempted interference. Attempted, because he was writhing on the floor before he could even reach the vile female. All the while, Farz and Michael stood by and let the calloused woman finish her exam. Well, Farz wasn't exactly standing. The serum she'd given him left him incapable of coming to Roux's aid. Most-likely *intentional* on Arzi's part.

Kayla had cried herself to sleep after Michael helped Roux to the lower bunk. The deplorable woman had left the room before releasing him from the torment. Entangled with his wife in the bunk, anyone who didn't know him might have assumed he was asleep. Roux was too good at masking his emotions, enough to lull his heart to a rate of his choosing. They both were.

Fixing his gaze on his younger brother, he waited.

"She sleeps heavier than you think." Roux spoke softly, his eyelids parting a fraction of their capability.

"Oh, I *know* she does..." Farz rolled his eyes at him for emphasis. "When she actually sleeps." Pointing toward the bunk above him, he snorted. "So does her brother."

His brother shifted carefully. But not enough to avoid showing the inaudible wince from Farz. Once he was sure Kayla wouldn't wake from the movement, Roux sat up on the edge of the bunk. How they were comfortable enough to rest, for any measure, Farz couldn't fathom. The bunk was barely wide enough for them to lie flat individually. He considered her side sleeping might have accounted for it. She continued to sleep that way once Roux slid away. Words failed him, a strange notion for him, watching his brother's sluggish movements. He bent forward, bracing himself in his open hands.

"Why would Arzi want Michael?"

Unsure if his brother spoke at the level he did to avoid waking the others, or if it was the lingering pain of what they did to him, Farz shook his head. The only reason he could hear Roux was through their implants. *That,* despite its convenience, was concerning. "I don't know..." He wasn't sure he wanted to know Arzi's plans for both of them. Roux's immunity didn't even phase her, which didn't bode well for any of them. The sooner their rescue party arrived, the better.

"I have to get them out of here, Farz." Roux swallowed, the sound rumbling through the implant's connection.

"If *they* don't find us, before she has your kid... I'm shooting myself."

His brother flinched, turning his gaze on him. "Don't say that!" The hiss of his voice carried more than he'd intended. Roux closed his eyes. "She's not that bad..." he swallowed heavy breaths.

Air clawed through his throat, pressing angrily against his esophagus. He didn't want to say it, couldn't say it. "You *know* what I meant."

"Five months—give or take." Shaking his head, he dropped his face into his hands again. "Arzi has a head start... it could take them longer to find us."

His brother struggled to steady his breathing, causing Farz to cringe in the darkness. "Just make it quick, when the time comes..."

"Farz..."

"I'm serious." His brother was the only one who could pull it off, especially if a certain *Siren* continued her efforts to pit them against each other. "I won't do that to her."

"And I won't let you."

"Good."

Farz stood from the bunk, walking the distance to the far wall. The compartment was bare anything but the retracting bunks. With a use for only three, Roux's insistence to be at her side behind it. The remaining walls were eerily blank.

"Is it as bad as Niv says it is?"

Roux compressed his nose, strangling his snorted reply. "Unfortunately..."

Farz rubbed a hand over his jaw. Their sister had warned them when they were kids that mating would take its toll on them if they continued their profession. The longer they were away, the pull would ease. She also told them that the same duration would make it even harder to leave their partner's side when the time to do so returned. He'd avoided the match his mother sought for him. Not just because he heeded their sister's warning, he couldn't stand the girl. The thought of being tied to her in such a way never carried the appeal he saw between his brother and Kayla. "I've never been more annoyed by taking her advice."

Roux grumbled, covering his face with both hands. "I am fairly certain Nivia only told us those details, because she was trying to scare some sense into *you*."

"You're probably right." Laughing softly, he continued to pace the confines. He'd never been the type to settle down, Nivia knew that. The number of women he'd associated with wasn't the issue, their reputations, however... "I should have ignored her."

"And end up leaving the poor girl behind to fulfill Mother's ultimatum?"

"You wouldn't have left if I was."

Roux watched him continue his trudge, following Farz with his eyes. "No, I still would have left. *You* would have stayed behind."

"And you'd be without backup here."

Huffing quietly, his brother stood up. "You're forgetting I've had contact with *Father* this whole time."

"And you're forgetting *he* sent you to the planet Arzi was hiding on. Not to mention, he's been pushing you toward Kayla for *eight years*! Who is to say he didn't send your *little* organization to Tinall and suggest they take on a *certain* brilliant young lady as part of their normal recruitment?"

"Father only encouraged me to pursue her, *after* I admitted how I felt."

"His childhood girlfriend's granddaughter... who looks a great deal like her." It was almost as if their father was living out his fantasy through Roux. Farz struggled to keep his groaning laughter quiet enough.

"If I'd known she was Caya's granddaughter, it wouldn't have changed how I felt. It doesn't now."

"Of course not!" Both of them flinched when Kayla stirred. Waiting for her to settle, Farz faced his brother. "You're stuck with her—for life, Roux."

"It was *my* decision. I don't regret it."

"You might not regret *choosing* the woman you love. But don't forget that I'll be stuck with her too, *if* we can't get out of this mess. And I *don't* see that happening in time."

"There is still a chance that she can't."

"No one has tested that theory, Roux. Are you willing to bet your marriage on it?"

His brother stopped pacing alongside him, eyes locked on Kayla. "No."

"The only thing I can think of... is having Kayla force me to stay away from her."

"You don't think her mother will expect that? She'd kill both of us for trying."

A sudden thought froze every nerve in his body. "Roux..." Farz stared toward the bunks. "Do you think she's trying to isolate the gene?"

Squinting, Roux moved to face him. The vessels in his eyes trembled. "No one has managed to. I don't see why *she* would try to recreate immunity. She's a Siren, Farz. She doesn't want people to resist her."

His brow raised, listening to his brother's counter argument. "Think about what you just said, *Dr. Tahali.*"

Roux stiffened, covering his face. "She's not trying to recreate it..."

"She wants to snuff the gene..."

Cursing, Roux finished the sentence. "By isolating the genes that hinder it. Having Michael and Robert around will ensure she has both to work with."

"Unless the immunity comes from Julie's side of the family, we're screwed."

"Farz, we're screwed either way. She has *us.*"

46

Nivia

She didn't see why he needed her around for backup. The twins could fully secure their vessel. If they didn't, it was on them. *He* could completely handle the issues her younger brothers left behind.

Of course, she didn't argue when the Admiral asked her to join him. She hadn't known, initially, what the troubles were. The request to bring her vessel to the outer reaches of the Vorn station's influence had been intriguing. It had something to do with her brothers, and the Admiral's need to rein them in—again, so Nivia Forran relented. Their mother would not be pleased that she was associating with the Admiral behind her back.

Not that she was the *only* one. Nivia was fairly certain her youngest brother kept in contact with the Admiral, even *after* he ran away from Arros society. She almost laughed at the memory. Their mother had been furious with his decision to leave and join the ranks of mere *doctors*. In her own opinion, Roux's choice was a noble one. He'd given up everything to help less fortunate cultures. Did she feel bad for Farz, being ordered to follow their brother everywhere he went? Not one whit.

The Admiral joined her at the airlock, his gun loosed—expression strained. "Do you really think you *need* that?" Nivia nodded toward his blaster.

"Nivia, we're dealing with Sirens..."

"Exactly, which is why *you* should put that somewhere safe. Or better yet, give it to me. I don't want any crazy vixen telling you to aim it at me."

The Admiral relented and handed her his firearm. "You're right, as always."

"You're right enough for both of us, *Admiral.*" She led the way, the airlock door easing open. Familiar with the layout of the ship her brothers used, she didn't have to check the map scrolling across the three inch wide screen—secured to her arm. She did, however, glance at it occasionally. "There is only one life sign. Let's hope *Roux* was right about them not finding her."

The Admiral moved in front of her, despite the growl she sent over the implant. He stood outside the doorway, of what Nivia was fairly certain was Roux's room, and nodded toward her. He then knocked on the sealed partition. Nivia followed his lead and stepped back into the corridor to allow their target to see them both through the doorway.

The woman inched into their view, shuddering at first. The lighting was still low. In their suits, neither of them needed the extra power usage. But if the reports were true, they were dealing with a half blooded civilian. Forcing back the urge to growl, Nivia removed her helmet—seconds after the Admiral did so. The woman before them covered her mouth with both hands.

"I wasn't expecting both of you."

Oh, no, she doesn't think... Growling at her colleague, Nivia elbowed him. *Great! This had better not be the reason you dragged me along! I don't need her, or anyone—for that matter—thinking I am my Mother!*

Her father laughed. *He laughed!* Extending a hand to the woman before them, he bowed. "Julie Erickson, I am Rivan Tahali. And this is my *daughter,* Nivia." He turned to her with a smile. "*Thankfully,* she doesn't look much like *their* mother."

Julie's hands flew to her mouth again. "OH! I am *so* sorry! I didn't know they had an older sister."

"I will lay that blame on the *boys.*" Nivia laughed, thankful their guest hadn't assumed she was younger than the twins.

"Spoken like an older sister." Mrs. Erickson chuckled for a moment, her gaze turning downward with her expression.

"We'll get them back." Her father nodded to her. "We don't have a lock on the communications dock Roux intended to use, yet. However, it is registering as active—so it's only a matter of time before we do." He extended his arm for Julie. "Come, I will ensure you have accommodations—until we reach the rest of your family. Mina, will no doubt insist you join Caya and Alan when we reach them."

Nivia slowed her pace, grumbling softly enough to avoid being heard by their half-blood guest. "Mother will gut me for arriving at the same time you do."

The Admiral smiled over his shoulder. Waiting for Julie to cross into the docking bay, he turned to her. "Go find your brothers. I will join the search as soon as *she* is secure."

47

Michael

Michael lay in a heap, pillow over his head, groaning about the hushed voices. Three weeks. The only reason he knew the length of time—his medication. The dosing receptacle, Kayla had explained, was good for a week's worth of medication. He'd just used the last bit of his *third* rationed to him the night before.

Thankfully, it wasn't an injection. Shuddering at the memories of the dreaded serum he'd watched his father and Farz endure, Michael pulled the blanket over his head. The taste wasn't the best, but it did the job. He felt less groggy, slept better, and could eat more of the *garbage* provided to them without feeling the constant buzz of being *unwell*.

True to Farz's theory, his hearing hadn't returned to the way it was with the new meds. Unsure if that was a good or bad thing, he pulled the pillow down over his ears. He'd never understood why Kayla was so grumpy about noises. The recent enlightenment brought with it a new respect for her—and their father.

Dad... He closed his eyes, deepening the darkness provided by his shelter. Arzi left with their father *three* weeks before. They hadn't seen either of them since. Meals were left unceremoniously and some crazy woman arrived once a week with his medication. Despite the ability Roux had to monitor Kayla's condition on his own, she insisted on examining her—every time.

He swallowed the glob of saliva threatening his pillow and wiped the escaped remnants away with his sleeve at his shoulder. Sniffing at the smell coming from the garment, he groaned. Kayla had been on him for several days about changing out of the clothes he'd been wearing since they arrived. Not willing to change into what *Arzi* gave them, he'd taken several showers in them. He'd stood in front of the heating vent a little too long afterwards—some days.

They had access to a tiny bathroom. The door only opened for Kayla. She unfortunately had to walk Roux and Farz in and out of the compartment any time they wished to use it. Agreeing with Farz, she only stood beside the door while he used it. Thankful for the freedom, Michael only needed her to open the door before he rushed into the minute privacy they were allowed.

"Mikey, go shower."

He peeked out from under the pillow to see his sister standing by the door. Michael rolled off the bunk and shuffled toward her. She lifted a hand to ruffle his hair before drawing it back to hold her nose.

"You really need to stop wearing your clothes in the shower. Try washing them while you're in there. Maybe hang them to dry while you're in there?" She was trying, but she sounded a little too much like *his* mother. The downward expression twitched into place—for both of them.

He didn't know how he'd showered and finished so fast, which left his mind spinning when he considered it. Standing in front of the heating vent, he fastened the closure of the pants—a size too big for him, wondering if the crazy siren assumed he and his father wore the same. He shook his head at the thought of wearing his father's clothing. The shirt in hand, he pulled it over his head—almost choking when he looked in the mirror.

Arzi was right, he looked like his father. Especially in the clothing left for him. Shuddering at the thought of the garments having actually belonged to him at some point, Michael rubbed his hands over his face. The decision to leave *his* clothing to dry by the vent made, he emerged to find Farz pacing, Roux sitting on the bunk he and Kayla shared—alone, and Kayla wrapping her arms around someone.

Air rushed from his lungs as she stepped away from the third man in the room. "Dad?"

The muscles of his father's jaw trembled, his eyes blinking away the evidence of tears. "Hey, Mikey..." he choked on his name, staring at the clothing Michael was wearing. "W... wh... where did you get those?"

His hand motioning toward the bathroom Michael, grumbled. "My clothes are still drying, and these were in there... it was the only stuff that didn't look like it was meant for them." Farz and Roux had at least six additional inches of height on him and were built half again as wide as he was.

His father turned to glare through an open door. A door that wasn't there before. At least he hadn't noticed it. "There's an S drawn with a red marker on the tag."

Michael shifted the shirt to inspect the tag. Sure enough, there was a red marking. Faded slightly, but it was there. *S… why would there be an S… Oh.* His stomach dropped a few inches, causing his movements to slow. "This *was* yours… wasn't it?"

Nodding, he moved toward Michael. "Mom used to mark which clothes were mine. Our maid could never tell the difference between Dad's stuff and mine." He swallowed, biting down on his lip. His eyes darted around the room, his mouth opening and closing several times before words tumbled free. "I didn't think she would keep them."

"That isn't what you were wearing when…" Kayla covered her mouth, shushing the gasp.

A nod escaped the trembles. His father wrapped both arms around him. "I've got to get you out of here, Michael. I don't know how, but I have to." The revelation left him incapable of moving while his father tightened his grip on him. "This is my fault son, I'm so sorry."

His sister joined the embrace. "I won't let her do anything to him, Dad, I promise."

"Sweetheart," their father pulled away. "You don't understand what is happening here. There is nothing any of us can do to change *this*."

"Change what, Dad?"

He opened his mouth, huffing after a few moments of silence.

"She won't let you say it? Will she?" Kayla groaned, backing away.

"What do you mean?" Michael felt his stomach muscles contract. His experience with Sirens had been nothing like he expected—from the description Roux and Farz gave back at the house. But from the bombshell they dumped on him, he couldn't really expect to have the same problem his father had.

Kayla shuddered, rubbing hands on her elbows. "Before you came, she did this… only worse. She wouldn't even let him speak."

His brows lifting, their father rolled his eyes. "She's done, and will continue to—do worse. It's just how she is." The latter, he said after checking over his shoulder.

"You've been on the other side of *that*…" Michael pointed to the doorway.

"The whole time, haven't you?"

"Yes..." his father exhaled, his hands fisting. "She's kept it locked."

"Why is it open now?" The others stared at him. Either they already heard the story or were waiting for him to hear what his father was going to say.

"They're moving *all* of us to another part of the ship. This has been a sort of quarantine... The Captain wanted to make sure none of us brought something from the planet with us."

Roux grumbled, climbing to his feet. "There isn't anything dangerous enough going around that would be worth quarantining for."

"Maybe nothing that originated there..." shuddering, his father continued. "Arzi left something behind. Whatever it is, the Captain is scared of it."

"She contaminated the population?!" The twins blurted their response as one, eyes bulging from them. Roux crossed the room, pulling Kayla to him. Farz simply shook his head. "She's insane!"

"We've already come to that agreement!" Kayla snapped, glaring at Farz from over Roux's shoulder.

"If he's scared of it, why did they send that *woman* in here?" The interruption might not have been the best idea, but no one glared at him for the comment—so he continued. "I mean, if we had something, we could have given it to her, Right?"

"Apparently, she was on the planet, so she was in this section of the ship with us, *anyway*." Their father sighed, putting his hands in his pockets. "She isn't going to give us much time. And I do not know what our living arrangements are going to be once they move us."

"Better than this box, I hope." Michael shrugged when the others glared at him. "Hey, you can't say any of you have been enjoying *this*." He waved his hands around for emphasis. Stopping short, he hurried into the bathroom for his clothes. Quickly replacing the tainted apparel with his own sopping clothes, he used one towel to rub as much water off as possible.

The others were gaping at him when he returned. "What? I wasn't going to give her the *satisfaction* of seeing me in those." He threw the clothes his father had worn, almost thirty years before, into the corner.

"Daddy?"

Kayla's gasp brought his attention to the glazed expression on their father's face. He blinked rapidly, grimacing for a moment. Throat tightening, head pounding with each breath, Michael stepped back. His sister had warned him of prolonged exposure to Arzi could do to both himself and Roux. Looking at her, hoping it didn't mean what he thought, he saw Roux wrap one arm around her abdomen—the other hand pressing against his sinuses.

Grumbling about the downside to being immune wasn't going to get him anywhere. Instead, he moved to stand between his father and the doorway.

"Michael..."

She walked through the door the moment his father spoke. Planting his feet, Michael stared her down, ignoring the spreading pain. Kayla said there were things Roux was taking for it. He wondered—briefly—if they could get away with giving Arzi another reason for their need. Looking over his shoulder, Roux dropped his hand to his side and forced a smile. He couldn't leave Kayla's side, even if he could—both he and Farz had restraining units. Michael was the only who might stand against Arzi.

The Siren laughed, standing in front of him. "What is it you intend to do, young man?"

He hadn't spent every weekend with his grandfather for no reason. The explanation they had given him was far from the truth, though it didn't change his appreciation for the sheltered life his family *tried* to give him. "You took him from us for *three* weeks. I am not letting you take him from us again."

"Spirited." She laughed again. "He is more like you than I first realized, Steven."

"Arzi, please, don't."

"I won't damage your boy, Steven." Arzi snapped her fingers.

Michael's lungs deflated at the sight of six guards filing into the room. Someone tugged him back by his wrist. It wasn't until the guards obscured his view of his father that he realized Farz was at fault. *Not today's battle.* The motion of his lips wasn't enough to ease his frustration. All the years spent learning self defense weren't worth a dime in the world of Sirens. Not when that Siren leveled the playing field. Without the restraining units, Farz and his brother were more than capable of handling the guards. Unfortunately, with the Siren in the room, Farz wouldn't do them much good without their specially designed gear.

Farz moved his lips slowly enough for Michael to read them, but not slowly enough for the guards to notice. *We'll get out of this, kid, I promise.*

Hand on his forehead, Michael grumbled his silent response. *Before, or after, she forces you to mate with my sister?*

The hunter grimaced, shaking his head. He pointed his finger toward the guards approaching them. Another hand clamped on his wrist, dragging him, along with the others, from their quarantine.

48

Roux

Clinging to Roux's shirt, his wife pulled herself as close as she could to him. He closed his arms around her, willing the migraine to pass. Certain that Arzi didn't know about the issue, he focused on Kayla—instead of his pain. Every bout of laughter from her *mother* induced him to tighten his hold.

"I won't let go of you." Not bothering to whisper, Roux pressed his forehead into her hair.

"Let him be possessive of his *mate*." Arzi chuckled, her voice coming from outside the room. "As long as he does what he's told—I'll allow it."

Roux shuddered, adjusting his position. He wouldn't correct the term. Sure, the mating instinct could easily be possessive. But every rush of blood through him screamed to *protect* Kayla from the woman sauntering around the room, possessiveness had nothing to do with it. He refused to look at her mother. Each sneer in his direction intended one thing, to prove she was in control. She could force the strength from him, cause him to drop to the floor at his wife's side, if that was her wish. Swallowing the memory of previous threats, Roux followed the others out of the room. The guards spread out around them, herding them toward the corridor he hadn't seen since his arrival. Instead of turning the direction he had, attempting to cripple the ship, they made their way into a lift capable of transporting them to another level.

He adjusted his hold on Kayla before he sat down. The motion would easily become disorienting for her. If they remained standing, it would be much worse. Across from them, her father trembled. His eyes roved the curve of her abdomen, further visible since he last saw her. Isolating the man's heart rate wasn't difficult. Michael's fluctuated between fury and terror levels. The guards were too steady to differentiate from each other. Farz's casual thrum was always easy for him to find. With Kayla against him, he could feel hers attempt to match his. The light flutter beside Robert was enough to disgust Roux, inducing his fingers to curl. And Robert, his matched the pulsing in the vessel of his eyes—the shiver of fear and defeat at his fingertips.

Robert wasn't the only one who'd failed to protect her. Though, unlike her father, Roux had a plan. Parts of one, at least. Unfortunately, it relied heavily on a man who'd lied to him. Someone he still trusted, despite the uncertainty of *his* motives.

Kayla shifted, wrapping both arms around him. The angle pulled her away from him for a moment before she compensated to rest her head on his shoulder. He stroked her cheek with the back of his fingers. The movement allowed him to see Farz lift his gaze from the boy beside him. His eyes reddened. Farz promised to watch over Michael—if possible. As long as they didn't push Arzi, they could bide their time. Unfortunately, Arzi was still flooding her aura. Which left Farz incapable of doing anything to help if she realized what he and Roux were doing.

Nodding to his brother, Roux forced a steady stream of breaths. The headache wasn't intolerable, yet, which meant she wasn't using her ability as heavily as he thought she would. Internalizing the groan, he watched the way his father-in-law reacted to Arzi's touch. There was less animosity in it, but it was still there. Roux's shirt wicked away the evidence of Kayla's tears, but not the sounds accompanying them.

Robert flinched, his gaze wavering between both of his children. "How's she been feeling?" The question hung between them, his eyes on Kayla—who hid from him. He leaned forward, touching her knee with a forced smile.

"She's fine, Steven." Arzi rolled her eyes, pushing him back against the seat with one hand.

"She isn't fine…"

"Steven, I don't want to hear another word about it."

His jaw hung open, eyes dampening with every breath.

"I'm okay, Dad." Her words rattled steadily, belied by the beating of her heart. It was something she knew everyone in the compartment would pick up on.

Michael glared at the Siren in their midst, his breaths like fog in the lift's chill. Farz nudged him with an elbow. "Don't."

Their remaining trip was accentuated by the silence. Arzi led them down a darkened passage into an atrium that left Roux and the others shielding their vision from the variation. Farz looked at him, his eyes wide. Neither of them had seen such elaborate details in any Arros Vessel. The air was clear and crisp, distinct from the passage—the door sealing behind them.

Most disconcerting were the rivulets of a water system weaving through the greenery and pathways. It had to be a refit. None of the vessels his father boasted had such superfluous arrangements, and nothing outside of the chamber differed from the norm of the Arros military.

"Our haven." Arzi smiled, inhaling the aroma of their surroundings. "Finally rid of the rotten moss smell of that horrid planet." With their attention on her, she folded her arms across her chest. "My *home* is yours now."

Kayla jabbed Roux with a finger, drawing his attention from her mother. She nodded toward Michael and Farz. Her brother spun slowly, examining his surroundings with a frown. His brother mirrored Michael, his eyes watching for any movement from the Siren.

"All of this is yours to explore." Sneering, she crossed one of the channels. "None of you are to leave this level—without consent." Motioning past the elaborate courtyard, Arzi strode toward the structures lining the dome.

None of the glass, or lighting, was natural. Each panel was a reproduced image of the void beyond the bulkhead. The lighting was simulated, emanating from the divisions of the structure above them. Roux shuddered, thinking what would happen to their supposed sanctuary if anyone were to attack the vessel.

The first door along the nearest wall opened. Arzi waved her hand with a flourish. "Michael."

He froze, mere paces from Roux, turning to gage his expression on the matter. Roux shrugged, squeezing Kayla's hand. Their warden had said the entire level was available to them. He only hoped she wasn't toying with them.

The boy peeked into the room, relaxing his shoulders after his inspection. "I'm not tired."

"No need to retire, yet, young man." Arzi laughed. "I assumed you'd wish to know more about your *temporary* home before making any decisions."

The way she emphasized temporary left Kayla digging her fingers into Roux's wrist with her free hand. Loosening his grip on her hand, he tugged free of her and wrapped an arm over her. Following the Siren only worsened the composure his wife could control.

"I hope this is acceptable for your *circumstances,* Ahni." Arzi smiled, genuinely—for an instant, before sneering at Roux and his brother. "There should be adequate room for *both* of them here."

Kayla's breaths and Farz's groan merged, deadening Roux's nerves.

"Ensure the *children* settle in before I return." Arzi strode away, Robert's hand in hers. He watched them from the corner of his eye until they were out of sight.

"C'mon kid. Let's check out your room first." Turning to Kayla, Farz nodded. "I'd rather not leave him in there alone if it seems *off.*"

"Good idea." Roux tugged her hand. "We need to go with them."

Sighing, she rubbed her free hand over her forehead.

Farz stopped outside the doorway intended for Michael. "Yours to explore..." his brother mimicked the Siren's words, tapping the restraining unit with two fingers. "Yeah, as long as she's within range." Using the same fingers, he pointed to Kayla.

"I'm sorry Farz." Kayla shuffled toward them, pulling Roux with her.

"Not your fault." He and Michael waited for them to move closer before they entered.

Michael swallowed audibly, spinning around to view his new accommodations. "This isn't what I was expecting." It wasn't spectacular, though it had its own facilities and closet—filled with clothing similar to the outfit he'd abandoned in their quarantine. "What is she trying to play at with this?" He held the sleeve of a shirt out to them.

Kayla muffled her shaky breaths with one hand, crossing to her brother. She wrapped both arms around him. "You don't have to stay in here unless you want to."

Farz stared at him from across the room. "Don't over think it. She probably thinks you like the same styles your father wore when you were his age."

"Does she not realize that was almost thirty years ago?" Michael cringed, releasing the hem. "We should have checked yours first."

"I thought you didn't like being couped up with us?" Kayla forced a smile for him.

"Being couped up with you three is better than being alone, with *that* to look at."

Farz threw the pillow from the bed at Michael before removing the rest of the bedding. "I'd be willing to bet there are only *two* beds in the *other* one."

Soon, the four of them stood in the middle of the accommodations intended for Kayla, Roux, and Farz. All of them groaned at the sight of the enormous bed on the far side of the spacious room. None of them moved for several minutes, continued grumbles breaking the silence.

Kayla took the first step away, taking one pillow from the bed and tossing it to Farz. "I can share with your brother."

Farz laughed, nudging Michael. "Should have dragged the mattress in here for you. What side do you want?"

"There is always time for that, later." Shrugging, Michael lobbed the pillow into a corner. He plopped down in front of it, using it as padding for his back. "This way, I can see when she comes in."

Farz smiled, chuffing his approval. "I like the way you think." He crossed to dump the rest of the bedding, along with the pillow Kayla provided him, on the floor a few feet from Michael.

"Do you think they have cameras in here?" Kayla's brother scanned the recesses of the room.

"Doubt it. Your sister might not be like her mother, but sirens are very *private* about their personal lives. I don't think Arzi would cross that line—or allow it in her own chambers—either."

Kayla and her brother shuddered.

"Thanks for that *delightful* image..." Roux grumbled, urging Kayla toward the bed, sitting down beside her.

"She expects you to be okay with this..." Kayla stared at the door that closed moments after they entered the room.

"I'd rather have Farz nearby... I know it's..." he rubbed the hairs at the back of his neck. "Awkward. But he's safer with *us*."

Nodding in rapid movements, Kayla leaned into him. "I keep thinking this is a nightmare, that we'll wake up at home and have Mom laughing about the ridiculous story I had to tell... but then... I wake up to *this*."

Roux held his wife to him, rubbing a hand down her spine in time with her breaths. "We'll get out of this mess, I promise."

The four of them flinched, heart rates speeding up as the door opened.

Laughing at their arrangements, Arzi shook her head. "Come with me, Ahni."

Kayla gasped, eyes shifting between her mother and Roux. She stood, pulling him from the bed with her.

"Just you." She tisked, waving a finger about. "Don't worry, they can't go anywhere." Eying Michael with a glare threatening retribution, she shook her head. "I wasn't aware you were so *familiar* with your brother."

Not daring to move away from where he stood at the foot of the bed, Roux allowed her fingers to slip from his hand.

"He's my little brother… it's normal to be overprotective of your younger siblings." Kayla shuddered with each step toward her mother, turning her head as she reached the door. The whispered affirmation for Roux left him cringing with the doors hiss.

Even hours later, Farz showed signs of Arzi's influence. His eyes were glazed and his muscles twitching. He hardly spoke a word—even when someone said something to him. Slapping the back of his head, Roux stepped away.

Farz blinked rapidly, shaking his head. "Crap, was I that out of it?"

Nodding, Roux strode across the room. "It's going to take months for you and Robert to fully recover from this, even if we get out before her order kicks in."

"You mean trying to force myself on your mate?"

Roux glared at his brother. He shook his head as he moved toward the door —but not too close. Every nerve in his body twitched with the need to know where Arzi had taken his wife, what she was doing to her, what she was saying to her.

"Breathe, little brother. I know right *now* that natural instinct is a beast wanting out. But you have to concentrate."

"Do you realize how much time we've been here?"

"Maybe three weeks?"

"The longer this takes, the closer Arzi's threat comes."

"You don't have to remind me, Roux. I'm already having enough difficulty keeping my distance from *Kayla*. It's a good thing that she's pretty tame compared to her mother. Otherwise, I'd probably have,"

Roux held his hand up. "Don't say it." If his brother hadn't stopped, he would've been facing a furious husband. One who would have begged his wife to subdue the idiot so he could beat some sense into him—without retaliation.

Farz arched an eyebrow. "I know that look. I'd be happy to spar with you, but your wife would have a heart attack if we did that."

"You're assuming I would allow a fair fight with what you were just suggesting?"

His brother laughed through his nose as he sat down on the makeshift bed beside Kayla's brother, swishing his drink in his mouth. "Still might be fun."

"Might be fun to watch." Michael laughed from his corner. "I'm betting on Roux and Kayla, though." He shook his head, burrowing into the additional blankets they found in their search of the space. With little else to do, they'd discovered the bathroom and various cabinets.

"You think he'd win?" Farz huffed. "If it was fair, I'd win."

"I doubt she'd allow him to fight fair. My sister would be horrified by what you almost said." The only visible part of the boy was telltale traces of dark hair poking out from between the covers and his pillow. "Why is it so cold in here?"

"We're in space, kid. It gets cold out here."

Roux ignored their banter, staring at the doorway—again. *I have to get them out of here.* Their father had a habit of arriving just when he was needed throughout most of their lives. The older they became, the less often it was needed. He shuddered, considering his father's presence at his and Kayla's wedding. She deserved to know who he was, but his father advised against it.

Hanging his head, he trudged toward his brothers. Yes, *his* brothers. Kayla's brother was his, would be *forever.* "I should have asked, before..."

Michael sat up in his heap of blankets, his head emerging a few seconds later. "Asked what?"

"Are you good with me calling you Mikey? Do you prefer Michael—or Mike?" Kayla always called him Mikey. For years, he'd assumed it was her brother's name, not understanding the human use of nicknames. He and Farz called their sister by a shortened version of her name, only because she'd hated her name.

The kid's smile widened and waned in an instant. "Everyone calls me Mikey. But you're welcome to use whichever."

He'd reach maturity in a matter of months, something Roux hadn't considered when they first arrived. Michael was supposed to be mostly human. The Arros maturity wouldn't have come for a while longer that way. There were far too many research documentations on the intermixing of Arros with other species. And too few in comparison where humans were concerned. It was about the pride of Arros and diluting themselves with lesser races. Fortunately, he'd read everything he could get his hands on *before* he met her family.

"Do you think your sister will approve if I stop using the endearment?"

"Term of endearment, you mean?" Michael laughed at his nod. "I doubt she'd even call you on it. I'm not really a little kid anymore."

"We should use what you prefer. You'll be mature—soon enough, it is only fair you have a decision about that." Farz grunted, laying back on his arrangement of bedding.

Internalizing his grumbles, Roux glared at his brother. Little brother was something their sister had labeled both of them with, regardless of their age. Farz latched on to the term, never quite relinquishing it—unless the situation called for it.

"Mature?" Michael stared at them, his eyelids cropping the visible amount of his eyes. "She kept saying something about that on the planet."

Farz grimaced, rubbing a hand over face. "I understand why your father sheltered the two of you, but this is going a little too far."

"He isn't the only one to blame for that, Farz. *Both* of their parents tried to protect them from *our* way of life."

Michael met his gaze, the blanket dropping from his hands to show his arms crossed over his chest. "Dad said you'd waited for Kayla to be a *legal adult* by human standards. I *distinctly* remember that."

Fingers dredging over his eyes, Roux sat down on the bed. He was old enough to have *this* conversation with a kid of his own—that thought wasn't reassuring. Especially since the conversation would have happened years before, giving the kid time to adjust to the situation. "Arros, develop their..." Roux groaned.

"Ability to mate..." Farz continued his train of thought, sitting up to face Michael. "In their teens. The more Arros blood, the sooner that process happens."

Michael traded gazes between them.

"I thought you were at least three quarters human *before*. Which would have your maturation hitting about twenty, sometimes later." There wasn't much record of anyone with less Arros genetics, considering anyone who married into their society—rarely strayed from it. The dilution rarely perpetuated with the offspring living longer than humans would.

"I do understand biology..."

"Human biology..." their voices merged, cutting Michael off.

"You're the one who decided to use that part of our genetics. You should be the one explaining." Farz covered his face.

"With. His. Sister." He ground out the syllables, glaring at his brother.

"Good point." Farz laughed, shooing Roux with a disguised flex of his fingers.

He retreated to the far side of the room, using the wall to slide down to the floor. Of all the situations he'd considered, being a part of her family, Roux never once entertained the idea of dealing with the woman who brought her into existence. Though, listening to the explanation his brother gave, topped that—by a long shot.

"The ability to mate for life happens when an Arros matures. Since you're half blooded… it isn't a *life sentence* for you. Because of that, that part of your hormones won't peak until you're seventeen, eighteen at the latest. Which was why your father mentioned the whole—*legal adult,* by human standards. Your sister would have reached maturity by sixteen…" He looked at Roux for confirmation.

He nodded, grumbling to himself.

Michael watched him from the other side of the room, blinking.

"When Roux first met her, she was… um… starting that process…" Farz coughed repeatedly.

Roux closed his eyes, their introduction projected against his eyelids.

The young girl sat alone in the last row of chairs, her hands folded across her lap. Waiting, he knew that feeling—a little too well. She was punctual. He had to give her that. The others chosen for the apprenticeship would trickle in soon enough, giving her little space to call her own. All of them would find their places among different rosters once their aptitudes were fully explored.

But this girl was different. He would make sure she found her way to *his* team. It wouldn't be difficult as a senior apprentice with enough political pull to get his way. Though she wasn't likely to respond well to that kind of attention. Smiling, he made his way into the auditorium. There were other ways to convince his mentor to take the girl on.

"Hello!"

The young lady lifted her gaze from her hands, a smile twitching into place. "Uh, Hello…"

He extended his hand, a customary *human* reaction. One he knew she and the other recruits from Tinall would respond to. "Roux Tahali."

She took his hand. Her smile brightened—he knew he was hooked. "Kayla Erickson."

"Mind if I join you? It's going to be quite a while before orientation starts."

Her shoulders bounced. "If you'd like."

Roux felt *it* again. The same thing he and his brother sensed when she arrived an hour earlier. *Siren.* Everything about his past warned him to turn around, ignore her, report her. But the soft-spoken girl intrigued him from the moment she walked through the doors of the university—temporarily commandeered for the company's initial orientation.

"You're here for orientation, too?"

"Nah," Roux shook his head. "I sat through mine two years ago."

Her mouth opened and closed, twice. Facing the podium, she nibbled at her fingernails.

While blinking the mild pressure in his sinuses away, Roux prodded her with a single finger. "You don't have to push me away, Kayla."

Eyes widening, she shifted in her chair to face him.

"Yes, I felt that… and no, it does nothing to me." Admitting his aversion to the sensation she kept a lot of control over, for someone her age, wasn't a topic for their first meeting.

"You're Arros?" She scrutinized every part of him, blinking in rapid motions.

Roux nodded, smiling at the surprise on her delicate features. "Last I checked."

Her shoulders shook. Kayla tried to hide the blush of her cheeks by dipping her head away from him, stomach rumbling.

"Hey, it's going to be at least an hour before this thing starts…" Roux motioned toward the door he'd been lurking behind. "And I can tell you haven't eaten anything in a while."

Heart rate spiking, Kayla rubbed her elbows. "I told my Dad I would stay in here until orientation started."

"Your Dad?" He knew the term meant father, but actually hearing it used—especially by a young lady with enough Arros blood to present the Siren genetics—was a different thing. "How *old* are you, Miss Erickson?"

She mumbled about turning fifteen a few months before, quietly enough that only the two of them could hear it. Not that anyone else was in the room to hide it from. Swallowing, Roux pat her shoulder. She was too young to be doing this alone.

"How about I ask a buddy of mine to grab us something? We can eat here while you wait." Sending a message to his brother, purely for appearance's sake, Roux sat back—watching her look him over.

"Do you," she fiddled with her hair, biting her lower lip. "Like working with the organization?"

"So far, yeah. It got me out of my corner of the galaxy." A half-lie he told many people. His previous profession sent him *everywhere*. Of course, he had a lot more time to enjoy himself since resigning.

Kayla smiled. "It is a liberating idea."

Laughing, he nudged her. "Never a bad thing." Farz grumbled his arrival over their connection. Roux stood, checking his hand-held device for good measure, taking small steps toward the door. "Don't go anywhere. I'll be right back."

"Your friend isn't joining us?"

Roux shook his head. "He's shy."

"And *She* is *literally* half your age!"

He ignored his brother's complaints, jogging up the stairs to meet him outside the auditorium. It wasn't uncommon for Arros females to marry young, or the males to be older when they do so. Farz knew that well enough. But being raised among humans, Farz was right. She and her family would see the gap in a different light. "She's also taking an enormous step for her future, and terrified. The least we can do is give her the peace of mind that not *all* of us are afraid of her kind."

"You... aren't." Farz held out the bag in his hand. "If she finds out you already had this planned, she'll slap you and never speak to you again."

"Speaking from experience, are we?"

"Just shut up and get back in there."

"The effect is not *temporary*... especially if you meet a full Arros girl. Just because you aren't bound by the effect the way a full Arros is, doesn't mean they..."

Roux's throat tightened. *Temporary*... Arzi had said temporary when referring to Michael's accommodations. *No*... Cursing, Roux stood up. The buzz of the restraining unit stopped him a few feet from the door.

"What is it?" Farz was at his side, a few feet further from the door.

"Temporary. Arzi said *temporary*, when she showed us Michael's room."

"Shit." His brother turned toward the kid, huddled beneath his blankets. "You don't think she's planning on actually using him like *that*..." Shaking his head, Farz growled. "*This* keeps getting worse. Where the hell is our backup?"

"Use me like what?" Michael stared at them, his hands shaking.

He and Farz turned to face Michael. Neither of them speaking as they watched the emotions boil over.

"How does Arzi plan to use me? Either one of you tells me what you think is going on, or I'll ask my sister to make *him* say it—when she gets back." He glowered toward Farz. "I am not afraid to ask her. Whatever you're not saying has to do with Arzi trying to trap my father more than she already has—I know it by the looks on your faces."

"I think it has more to do with trapping your sister. She has a pretty good grip on your father's chains already." Farz groaned.

Michael altered his glare's direction, moving to stand directly in front of Roux. "Don't assume I'm afraid of you. You may be dangerous, but I can walk out that door—you can't."

Roux pressed his lips together, blowing air through his nose. "Michael, *she* said your room was temporary. What do *you* think that means?" Unsure if he really wanted to shed light on what was undoubtedly the situation Robert wasn't allowed to speak of, he turned away, staring at the door—again.

"I don't know. Everything since she dragged us out of your place has been *temporary*."

Placing a hand on the back of his neck, Roux bent his head back over it. "She has someone lined up for *you*."

"What?" The boy's retreating steps had a slight echo. "You've got to be kidding me... why would she do that... how would that trap Kayla, how would that..." he went silent, aside from heavy breaths, followed by amplified cursing. "No! I won't let her do that to my dad... Kayla... Me!"

"She's gotta know he's immune by now, Roux."

"If she's after Caya's line, she will do whatever it takes."

"Who would she be dealing with? You may not be keeping up with what we used to do... But I have. And there isn't anyone needing *that* type of service."

Roux glared at his brother, stuffing his fist in his mouth. *"Just because we don't know about it... doesn't mean there isn't someone she'd be willing to trade favors with."* His garbled mumbles, spoken in Arros, would reach Farz, and Farz alone. Hoping Kayla was right about Michael's inability to understand it, he held his breath.

His brother's expression fell. "I hate it when you're right."

"Right about what?" Face red, hands shaking, Michael pulled at Roux's shirt—forcing him to look his way.

"Sirens aren't against trading favors… or drudges."

"Drudges?" Michael shook his head, pacing away before he stopped by the door. "You mean those idiots out there who do nothing aside from what she tells them to?"

Nodding, Roux ran a hand through his hair. "You're a more valuable commodity, though."

"Why is that?"

"Your grandmother's bloodline, add in the fact that you're only half Arros, *and* you're immune."

"But she can't make me do anything…"

"Yet." Farz grumbled from the bathroom doorway. "She can't make you do anything, yet." He held both arms out, palms facing inward. "Think of it from this perspective: *if* she knows someone who needs a mate, someone with your *particular* bloodline is *very* attractive. Say she makes a deal for you, and threatens your sister or your father to ensure you end up mated with *whoever* they are."

Michael paled, his hands frozen at his chest. "But I wouldn't be stuck with whoever that is, right?"

"Sure, but you'd most definitely have *feelings* develop for *her*. Because there is an element to that with our biology. Even being half Arros—you should have those instincts." Farz grumbled, leaving the doorway. "Which brings us back to your father… *he* had feelings for Arzi. It's harder for him to resist her than it was when he was your age, because of what I *just* explained."

"Wait…" Michael pivoted, his attention on Roux. "*He*," hooking his thumb over his shoulder, he continued. "Was saying *your* natural instinct wanted out… as in you're biologically *obligated* to be around my sister?"

Roux shrugged. "More or less." It was a bit more complicated than that, but he didn't want to get into the details with his wife's younger brother.

Gaping, Michael stared at him. "And my sister, is she… that way with *you?*"

Roux nodded, inhaling through his nose.

"I was *trying* to explain that *earlier*."

"You could have just said it *outright*! I'm not an idiot!" Closing his eyes, Michael pressed fingers along his forehead. "So you're saying… if she finds a way to make me agree to *that*… I'd be stuck having those kinds feeling for some crazy Siren that I don't even know or care about?"

"I'm not the one you should ask that question."

"If that's what my dad has going on with Arzi... what about my mother? She's half Arros... Doesn't that mean he'd feel that way with her?"

"Possibly."

"*Possibly*? What kind of answer is that?"

"Your mother is half human, and so is your father."

"Obviously..."

"*They* can have children together, *without* mating the way Arros do."

All three of them froze at the sound of the door opening. Roux turned on his heels, a breath escaping him at the sight of their visitor.

"Am I interrupting?" Robert rubbed a palm over his glazed eyes.

"Dad?" Michael spun to face the doorway. "What are you doing here?"

Robert checked both directions outside the door before entering. He watched the door close; the tension bleeding away once it did. "*Technically*, Arzi never said I couldn't *explore* on my own." He tapped his chest, where the restraints rested for Roux and his brother. "The only restriction I have..." he turned toward the door. "Is not leaving this level of the ship." He looked around the room for a moment, his hands trembling. "Where's my daughter?"

"You don't know?" Farz grumbled, dropping into his bedding. "*She* came by for her *hours* ago."

Her father turned to question Roux, his expression taught. "She left me to do *something*... but I have no idea what that is. Or why it would involve my daughter." The latter, he added—seeing Roux's glare.

"Dad..." Michael covered his face with one hand. "Do you love my mom?"

Robert's jaw dropped open. An audible click reverberated through Roux's head—being the closest to him. Blinking rapidly, his breaths matching the pace, he huffed. "Why would you ask that?"

"Do you *love* my mother?" Michael growled, inducing Farz to jump up from the floor to hold him back.

"Of course I do, Michael..." Robert struggled to steady his breathing. "What is wrong with you?! Why would you even question that?!"

"I saw the way you looked at *her*!"

Chin dropping to his collarbone, Robert shook. "Michael... I... I can explain."

"We've already done that for you." Farz stepped back, letting Michael sag to his knees.

Robert slid to the floor, forcing his son to look at him. "I love all three of you, Michael. You, your mother, Ka... k..." groaning, he bit his lip. "Your *sister*… No matter what Arzi does, or doesn't do. That. Will. *Never.* Change."

"Did she force you to stop calling her Kayla?" Michael's eyes reddened.

Nodding, his father closed his eyes. "She wants me to call her Ahni. Thankfully, your sister hates the name. Arzi hasn't corrected any other term I use in its place."

"Do you love Arzi?"

Robert swallowed, quietly. Turning to gage the expression of both Roux and his brother, he nodded. Before Michael could complain, he held out his hand. "Not in the way you're thinking. Your mother is the only one I've ever *loved* like that."

"Did you even *try* to mate with her?"

Roux spun away from them, his eyes threatening to fall from their sockets. Farz cursed, retreating to the bathroom. As much as he wanted to join his brother, Roux couldn't abandon them to the potential of Arzi walking in on their conversation.

"Yes…"

Stumbling over his own feet, Roux stared at his father-in-law. "What?"

Taking several steadying breaths, Robert placed a hand on Michael's shoulder. "Before I married your mother… I," his eyes couldn't decide what direction was best. "I was fixated with being around her. I should have realized what happened when I did it. But I didn't know how that was supposed to work with humans. I thought she was then…" Robert laughed quietly. "My parents weren't exactly open about that part of their marriage."

"You and Mom…"

He nodded, his eyes still closed. "Your mother is half Arros. She would have known what I was doing—even if she *was* keeping it from me."

"So, you're not just missing her, you're *missing* her?"

Robert glared, softly, toward Roux. "How much have you told him about *this*?"

"Just the things *you* should have!" Farz bellowed from the bathroom. "Y'know…" he leaned against the door frame, shaking his head at Roux. "I think I see why she liked you from the start, *little* brother… You're just as bad as her father is."

Kayla's father sighed. "I only kept things from my children, to keep them safe from all of this."

"Lot of good that did…"

Tossing his brother the worst glare he could muster, Roux contemplated letting Kayla subdue him after all. Maybe give both Robert and Michael a turn, before beating him to a pulp himself.

Rubbing both hands across his face, Robert shuddered. "Yes, Michael. I *miss* her. And *that* is keeping Arzi's control to a minimum."

"Okay, first thing we do when we get out of this—get the kid a girlfriend." Farz laughed, earning glares from all three of them.

"Farz, if *anyone* needs a girlfriend—it's you."

His brother raised an eyebrow. "We've been over this before, little brother. I. Do. Not. Do. *Relationships*."

"Your behaviors, say otherwise..." Roux held his hands out for Michael and his father, pulling them to their feet. "If either of them sees you two like this, it will not end well. Whatever you two need to discuss, it needs to be done in there." Directing them to the bathroom with a nod, he glared at his brother. "Keep in mind, we have no way of knowing when they'll be back."

"My *behaviors* are none of *their* business." Farz moved out of the way, shaking his head at the look Michael gave him.

"Farz..." thinking better of mentioning the habits his brother had being none of his business, he shook his head. He sat on the end of the bed once the bathroom door closed, dropping backward with a sigh.

His brother dropped back on the bed next to him. "Hey, this is *cozy*."

Reaching above his head for the pillow, Roux slammed it against his brother's face. Unfortunately, that created *another* problem.

49

Kayla

The sounds coming from beyond the opening door left Kayla's breaths falling in rapid motions. She recognized the voices, though the words were spoken too quickly—in Arros. If it weren't for the addition of crashes and groans, she'd have walked in on them—that instant. Her mother's laughter was a *bad* sign. Kayla leaned carefully across the threshold.

"Roux!" The momentary distraction allowed Farz to land another blow, knocking him off balance. Her husband rolled away from his brother, landing on his hands and knees. "What are you doing?!"

In glancing around the room, she verified that nothing—aside from the bed—looked different from the way it was when she left. Hoping she'd caught the argument early, she ran to his side. "Roux?"

He spit blood on the floor, cursing his brother's temper.

"My temper? *You* started this."

She glared down at Roux, his split lip and the darkened patches around his face glaring back at her. With the decision to forgo covering her face with both hands, she curled her fingers. Roux had a temper, but she knew better than to think Farz hadn't incited the brawl. Her father and Michael peered through the bathroom door, both frozen there. Michael watched her assess her husband. Their father stared across the room at the Siren throwing her head back with laughter.

The motion to look up at her was halted by Roux tugging at her hand. He shook his head. "Don't. It *was* my fault. I hit him first."

Sitting back on her feet, Kayla scowled at Farz. She wouldn't let it end there. "What happened?"

Michael shrugged. "Dad came by to check in on us. Next thing you know, Roux hits Farz and..." Michael waved about himself, his eyes never leaving Roux.

"Perhaps we should let them work this out—in our absence, Steven." Arzi shook her head, laughing as she turned to leave.

Kayla's father helped her and Roux to their feet, wrapping both arms around her. "I'll be back to see you soon."

All composure fled the moment the door closed. "What were you two thinking?" Her voice reached a level that had them all covering their ears. Not bothering for herself, Kayla glared at the three of them. "This..." she waved her hand around the room. "Just cost me any time I could have had talking to my father!"

Roux flexed his jaw. He wiggled it from side to side while wringing his hands together. "It was my fault."

"No, I won't take that answer!" Kayla trudged toward Farz, her head rattling with every step. The closer she came to stand in front of him, the wider his eyes seemed. He ground his teeth, attempting to turn away from her. But she wasn't having that, not when she wanted answers. "What did you do to make him angry?"

Swallowing, Farz looked at his brother while biting down on his lip.

"Kayla!" Michael's voice merged with her husband's, the two of them rushing to her side.

Roux forced her to turn and look at him, his hands on both sides of her face. "Kayla, breathe. Please, Kayla, you *need* to let up on him."

Kayla recoiled, gasping. Roux pulled her to him. He whispered encouragement towards the bed. Once sitting, she glanced up from the floor. Farz panted, holding his chest with one hand and biting the knuckles of the other. "Farz... I... I... I didn't mean to..."

"He knows." Roux sat beside her, stroking hairs away from her face while his brother retreated to the bathroom. Farz closed the door behind him.

"At least that door isn't barred from use without your help." Michael laughed shakily, sitting down on the opposite side of her.

"Roux, is... is he alright?" Sobs tore through her throat, destroying any clarity her words normally held.

"Shhh, Kayla, it's okay. We've all been under a lot of stress." Roux glanced toward the door, closing his eyes. "Farz just needs a minute to compose himself."

Michael draped his arm over her shoulder while leaning his head against hers. "Dad is okay. We spoke with him *before* they started off on each other."

Calm rolled through every nerve in her body. The effort expended left her brother leaning more against her. "Mikey, be careful... it can be exhausting—sometimes."

He blinked, stretching his eyelids. "I don't think I've ever done *that* on purpose before."

"Thanks, Mikey." She pulled him in for another hug. "Is he really okay?"

"Yes, and no." He shook his head. "Well... as okay as you can expect right now."

"I won't let her take you away from me." Her grip tightening around him, Kayla pushed the thoughts away.

"I'm not going anywhere, sis."

An internal battle waged as she fought to keep the calm he'd given her. She rubbed a hand through his hair. "This is my fault, all of this."

Roux exhaled behind her, rubbing his hands up and down her back. "Kayla..."

"This is more my fault than yours, kid." Farz grumbled, his voice pained.

Releasing her brother, Kayla clenched Roux's hand. "How is any of this your fault?"

"The sensor... I was going to fix it."

"But *I* told you to let her and Robbert do it." Roux's response had the two of them staring at each other.

Was that why they were fighting? Did Roux blame his brother for not maintaining the sensors—causing them to be out in the open for her mother to find? Kayla shook her head and leaned against her husband. She'd chosen to drag her father along, but it was almost Michael who went with her. They could easily shift blame to any detail in their situation. It would only make it worse. She prodded Roux to look at her. "Roux, why did you hit him?"

"Because Farz *insinuated* that if you weren't so composed, he'd have slept with you before now." Michael's voice rattled through her head as she traded glances with her husband and his brother.

Her mouth dropping open, Kayla released a strangled gasp. "You're the *exact* opposite of Roux, aren't you?"

Farz nodded, his glazed expression never leaving her.

Kayla fell back into her husband's arms and buried her face in his chest. "You should have told me..." her muffled response heated the shirt where her lips met it. The research the two of them had been working on for years, Roux's side project he'd enlisted her help with, was to help his brother. "Does he know?"

Roux rattled his head, stroking his hands down her back.

"Know what?"

She watched Roux, his eyes focused on the patterns of the floor, his breaths steady. With an effort to stifle the groan, she prodded him. "Roux... You've been working on it for years..."

"We've..." he smiled for her benefit, moving strands behind her ears. "And we're not there—*yet*."

Kayla had assumed his choice in the side project was to soothe her own concerns about how others would react to her. She'd failed to realize the major motives behind it. "You wanted me to meet him. That's why you worked so hard on it. Isn't it?"

Michael backed away from Farz, his arms folded over his chest. "I don't know what either of you are talking about, but I'm guessing it has something to do with your long hours in the examination room."

Roux nodded for both of them, lifting his gaze to meet his brother's. Kayla watched both of them. Farz closed his eyes and turned away from them. "*You've* been trying to isolate the gene, haven't you?" He disappeared into the bathroom again, but left the door open. "You are wasting your *time*, little brother."

Her husband blinked in rapid succession. "We've been trying a *different* approach." He stroked Kayla's shoulder with his fingertips, eyes on his brother's retreat.

She swallowed the saliva pooling in the back of her mouth. The *different* approach was using *her* Siren genetics in a way no one had access to. Roux was so concerned that she would decline when he presented her with his idea. They'd been dating for over a year at that point. But Kayla knew him well enough to judge his words for what they were, not what she would have assumed when they first met. Her altruistic best friend wanting to give her the chance to live a normal life.

"*Any* progress you've made is gone now."

Kayla squinted, attempting to measure the reaction she could see from Roux. He rolled his eyes—almost playfully. "Farz, any progress we made is safe—with *father.* He is the only one who knew we were working on it." He held her face in his hands. "It wasn't just for Farz." He laughed. "Okay, maybe it was *partially* for Farz when I first considered it."

Floodwaters threatened to rage from her eyelids. Sniffing the sensation away, Kayla hugged Roux. He *hadn't* omitted everything. Her husband loved her enough to give her details she wouldn't worry over, enough that everything he told her would fit between the pieces of his life he had kept from her—when the time came.

"Your father, grandfather, Michael, Farz, *Me*..." Roux held her tight to his chest. "I just wanted you to live your life, unguarded, free of the fear you live with every day."

Sniffling breaths, she pulled him down. Arms around his neck, she kissed him. Leaving it brief for the benefit of their brothers, she shook her head at him. "I love you, Roux Tahali."

His smile wavered, breaths short. "That makes it worth it." Pressing his forehead against hers, he sighed. "Farz, *if* we're right, it won't be a perfect fix. But you will be *immune*—to Kayla."

Facing her husband prevented her vision of Farz's reaction, though she could hear the acceleration of his heart rate—her brother's too.

"You're using my sister's blood? When she's pregnant? Are you an idiot?"

Farz laughed from the bathroom, the echo oddly vacant. "You realize they've been in a relationship for eight years, right? Having sole access to her for that long..." Kayla turned to see him shake his head. "He wouldn't need it anymore."

Pressing her lips into a thin line, she rubbed her abdomen—intentionally. Roux was far more protective than her brother realized. Even with the altercations they've had over the matter. The flutter of movement toward her hand interrupted her laughter.

Roux shifted his position, his pupils dilating. "What's wrong?"

She laughed again, tears cascading from her eyes. "Nothing..." shaking her head at the concerned glances all three of them gave her, Kayla pointed with her free hand. "I can feel him moving."

Roux pulled her into his embrace, before pressing a hand to the exact position she had hers. After a moment, he pulled his hand back and stared at her. "*Him?*"

It was her turn to be honest. Kayla gulped air, pressing her hands against her lap. "Yes, *him.* That's where she took me." It had been the most thorough examination she'd ever had in her life. Not that her father had allowed many

doctors near her when she was growing up. The few times she had needed medical attention, her grandfather found medical doctors who specialized in Arros biology—and discretion. Joining as an apprentice, they gave her a detailed examination for their records. But Roux pulled strings to avoid her genetics raising too many red flags. Her biological mother wasn't looking for superficial answers. Part of her wondered what her mother was really up to.
"Arzi was concerned all of the *excitement* might have affected our child." Her husband lifted her from the bed, pulling her into his lap. "Your son is fine, Roux." He would stay that way as long as his grandfather arrived before he was born.

"Right now," Roux exhaled. "I am more worried about his mother."

50

Rivan Tahali

Fire ignited beneath his skin, the tingles lingering beyond the slap. "My son's daughter!" She slapped him again, cursing him in their native tongue. "You knew who she was the whole time! Did he?"

"No," Roux barely remembered the details of that night. Mina knew he'd not only helped them leave, but involved Roux. She made sure both of their sons couldn't remember any of it, solidifying Rivan's distaste for his mate. "Roux doesn't remember he was there."

Caya covered her mouth with one hand, slapping him again. "You would use a toxin on your own, son?"

"It was Mina's doing—not mine."

Caya's eyes widened. "You let her do that to them?"

"She did it before I intervened." Shaking his head, he rubbed a hand over his face. "It was for the better. One day, it will come back to him."

"And he'll hate both of you for it, Rivan." Caya growled, her face heating. "All of this was your doing. You wanted to draw *her* out."

"I never intended for Arzi to *actually* find them."

Head thrashing from side to side, she slapped him—again. "You're a hypocrite, Rivan. All those years you came to me, *worrying* about your sons. Your mate may have had them trained to destroy lives, but you orchestrated lies for them to *live*. *You* are no better than *Mina*."

Hanging his head, Rivan exhaled through his nose. He'd known his dearest friend would be angry with him, despite his intentions to protect her granddaughter. "Without my sons, Steven would never have escaped the first time, and Arzi would have found all of you—a long time ago."

"You knew where we were?"

Nodding, Rivan braced himself for another round of abuse. Thankful his mate wasn't present, for many reasons, he shuddered in silence. "I couldn't let you suffer at her hands. Not again."

"And you thought throwing your sons into *this* would make it any better?"

"Farz and Roux are capable."

"Recent events do not entice me to agree with you."

"Roux would give his life to protect her. Farz would give his, to protect his brother."

"And are you prepared to lose *both* of them?"

Rivan dropped into the chair behind him, rubbing his hands over his face. He hadn't known Caya's son would arrive until it was too late. It was stupid, but he couldn't blame her son for being concerned about his daughter. Not knowing the danger was close enough to draw Arzi's attention directly to Roux and Kayla the moment Steven arrived was another strike against him.

"At least *some* of the young man I cared for remains." Caya paced away from him. "What am I supposed to tell my husband?"

"What he needs to hear."

"That's *rich,* coming from you, Rivan."

The door opened. Caya's mate entered, their younger children squabbling behind him. "This isn't the time to discuss it. Ask your mother how she feels about it *later.*" Noticing his wife's scowl and Rivan's presence, he stiffened. "What is *he* doing here?"

Her eyes threatened to tear a hole through Rivan's chest, but the expression softened with her attention on Alan and their children. "I wanted an explanation, and *he* wanted to give it in a place Mina wouldn't intrude upon."

Pressing his lips together, Rivan stood. He nodded to her family. "I've returned your son's wife to you. Farz and Roux smuggled her away before we lost contact with them."

"Julie is here?" Their daughter rushed by them, barreling toward her room.

"Eva, she's resting. Don't pester her."

"I won't!" Everyone, aside from her father, winced with the delighted squeals coming from beyond the door.

"Brandt," both of his parents glanced in his direction, their gazes wavering. The boy nodded, hurrying from the room to join his sisters.

Alan Morris waited for the door to close before he turned on Rivan. "What are you doing here?" He held a hand up. "And don't give me the excuse about returning Julie to us. You could have sent her across the ship, *alone.*"

Caya crossed her arms, closing the gap between her and Alan. "He's known where we were this whole time." Her mate moved to stand between them, his eyes flaring.

"I never contacted your mate. Our past was over, a *very* long time ago."

"I'm supposed to believe you? I know my wife wants nothing to do with you, but I wouldn't put it past you—to not accept that."

"Dear," she held his shoulders. "Rivan was here to explain *other* things."

It was true; he cared more for Caya than he did for Mina. But that was a very long time ago. "I came here to make sure Mina wasn't keeping you in the dark."

Caya rolled her eyes at him. "Perhaps you should explain why you pushed your son to pursue our granddaughter."

Her husband's green irises faded, hands fisting. "Does Kayla know?"

Caya answered for him, her hands shifting to Alan's waist. "No, and neither does Roux."

Pivoting between the two of them, the skin between his brows compressed. "But he knows who we are. He was part of *everything*..."

"They obscured his memory of it." Caya held her mate against her.

"You gave your son a toxin? Are you insane? He was sixteen!"

Flinching at the volume, Rivan stepped back. "Mina did what she felt was needed to protect our sons. You both know that this will only end when *she* is dead. If anyone ever found out Roux and Farz were involved—then, their lives would have been just as much at risk as *yours* were."

Alan shook his head, grasping at Caya's hands around his waist. "Your son doesn't know he was involved in helping us disappear, and now he's married to our granddaughter."

"I only encouraged the feelings he already had for her. I didn't intend to place him in her path for that purpose." He knew Roux would feel obligated to protect her. Putting him at her side ensured Arzi wouldn't win. "Honestly, Alan, Caya, I hadn't considered my son would fall in love with her."

"I'm sure you didn't." Caya huffed. Alan turned to her. "Please consider, our children do not know us by the names you do."

"Nora and Dennis Erickson? You couldn't decide on something less *average*?" He didn't bother holding back the laugh. *Of all things...*

"Don't, he isn't worth this..." she held her husband's arm back. "Rivan, you need to leave. Your place is with Mina."

"Everything I have done has been to protect you and your family from *them*." Stopping at the doorway, he turned to face them. "Consider your younger children in this. If we do not stop them, they will come after Brandt and Eva. She already forced the location of your home from Steven. You won't be going back there. Anything you left behind was either destroyed or taken by her drudges."

Caya buried her face in Alan's chest, her hands clutching his shirt. Her mate wrapped both arms around her, his eyes shifting from the door to her and back. "If we never see them again, it's on you."

"I will do whatever is necessary to bring them back to us." He meant it.

51

Nivia

Acid roiled from her stomach, threatening the lining of her throat with every breath. As a captain in the Arros military, she'd seen so many things mere civilians would gag over. *But this...* Nivia blanched, turning away from her commander.

"I could relay the information to the Admiral instead."

Shaking her head, she strode away. "*He* needs to hear it from me."

"It wouldn't kill him to get it from someone else for a change." Her second in command forced a smile, one in which all of her teeth showed. The sound of them grinding together proved even she was just as disturbed by the news.

"You know as well as I do, he'd prefer it came from me."

"What he prefers, and *what* you need, are two different things, Madam."

"Commander Vani, as much as I appreciate the concern, *they* are my brothers..."

Vani sneered at the data before turning to face Nivia. "*This* isn't their doing. And even if it were, you've been cleaning up after them long enough."

"If only it were that simple, Marcielle."

Commander Vani nodded as she turned away from her. "I'll relay the information to your private archive."

"Thank you, Commander."

Nivia trudged through the corridor, keeping the blatant lie plastered to her expression. The rest of the crew didn't need to know what had happened to the mining planet her brothers were on. The lack of evidence that Roux and

Farz were there was the only thing keeping her strides even. If they'd been on the planet when the devastation took place, there would have been bodies to account for.

Once the door to her chambers closed, Nivia leaned against it, granting the air trapped in her throat—the freedom it desired. With a hand to her temple, shaking fingers sought the pressure points to relieve the strain on her head. "Breathe, Nivi, breathe." Two weeks since she left her father's side, and all she had was a lack of evidence. Last reports from Roux, had detailed Farz being held by Arzi with the others. If their luck held out, she'd still believe she had the right brother.

After several breaths, she made her way to the communications console. Separate from the entire server on the ship, it had a direct link to her father's personal unit—and that of Farz's. She'd never been *overly* fond of his antics, but she loved him—and Roux.

The Admiral answered slower than he normally would, sweat covering his brow. "Thank you for saving me from your mother. She was about her favorite past-time when this came through."

Her mother's favorite past-time, railing on their father for his distance and his insistence on meddling with the *twins*. She allowed the chortle before sobering. "Arzi is at it again."

Eyes wide, her father moved closer to the screen. "How many casualties?"

"Not a single living soul, creature or otherwise, survived what she left behind." Her mind heaved at the thought of what might have happened if Arzi hadn't known her daughter lived on the planet as she started the data transfer.

He cursed, rubbing a hand over his jaw.

"I've never imagined I would be glad to know they're in the hands of a Siren. But..."

Nodding, her father's attention shifted to the data she'd sent him. "The alternative..." The Admiral closed his eyes. "We'll find them, Nivi."

"Caya and Alan?" Nivia had always liked them. Caya was a socialite, much like her mother, but she wasn't the type that made Nivia feel tainted associating with. Alan was a good man, despite what her mother thought about his being *human*. They'd raised a gentleman. At least it was what she could remember of Steven. She doubted Steven remembered her, but she liked his temperament. Had he not been confiscated during the raid, Nivia imagined he would have chosen a military role. As the child of his *influential* mother, he'd have found his way to *her* bridge. Preferable to the events of his life, for all parties involved.

Her father's expression faltered for an instant. She'd known he was fond of Caya, despite the unfortunate alliance he'd been forced into with her mother. "They have two younger children now."

Unable to give him the condolence he wished for, Nivia raised her brow. She knew he'd put their past behind him, also that he'd never quite moved on. "Putting their lives on complete hold would only have drawn more attention to them—smart of them to blend with the communities they chose."

"And stupid."

"Possibly. They weren't aware of how close she came to finding them. They're lucky they had the younger children..."

"Undoubtedly. I don't think *she* was expecting Steven to have a family of his own—aside from the girl."

"That *girl, Father,* is your daughter now."

He shifted in his seat, glaring over his shoulder toward the camera. "I never said she wasn't."

"You should have included me in this *before*. Roux was young," and still was, in her opinion. Her brothers were never allowed the childhood other Arros were given. Neither was she. The difference was, she had the choice in it. Her brothers never had the luxury.

Her father faced the screen fully again. "You were too visible, and your brothers agreed with me."

"Brothers? Father, you told me it was only *Roux*."

"I consulted both of them."

"And you used *it* on both..." He didn't have to answer. She knew it from the thin line adorning his face.

"*That* was your mother's doing... not mine."

"And you let her?!! They were boys! You should never have gotten them involved in the first place!" She didn't need to add what she would do to him and her mother if they *ever* did the same with her son. With the urging of the anger from her voice, she glared at him.

"What choice did I have? Caya came to me. I needed a discrete means of getting them off the planet and out of Arros controlled space." Exhaling, her father shook his head. "Before you accuse me of choosing at random, I'd never do that with your boys. They've led a very different life than your brothers have. *They* were the best choice."

Grinding her teeth loud enough for him to hear over the connection, Nivia followed it with a growl. "Before my sons existed, I would have agreed with you, *Father.*"

His expression dimmed, head drooping. "Caya agrees with you."

Massaging her forehead, Nivia groaned. "Of course she does. *She* was the one who gave up everything to protect her son from Arzi."

"I will find them, even if I have to do the same."

"It's safe to say she didn't head toward Vorn."

"Nivia, we don't have time to argue about this. Kayla isn't just mixed up in this alongside your brother. She's carrying his child. I can't in good conscience allow that *woman* to have *my* grandchild."

Her jaw slid open, locking into position. Hand over her gaping expression, Nivia hissed. "You didn't think I should know *before*?"

"If you knew, your mother would have known. Roux wanted discretion for as long as possible. He hadn't even told Farz, last I heard from him..."

"He'll know now!" Grumbling, she sent a message to the Commander to join her. "How long do we have?"

"Less than four months."

"Get back to mother, promise her whatever is needed for her to allow you to leave." Rolling her eyes at him, Nivia groaned. Their arrangement was worse than most she'd seen in her sixty years of life. Thankful her own match wasn't filled with the hatred her parents harbored for the other, she cut the connection.

The chime at her door came before she could compose herself. Knowing it was Marcielle Vani, she allowed entry amidst calming breaths. "Close the door and *secure* it."

Marcielle nodded, her expression grim. She turned to do as directed, facing Nivia with her hands clenched over wrists behind her back when she'd done it. "Madam?"

"My brother narrowly avoided wiping out our chances of keeping Arzi at bay."

Patience was never in Commander Vani's repertoire. She crossed the room to stand beside her. "The attack? Neither of your brothers were there, Captain."

"The result of searching for Roux's expectant mate, who also happens to be the daughter of the woman we're dealing with."

Vani's eyes widened. "Arzi's daughter! Your *brother* mated with Arzi's daughter!" Her hands shook with the briefest of motions.

"Thanks to the Admiral's *discretion,* not even Roux knew that detail." *Until it was too late.* Not that she imagined it would make a difference. Roux was in love with the girl long before he claimed her. *Love* was dangerous in their society. At least in its genuine form. They made most arrangements based on some sort of deal, political or otherwise. Thankfully, the twins had declined the women offered to them. They'd used their profession as an excuse. Nivia almost smiled, knowing her warnings had been the root cause for their caution.

Commander Vani groaned. "We'll be working triple time to find them before anything happens to that child."

"Make sure we split the crew to account for the need. Put Lieutenant Cu on telemetry, rotating out with Mekk when necessary."

Marcielle nodded, adopting the glare of command.

Sighing with her commander's egress, Nivia dropped into her bed. It was going to be a long string of nights, one she needed a good *solid* sleep to bolster her for.

52

Commander Ban Tuhani

With the dismissal of the latest recruit, Commander Ban Tuhani slipped through the door. Months since his last reprieve, he knew it would not last. Admiral Tahali's first correspondence promised to make it up to him and his mate. The Admiral's all hands on deck order was void of any details about the mission. But Commander Tuhani was one of the few who would meet with the Admiral personally for that part of their assignment.

Unfortunately, a personal meeting with Admiral Tahali wasn't possible for the present situation. That left Tuhani to use his Command authorization codes to contact the Admiral's personal channel. The conversation promised to be interesting. More so than his vacation with the family had been—not that he intended to tell anyone that.

Behind the well-worn desk, he dropped into the decrepit chair. He'd had far too many arguments from the same position, his desk evidence of those physical and verbal altercations. He ran his hands along the largest scuff and smiled—one of the Admiral's sons was responsible for that one.

Ban pressed down on the center of his desk. It lifted—faint scratching accompanying the movement. He waited for the screen to extend, allowing for the use of the keypad, Tuhani leaned back in his chair. His fingers traversed the archaic glass top of the keypad, designed to allow the system to scan his biometrics. The Admiral had promised to replace it years before. Saliva swishing from side to side, he wondered if this mission would be the tipping point—forcing him to spend more on the dying facility. They had plenty of funding for the ships, their men—and their equipment—but they often left the training grounds and offices on the chopping block where the budget was concerned.

"Ah! Commander Tuhani! Punctual as always." The Admiral rubbed his face, his gaze meeting someone out of range of the camera.

The curt greeting to his superior, Tuhani fumbled with the settings of his display. He didn't dare mention the damage the young man made causing difficulties with the device, yet. Once the image was clear, he smiled. "Admiral. What can we do for the Empire?"

"*They've* run into some difficulties."

The Commander kept his expression blank. It wouldn't do him any good to show the Admiral how *unsurprised* he was about his sons running into trouble. They had a habit of it—even when he was their commanding officer. "What kind of trouble would require you to contact *me,* Sir?"

"They've found Arzi."

His hands latched onto the front of the desk, pulling him closer. "I thought your *sons* were retired?"

"So did I," the Admiral exhaled heavily. "It would seem, Commander Tuhani, that *you* have rubbed off on them."

"I can't say I'm surprised, sir." An internal smirk spread. He knew it was only a matter of time before the Forran boys grew tired of the monotony of normal life.

"I need your best extraction team ready, coordinates will be provided en route."

"Please tell me they didn't strike the hornets' nest by *themselves*."

"Something along those lines."

Shading his eyes with one hand, he bowed his head to avoid showing the smile to the Admiral. Roux and Farz Forran were two of his best, but they also had a bad habit of biting off more than they could stomach. Fortunately, they were his best for a reason—often finding the most ludicrous ways to survive their quandaries. The Admiral could have been calling in support, merely for appearance's sake. Unfortunately, his expression claimed otherwise.

"I believe, Admiral, that you owe me a new desk. Add on an explanation of *'something along those lines'*, and we'll be even." Smiling in full view of the camera, Commander Tuhani tapped the desk with his fingers.

"Ban, when this is *over...* A drink, and far more than that—*will* be supplied.”

53

Robert

He watched the supernova, even from a distance—and the convince of a sheltered room far from the exterior of the ship—was beautiful. Part of him wished they were closer. Another plead for the means to free his children, not wish for their deaths alongside him.

"Are you still upset with me?"

Robert turned to face her. "You intend to take my son from me, Arzi."

She moved to stand behind him, wrapping arms around him. "Oh Steven, he won't be gone. You'll see him as much as you like, I promise."

Jaw slack, he dropped his chin to his chest. Robert clenched his eyes closed. That was less comforting than it was several weeks before, when she'd told him of the arrangements for Michael. Her sister being born *after* he and Kayla were rescued, he hadn't known about her existence—until Arzi volunteered his son to be her mate.

"He will be well cared for, as you are."

"And Ahni?"

"Oh, Steven... She is well cared for. You've seen it with your own eyes."

"Neither of them *wants* to be here." The words dragged through him, like fingernails clinging to the lining of this throat.

"But we know what's best for our children, don't we?"

"Mina will hunt *us*."

"Let me deal with *that*, Steven." Arzi padded toward the closet, mulling over her choices. "You should enjoy the time you have with your son before we reach the others."

The pressure of the command in her voice caused the rush of his senses overloading, Robert crossed to the door. He never felt worse, the dismissal only solidifying his fear. Unable to even tell his children what kind of trouble they were heading for. Farz, Roux, and Michael had come to the correct assumption that Arzi planned to hand Michael over—but not to who. Only able to confirm how close they were weighed heavily on him. Unfortunately, none of them had the heart to tell Kayla what they knew was happening.

His feet carried him to the familiar patch of greenery, Kayla's favorite place to wander. It was fairly common to find her there with both of Mina's boys at her side—and Michael not far off. The dutiful father and uncles to be attended to her every need—as far as she would allow them.

Kayla sat on a bench with Roux at her side. Their backs to him, watching Farz assist Michael in his stance. The twins insisted they build upon the techniques Robert's father taught him. Arzi hadn't complained about the matter when she noticed the actions. She knew Robert could protect her as a last defense—not that it would *ever* come to it, wholly encouraging Farz's attention on the young man who would one day defend her younger sister.

With a look over her shoulder, Kayla waved to him. "Morning, Dad." The feigned smile was ever present on her face, even when her mother wasn't around.

He nodded to her and Roux, moving to stand beside the bench. He watched his son's focus waver for a moment before closing his eyes. "How are you feeling today?"

"Tired... I think I might have gotten a few solid hours of sleep last night, though."

Roux laughed softly, rubbing hands down her shoulders. "Let me know when you are ready to get back, so I can tell them." He nodded toward their brothers. At notice Robert's shifting stance, his son-in-law glanced up at him. The damage from their physical altercation was no longer visible, though Robert's eyes often drew the discoloration for him. Arzi refused to give them any of the serum for their lack of *control*. As full Arros, they cared little about the damage that would heal on its own. Neither of them showed a single mark from the bloodied fist fight he and Michael witnessed.

Unable to blame them for the altercation, he'd stood by—preventing his son from intervening. It was only a matter of time before it happened again. Arzi was constantly goading Roux into attacking his brother. Her ordering Farz to stay near Kayla at all times was hard enough on Roux. But Robert knew the effect on Farz was far more difficult, knowing Kayla was Roux's—but not being able to resist the need to be around her. His shudders at the images brought Robert out of his thoughts.

"Farz is the best for this…" Roux glanced toward the tumble Michael took—failing to avoid Farz's *lesson*. He didn't need to tell Robert how hard it was to leave Kayla's side in her condition.

Of the two, Robert preferred Roux. Having the time to acquaint himself with *both* of them, he knew his daughter had been right about her mate's nature. They were *very* different in most ways. Farz was calloused, but he showed a softer side with Michael. Robert wasn't sure if it was their situation, or that the two of them had come to terms with being part of Roux and Kayla's lives—even if they got out of the mess they found themselves in.

Roux watched them spar, his eyes taking in every movement. Unable to help but observe Kayla's mate, Robert mentally slapped himself for not realizing who he was when they first met. Roux's mannerisms hadn't changed in twenty-two years, not that he saw much of them before. Purposely smothering the memories of his initial impression of Roux, Robert dug through the recesses of his own mind for the fragments of what he once knew of the *Forran Twins*.

He shuddered at the thought of the process Rivan Tahali went through to suppress Roux's memories of the encounter. *Encounters*. Neither of them could remember the few times they'd actually been in the Morris Household—with their mother. *How could he do that to both of them?* Robert's mother had made it sound like the fling she'd had with Rivan when they were kids was in the past for *everyone* they knew. Going through the trouble to erase any notion they might have of seeing how Robert's mother once felt for him was laughable, despicable, even. And *he* was Kayla's father-in-law.

He pushed the thoughts away, diverting his attention to his daughter. Fatigue setting in, she leaned into her mate—smiling genuinely. He took some comfort in genuine affections between them. It ebbed a small amount of the sting from their predicament.

"Kayla needs to rest." Roux tucked his arms around Robert's daughter, lifting her from the bench.

Still coming to terms with their ability to communicate with the faintest of effort, thanks mostly to Kayla, ensuring he couldn't tell Arzi about the implants, Robert couldn't believe how in sync they really were. Robert imagined playing off their differences, made them a deadly team.

Tugged away from his lesson, Michael fell in beside Robert. Sweat dripped from every exposed surface of him, and undoubtedly every covered area as well. "Hey Dad." In the recent weeks, his son had dropped the, *'how are you?'* from their conversations. And while it made sense—since none of them were going to answer honestly—he missed the casual normalities they had *before.*

Unfortunately, he couldn't bring himself to do the same for his children. "How you feeling, Son?"

Michael lifted a brow and spread his arms. "About as good as I can be after Farz kicks my ass."

His sister laughed, shaking her head at him. "Trust me, he hasn't done that *yet.* I'm pretty sure you'd still be laying there, *if* he wanted to seriously injure you."

"Beating the snot out of me, and leveling me like a pancake, are two *very* different things."

"If your sister's life depended on it..." Farz laughed. "I couldn't get close enough to you before my brother finished you off." Everyone stared at Farz. Casually strolling away from them, he shrugged. "Just stating something that most of you are seeming to forget about."

Knees refusing to allow movement, Robert swallowed the pocket of air trapped in his throat. Roux looked over his shoulder at him, his eyes softening with every breath. Neither of them said anything in those moments.

"He'd never hurt either of you." Kayla's expression was shielded behind her mate. His eyes turned cold in the briefest moment before he returned his attention to the others.

Robert down on his lower lip. He dragged rebelling joints to follow them. The gaze, intended for him, meant one thing: Roux blamed *him* for their situation. Accurate, but cold. His daughter's mate wouldn't hesitate to kill him if he thought Kayla's life depended on it.

He found his normal perch at the table and adjusted his position to allow him to partially face the bed where Roux set Kayla down. Michael disappeared into the bathroom, groaning about his own smell. Hardly paying heed to any of the motions, aside from his daughter's, Robert sighed.

Arzi's sister wasn't bound to treat his son well. Arzi cared for Robert as his mate, but she was manipulating him at every opportunity. Her sister would have to find *other* ways to manipulate his son. Unable to put it past either of them to use Kayla, Robert rubbed knuckles over his eyes.

"Things have gotten worse, haven't they?" Farz sat down across from him, folding one arm over the other on the table. "I wish you could tell us *how* much."

So do I. Sufficing for a grimace, Robert propped his head up on both hands.

"Of the four of us, I understand—more than you think." Farz inspected the nails of one hand, flicking debris from them.

"I don't doubt that..." Robert closed his eyes, attempting to ignore him.

Roux's brother spent every moment possible spouting ideas to him, hoping for some spark of recognition in his expression. It wasn't efficient by any means, but it kept him distracted and *away* from Kayla.

"Farz, can you leave him be for once?" Kayla yawned, turning away from them. "This is his reprieve from my *mother...*"

Grumbling, he slid back in his chair and rested his feet on the table. His gaze drifted to the door of the bathroom. "I can't guarantee anything we teach him will do him much good here."

Robert suppressed the groan. They'd had *this* conversation several times, though Farz seemed additionally concerned in the renewed topic. "What does his being immune mean for him?" Sludge ran through his veins. He adjusted his position to allow eye contact with both of them. "If *he* gets out of this..."

Roux glanced down at Kayla, crossing one knee over the other, where he sat beside her on the bed. "*When...* we get out of this," he shrugged. "He can technically choose anything he wants to. He doesn't have to go back to Arros and train as a hunter... if *that* is what you're referring to."

"*That* decision was made for us." Farz interjected, dropping his feet to the floor.

"Unlike, my *brother.* I do *not* miss it." Roux shifted to lie beside Kayla, eyes trained on the ceiling.

There wasn't much comfort he could take from the statement. Robert watched his daughter shift to wrap her arm over Roux's chest. Farz huffed across from him, shaking his head at his brother. "You say you don't. But you're the one who climbed a cliff in a downpour *and* attempted to disable this ship *alone.*"

Fingers clutching at his chest, Kayla pulled herself closer to Roux. "You did what?"

"I thought he already told you I attempted to take this beast out of the equation." Roux avoided her gaze, glaring at his brother. "I'm laying here, right now, because I got *caught* doing it."

"No," shaking her head, she sat up. "The other thing he said."

Roux closed his eyes, pressing fingers into his forehead. "I was trying to keep up with them when they took your mom, Michael, and *Farz.*"

"You could have fallen. What would we have done then?!"

"I didn't."

"You *could* have!"

"Kayla, I didn't. I knew what I was doing."

Exhaling rapidly, she glared at him.

Robert flinched with every movement his son-in-law made. The last thing he needed was to make Roux angry. He'd seen enough of what the twins were capable of. Any more and he might regret letting Kayla leave home—to a greater extent.

Roux sat up. Grumbling toward Robert and Farz, Roux rubbed both hands over his face. "I was trying to find you," motioning toward his brother, he growled. "And *you!* You said you wouldn't tell her!"

"No, I said it was fair for her to blame me for you *having* to do it. I never agreed to *not* telling her."

"Would the two of you, please, calm down?" Robert held the sides of the table. "We don't need another exhibition of how much of a beating the two of you can dish out—or survive." The latter part set Kayla rolling away from them, her hands trembling.

Farz leaned back, his feet once again rested on the table.

Roux exhaled a shaky breath, covering his face. "Our father used to take us climbing when we were boys." Turning, he placed a hand on the bed. "I continued to meet up with him after our parents separated." Inhaling and exhaling slowly, Roux tugged at her arm. "I knew what I was doing. If I thought I was going to fall, I wouldn't have done it."

"You never told me you enjoy climbing..."

"An adrenaline rush..." shaking his head, Roux huffed. "It's better than killing people."

Incapable of stifling the snort, Robert smiled as apologetically as possible when his daughter glared at him.

"Why did you stop?"

Raising both brows, Roux looked around the room. "I haven't ever stopped."

"Doesn't it seem, I don't know, *strange* to you... that he would be in peak physical condition for a doctor?" Farz chuckled, folding his arms over his chest. "You think his devilishly perfect physique is from running every morning? It takes a lot of work to look and *be* this good. Granted, we're both losing our edge—a bit—cooped up as we are, but you've had to realize how ridiculously easy it is for him to carry you." Farz held his hands out, eyes wide. "I'm not saying you're fat, but marriage to my brother has been *good* to you."

Kayla scowled, her eyes trailing between the two of them.

Beckoning her to him, Roux pulled her into his lap again. "Farz has a fairly decent setup at his place." He rubbed one hand over the back of his neck. "We weren't running *every* morning. Though, honestly, I *did* run there."

Farz stood up as the door opened.

Tightening his grip on the table, his back to Arzi, Robert watched Roux and Kayla from the corner of his eye. Whatever she had planned, he couldn't protect them from it.

"Come with me, Dr. Tahali."

54

Roux

Roux tightened his grip on Kayla's wrist. Gentle prodding from his wife remedied his mistake. Her mother's presence, even though it was less frequent than any of them expected, brought the threat of losing what differentiated him from his brother. Neither of them knew he and Farz stumbled onto that little detail. One was completely oblivious to the plans. The other was purposely hiding the intent.

"Come with me, Dr. Tahali…" her mother repeated the order, glaring across the room. Her gaze drifted toward his brother, a sneer appearing. "Farz…" the melodic hum of her inflection left his brother blinking like an idiot.

"Leave him out of this!" Growling, Roux moved to stand between them.

Her tongue struck her teeth, the noise grating in his ears. "Oh, but I *need* both of you." She ushered him aside with a wave of her hand and laughed. "Bring your brother with us, will you? I don't think he wants to cooperate."

Before Roux could react, his brother wrenched an arm behind his back—the momentum landing them on the floor. Kayla's whimper had both of them staring up at her. Her eyes darted between them, hands shaking. The rhythm of her heart wasn't as erratic as it should have been, despite the shock on her face. His breaths felt foreign to him as he stared at her.

Kayla's nails, bitten beyond her normal nervous habits, were the first thing he noticed from his position. He'd known she was doing it, though he hadn't seen how red the tips of her fingers were. Her expression had Roux struggling against Farz's grip on him, his stomach rolling with every breath. She only did that when she feared what people would do around her. "Kayla?" The distraction allowed Farz to lug him to his feet, pushing him towards Arzi.

Four quick steps toward him, Kayla stopped. The tisking from her mother causing her to cringe. She worried her bottom lip with fisted her hands.

"I'll return them to you, as they are, provided..." her mother ran a finger along his chest, stopping on the restraining unit. "He cooperates."

Relinquishing his efforts, Roux hung his head. She hadn't used the full potential of her toys yet. Once she did, he'd have no way to stop her. The only thing stopping him from lashing out, ending her life where she stood, was his inability—his objection to injure his brother in his present state. Arzi was fully aware of what he and his brother were capable of. She wouldn't let him close enough. If he tired, she'd likely kill him—in front of Kayla.

"Stay with her, Steven. She needs extra care for the foreseeable future."

The familiar murmur of pain was strangely absent as his brother dragged him toward the doorway with the Siren at the lead. Breaking eye contact with his wife, Roux's expression lingered on that of her mother's. He'd assumed Kayla was the only one who could lead them about, wrongly. Grumbling internally, he bit down on his tongue. When he looked back through the doorway, Robert held his daughter to his chest—whispering soothing words into her hair.

Farz muttered an apology, digging his fingers into Roux's wrists.

"You are close, nearly inseparable, I understand." Arzi laughed at them, leading the way through the corridor—toward the lift. "All the better that you should *share* her."

Roux made to pull away, hoping to take advantage of his brother's distraction. Anticipation of the movement allowed Farz to have him in a headlock before he could reach Arzi. "Shouldn't she be allowed to decide on that *herself*?" The words couldn't carry the sting he'd intended, his brother's arm tightening around his throat.

Standing with her face in his, Arzi raised an eyebrow. "She did. She chose *you*. And if she wants to *keep* you, her decision will include *both* of you." She waved her hand as she boarded the lift. "Let him breathe properly. Ahni will complain if he's damaged."

His brother's hold loosened and fell away, though he stood between them in the lift. "You think Kayla will let you destroy her life, and *his*?" Roux motioned with both hands toward Farz's chest. "She isn't like you, Arzi. She never will be. You'll only encourage her to *hate* you."

She sat down, crossing one leg over the other. "The decision has been made."

Blinking the pain from his perception, Roux watched her reaction. *You're not in control of this situation... are you?* Not daring to vocalize it, he stared at her over his brother's shoulder.

Facing him, his brother blinked twice, then four times, then three, and two again. The combination for the locker they'd used for private messages between them—when they were young. Roux heaved as quietly as possible. Farz was still minimally in control. Unfortunately, that control didn't extend much of a helping hand to him in their situation.

Urged through the doorway, Roux couldn't move beyond the threshold. Every nerve in his body misfired, sending him to his knees.

Farz held a hand out to him. "Roux, now isn't the time to..." eyes widening at the sight before them. He cursed, barely loud enough to register on the implants. Farz clenched his eyes shut, waiting for Arzi to pass by them. "This is where she..."

His brother's gaze on him once more, he nodded—Arzi's laughter punctuating his shudders.

"Secure him." The Siren tapped fingers on back of one of the two chairs in front of her.

"Roux..." Farz dragged him by the arm. "I'm sorry."

Shaking his head, Roux glared at Arzi. "What do you achieve with furthering this, Arzi?"

She waited for Farz to do as he was directed before motioning toward the second chair. "Take your place."

The man Roux recognized from the facility materialized out of the darkness. Tensed appendages hurried about securing the beast his brother could be to the chair. Arzi dismissed him with a wave of her hand. "The two of you are necessary." She laughed, shaking her head wildly—hair flayed out around her. "One day, you, *her* brother, and anyone else born with the recessive genes will be incapable of escaping *us*."

Arzi ran the back of a finger down the side of Farz's face. "I am told you both resemble your father..." her smile widened. "I am also told..." she sauntered toward Roux. "He is fond of *you*." Arzi repeated the action Farz's expression appeared to enjoy. Roux flinched away from her.

"It is clear you care for my daughter, *genuinely*. Your cooperation, however little you've shown, proves you care for your brother too. I wonder..." skirting him, she trailed her finger over his chest. "How much of your affections extend to your father?"

Heavy breaths expelled through his nose, Roux clenched his teeth. Arzi didn't know who their father really was. She couldn't have found that out. There were few people privy to that information. If she really knew, their military was far more compromised than he first considered.

"The Tahali lines are *legendary*! They've evaded us... until now."

Farz ground his teeth together, drawing Roux's attention to him. "My brother's fascination with the name means nothing. We're Forrans."

"*You* will not speak until I'm finished here."

"Farz..."

His brother glared, nostrils flaring.

"How interesting. He can't fight it, but he is still trying to protect you. That doesn't quite match his reputation. Though it makes this *entertaining*." Arzi stood between them, blocking Roux's view of his brother. "The two of you are exquisite specimens. I wouldn't mind seeing your *father* for myself."

"You think you understand, but you don't. Our father won't stand idly while you ruin more lives than your mother and grandmother combined."

"You are a rare entity for our species." He opened his eyes to see the Siren looming above him. "You, willingly, mated with my daughter." She laughed in his face. "A hunter of your caliber... mated to a Siren."

"I married the woman I care for!" Meeting her gaze, Roux forced air through his teeth. "She's not a monster, though you would have her be."

Arzi's eyes lilted between him and his brother. "Monster..." she sneered, walking away from him.

Roux followed her traipsing movements with his eyes, turning his head when he couldn't see what she was doing beside his brother.

"Do you think I'm a monster, Farz?"

His brother stared at her.

"Farz, you can answer me... Do you think I am a monster?"

Eyes shifting toward him, his brother swallowed. "Yes."

"And my daughter, do you feel the way your brother does about her?"

"Depends on the aspect." Each syllable pulled from him was dull on Roux's ears. "I don't love her. But she isn't a monster."

"We'll see how you feel about her when she's yours," Arzi smirked, her eyes pulling Roux's from his brother. "Your research, it's intriguing." She pushed off Farz's knees, standing upright again, making slow strides between them. "We've been perusing the data my men brought back from your *home* on the planet."

Nerves rooted in place, Roux's breaths caught in his throat. If she'd accessed his work, there were many things that could go wrong. Attempting to push the worst-case scenario from his mind, Roux watched the Siren's pace.

"It's quite fascinating. I am not sure what you're trying to achieve by it..." Arzi waved her hand. A technician emerged from the darkness at the command—handing her two vials. "However, I made some changes—to *perfect* it."

Eyes fixed on his brother's gaze, Roux pulled at the restraints. It wasn't ready. In the present state of development, it could easily do the exact opposite of their intentions. Arzi had two vials, not one. Air raging wildly through his esophagus brought with it the risk of damaging his vocal chords. Being around Kayla, it if didn't work, would be detrimental for his brother and potentially excruciating for Roux.

Ingesting the flow of curses, Roux closed his eyes. His reluctance to watch her mother ignore the safety measures his research required left his head sinking to his chest.

"Afraid to lose your immunity to my daughter?" Arzi trailed the nub of the vial along the exposed skin of his neck. "I thought you loved her?" Stopping at the base of his jaw, behind his left ear, she laughed. "No, no, this shouldn't do that. But if it does what I hope to achieve, no one like you will ever be capable of hiding from us—enabling us to wipe out every one of you."

All eight diminutive needles pierced his skin, flooding his nervous system with over ten times what he would have done—if it was ready for testing. His brother's teeth crashed together, hands wringing against his restraints. Risking the glance in Farz's direction, he shuddered. Arzi hadn't yet reached him, her eyes still fixed on Roux.

Farz pulled against his bonds, less vehemently than he would have outside of the Siren's influence, his eyes twinging with each motion. Unable to fight her direction, the groans barely carried through the implant. His brother fought to keep his eyes on him—even with the Siren's movements in his direction. The wretch knew she was right about them. Farz was always protective of him—though he'd never openly admit it. She would use that against them at every turn.

Arzi was no less delicate in her measures with Farz. "Note *everything*." She left them to the lone technician standing ready to record everything he could observe from them.

"Farz," his brother looked at him, the vessels of his eyes pulsing. "I'm sorry."

Rubbing his eyes with one hand, and the back of his neck with the other, Roux stretched the muscles of his spine. The last thing he'd remembered, Farz was growling at the technician. He blew air through rounded lips and turned his head to face his brother. His heart-rate was always a betrayal of his position.

"You might want to put those on before she comes back in here." Farz leaned against a slab, the height of what a table would have been, though it didn't look to be designed for the type of use his stomach urged for. He motioned toward the pile of his clothing, discarded in a heap on the floor. "Trust me, you don't want her eyes *roving*."

Groaning, Roux glared at him. "No, I don't." Thankful for the lack of blood stains to divert Kayla's attention from, as apposed to the last time, he rolled from the cot to retrieve the clothing. His hands froze at his sides before he could reach for his shirt. "Why did they do *this*?"

Farz stood, looking over his shoulder at the contraption. He shrugged. "Woke up here a few hours ago—like you are now." Noticing Roux's expression, he shuddered. "No one has showed up yet. So, I'm assuming if we go anywhere near that door…"

Nodding induced another groan from his brother. Roux pulled the shirt over his head. "How are you feeling?"

Farz scratched the left side of his neck, shrugging his shoulders again. "Glad she didn't try the right. But I guess she was going for consistency for *observation's* sake."

The injection wouldn't have damaged their implants, the length of the needles being far too short. Roux chuckled softly.

"She obviously made some alterations…" pointing to the cot, his brother groaned. "I doubt you'd have wanted me passing out when you tried this on me."

Nodding, Roux sat on the edge of the medical bunk.

"You said it wasn't ready." Huffing at the once again repeated motion of his head, Farz ground his teeth. "Whats this going to do to you?"

"Worst-case scenario? I…" interrupted by the doors hiss, Roux and his brother jumped to their feet—spinning to brave their tormentor.

"Roux!" Her strides brought him to her before his brain could register her presence.

Blinking, Roux looked to his brother in the same moment he wrapped his arms around his wife. "Kayla?"

"I was so worried! You've been gone for *hours*!" Rapid breaths escaped her, strumming against his shoulder. "She told me I needed to bring you back... and... I didn't know what state *either* of you would be in."

"We don't even know." Farz grumbled, shifting his stance to face them.

With a shake of his head, Roux pointed toward the door. "Is Michael still with your father?"

Kayla nodded. "She told dad not to leave until after we come back."

Following his wife from the compartment, Roux exchanged glances with his brother. If Kayla was free to move about the ship, it could prove useful. But he wasn't willing to risk her, or their child, to do what he had in mind. Any hint of action beyond the desire to eradicate his research wouldn't end well—for any of them.

Roux dropped into the seat once they boarded the lift. His head was aching, not in the way it normally did when Kayla was overly emotional. Blinking, he looked up at her as she growled at his brother.

"Farz, sit down. You look like you're going to fall over."

His brother arched an eyebrow. "I won't fall over, you..."

"I'm not incapable!" She spun to face him. "I may not look it, but I am angry right now. I am sick and tried of the games my mother is playing with *both* of you. *You* dragged your brother away from me! I don't want to think about what else my mother forced you to do to him." She jabbed a finger into his chest. "I won't let her use you against Roux. He has enough to deal with," absently rubbing her abdomen, Kayla hissed. "You can't hurt him at her whim! I. Will. Not. Let. You. You will never obey my mother again. Now, Sit Down!"

Farz angled his view of Kayla, her gaze level with his chin.

Roux knew his brother obeyed the command but couldn't see the rest of his actions, the sudden onset of nausea forcing him to double over. Wracked with dry heaves, he held the bottom of the bench for support.

"Roux!" Kayla dropped to her knees, wincing with the effort. "What's wrong?"

Body shaking with every breath, Roux attempted to take her hand. "Kayla..." rattling his head, their eyes level, Roux clenched his shut. "L... le... let... up..."

Both hands flying to her face, Kayla slumped back on her feet as everything around them spun for an indeterminate amount of time. Roux slid from the bench into her arms, blinking the unsettling nausea away.

"What did she do to you?" Tears gushing from her eyes, she sobbed against him.

Following her gaze, Roux's stomach rebelled. "Farz?" He shuffled the minimal distance toward him on his knees before snapping fingers in front of his brother's face.

Farz's head rotated toward them, slowly. "This... isn't... good."

Roux swallowed, trading glances with his wife and brother. "Kayla, how hard were you trying to *compel* him?"

She swallowed several times before meeting his gaze. "I shouldn't have... I'm sorry... I... I can't watch him hurt you."

"You won't have to." Farz's eyes were the only things that moved aside from his jaw. "You just," he gulped, the motions slow—exaggerated in his dazed state.

Roux pinched the bridge of his nose, his stomach churning with every inhale of his wife's presence. "*Your* mother, she used *our* incomplete process."

Kayla's eyes increased in size. "But we were years away from being able to safely test it. It could easily have the exact opposite effect..." pulling away, Kayla sobbed into her hands. "It made your reaction to me worse, didn't it?"

Roux prodded her jaw softly, urging her to look at him. "You need to be careful. She gave it to both of us."

"Hours. You've only been gone for *six hours*..."

He and Farz both groaned.

Rubbing his eyes with the palm of his right hand, Roux fought to steady the remaining nausea. "Kayla, she gave us ten times more than she *should* have."

His wife flung herself into his arms.

Farz blinked rapidly, staring at the door. "This isn't good."

"The first thing we do when we get back to them," Kayla's hands shook. "Is make sure Farz and Dad can't tell her what it's doing to both of you."

55

Rivan Tahali

"I don't know how you got away from mother," Nivia shook her head at her father. "But I get the feeling that she is going to blame me."

"She won't." He'd perfected his means of escape many years before. Mina would never imagine their daughter had anything to do with his egress. His mate adored and loathed him. The latter more often than the former—with his attentions elsewhere. The smile spread without hindrance. Nivia wasn't an idiot. Hiding his emotion wasn't something she tolerated from him.

"Everyone assumes Roux is more like you." Shaking her head at him, she crossed her arms over her chest. "If *only* they knew."

Taking on his mantle of Admiral, the laugh was suppressed. "You said it was sensitive."

"Yes." His daughter turned away. She slid her fingers over the display—expanding the details for him to read over her shoulder. "I have reason to believe that we have a problem that reaches farther than it *should*."

Waiting for her to continue, Rivan clenched his fists. It would not be a pleasant conversation.

"Arzi *knows* who they are."

"What?"

His daughter shuddered. "We connected to their implants, receiving only—at the range we are now."

"They're both alive?"

Nodding, Nivia moved from the console. "Listen for yourself…"

"I am told you both resemble your father… I am also told… *He* is fond of *you*. It is clear you care for my daughter, *genuinely*. Your cooperation, however little you've shown, proves you care for your brother too. I wonder… How much of your affections extend to your father…"

Heavy breaths registered from the connection, the display confirming what Rivan already knew. *Roux*… The sound of teeth clenching came from both of his sons.

"The Tahali lines are *legendary*… they've evaded us until now…"

"My brother's fascination with the name means nothing. We're Forrans."

"*You* will not speak until I'm finished here."

"Farz…"

Heavy breathing from the elder of his twin sons. Rivan cringed, curling fingers into his palms.

"How interesting… He can't fight it, but he is still trying to protect you. That doesn't quite match his reputation. Though it makes this *entertaining*. The two of you are exquisite specimens. I wouldn't mind seeing your *father* for myself."

"You think you understand, but you don't… our father won't stand idly while you ruin more lives than your mother and grandmother combined."

"You are a rare entity for our species. You willingly mated with my daughter."

Arzi laughed, the volume betraying her proximity to his *immune* son.

"A hunter of your caliber… mated to a Siren."

Nivia cut the recording before he could deduce what Arzi intended to do with them. His heart hammered against his chest with each pulse of blood. "What has she done to your brothers?"

"What do you know of Roux's research?"

Rivan dropped into the chair beside her, holding a hand to his forehead. "Please, tell me she didn't get her hands on it?" The slow bob of her head made his stomach churn. "She will take his work, bend it to her own needs, and use your brother to do it."

"She has already made the first step." Nivia sat across from him, pressing wrinkles from her uniform. "Farz's sensitivity has increased, as have Roux's symptoms."

Blowing air through his nose, Rivan dug fingers into his scalp. "This is my fault."

"I won't argue with you on that…"

"Where is she taking them?"

"You can't go anywhere near the extraction, Father. It's too dangerous. If she has even the slightest suspicions of you being there..."

Rivan swallowed the air he'd intended to expel. "She has your *brothers*."

"Let *me* handle this. She cannot know you are anywhere near us."

The pressure of his jaw threatened to crack the molars in the back of his mouth. "I will not stand Idly, while you risk your life getting them back."

"I never said you *couldn't* be involved. I have every intention of sending them to *you* once we get them away from Arzi. We don't know who is giving her information, and as you said before, *I* am too visible."

"Caya, I'm sorry to be sending this in this way." He exhaled, pressing delete on the recording. *How do I tell them this?* His daughter sent as much information as she thought he needed. Though he was fairly certain she was keeping details from him for his own good.

It was, however, enough to know there was little chance they'd get everyone off the ship—if Arzi didn't die at the hands of Tuhani—or his men. Arzi wasn't likely to let Steven slip through her fingers—again. Her informers would make a clean extraction difficult, which was why he'd agreed to stand down, let the hunters—and his daughter—do their jobs.

With the input device shoved aside, he turned from the camera and rolled his chair away from the desk. He couldn't, in good conscience, tell Caya anything—yet. She'd want to know how her son was doing, how Kayla was doing.

None of them were *doing* well.

Caya wouldn't handle the news any better than he was. She needed to be strong for her *other* children. For her mate. Rivan turned the light off, leaving the war-room locked behind him.

56

Commander Ban Tuhani

"Our objective..." Commander Tuhani turned to face the eleven other members of the extraction team. Every one of them either knew the Forran boys by reputation, or served beside them directly at some point. They'd recognize Farz and Roux without consulting the tracking data they would have once they were close enough. But it wasn't just the *twins* they had to get out—preferably alive.

Ban pointed to the display behind him with his left hand. "I don't think I have to explain who this is..." he shook his head at the terse laughter coming from his men when Arzi's image appeared behind him. "Five friendlies, two of our own included, made it off the planet—but not far enough to outmatch her. They're being held. We don't know their condition yet."

Both Roux and Farz were alive, that much they knew. He'd been told their implants were registering vitals. But they did not share the specific details in their orders. Tuhani couldn't blame the Admiral for keeping that information to himself. With the Admiral's consent, Ban would monitor everything from audio to body temperature, on both of his sons, once they came close enough.

Careful to smother the tremor in his demeanor, he continued his commentary. Their implants weren't standard issue. Being who they were, the twins were literally aristocracy among the grunts of the military force. It never gave them the leniency most might have assumed. Tuhani ran them just as hard as every other man and woman in his ranks—harder sometimes.

"Prudence is warranted here. We can't just smash and dash, gentlemen. We have civilians to consider. Do not make the mistake of trusting our men to run the show once we rendezvous. They've been in enemy hands for too long." The hum of multiple grumbles induced him to close his eyes. "You all have your orders. Do not engage until *I* give the word."

57

Kayla

Laughter came to an abrupt halt, their surroundings shaking violently. Roux vaulted across the room, pulling Kayla from her chair moments before it fell to the floor. The rapid motion left her shaking, legs struggling to hold up the extra weight she was putting on.

"What was that?" Michael's eyes darted from Roux to Farz.

Expressions passed between them, faster than Kayla could keep track. Lights flickered between their normal hue and a blaring red, giving the snarky smile on both their faces—an eerie hue.

"*That* was a warning shot!" The joy in Farz' voice didn't translate to the nerves fraying in Kayla's body.

"Tell me why you're so happy that *someone* fired on this ship?" Kayla's father scowled, closing the gap between them.

"A warning shot is designed to rattle and potentially disable—not break through the hull." Farz rambled on about the military reasons for it while Roux moved her to the bed, pulled a pillowcase off one pillow and handed her the other. In the empty case, he began tossing various items from around the room into it.

"Our sister is fond of the tactic." Roux whispered, handing her the stash of food and water.

"You think Nivia is here?"

Roux smiled, his teeth showing. "There's thinking, and knowing." He tapped behind his right ear. "She just pinged us." Blood rushed through her as Roux lifted her from the bed. Help had *actually* arrived.

"Why didn't she ping you *before* she fired on the ship?" Michael grumbled, staggering toward them.

"If Arzi was around, that would have been a dead giveaway." Farz shook his head, reaching for the bedding before he raced to the door.

"Where are we going?" Michael's tone suggested he was angry, but the trembling veins of his eyes betrayed him.

"Your room. She won't expect us to hide there." Roux adjusted his hold under her legs. "She'll have to look for us, and that'll give the extraction team time to board."

Kayla's father moved to follow them, his breaths deepening with each stride. "I can't leave this level, and neither can either of you."

"There are ways to get around that." Farz grinned. "At least for you, it will be a little more difficult with *us*."

"How did your sister know *where* to find us?"

"I planted a port, somewhere Arzi would never find it. It amplifies the signal from our implants." Roux hurried through the door, careful to hold Kayla close to him, his pace increasing with each step. "Tracking, audio, everything." He smiled. "Our sister is listening to this conversation right now."

Breathing shakily, Kayla wrapped her arms around Roux's neck. It felt too good to be true. Arzi hadn't been gone for long, and she wasn't likely to stay away after a threat from an attacking vessel. "Roux, we don't have time to get away from her."

Farz rattled his head, his gaze locked on the direction of the exit. "She's not coming, yet. We have time."

Her father clenched his eyes closed for a moment, shaking away the look he'd given her almost every day. "It can't be this easy."

"Oh, it isn't." Farz groaned, slapping the mechanism to Michael's domicile. "Inside now!"

Roux moved completely into the room. Turning to face the door, he backed away as far as he could once Farz entered behind her father and brother. "Kayla, whatever happens…" he breathed deeply against her hair.

"Maybe we should drag the mattress in here," Farz looked into the bathroom. "Just enough room for it in there."

"You are NOT shutting me in there."

"Shhh." Roux rubbed his hand down her back. "No point in doing that."

Roux stepped up on the bed—her still in his arms. Back to the wall, he slid to a sitting position. "The point is to *keep* her calm, Farz..."

Kayla avoided eye contact with Farz, biting at the already shortened nails from her fingers. It hadn't been the best idea to force him to keep everything from her mother. While it kept her from knowing Roux was worse off every time she slipped up and used her aura, it had also made it much more difficult for his brother to keep his hands off her. Unfortunately, it hadn't negated any of her mother's previous orders of him. Agreeing that everyone had to play along with Arzi's demands to some extent, Roux made sure Michael was on board with their plans months before.

Months... Capable of going into labor any time, Kayla dreaded the accentuated *problems* that would create. Farz was always watching her. He couldn't help it, but it was rather disturbing when he smiled at her a little *too* longingly. She tried focusing on the potential inability to do what her mother wanted her to. It kept her sane—to an extent. But even Roux worried she *could* do what her mother required of them.

Swallowing, Kayla prodded his chest. "How far away is this extraction team?"

Eyes unfocused, he held out a hand to quiet her. He cringed. "It's going to cut it close, but we can distract her—if needed."

"You can't distract her, Roux!"

Roux grumbled, hanging his head. "Hard to explain that. No, Arzi hasn't done anything stupid *recently*..." sighing, he turned to Farz. "Care to explain it to her?"

Farz shook his head. "*You* explain it to her. I'm going in there." He pointed to the bathroom.

"Yes, Farz disconnected his feed, no, he's fine—for now at least." Roux cringed. "Niv... he can't be left alone with Kayla, even after we get out of here... Stop for a second, and I can explain." Sighing again, Roux stroked Kayla's cheek. "It is going to be okay, I promise... Niv, Arzi wants him to..." he coughed, rubbing a hand over his forehead. "Once she has the baby."

Her husband cringed. The door to the bathroom opened, Farz stuck his head out, glaring at Roux. "Sometimes, I hate that she can get through whenever she wants."

The compelled smile didn't reach Roux's eyes. "She's screaming at him."

Michael laughed, covering his mouth in the same instant. "Can't say I can blame her."

Roux *did* smile then, shaking his head at Michael. "Unfortunately, I can't avoid hearing the thrashing she's giving *him.*" He nodded to where his brother retreated once more.

"Can anyone connect to your communications link?" Michael fished out a granola looking bar from their stash.

"Any officer," Roux watched the bathroom door. Kayla, still sitting in his lap, leaned against his chest. "With the appropriate access codes," he rolled his eyes before turning to his head to face her brother. "But our sister doesn't need that. Nivia's is sort of hard wired in. If she is close, she can connect directly to ours. *If* she wants to."

The thought crossing her mind, Kayla shifted, sitting beside him on the narrow bed. Pressing her back to the wall, she took his hand in hers. "You've talked to your father using yours, haven't you?"

He laughed. "*No.* Not since we met. Farz would have heard everything, and I didn't want him to know I was still in contact with our father." He pulled her hand to his chest. "But he linked to me on occasion—when he was close. He's the only one who can drop in to either of us—individually. Not that it really matters. We *were* usually close enough that both of us would discuss it, anyway."

Kayla's father sat down in the chair across from the bed, shaking his head at them. She cringed, thinking of what she had to do to prevent him from mentioning anything they said in private—when her mother wasn't around. He could tell her vague details, but nothing that would compromise their situation—more. She looked forward to releasing him from the obligation once they were out of her mother's clutches.

Life had gone smoothly. As smoothly as being held captive by her mother could, the threat of her having to take Roux's brother on—looming over them.

"This is cutting it close, isn't it?" Her father rolled his sleeves up, flicking something from the cuff before he faced them. "Them showing up, now."

"They were following the trail I could leave. *And* we sort of had a head start."

Her father nodded. Hands pressed against his thighs, he blew air through his nose. "I don't enjoy waiting in here."

"Me either." Michael stared at the closet doors. None of them had even bothered to mention what they found in it the first time they explored the confines.

58

Commander Ban Tuhani

"Sir,"

Commander Tuhani imagined the customary grimace that accompanied the tone coming from his partner.

"Why does this feel like we're getting off easy?"

Considering the answers, Ban grumbled to himself. "We're not dealing with *her* mother, remember?"

"True, but..." Von's attention wavered. "Her daughter and Forran are here. You'd think Arzi would take that a *little* seriously."

The lack of guards huddled around the levels his advance team reported when they had gone as close as they could to the Admiral's sons, was unsettling. Her entourage... He shuddered at the thought of what those *men* went through at her side, never more grateful for his immunity—even with the mild discomfort it brought with it.

"*His* brother too. I'd wager she knows what they are and doesn't think her daughter needs the buffer of expendables in comparison."

"I hope he's right about not *all* of them being this bad, for his sake." Clearing his throat, his junior partner—often his second in *other* situations—stood beside him. Unable to physically see the other, they relied heavily on their tech. The tracking on the display inside his helmet took up a third of the visual range, designed to be faint enough for him to see through.

Grunting his agreement with Von, Commander Tuhani made his way around the corner to the position they'd agreed upon. The kid who stormed out of his office after handing in his resignation had ideas that would have brought the Arros empire to its knees. Ideas that would make Commander Tuhani's profession obsolete—if he was right.

59

Kayla

Having somehow fell asleep against Roux, Kayla woke up to his startled movements. Her hands grasped at his shirt as he stood, lifting her into his arms—again, Kayla whimpered at the sight of her mother standing in the doorway.

"You're backed into a corner, Arzi. You know it. Our mother will never let you keep us."

"I can still take what is mine." Her lips twitched, teeth bared. "Steven, we're leaving." She nodded to the single guard at her side, the only one she'd dared to bring inside the small room. "Bring the boy."

"No!" Kayla's lungs expanded painfully, her eyes locked on her father. Roux shook a single finger in her face, the others he tightened around her arm, his reminder for her to stay calm. No amount of steady breathing would help them as her mother toyed with her father's control of himself.

"I can still kill both of you, remember that…" She backed away, allowing Kayla's father through the door.

"Kayla!" Michael lashed out at the guard approaching them, taking the blow intended for Roux as he moved between them. Her brother fell to the floor and didn't move.

"Michael!" Roux practically tossed Kayla to his brother, who caught her with little effort. Her husband threw the guard against the wall and knelt beside Michael, hissing with the movement.

"He's mine! If you want your mate, you'll leave them to me." She held the control for the restraints in one hand, rattling it for emphasis.

Every part of her screamed, no sound escaping beyond the hand over her mouth. Debating about biting his brother, Kayla glared up at him. Farz shook his head as he tightened his grip on her. Her gaze returning to Roux, Kayla shuddered at the sight of his retreating steps. *No! You can't let her do this!* The attempt to struggle against Farz was useless. She knew he was stronger than Roux and she could hardly do anything for herself—as it was.

The guard shook his limbs before lifting Michael from the ground. His glare settling on each of them, he backed away. Arzi ripped out the controls for the door from the outside, causing the door to close like a trap. Her father's efforts to regain control faded from view in an instant. "Dad!" Her scream caused both of them to flinch once Farz's hand left her mouth.

"Find something sharp!" Farz dumped her on the bed before racing across the room. He and Roux dug through every cabinet they could find. Farz turned over the chairs, kicking at the legs beneath them.

"Sharp, what is sharp going to do for us?"

"What about this?" Farz held up a jagged edged chair leg.

"No, we're not using that!" Roux barked at his brother, disappearing into the bathroom.

"It could work on the panel, though. We still have to get out of here. She could send guards back for us." Farz didn't pay her arguments any attention. "Niv... She has a jig, it is connected to the restraining units Arzi dumped us with. We can't go anywhere without being near it—and thus her..."

"And I'm not dragging my wife anywhere right now."

Kayla's head spun. Pressing fingers to her temples, she focused on keeping her ability honed—controlled. They didn't need her panicking to the point that she incapacitated them—unintentionally. "Wait! You want to use that to get *it* out of my arm! Are you crazy?"

"I'm not letting him near you with it, Kayla." Roux's efforts came back less fruitful than his brother, at first glance. "It isn't as sharp as I'd like it to be, but it's better than *that*." He motioned to the frightening shank his brother held.

He made his way to her with the thin metal contraption protruding from his fingers. "Tweezers?"

He knelt down beside her. "Kayla, the longer we wait, the farther she gets with your father and bother."

Exhaling, she nodded to him.

"Where is it?" Roux held her right arm, brushing fingers along her biceps.

"There." Farz jabbed his finger toward the area above Roux's thumb.

Her husband prodded the area with his fingers. "Got it," he looked her in the eyes, his smile wavering "Kayla, this *will* hurt."

She grasped the blanket with her left hand, shoved a clump between her teeth, and looked away. The slash of the pointed end ripped a scream through the material, blocking the volume from her husband and his brother. Not daring to turn toward him, she watched him use the tweezers to pull the jig free. Each movement produced tears and earsplitting cries muffled by the blanket.

"It's out!" Roux jumped to his feet, snatching the chair leg from his brother.

Farz dumped the pillowcase out on the bed, flipped it between his hands and wrapped it around her arm. "Go! I'll stay with her."

Roux's grunts were followed by the sound of pops and screeches as the door opened.

"Wait! Roux, she can still stop you!"

"Kayla is right, Farz. I can't even get close to her." Roux knelt beside her again, holding her face in his hands.

Farz groaned, throwing his head back. "Give it to me."

Roux tossed the bloodied device roughly the size of a small coin. His brother caught it—bolting from the room in the same instant. "He'll get to them."

Kayla didn't dare mention Farz being less capable, even with the mandate to not obey Arzi.

60

Farz

Farz rounded the corner toward the lift. His fingers clenched around the jig as he placed it in the zippered front pocket of his pants. Strange enough, her blood had the faintest aroma of her. *That is just screwy.* He smelled his hand, verifying it wasn't just in his head. "Is it just me, or does her blood smell *oddly* sweet to you?"

"You can't be serious?" He could almost see the disgust on Roux's face when he grumbled his response.

"No, really, it smells good." Cringing, Farz shook his head. "Okay that sounds weird, now that I think of it. Do you think it has something to do with what Arzi did to us?"

"It could be... Nivia, we *need* to explain something to you."

Grumbling, Farz ran by the lift. Their sister was going to kill them.

"We already know what she did..." Nivia's voice was tight, her teeth chattering—slightly. "We've been receiving audio from your implants for some time."

Lovely... Farz slowed his pace, slapping a hand to his face. "So you know she's made Roux's reaction worse and that I can't stop looking at her chest."

"Keep talking like that, and I'll kill you myself." His voice lowered, Farz assumed to speak to Kayla because the connection cut again.

"No need to be shy. It isn't like I haven't heard your pillow talk before, little brother."

"Really, Farz? You're an Ass."

"You're just now realizing this?" Roux laughed

"I rarely seek either of you out, intentionally..."

"Aw, now I'm offended."

"Shut up, Farz!" They both growled over the connection.

"Back to the matter at hand. Roux, is there *any* way you can get to a computer and access your files?"

"I don't know where the nearest terminal is." Roux groaned.

"*She* has access to everything from her *chambers*." Kayla spat the last word like it was a plague. Farz couldn't really blame her for it.

Their sister sighed. "Roux, you need to get in there and deal with *your* problem. She cannot, I repeat, *cannot*, do to others what she has done to you two."

"You're assuming he can,"

"Neither of you do anything, without an exit plan..." Nivia left the words hanging. Roux had a few tricks up his sleeve—even where computer warfare was concerned.

"I can do it."

"Do as much damage as you can."

"You want him to break into Arzi's chambers? Are you insane?"

"Farz, Niv is right. We can't let her leave with my research."

"Roux, you can't leave that room! And I am too far from you to come back. If I do, I'll lose Arzi. Kayla's father and brother will disappear with her." Groaning, Farz slowed to check around another corner. "Don't tell her I said that."

"I wasn't planning on it." His brother made excuses to his wife before speaking to him again. "If I don't get there, she'll wreak havoc on our forces."

"How are you going to get through every door between you and there? Hm? Kayla can't exactly drag you."

"Let me figure that out. You worry about Robert and Michael. And Farz, be careful."

"You too."

Shaking his head, Farz dropped into the access hatch. If he'd considered Roux's research *before*, he might have insisted on escorting them to the lift at least. Sliding down the ladder, he counted levels in his head. If he timed it right, he could reach the smaller launch bay before her. She wasn't exactly dragging her feet with an enemy fleet closing in, but she hadn't seemed to be in much of a hurry either. *What is she playing at?*

"Roux, we might not have as much time as we thought. You've got to get moving!"

61

Roux

It was a terrible idea. But he didn't have a choice and there wasn't time to consider other options. It was going to take Farz too much time to get back to him. Kayla sagged against him, tears wetting his sleeves. Unable to give her the reassurances he wanted to, Roux squeezed her hand. It wouldn't remedy the pain of her heart, but it would at least give him some way to show he understood she was hurting—more than she wanted to show.

They stood inside the doorway, just shy of a few feet, the two of them looking at each other. "Okay, we have to do this fairly fast, and I can't carry you."

"I can go wherever, so..." Kayla sniffled while wiping tears from her face. "You sprint it... I can come out after you do."

He grimaced with the effort to let go of her hand. Nivia grumbled over the implant. Time was of the essence. Her team was only fifteen minutes from reaching the ship. Minutes they might not have. And definitely too much time for Arzi's drudges to take what they wanted and run. Not to mention, she still had time to change her mind and come back for Kayla. She was already slipping through their fingers with Kayla's father and brother.

Roux shook the jitters from his hands, smiling for Kayla's benefit. He took several paces backwards—towards the bathroom, then sprinted across the room. Just before reaching Kayla, he bent his knees—leaping through the doorway. He fell to the deck outside the room, breathless, holding his chest where the restraint sat.

Kayla hobbled through the opening and knelt at his side. He waved off her attempt to drag him further from the door, glaring at her. They'd already discussed the problems tied to her exerting herself. Her pulling his massive build would only slow them down in the long run. He rolled to his feet, ignoring the lingering zing of pain, and helped her stand instead.

"One down..." he cringed, taking her hand in his. "At least four to go..."

"How are we going to get you out of the lift—if it works the same way?"

"Hope Farz gets to your mother first?" He shrugged, earning a smack to his shoulder. He looked around at what they'd labeled as the atrium. "We know your mother's area was that way." He pointed off in the distance as he considered the time it took for Arzi to return on more than one occasion.

"Roux... I already know where we're going." Kayla shuffled in the direction he'd indicated.

"You never..."

"You, Farz, Michael, and Dad are her prisoners... remember that." She grumbled something he'd commonly heard from her but didn't understand.

He hung his head and followed his wife down the paths that looked far too tranquil for their mission.

"I wasn't insinuating that I'm fine with how she treats any of you."

He would never assume it. He'd watched the vibrancy he loved fade from her and hadn't been easy. No amount of wanting their child to see a side of their mother they wouldn't in the present situation was going to help. "I know. We're almost out of this."

"Not if she gets away." His wife stopped and stared at the door in front of her. Kayla rubbed her stomach with trembling hands.

"Can you open it?"

Kayla nodded, releasing his hand. The door opened with a touch of her finger to the mechanism. His wife moved into the room first with her eyes closed. Roux followed her a little too quickly, almost falling over. The lack of any pain, physical or otherwise, had him staring around the minimalistic design—similar to the other two rooms he'd seen.

"That seems a little too easy. It didn't even do anything." He pointed to the restraint device.

"I don't think she imagined you would ever *intentionally* come in here." Kayla shuddered, easing her way around the bed. She pointed toward the console the other two rooms didn't have. "You sure you can get in from here?"

"Only one way to find out." The screen blinked twice before settling on the most recent work her mother attended to. *No* security? He swallowed saliva, hoping it didn't mean what he thought.

"She has security on the exterior doors. Most of the idiots can't even get through it. I wouldn't be surprised if they had restraining units on them…" Kayla rolled her eyes, absently massaging her stomach.

He curled his fingers into his palms, smothering the shudder. "She's started uploading everything." Roux ran his hands over his brow. He searched for his files—but nothing came up. His lips between his teeth, he rattled off things she could have labeled it as—in the silence of his head. Kayla watched the door, her hands shaking. *Kayla… no… Ahni…* The decision to search under his wife's birth name brought back four records. Two of which made his internal struggle spill from his mouth.

"What's wrong?"

He rattled his head for her, pointing toward the door. The last thing he needed was for her to see what he just did. She growled at him to hurry. Exhaling through his nose, Roux pressed the icon labeled *'Ahni's son'*. Of course, she'd hide his work there. Fingers trembling at the thought of what Arzi would do with his research *and* his child, he pulled up the records—fingers flying over the input. *I will never allow you to manipulate my son.*

Moving away from the console, he turned to Kayla. "It's done. We need to go, preferably, *before* she realizes what I have done to her system."

Their passage through the opening to the opulent enclosure was less difficult than expected. Though he insisted Kayla let him lay there for a little longer than she was comfortable with. Her gaze shifted erratically in every direction for signs of trouble while she waited.

Stopped outside near the lift, Roux kissed her hand. "Hold your hands over your ears and don't watch—once you get us going."

She practically shoved him through the doorway, growling about his callousness on the issue. It didn't help matters when his body convulsed, mid-fall, his knees banging against the front of the bench inside it. Rolling to the floor, attempting to keep his arms from tangling with her legs, Roux held his breath through the pain.

62

Commander Tuhani

"Tuhani, please tell me you *are* listening to this."

"*We* are." Refraining from commenting on the banter between her and her brothers, Ban shook his head. The Forran Twins were always an odd pair, but they'd give their lives for the other.

"Farz will need help. Arzi still has the command unit for the restraints."

Commander Tuhani grimaced behind the shelter of his suit's cloaking. The tone of Captain Forran's voice wavered with each word. He knew she had every reason to be concerned for the boys, but she was too close to them for this mission. Why the Admiral dragged his daughter into the fray, he would never understand. Though she was quite useful when he considered it. Her crew took on a vital role in tracking down the details of where they were going. Nivia Forran was a bloodhound on a mission. A mission to save her younger brothers—from their own folly.

"He won't be alone..." swapping channels, Ban relayed the orders to his fifth team. He and his partner weaved through the corridors toward the lift. If Roux and his mate were successful, they'd need help getting out. They'd need it either way. He just hoped whatever they were risking their lives to do was worth the effort to move from their present position.

"The *Doc* is three levels above us—but he's moving again, Sir. Forran is approaching team five."

"I see it." cutting off the retort for using the label every hunter under his command used since Roux left their squadron, Tuhani moved away from the alcove they used to wait out their orders.

Four hours, waiting for the right moment. He could have reached Roux and the others, at least given them a heads up on the situation, but that would have made getting them out more difficult. Reminding himself they had one shot, he grumbled for his partner.

"They certainly have a way with people—don't they?" His second peered around the corner, eyes trained on the drudges rushing toward the launch bay. Team five waited just outside it.

"Sir… Forran bypassed Kern and Mani. They're amending their position to intercept."

Ban increased his pace, running toward the lift. "Naz, Corran, cover their slack! Mani, do *not* let her get off this ship!"

63

Kayla

Kayla tried fighting the trembles of her fingers, arms, legs, and every bit of clarity in her mind as she covered her mouth. The lift was going too slow, and the compartment was too small to keep him far enough from the entry. Continual spasms prevented him from reaching the bench, laying at her feet.

She bit the knuckles of her right index finger and slid to the floor. She struggled with the hem of her shirt for moments that felt longer than they should have been in the lift, before she tore a length free. A battle with unsteady limbs, she folded and rolled it into a cylindrical shape.

"Roux, please don't bite me." Her voice came out in a squeak, her hands drifting toward his mouth.

Beads of deluge ebbed from his eyes. Minimal movement of his head begged her to stay away from him. Ignoring his protests, she slid closer to him. She shifted her weight, allowing her to pull on his shoulders and bring her legs around him. The sluggish movements finally had her holding him still between her knees. Bending forward was even more difficult in her state. If she could wedge the material between his teeth, it would at least stop some groans—and damage to his lips or tongue. The success left her with her hands at the sides of his jaw. She leaned back against the curved end of the bench, rubbing her hand under her nose. It wouldn't help to complain about her own pain at that moment. He'd only blame himself, even though he was worse.

The lift halted, sending her shoulders against the edge of the seat. Pain filled breaths ripped from her throat as she prodded her husband. "Roux..."

He was still shaking between her bent knees and her pants were saturated from his sweat. With the back of her fingers trailing over his brow, she noticed the traces of blood coming from his ears. *NO!* Alternating movements with her legs, she groaned loudly with each failed attempt to keep her knees from hitting him in the face. "Sorry! Ugh! I'm useless!"

Spilled into the corridor, Kayla rolled to her side. While tossing ideas of how to force him out of the lift through the recesses of her head, she dismissed each one for various *stupid* reasons. She couldn't push him out. There wasn't enough room to even get over him to wedge between him and the seat. Couldn't pull him, either. Not this late in her term. She had more than a month left. But that kind of exertion could easily hurt her—if not force labor. One hand slapped to her face, she reached for him with the other.

"Roux, wake up, please! I can't do this without you."

Something touched her, covering her mouth in the same instant she was pulled away from the lift. Unable to scream for help, her limbs flailed. *Roux!* Her eyes expanded in their sockets. Her head pounded with each intake of air through her nose.

"Shhh, it's alright... we're here to help." The male voice was faint, almost nonexistent. "Get him out of there before that thing kills him."

Panted breaths brought the threat of passing out in the arms of whatever held her off the ground. Roux's body lifted from the floor, held an invisible force that pulled him toward her and her *rescuer*. If they were—*such*.

"We've got to get them out of sight."

"She's going to pass out on you, Commander."

The grip over her mouth loosened, air rushing to her lungs. "Is he..."

"He'll live, but we've got to get you two off the ship now."

Strikes at whatever appendage held her away from Roux, Kayla elbowed the man behind her. "No! His brother is still out there. My father and brother too!" The two voices were silent, movements still heading away from where they needed to go. "Please! She can't take them!"

"Young lady... you and your mate are in no condition to assist Farz and the *others*. We are getting you off this ship. Now!" They changed direction again, arguing with someone else in Arros. "This way." The voice in her ear escalated. "I need you to keep it together, kid."

She watched Roux shoot through the doorway, nearly stumbling in her attempt to follow them. The door closed, an air pressure seal hissing moments before a helmet flew across the room—revealing the face of the *Commander* who came to their aid.

"Set him down." The disembodied head reached her husband, dropping the rest of the cloaking from his suit as he knelt down beside him. "Forran! Wake up!" He slapped both sides of Roux's face. "Secure him. We leave now. The others can handle Arzi's forces."

The second form appeared before her, flipping the latch on a helmet. He placed it under one arm and pointed toward the far corner of their shuttle. "I would feel a lot more comfortable if you stand over there... please." He massaged fingers over his forehead.

"You..." She backed away in the direction he showed. "You're immune too..." forcing breaths the way Roux taught her, Kayla fought to pull her hormones—and everything else—in check.

"And you're a Siren." The younger man of the two shook his head, laughing at something in Arros she'd never heard before.

Looking over his shoulder, returning from the cockpit she couldn't see from her position, the Commander pressed his lips into a thin line. "Hell of a choice... that's for sure." He turned his attention back to Roux, jamming a vial into his chest.

Gasps rent the silence as her husband shook more violently than he had with the device's effect on him. Struggling to contain herself, Kayla pulled her knees as close as she could with the ever-growing bump that was her child. Unable to remember how she sat down, she wrapped her fingers around her knees.

"Kayla!" Roux's voice tore at her eardrums.

She had every intention to crawl closer, but stopped at the Commander's hand held out toward her.

"Your mate is safe. She's right here..."

"Commander?" Jerking from side to side, eyes blinking in rapid succession, Roux turned to their rescuers. "Von... Tuhani? What the hell are you two doing here?" Noticing Kayla over their shoulders, he shifted. "Kayla!" Tethered to the stretcher along the wall, he glared at the man he'd addressed as Tuhani—wincing with every movement.

"Mated to a Siren..." Commander Tuhani laughed. "And I thought *Farz* had the dangerous taste in women."

Mustering the best scowl she could, Kayla felt her nostrils flare.

"She's going to panic... either let her come to me, or get me off this thing."

Von stepped aside, motioning toward the space he'd been standing in. Not waiting for the hunters to change their minds, she shuffled toward him on her knees.

"Breathe, Kayla, look at me..." Roux rubbed his cheek against her hand. "Ban won't let anyone near us, we're safe."

64

Farz

On his toes, leaping back, Farz avoided the fist aimed at his face. *And* the kick intended to knock him off balance. Glaring into the eyes of a human, he shook his head. "Mistake one... You are trying to contend with someone who was born faster and stronger than you are." He threw the feeble excuse for a man against the wall, bones cracking on impact.

Farz let the body drop to the ground, stepping over him. Pity wasn't in his vocabulary. At least it wasn't before he and Roux met Kayla. Their line of work had no room for the sentiment. Targets and objectives. Someone else always had the unlucky task of sorting out whose lives were worth pity.

"Forran..."

He froze, focusing on the direction of the voice as he threw his hand out. It met with the materials he knew well, his hand disappearing with the effort. The laughs sputtering from his target were quieter than they would have been without the equipment he tightened his hand around.

"We're here to help..."

"Mani?"

"One and the same... She has seven guards on her, her mate, and the boy."

Biting back the argument, Farz nodded. "The priority is the kid. She's less likely to fight for him and she won't hurt his father."

Mani grunted in agreement, still invisible to Farz. "Let us take the lead, take out a few of them, *before* you try doing anything stupid."

Sure, he'd let them have the fun. If only because Arzi was likely to turn the power to full on the contraption requiring surgical removal. She could kill him in an instant. The thought hadn't even phased him until Mani held him back. "The boy is immune. She's using his father to keep him in line."

Mani pressed his hand to Farz's chest. The angle betrayed his position directly in front of him. "Future investment?"

"Possibly..."

"Kern, get as close to the kid as you can. I don't want Arzi knowing we are here—yet."

The gene presenting itself was less common in recent years. The hunters would find Michael a tantalizing addition to their ranks. Especially when they realized he was a Skym too. Roux was going to kill him for letting that detail slip. Even if it was exactly the push they needed for the kid to matter enough to rescue.

Kayla was important because of Roux. But Michael was excess baggage. Young, impulsive, and likely to get in their way if his father needed help. As long as they knew he was a potential weapon against the woman they were chasing, they'd be all for keeping him alive. Even if it meant having to drag him, kicking and screaming, away from his father.

65

Robert

Heart leaping through his throat with every step away from his daughter, Robert ground his teeth together. His eyes darted between the guard carrying his son and Arzi. "This ship is under attack, and you left *our* daughter back there!"

Arzi ignored him, barking orders into the void.

Blood pulsing behind his eyes, Robert shuddered. If Kayla was right about Roux's migraines, he wouldn't be able to get close to them. Even if they caught up. Arzi wasn't going to let him go. His ability to fight her aura couldn't match the level of control she pushed on him. At some point, she'd be too exhausted to continue. But he'd be long gone mentally before she hit that point.

Six guards formed a circle around them, their eyes scanning the darkened corridors. The lights cut just before they reached the corridor leading to *wherever* they were going. Robert had never been familiar with military vessels. In the four months they were trapped aboard the monstrosity, he'd only paid attention to the dome. He did not know if it worked like this, lights cutting out when they were under the gun—so to speak. Unfortunately, the posture of the guards told another story.

This isn't supposed to be happening. He chanced a look over his shoulder to ensure his son was still breathing in the drudge's grasp, sucking in a breath at the sight of Michale's head injury. It happened so fast. He hadn't even noticed the blood until it glinted in the flicker of emergency lighting.

"Arzi, he's bleeding…"

"I can see that." She laughed. "Maybe next time you won't let him behave that way."

"Let him…" the whine expelled through his teeth sent shivers down his extremities. "He was protecting Kayla."

She barely moved her neck, eyes angled toward him. "Do not focus on his injury. Keep moving, no matter what happens here."

Air ricocheted through his chest cavity. *You left Kayla behind. If anything happens to this ship—she could die, and now you won't even let me worry about my son… Arzi… How could you do this to me?* Robert shook the melancholy away. He was slipping, Kayla had warned him he was. But he didn't see it the way she did.

"Do not let them take my mate!" Arzi's voice had Robert covering his ears, his feet tangling with each step. She wrenched his arm forward, dragging him closer to her.

Blinking the strain away, Robert watched the guards split off to spread out around them. *Wait… what happened to the other guy?* Behind them in the distance, the emergency lights illuminated something. He shuddered as Arzi pulled him farther from what he knew was the missing guard.

"Michael…" reaching with his free arm, he found his son's wrist and tightened his fingers around him. He didn't care what the guard had to say on the matter.

Their pace wavered and turned, with his perceptions ebbing from him. Arzi was pushing her aura out like fog. His eyesight blurred with every step at her side. Unable to tell if it was the tears she wouldn't allow or the effect she had on him, he curled his fingers tighter around Michael's wrist.

The three remaining guards—aside from the one carrying his son—split off. They took up the rear as they reached what appeared to be a small loading bay. In his bleary state, it could have been a trash tube—for all he knew.

Arzi screamed at the guard. Robert's haze dropped away as she pulled Michael from his grasp and tugged Robert through the airlock. Thrusting Michael into his arms, she turned away from him. "Take careful care of your boy. We wouldn't want him damaged before we reach our destination."

Breaths ripping free of his lungs, he lifted his son's chin. "Michael?"

Eyes twitching, hands trembling, Michael blinked several times before their gazes met. "Dad…"

Motion outside the airlock drew his attention as Robert looked up from his son. The cycled lighting illuminated the rapid approach of the one person who could help them. Arzi still had the restraint's remote on her—but she wasn't holding it. Pupils dilating, the light of the chamber drew mist from his eyes.

"Take care of your mother." His arms extended fully, pushing his son through the closing airlock.

"What have you done?"

Turning to face her, Robert dropped to his knees with the motion of the shuttle disengaging from the ship. "You can't hurt him now."

66

Michael

Michael fell away from his father, landing hard on his left shoulder. The popping sound ripped from him with the cries of pain. He blinked tears free of his eyes, struggling to breathe. What was his father thinking, shoving him through a closing airlock?

"Michael!"

He turned his head to view the sounds rumbling toward him. Passed the bodies in a line toward the only direction they could have traveled from. Gagging, Michael looked away.

"Michael!" Farz pulled him to his feet by his injured arm. Farz's eyes pulsed with the groan escaping him. "Your father just saved you. Don't let a little pain ruin what he gave you!"

Thankful that Roux's brother adjusted which arm he held, Michael stumbled to keep up with his pace. "How did you get here without Kayla?" He regretted the question the moment Farz held up the bloodied jig, gagging—again.

"She's fine. Roux is with her… they're safe." His eyes glazed for a moment, scanning the recesses of the nearby walls. "Our help was closer than I thought they'd be."

Michael jerked away from him, wincing with the motion of his left arm. "Then why don't we…"

"She's gone, kid. Unless you have an exposure suit hidden somewhere nearby with enough punch to catch up to that shuttle of hers…" Farz shook his head. "We'll get him back. We just gotta get ourselves out of this *alive* first. Okay?"

They walked for several feet with Michael's head throbbing. Farz stopped to inspect his injury. "Kern?"

"Behind you."

Michael turned to face the voice. But no one was there. He shook his head, blinking with the regretted motion. He winced as he took in the expression on his rescuer's face. Was Farz talking to someone that he couldn't see? Remembering the discussion about the suit Roux used to get into the bunker, Michael's eyes widened. "Hunters?"

Farz only nodded, grumbling in Arros to the man who followed them. He picked up on a few words here and there. But not enough to understand what they were talking about. He knew Farz was pissed, that much was easy, the ability to read him had become easier over the last few months.

Farz's expression softened once he noticed Michael's attention. "I'm sorry, kid. She got through there while they were killing the last one. You're damn lucky your old man shoved you back out."

Tremors of air raked through him, his body convulsing with the fear. His father was gone. He couldn't save him from Arzi. *What good was all that training?* Flinching with the pain bending at the elbow brought with it, Michael bit down on his hand to ease the shaking of his nerves.

Everywhere they went, they stepped over more bodies. Unable to stomach the sight after another hall of drudges, Michael closed his eyes. Farz led him less gruffly. More voices merged with the blurred dialogue rumbling in his head. He limped beside them uselessly, unable to count the voices any more than he could understand their words. Moments dulled with the pain radiating from his shoulder and his head. If it weren't for the gentle prods of Roux's brother, he would have collapsed in a heap somewhere among the trail of bodies.

67

Roux

While glaring through the transparent partition, Roux paced the interior of the isolation chamber. Protocol was merit no matter how much he argued with the medical staff about the situation. They wouldn't listen to him until after they made their assessment. Just over four months in close quarters with a Siren was enough to alarm the most iron stomached medical personnel. But he'd mated with one, *that* was enough to encourage careful observance of them both.

It wasn't until his father sent instructions to allow the two of them to stay together that they even considered it. Kayla was huddled under a blanket behind his parading movements. Commander Tuhani had compared him to a predatory animal defending its pack. It wasn't a joke. He'd have done the same. Many species made similar comparisons when referring to the protective instincts of Arros males.

The medical team dispersed with the arrival of the Admiral. Roux's shoulders sagged for an instant. Closing his eyes, they squared off with his exhale. "Father..."

"Roux..."

Kayla blinked, tightening the blanket around her shoulders in his peripherals. "Farz' link isn't active and these idiots won't even speak to me."

Admiral Tahali nodded, stopping a few steps from the partition. Lips pressed into a thin line, Roux's father exhaled through his nose. "Sedated." He indicated the woman in their company before he continued. "Apparently she, and her mother, did a real number on him."

"Anything Kayla did was *unintentional*."

"I'm aware of that. But they want to see it for themselves. You know how these types are." The Admiral shifted his footing. "They've finally approved the medication for you. Should see it soon."

He rubbed sweat from his brow with his sleeve. Roux chanced the look in Kayla's direction. "She hasn't intentionally used her ability since we got here. Can't they see that?"

"I just said, they'd approved it. Son… They're *hesitant* to accept her presence, but they're not *against* it. It will take time for them to understand your choice. Don't let their precautions rile you."

"He's sick, and they've trapped him like an insect on display. There isn't enough ventilation in here to prevent him from getting worse. I can't hold off the minimum anymore… not as I am…" his mate opened the blanket, revealing her rotund belly.

"Which was why they insisted on keeping the two of you apart…" his father pressed fingers into his brow. "But I knew I'd never hear the end of it from you."

The motion to shift his shoulders was oddly relaxing without the restraining unit to hinder the full movement. His only positive experience with his *father's* medical staff had been their efforts to remove the restraining units from him and his brother the moment they arrived aboard the vessel. The skin still held an uncomfortable itching sensation that rarely faded. But it was healing quickly.

"Taking into consideration, she's been doing what she can to hold it off— they realize she isn't out to hurt *you*."

Not daring to argue with his father, Roux sat beside his mate. "I'll be fine." She leaned into him while breathing heavily against his shoulder. "It isn't as bad as you think, I promise."

"I assume my son explained why you and I couldn't be properly introduced before?"

Kayla nodded and Roux's hand.

"I hope you'll forgive me for the deception. I was concerned my attention would give you reason to push him away."

Roux grimaced. He turned his head to allow a view of both his father and mate. "Our meeting wasn't chance…"

"No." Roux's father pulled a chair toward the glass. "I should have warned you. But I was concerned how you would feel about my intervention. *Especially* after you told me…" he gestured toward Kayla.

He rubbed a hand down her shoulder. "He's known about my interest from the beginning." Kayla leaned against him, forming an o with her mouth.

"I assure you, I wasn't trying to force the two of you together. Though I am glad to see it worked out for both of you."

Lifting her chin with his free hand, Roux smiled for his mate. "I wouldn't trade the last eight years for anything." He closed his eyes, leaning his head back. "When can we get out of *this*?"

"Once they've ensured the medication helps, they'll move both of you." His father sighed. "Farz will remain where he is…"

"And my brother?" Roux opened his eyes in time to see Kayla clench her fists.

"He'll join the two of you. All of you will continue to be under observation for a few days once they let you out." He pressed hands over the pant legs of his uniform. "You should be out of here within the hour… as long as you take what they give you."

He left Kayla behind in the quarters his father provided them with and made his way to the care unit. The Admiral gave express consent for him to head up Farz's treatment. None of the medical staff argued against it. Most of them wanted nothing to do with the long hours and care Farz needed. Several of them shied away from Roux any time he crossed their paths. He hadn't considered mating with a Siren would earn him a greater degree of intimidation than he had as a hunter alone. While it gave him a bit more room to do his work, it was going to cause more problems in the future. Especially when Kayla could accompany him.

The sight before him when he entered wrung out his veins. Light-headedness spreading, he leaned against the nearest console.

"That bad, eh?" Farz sat on the edge of the bed beyond the barrier between them. He rubbed fingers over bloodshot eyes.

"I wasn't aware you'd be awake yet."

"If I'd known they would send you, I might have…" he tapped behind his right ear. "Apparently, I need to be awake for *some* of this."

Roux crossed to stand near the partition, grimacing for his brother. "Unfortunately."

"How is she?"

Inhaling and exhaling through his nose, Roux shook his head. "She is fine, but you really should focus on your treatment."

Farz lifted an eyebrow. "Really? You're going to treat me like one of those crazy medics does?"

Roux fisted his hands behind his back, slowly blinking the retort away. "Farz, I'm the one standing here."

"And they're the ones scared as hell, hiding in the corners." The laugh only accentuated the dark circles under his eyes. "But seriously, little brother... she's good, and the baby is okay?"

"Yes."

Farz slipped off the edge of his cot. "I'm glad my *nephew* and his mother aren't in worse shape than *I* am." He began pacing. "How's the kid? They won't tell me anything about how he fared in all this isolation."

"He's with Kayla now." He shook his head, raising both brows. "I am not entirely sure how well he's doing. Neither of them are very open about it."

"You're the doctor, and you can't tell if they're okay?" Farz laughed. He pressed fingers into his forehead afterwards.

Roux blinked in deliberately slow movements before shaking his head again. Leave it to his brother to make jokes when he was facing extreme withdrawal manifestations. "I don't play nice with people who have emotional scars."

"If memory serves..." Farz groaned, deciding to return to his bunk. "You did pretty well with *her*."

"It is too soon to push the issue." Groaning, Roux thumped the glass. "I'm not here to discuss my mate and her younger brother. I'm here to care for *my* brother."

"What's next on the list for *detoxification*?" Farz stressed the word with a flourish of his hand through the air.

Roux turned away from Farz and walked toward the station that his father locked down for him. "Well, I have more blood-work to go over. It might be just what we need to complete the process *we* started."

Farz held a hand over his face. "Please tell me you can fix what Arzi did to us. It's bad enough being sensitive to it. I don't need to be stuck in one of these things every time I stop by the Tahali residence to check in on you."

"I can't make any promises yet. For now," Roux tapped fingers along the edge of the console. "We're *hoping* the current process doesn't fail when measured up to your newfound *sensitivity*."

"I can hardly stand up for a few minutes at a time, and you're joking about *that*?"

68

Kayla

She tossed the towel she unraveled from her hair at her brother and ran for the door to the bedroom. "Roux isn't supposed to be back for at least an hour. He wants to make sure Farz is okay."

Michael flung it back at her. It hit the wall by the door, missing her by at least a foot. He sat at the table with his back to her. She rolled her eyes, hobbling back to the table. "You could easily have pegged me with that thing." Kayla pointed to the sopping cloth.

His head rotating to look at her, Michael raised an eyebrow. "I know what your mate is capable of, Kayla."

She sighed. "*Roux* knows the difference between teasing and anger, Mikey." Kayla rubbed the shoulder at her side before leaning in to hug him. "He'd probably join '*the battle of the wet towel*'."

He laughed, shoulders lifting to dislodge her. "He's good to you, right?"

Her brows bunched. "You know he is."

"What I *know* is... your *mate* is a very dangerous individual."

"Michael," She hugged him again, sighing. "You saw how he was in *our* home." After waiting for his nod, she continued. "*That* is the Roux I know and love. *He* is the one I married. Beneath that is years of training..." Her chin burrowed into his shoulder. "And yes, it is terrifying. But he would never hurt me, or you... what he did that night..."

She sat upright in her chair, the attempt to blot out the memory of watching her husband pin her brother to the floor failing. "He only stopped you from doing something he *thought* you wanted to do. Roux doesn't understand that we aren't violent." Sure, they all had tempers, but no one in their family ever raised a hand in anger. Jokingly, maybe, but never intending to hurt.

"Dad isn't like that."

"No, he isn't. But Dad has *other* issues." She didn't dare add that their mother would probably have slapped him upside the head for yelling at her. Julie wasn't opposed to teaching them manners.

Michael laughed, air blowing through his nose. "That *he* does."

They both turned to the exterior door of the residence of their confinement to at the sound of a chime.

"We're not supposed to have visitors, are we?"

Shaking her head, Kayla stood. She wished for a way to contact Roux, the way Farz could, making slow steps toward the door. *It could be his father. Stop acting like someone is going to hurt you everywhere you go, Kayla.* She'd been perfectly at ease with life and its changes before her mother found them. But since... Kayla cringed. It was going to be difficult to avoid second guessing every situation.

"Sorry to disturb you." A female officer nodded, her arms crossed behind her back. "Lieutenant Dannari, I came to ensure you were *well* cared for. May I enter?"

Kayla backed away from the door, extending her hand toward their modest abode. "Not a problem. We were just discussing the rations requests."

Her brother raised an eyebrow with a roll of his eyes. Truthfully, it had been her intention to ask him what he wanted—after the *Towel War.* His expression shifted, eyes narrowing on their guest.

The Lieutenant smiled at Kayla, failing to notice her brother's attention. "The Admiral wants only the best for his family. I can take the order in for you, if you'd like me to wait for it."

Michael shifted his position, standing behind the woman. He lifted his eyebrows, mouthing the exclamation *SIREN,* with a rub of his nose. Veins hardened, her limbs freezing in place. Kayla shuffled toward the table, attempting to remedy her mistake. "I'd actually like to wait for Roux's input. Thank you, though."

Her brother moved, his hands grasping at the Siren's throat. Anticipating him, the Lieutenant threw him to the floor. "Nice try, young man, but you're no match for a seasoned officer." She drew her weapon and held it over him.

"Now, let's not make this harder than it *should* be. You're both coming with me. Try anything, your brother suffers for it." She dug the heel of her boot into Michael's ribcage, following the motion with a nudge of her toe to his chin. "Get up!"

69

Roux

"Dr Tahali! Just who I needed to find."

Roux turned to face the female barging into the room. Her cheeks were flushed and hair slightly disheveled. "Can I help you..." not knowing her name, Roux insinuated the question with a wave of his hand.

"Yes, you very much *can*." She crossed to the gurney tethered to the wall. Tapping it with one finger, she laughed.

Trailing her with his eyes, Roux's stomach churned. He shifted on an unsteady footing as his eyes darted for balance. He fell before he could warn his brother or their father.

70

Farz

"Roux!" Farz's throat rebelled. His legs failed him in the attempt to reach the partition faster than his sluggish reflexes would allow.

The woman, an officer of his father's crew, hefted his brother from the floor and dumped him onto the gurney. She laughed at Farz's attempt to stand. "Without your brother's help, they'll never fix what she did to you." She made her way to the partition, her smile showing teeth. "And you'll die from their efforts to put you through detox."

"Father!"

"He can't hear you, Farz... by the time anyone realizes I've taken them, we'll be long gone."

Farz rolled to his back, reaching for the side of his cot. He watched the woman saunter away, humming with the effort to secure his brother to the gurney.

"Where is Kayla..." Roux's groans were faint even over the implant, spurring Farz's effort to reach for the bed.

"You'll join your mate soon enough, Dr. Tahali." The woman ran fingers down the side of Roux's face.

For once, Farz was thankful for the partition blocking everything from him. In his state, another overload from a Siren would be excruciating. Roux's *newfound* sensitivity hadn't robbed him of his immunity, but he couldn't do a damn thing to protect himself under its effects. Arzi had, for all intents and purposes, made Roux worse off than Farz. He was supposed to be taking something that would help. Though, considering the situation—Farz groaned. His brother's wife did everything possible to keep her aura in... *This woman wants Roux incapacitated.*

The scratching sound of the wheels crossing the threshold spurred further groans from him. "Father! Please tell me you heard that!" The complexity, let alone the existence, of their implants were known to very few. Whoever this woman was, she wasn't privy to her commanding officer having a direct link to both of his sons. Or that he was, in fact, listening in on Roux's discussion on how to proceed with detox.

"I did! Commander Tuhani and I are on our way."

"*Don't* get near her, she's a Siren." He dropped his hand to the floor. If this Siren had Kayla stashed away somewhere, she almost certainly had Michael, too. He'd allow no one near his sister, not after everything they went through with her mother. The kid didn't deserve the life waiting for him if Arzi got her way. Successfully rolling to his side, Farz groaned again.

"Leave that to me, son. I won't let her take them."

71

Commander Tuhani

Commander Tuhani barreled through the doorway, tossing the Admiral components of his exposure suit. Time was of the essence, but he wasn't going after Roux alone—not with a Siren on the loose. Who was this woman who hid among Tahali's ranks, and how had she hidden from every screening that would have shown what she was for so long?

Few were privy to the connection Rivan had with his sons, even fewer knew he could hold his own. He just needed a *little* help when a Siren was involved. Fewer still knew he and Ban were on a first name basis. In private.

Ban smiled, assisting the elder Tahali with his gear. He'd always been a tad jealous of the equipment he and his boys had access to. Unlike the Admiral, Commander Tuhani was expendable. Not that he was easy to kill, he just didn't merit the attention Rivan and his sons dealt with. He fueled his pace with ashes of his jealousy, revolving on his heels. "Lets do this."

"She'll regret her actions."

That she would. Ban knew it too well. Rivan Tahali wasn't the type anyone would want to make an enemy of. Checking the signal, the Commander led the way. It was the Admiral's vessel. He should have been giving orders. But as merit for the situation, he deferred to Ban's expertise. In any other situation, he'd have complained about Tuhani taking charge.

"She's headed for the cargo hold."

Missing his own gear, Ban resisted the grumbles. The body armor he wore would block anything short of point blank. Fortunately, the Siren would not start shooting holes in anything. Aside from them. She'd be careful how she dealt with the situation, as her cargo was precious to more than herself.

72

Michael

Michael tugged at his bonds, alternating wrists. Whatever Lieutenant Dannari had given his sister, she was still out. He shuddered at the thought of what it would do for his unborn nephew. The matching tethers above his knees and over his ankles looked like they'd been taken from somewhere in the cargo hold. At least six inches wide, the edges bit into his skin as he struggled with his minimal movement. He elbowed the edges of the confines, giving up on calling for help with a muzzle that was practically glued to his face. He'd be a bloodied mess by the time anyone heard him. But he didn't care.

He failed to fight the budding sneeze. *Sorry.* Kayla wouldn't hear the muffled apology for kicking her shins amid the spasm. It wasn't his sister's fault he was reacting to her aura. Complete control went out the window over the last several weeks. Increased stress didn't help matters. Poor Roux. Even with the medication they'd given him, he could barely breathe when she was next to him.

Michael felt a little selfish griping over his minor symptoms as he rested his head on Kayla's shoulder. The box the woman shoved them in had him laying on his side. He hoped she was at least comfortable. Thankfully, their kidnapper hadn't even considered binding her. Sure, she was pregnant and couldn't move fast enough to save her own life. But the Siren who dragged them both to the docking bay had him to goad her with. Clenching his eyes closed, Michael tried not to think of where they were headed.

Exterior scratching noises brought his attention to the lid of whatever they were in. It opened with less of a bombardment than he expected. Not that he should have been surprised. He was on a ship full of Arros. They were all sensitive to loud noises. Unable to differentiate between colors or objects, the harassing contrast of light to blame, he noted something large blotting out the light. His eyes adjusted in time to gaze into the startled expression on Roux's half obscured face.

The woman had to be strong to lift Roux over the opposite side of the container by his elbow and just above his knee. That, Michael considered, would have been difficult for most people. Though he imagined Farz could have done it. His sister's mate was bound similarly as he was. Michael shifted his nose to stifle his reaction as Roux's eyes twitched with the movement to inspect their surroundings. Wedged in on either side of Kayla, there would be little movement capable until they were released from the prison.

Praying Roux was coherent enough to keep his connection to his father and brother open, Michael avoided the gaze of the woman closing the container. With his attention divided between Michael and his sister, slow breaths rattled from his noise. Roux shuddered, taking in what Michael assumed was the blood dripping from his wounds.

The veins in Roux's eyes trembled, his nose twitching from the aura Kayla couldn't keep at bay in her unconscious state. His jaw moved, stifled by the mirror image of the muzzle on Michael's own face. It sounded like: mlm wimums ovwou wus. Though Michael assumed it meant something more along the lines of: I'll get us out of this. There wasn't much chance for that when considering that all three of them were contained.

He gave it a few minutes at most before they'd feel movement of some sort. And just like that, they'd be back in Arzi's clutches. Grumbling, Michael's eyes drifted to his sister. *She doesn't deserve this life, neither does her baby.* Meeting Roux's glazed eyes, he amended his thoughts. *You don't deserve this, either.* Kayla was right. Roux wasn't a monster. He'd spent a great deal of time trying to protect Kayla from the life he lived before they met. It was time for Michael to treat him with the respect his brother was worthy of.

73

Commander Tuhani

Ban watched the woman heft the lid over the apparatus before her. They might have reached her before she smuggled them away. But if the guards making their way across the ship didn't hurry, Dr Tahali would slip through their fingers—his brother's life with him. He moved out of the shadows, rising his gun. "Lieutenant Dannari, the Security Officer would have words with you."

"Sent to deal with me alone..." she laughed, running a single finger over the length of the chamber. For an Arros female, this Siren was large. Built like many of the members of the hunters he commanded, she would give them hell with the training. "The Admiral is weak. He can't even resist the urges to *obey* his son's mate." She stopped trudge at the control panel, punching the command in with one hand, and watched him. "I'm doing Tahali a favor..." sneering, she laughed at Tuhani. "In the short term. But he won't escape the realm we will *rule*."

Teeth clamped down on his lower lip, Commander Tuhani glanced at the tracking panel on his wrist. He needed Rivan in position. Every second it took for the Admiral to get there, his son and his mate slipped farther from consciousness. He didn't need the proximity to recognize the containment vessel intended to keep valuable equipment at steady and exceedingly low temperatures. The conditions wouldn't pose *long-term* effects on the three adults inside the chamber. Even with their quarter and half human genetics, Kayla and her brother would survive. Roux's unborn child, *however...* Tuhani lifted both hands and stepped away. "You don't want to do that. What would Arzi say if you damaged the child her daughter carries?"

The Siren activated the chamber with her fingerprint. "Further *posterity* won't be an issue with her mate at her side."

Ban eased back toward the doorway, shaking his head. "I've spent some time with the young lady in question. I doubt she'd find your reasoning *acceptable.*"

"Your stalling won't save them. It only makes the inevitable draw nearer." She lifted the weapon in her hands and stepped closer to him. "Your head will be an added bonus."

Ban curled his fingers into his palms, a smile growing. "I think I'd rather send her *yours*."

Rivan closed in, the darkness hiding him from the siren's view until the moment he struck. His hand closed around her throat before she could scream. He pinned her to the ground mere inches from the crate. "You would dare take *my* son from me?" The Admiral lifted her from the ground and bashed her head against the container with the movement, ripping consciousness from the screaming wretch.

Still holding her throat until the woman's heart rate lulled, Rivan nodded toward the discarded remnants of the freight tethers. Tahali flipped the safety of his helmet away after taking the time to ensure they sedated the woman. Curses against the uselessness of tests intended to weed out the very problem they faced bled from the Admiral as pulled his officer's hand up. Not caring for the pain the angle might cause her, he placed it on the biometric lock.

Tuhani pulled the Siren away from his friend. The hiss of the lock disengaging punctuated the breaths coming from him. Four men barreled in, tugging the seductress away from Ban. The sheer vulgarity rumbling from them would have made even the Commander's steel-hearted mate squirm.

They each took hold of one end, hefting the cover from the box, exposing the occupants to the controlled temperature of the cargo hold.

"Roux!" The Admiral pulled his son by the shoulder, helping him to the side of the container. His son shifted as much as he could in his state and sat upright on the edge while Ban pulled the boy clear.

Tuhani ensured the injuries were only superficial—despite the amount of blood—before cutting Michael's bindings away. The boy never took his eyes off the crate, hands shaking. He followed the boy's gaze with the remaining tether falling from the kid's ankles. Rivan's hands clenched at his boy's shoulders, their expressions frozen on the other. Roux's eyes moved sluggishly from his father to the young woman still laying in the crate's bottom.

Ban nudged her brother aside and bent to retrieve Dr. Tahali's mate. Her skin, like that of her brother's—and no doubt Roux's, was cold to the touch. He lifted her in his arms, making his way to the door. Her mate's muffled growl set Tuhani laughing through his nose. "None of you are in any condition to carry her."

Roux nodded, his father removing the stifling device from his face. Another glance in his father's direction—he closed his eyes. "You alright Michael?" Roux winced with the movement to stand, pulling his mate's brother to his side to inspecting the injuries. Dr. Tahali grimaced. "Your sister is going to *kill* me if we don't take care of those *before* she wakes up."

The young man shuddered, looking down at the device Rivan discarded at their feet. "Considering the circumstance. I don't think she'll be angry with you."

74

Michael

Barely able to keep his eyes open, Michael leaned on his sister's shoulder. She prodded him with a finger, a slight smile parting her lips as she draped her arm over him. They were safe. Safe as they could be with twenty armor clad guards. All of them wore exposure suits.

He wasn't sure if the precaution was solely for the problem they'd encountered a few weeks prior, or because his sister was still having trouble keeping her own aura at bay. They were at least respectful. She was, after all —married to their Admiral's son. That and she hadn't once tried to talk to any of them, much less look at them in the two weeks they'd been a constant fixture.

Michael overheard one of them mentioning she was the most standoffish Siren they'd ever heard of. He wanted to laugh in their faces but that wouldn't have helped him much. He was excessive in their efforts. His life didn't mean nearly enough to let him mouth off like that. At least he'd thought that initially.

Commander Tuhani stood a few feet from them with his gaze fixed on Michael. He nodded to him. The same smile plastered on his face. No doubt hoping Michael considered their discussions. Roux hadn't left them alone with anyone he didn't trust implicitly. That often left Von and Commander Tuhani around the billet they spent most of their time in. Tuhani spent every spare moment talking up the benefits of what he and the other hunters were doing to protect not only Arros—but all humanoid species that were vulnerable to Sirens. Finding his familial connection to Kayla unique and intriguing, Tuhani boasted the benefits of knowing the difference between a good and a bad one.

Kayla didn't know. Not sure if he wanted to tell her, Michael sighed and sat upright again. He knew what she thought about Roux's former profession. And while it scared him a little, Michael saw the benefits of his genetic disposition. Roux wasn't an awful person. He'd come out of the line of duty and was still a good man. Farz was a bit odd, but he wasn't so bad either.

He had spent little time around Roux's brother since they were rescued. He'd explained that his brother was going through withdrawals. Much like a junkie would. Roux didn't know how long Farz would be under his medical watch. Speaking of Roux—he walked through the gap in soldiers making his way to them. He nodded toward Tuhani before taking a seat next to Michael's sister.

Amazed at how much room a shuttle could boast, Michael shook his head. Farz was apparently on the other side of the guards, sedated and secured to a gurney that was out of sight. They couldn't let him near Kayla yet. He couldn't imagine the stress it was causing his sister, knowing Farz was still hung up on what Arzi intended him to do. Michael considered the opposite side of the situation, a shudder escaping. Farz was just as screwed over in most aspects.

The shuttle jostled lightly, the docking mechanisms engaging. Michael's heart raced with the impending reunion beyond the airlock. Not that they'd have the opportunity until the wall of brute force vetted everyone surrounding them. That and Roux said they were going to get them settled in before his mother allowed anyone near them.

Michael jumped to his feet, extending his hand to assist his sister. She smiled, though she held tears back with each breath. He hugged her in a bear-like hug their father used when they were young.

"It isn't your fault—either, Michael."

Closing his eyes, he shook his head. "I should have done something..."

"Mikey..."

Interrupted by the gasps behind them, Michael turned to face the one person they let through the barricade. "Mom!"

His mother held both hands over her mouth. Tears flowed down her face. Flinging both arms outward, she pulled him and his sister toward her. No one spoke, waiting for his mother to take the moment with them. A moment he'd dreaded would never happen.

75

Roux

Roux was nearly asleep in his chair when Caya Morris entered the makeshift maternity room. Elbows braced on the bed, hands holding his head up, Roux blinked at the bombardment of light from the corridor.

"I can come back another time."

He slid his chair away from Kayla's bedside as he stood on barely responsive legs. "No, it's fine."

She smiled, shaking her head. "The three of you are exhausted. You have every right to turn *everyone* away."

Roux straightened his posture. "Not everyone." Julie had come and gone several times over the night. Without her, he'd have passed out hours before.

Caya smiled again. "Brandt and Eva are excited to see their nephew. Alan is keeping them occupied for now. But I can hold them off for a few more days if you'd like."

"Once she's had some time to rest..." he glanced toward his wife. "I think she'd appreciate the visit."

Kayla's grandmother approached. Her tired eyes scanned the room before stopping beside the cot at his side. She smiled down at his son. "He's so precious, so perfect, and so delicate all at once."

Roux bobbed his head, reached down, and lifted his son in his arms.

"Twenty-three years ago, you stood by her father. He held her the way you do now with your son."

"I don't remember any of it."

"Memories are *fragile,* even without meddling."

"You've spoken to my father."

Nodding, Caya came closer. She shook her head when he made motions to hand her the child, wiping tear coated cheeks. Kayla's grandmother smiled down at her great grandson. "Julie didn't say if you'd decided on a name yet."

He twined his finger among his son's tiny hands. "Alan Rivan Tahali."

Caya held both hands to her chest, blinking further tears away. "He'll tell you it is an awful name. But be sure to understand—he is only deflecting the attention. My husband will feel honored by the choice." Laughing softly, she stroked Alan's cheek. "Your father will no doubt boast of this little one carrying his full name."

Smiling, Roux laughed quietly. His father would indeed. But that wasn't the reason for the name. "I gave her the choice when we married... She chose Tahali—she thinks Roux Erickson would sound terrible."

Caya covered her mouth, muffling her laughter. "It does!"

His shoulders shook, stirring Alan from his slumber.

"How is Farz doing?"

Steady breaths expelled, Roux set his son in his cot. He gently stroked fingers over his head until he slept again. "It could take some time before it's *safe* to let him near her."

Her grimace spread quickly, half hidden by her hand. "I can't imagine..."

Closing his eyes, Roux made his way back to the chair. He'd shut his connection to Farz down the moment he knew Kayla was going into labor. His brother didn't need the added discomfort in his state. Hoping for more time didn't get them anywhere. While he and Kayla were close to something, their attention was fragmented in the weeks following their rescue.

"Roux... I heard what happened. How are you handling all of this?"

"Niv scrounged up some of the heavy stuff. I haven't felt a thing all night." He shook his head. "Drowsy... but I've managed to stay awake."

"I should let you sleep. The two of you have earned it." Caya nodded to him while backing away.

"I'll let her know you came by." Waiting for her to leave, Roux lifted the blanket and slid into bed beside his wife. With an arm around her, he allowed sleep to take hold.

Looking out the window of the high-rise apartment his mother insisted she decorate, Roux groaned. It gave a perfect view of the entire city. The city he was born in. The city *she* would have preferred his son be born in. But that wasn't how it happened. At three weeks old, his son was on his way to be a well traveled Tahali. With the best of them.

Thankfully, his mother was understanding of that fact. Especially since she was present for the event. She wasn't pleased, however, that he hadn't allowed her entry. Michael, Julie, and Caya were the only ones Roux permitted in the room they'd dubbed the maternity wing aboard his mother's ship.

He scanned the line of buildings in the distance, his gaze stopping on the training facility. "Has Michael spoken to you yet?"

His wife fastened the sash at her waist with one hand, the other she ran through her damp hair. "I haven't seen him since this morning. He said he needed to talk to mom about something. He left before I made sure he'd eaten."

Roux rubbed his right hand over his jaw, the left through his own hair—digging fingers across his scalp. *It's now or never,* a phrase he'd learned when he was a boy. Truthfully, studying some of the human habits were the more entertaining memories of his childhood. Exhaling, he turned to face his wife instead of watching her reflection in the window. "Tuhani has convinced him he'd make the greatest difference among the hunters."

"What?" The brush in her hand dropped to the floor. "Does Mom know?"

Exhaling, he increased the pressure against his head. "If he hasn't told her by now, she'll know before the week is out."

"What is he thinking? Roux, you told me he didn't have to make that decision!"

"Kayla…" His hand sliding down to cover his eyes, Roux grumbled. "Your father is still out there. He has it in his head that this is the surest way to get him back."

Kayla lowered herself into the chair beside their son's bed and stared at the wall. "He's going to get himself killed…"

"I won't let that happen."

"What can you do about it, Roux?" She kept her voice low. Their son didn't wake from his rest over nothing. But neither of them wanted to relinquish the reprieves they had. Once her shoes were secured, she stepped quietly toward him. "You resigned eleven years ago!"

"My mother is forcing my hand."

Kayla stopped her motion toward him, her eyes closing. "Please tell me this has nothing to do with *us*."

"Us? No..." Roux shook his head. "Well, not in the way you're thinking..."

"Not in the way I'm thinking? Roux! She's forcing you to go back to that life because of *me*, whether it is because you chose me behind her back. Or that I am, in fact, the very thing she's had you *hunting*. It is very much about *us*."

"If I don't willingly return to my duties, she will leverage *our* son the moment he shows any sign of being like me."

Kayla blinked, her eyes flaring with each motion.

"It was either do this to protect Alan, or let my mother have her way with his future."

"She has no right to dictate our child's future—or yours."

"Kayla..."

"No, I won't let her do this to you."

"It *was* my decision."

"One she forced you to make."

Roux let his chin drop to his chest. "Kayla, it won't be the way it was."

"You can't guarantee that, Roux."

He moved to stand in front of his mate, stroking her cheek with the back of looped fingers. "It's a command position, Kayla. Farz and I won't be sent out the way we were before."

"Command?"

He pulled her into his arms. "Kayla... I swear it won't be what you think. They would never expect me to take another Siren's life—without profoundly *justifiable* evidence."

"When?"

"I report in tomorrow morning. My presence is required for Michael's assessment and subsequent procedure."

"*Procedure?*"

Roux folded both lips between his teeth, nodding. Michael promised he would mention it to his sister before he left. Grumbling internally, Roux pressed his forehead against Kayla's. "Despite your grandfather's heritage, your grandmother's gives Michael the same *advantage* Farz and I have."

"An implant?" Her eyes widened, hand slapping to her mouth. She shoved away from him, moving to Alan's bedside. "Roux..." her head thrashed from side to side. "Why would he *need* it?"

Chopped breaths escaped his attempt to stifle his hesitant laugh. "If he's going to join *my* team, it will be *required*."

She spun to face him, falling back against the seat. "What!"

Unable to move from his position, Roux rubbed hands on his elbows. "Because of his age and heritage, it was the only choice."

"Your mother is using my *brother* to force your hand!" Alan stirred beside her, inducing a cringe from both of them.

After waiting for their son to settle, Roux crossed the room to sit beside her. "*Yes*, she *is* using Michael to force my hand. I had to choose. Let him and Farz continue without me—which you'd never forgive me for." His brother's behavior was bound to rub off on the kid. Kayla would forever blame him for it. "And let her dictate Alan's future..."

"Or report for duty, protecting both of them..." his wife collapsed into his embrace, shuddering in his arms. After several moments of silence, her sobbing into his chest—him holding her with shaking hands—she looked up at him. "You and Farz had better keep him out of trouble."

He ran a hand through her hair. It was much longer than she preferred, making her look more like her Aunt Eva than either of them was comfortable with. "I will do everything I can to ensure we give him the best ability to do that for *himself*."

Stroking the fastening of his shirt, she looked up at him. "How long will you be gone tomorrow?"

His throat knotted with every breath, words failing to reach his tongue.

"Roux?" She slid away from him. "I thought the medication Nivia gave you was working?"

"It isn't that," taking in her trembling appendages, he rolled his eyes. "I promise I'm fine."

"What *is* it then?"

"I won't be returning for at least a week."

Her eyelashes blurred. "What? I thought you were just supposed to oversee Michael's process."

"My presence is required..." Roux cringed, rubbing behind his left ear. "Because he isn't the only one going *under*." Despite her understanding of minimal procedures for the varying devices of similar nature, his wife wasn't part in Arros society—and thus wouldn't know the reasons behind it. He'd never intended to explain the process to anyone—much less his mate. "Farz and I will both require our implants to have *direct* modifications to allow for the *addition*."

Her jaw opened and closed multiple times before she leaned against him. "He'll be..." her breaths heated his chest. "Connected directly to yours?"

"Unfortunately..." he squinted, pressing both lips together. They'd be pale for his mate's observation—of that, he was certain. "I'll have both of them pestering me at their whim."

Kayla pulled away from him. "Do you have any idea how horrible of a decision that will be—on your part?"

Roux laughed through his nose. He couldn't help but let his chest heave with the breaths rattling from him. "I doubt he will be anywhere as *difficult* as Farz is."

Kayla lifted her brow and shook her head. "He's seventeen. Honestly, I don't want to know what influences he had after I moved away. But I know that not every thought that crosses the boundary of his speech is the best idea."

With both hands in his, before she could slap *sense* into him—she'd done it a few times in their relationship, Roux kissed her. "Trust me, I am well versed in how to deal with *that.*"

Crawling into his lap, she rested her head against his chest. "So you'll be gone for a week?"

"Minimum, yes." Moving hair from her face, he exhaled.

"And after that?"

"Michael will need to live with us for a while—while he adjusts to the enhancement, Farz too."

Her eyes widened at the mention of his brother. "Don't worry. It won't be here..." exhaling, he pulled the document out of his pocket. They didn't have the room in the small domicile his father's family provided on short notice. "As a commander, I will be required to live near the training grounds. Given our *situation,* the only place they have available allowing Farz to keep his distance from you until he recovers *fully...*" from what her mother did to him. It also had room for the two of them to continue their research—another ultimatum set by his mother. He handed her the slide that would allow her entry to the residence they'd inhabit for the foreseeable future. "Is *inside* the facility."

Kayla gaped at him.

"Someone will escort us there later this evening." Tugging at her hand, Roux rotated her to face him—her legs wrapped around his waist and arms over his shoulders. "Say something, anything..."

"*Inside*... the training facility?"

He nodded.

"Well... I guess the question about who was going to keep an eye on *us* while you were gone isn't necessary."

Laughing, he bit his lower lip to stifle the noise. "Your family will stay with you while Farz and I are not present."

"All of them?"

"Anything you need will be provided before I leave," he kissed her forehead. He knew she would not like the rules. "The door won't open for anyone but Farz, Michael, and myself."

"They don't trust me to open my own door?" She held the key-card up. "Whats the point of this, then?"

Another sigh escaped him. "Considering what happened aboard my father's ship, Commander Tuhani doesn't think it's the best idea to let *anyone* through that door while *I* am *incapacitated.* That includes you, and our child, until things return to normal. Which is why your grandfather has agreed to bring the family there, to stay with you the *entire* time."

76

Kayla

Incapable of holding her breath any longer, Kayla huffed and dropped into the lonely chair by the door. The locked door. She knew it was going to stay that way for another week, but it didn't make her feel any less light-headed. Head in her hands, she shuddered dew-less tears.

"It isn't forever, sweetheart." His voice behind her, Kayla's eyes threatened to release floodgates. "Oh, Kayla, come here." Her grandfather tugged at her arm, pulling her into an embrace.

"I can't lose them too, Grandpa."

He wiped the beginning of tears from her face, his eyes threatening to follow her lead. "You aren't losing them, Kayla. They'll be back before you know it."

Inhaling the sobs, Kayla hugged him tighter.

"Why don't we find something to do to make this feel a bit like home for you? It might keep your mind off what is going on out there and help the time pass, eh?" He led her to the back room, allowing the voices of her aunt and uncle arguing about where the proper location something should be. They both laughed.

"Your Gran won't let them hold Alan. She wants them to do something productive first..." he stifled a laugh. "Not sure what else she expected them to do."

Kayla laughed, leaning into his side. It was good to have him there. Even if she wanted to cry every time she saw the pain in his eyes at seeing her. They all missed her father. Until they could find out where Arzi fled to, they'd live with that sadness. None of them needed the reminder. The ability to find him slipped away with every passing day. The Siren who'd attempted to take her, Michael, and Roux, didn't even know the exact location. Her contact wasn't anything more than a number. A number to a military authorized burner frequency that had been deactivated.

Eva greeted them with a stack of plates on top was a bin of flatware. "Aren't these the most beautiful dishes you've ever seen?!"

One look at her grandfather and Kayla almost died laughing. Apparently, he had seen them before and they weren't exactly a wonderful memory. Though, she imagined by the cringe on his face, that it wasn't all that bad either.

"Your mother is going to break those the moment she sees them." His head rattled from side to side as he pointed toward a box in the corner. "Put them back before she comes out here." Looking down at her, he shook his head again. "Don't ask."

Julie covered her mouth with both hands, tears streaming down her face, attempting to muffle the laughter. Kayla's grandfather shrugged and followed Eva to the box—ensuring she covered them enough to block the evidence from her mother.

"I'm not sure where Roux's mother found those, but I doubt we'll be using them until after the boys are back." Her shoulders shook with the remaining laughter.

"What is so funny?" Gran snapped from the other room. She cooed for Alan, singing a song Kayla remembered from her childhood. "Please tell me Mina didn't send those awful dishes."

Eva and her father turned, shaking their heads. "No, Mom, she sent some weird decorations. Kayla doesn't like them, so we just put them back in the box."

Julie's gaze locked on Kayla's. They almost burst out laughing again. Eva was always guilty of being Grandpa's partner in crime. Some things never changed. Hoping those things would bring her through the things that would never be the same, Kayla crossed the room to survey the plunder of marrying into Arros' High Society.

About the Author

M.J. Rosay grew up in very small town. So small, that it's name means "where is it?" in the local Native American language. She had the bad habit, back then, of dreaming up tales of far off places and exotic people—she hasn't really grown out of it. Recent years have her still daydreaming, camping, playing video games, and traveling the country with her family.

Thanks for reading Resurgence: The Arros Siren Conflicts: Book 1. If you liked this story, stay tuned for Book 2 of The Arros Siren Conflicts.

If you'd like to be notified when its available, sign up for updates at: www.subscribepage.com/the_arros_siren_conflicts

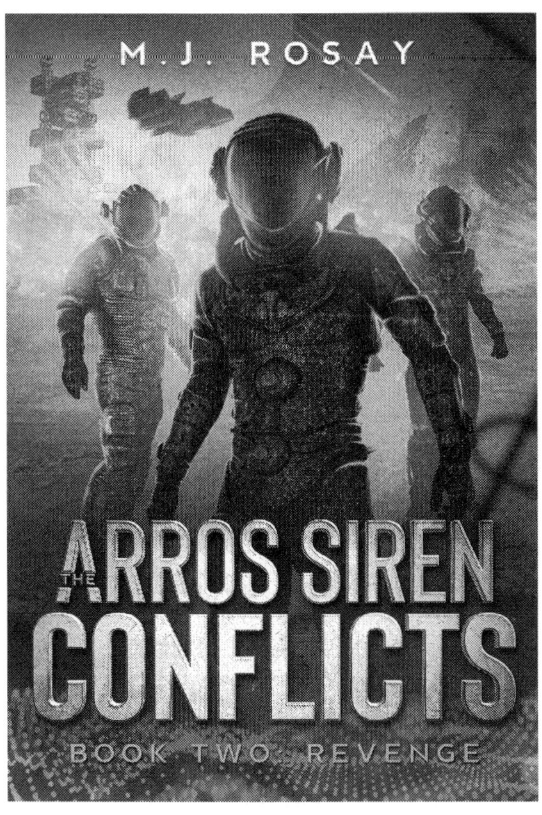

Other stories by M.J. Rosay

The Arros Siren Conflicts

Resurgence

Revenge (Coming Soon)

Heirs of Denuitia

Book 1 (Coming Soon)

Made in the USA
Columbia, SC
09 November 2022